The Heart of a Warrior

Book 3 of:

The Curse of the Tribe

JERRY L. MAURER

ISBN 978-1-962363-52-5 (Paperback)
ISBN 978-1-962363-53-2 (Ebook)

Inquiries and Book Orders should be addressed to:

Leavitt Peak Press
17901 Pioneer Blvd Ste L #298, Artesia, California 90701
Phone #: 2092191548

Chapter 1

Noh Tay Dah didn't know what hit him! One minute he was carrying an arm load of wood from his wood pile and the next he was lying face down in the snow. There was no feeling, seeing or hearing as the blowing snow drifted over his inanimate form and began to cover his very presence in this life.

He had been musing on the wonderful turn of events that had brought him here. He had found a wonderful wife who had been a captive of the much feared "White Faced Tribe" known for the white covering that they painted on their faces and bodies to make the warpaint stand out. They were also known for their slave capturing raids on other, usually smaller, tribes. That's how he had found his wife, Deh Neh Totsi. She had been brought in from a raid far to the south. They had fallen in love and were married. He had felt pride in his two healthy children. He thought of his daughter, Lay Leh Tso, who had seen six summers, and his son, Yah Doh Nay, who had seen five.

They had fled from the Whiteface because they mistreated his wife and children.

It was on that journey that they had stumbled upon Sunflower and Azalia, Chee and Blossom, and the boys, Lobo, Impala and Little Badger. He had to smile at the memory because Sunflower had scared him more than the Whiteface.

A wonderful friendship had developed. They had brought him many unusual gifts in the months that had followed. Strange things with strange names made of a strange substance, stronger, harder and sharper than stone. There were names like "saw, hatchet, knife" and for his wife "pots, pans, skillet" and many other things. The boys had taught him how to make a pole to fish and gave him other strange things like "line and hooks."

As he was making his way back to his stone cave and family with a smile and a warm heart, everything went black and he remembered no more.

Deh Neh Totsi looked up from where she was preparing the evening meal. Noh Tay Dah was taking a long time to get an arm load of wood. There were times when he paused to look down their valley and out over the mountains to breathe in the view and the fresh air. Today there would be no view. There was a blizzard with snow obliterating any view more than three or four steps ahead. What was taking so long?

She heard the movement of the deer skin flap that served as the door and she looked up. Noh Tay Dah was a good husband and she smiled with warmth and pride every time he entered.

With a jolt of surprise and fear she gasped. It was not Noh Tay Dah! A strange warrior entered followed by another and a third pressed in behind them.

"Who are you and what do you want?" She rasped out through clenched teeth. She reached immediately for a knife and the children scrambled to get behind her.

"You and the children will come with us and no one will be harmed." The first warrior growled. "And don't wait for your man. He will not help you."

Again, the pangs of fear and dread struck her like a falling rock. It almost took her mind off of the present danger.

In a moment she had her wits about her and her mind came back to the present.

"Better to die here with my husband than to freeze to death out there," she snarled defiantly.

"I say truth! Two of you will not walk from here before I die," she said with determined conviction.

Deh Neh Totsi had discovered months before that a knife would make a great weapon. She had an older, large knife that had been given to them at the first encounter with Chee and the little band of hunters. After she had received the more specialized, skinning knife and slicing knife, this knife had fallen into disuse. It came to her that it might make a weapon if it could be thrown with accuracy. She had practiced with a few short sticks, then she had carved a similar sized knife out of a piece of wood. She practiced for weeks, throwing it into a dirt wall where it wouldn't shatter. Soon she could stick the point into the dirt every time. She then practiced with the real knife, throwing it into the soft dirt. Finally, she took the real knife out to try it on a rabbit. She had gotten within several steps of the prey and brought it down on the first try.

"You think you can fight against spears with a knife?" He said, with some derision.

An answer, she flung the short skinning knife which stuck less than a foot from his head into a log that was leaning against the wall of the cave.

His eyes widened. She had two bigger knives in her hand and there was little room to maneuver in the confines of the cave entrance.

"I see that you might strike two of us but then you will die and we will take your children," he said evenly. "Come with us peacefully and I will see that no harm will come to you or the little ones."

Realizing the need for time and the protection of her children, she gave in. Tossing the slicing knife at his feet she returned the hunting knife to the sheath at her waist.

He almost smiled at her audacity in keeping the knife, but shrugged and motioned for her to leave.

"We are not ready for the cold," she said determinedly. "We must put on the winter coverings."

She turned to the children and said, "get your coat and boots on and each take a small pack."

Making sure that they were warmly dressed even before putting on the heavy coats, she stuffed an extra shirt and pants into their packs and with her body turned to cover some of her actions, she put a couple of cans of food in each pack and helped them put them on over the heavy coats.

Her own pack included a blanket in addition to her extra coverings, along with several cans of food. She stuck a can opener into a coat pocket. She also put in several things that her captives wouldn't understand even if they saw them.

The container of little sticks that started fires, the small package that unfolded and unfolded into a poncho. She also made sure each of them had an extra pair of gloves.

With extreme sadness she looked around their little home, still filled with their things. The children had each picked up the little stuffed animal that Blossom had given them and she stuffed them into the top of her pack.

The captors were looking on with great curiosity as she passed over the valuable skins and hides for these strange items. Other than the knife she had returned to her belt, she had passed over a hatchet the likes of which they had never seen and cooking things made of the strange unknown material, to take the strange coverings.

Turning to the leader, she looked him full in the face and said flatly, "we go."

The warriors stepped aside as she and the children exited their home. The rest of the raiding party scrambled to rush in and take all they could carry. They snarled and argued as they grabbed the family's belongings. She hadn't realized that they had accumulated so much. All this would slow their captors down and tire them out, making it easier for the children.

As she passed nearby the motionless body of her beloved husband lying in the snow, now almost entirely covered by the drifts, she could not help but wail out a long cry of despair and goodbye. The children screamed and cried out also as they suddenly understood the severity of their situation.

She almost succumbed to the temptation to fight to the death here and now. Only the cries of her children checked that temptation.

She began to kneel down to gather them in her arms to comfort them when one brute gave Yah Doh Nay a shove, sending him sprawling into the snow.

"Get going!" He snarled.

Deh Neh Totsi straightened up and faced him with such fury that he stepped back.

With a ferocity and intensity that dropped her voice almost to a whisper, she said through clenched teeth, "when Chee comes, you will fall."

She then threw back her head and screamed into the sky with such force and intensity that it froze every one of them in their tracks.

"Chee eeee!" She screamed and as her volume faded the echoes came rolling back, she dropped her head, grabbed the children's hands and started down the hill.

Within a few minutes, the marching order was established. Most of the band went ahead to break the trail, then Deh Neh Totsi and the children had an easier path to follow with two more warriors following them to make sure they did not lag behind.

In another half hour their home seemed far away and in another time. Their future looked as cold and bleak as the swirling snow in the gusting wind.

Back at the little cave home, the form of Noh Tay Dah was almost totally covered in the drifting snow.

But suddenly, there was movement. The form attempted to rise but sagged back into the snow. Again, there was movement and he got to his knees. With great effort he got to his feet where he swayed for a moment as the snow flaked off his form. He tried to take a step but his legs were weak and frozen. His head felt like it would burst with pain. With another great effort he opened his eyes. The snow was not the only thing swirling. Everything he tried to focus on was swirling, and the motion left him nauseated and he closed his eyes.

He took a tiny half-step and almost fell, but he tried again with a little better success. He opened his eyes again and the spinning movement almost made him fall.

Opening his eyes for only a glimpse and then taking a step he began to stagger towards the cave. As the swirling disorientation diminished, he could open his eyes a little longer. He still could not focus and he was seeing two of everything.

The first scene he could observe with any clarity was that the half teepee of poles that protected the entrance to the cave, had been torn down exposing the doorway.

It came through the fog in his brain that something was terribly wrong. Staggering a little faster, he called out as he approached the entrance.

"Deh Neh Totsi!" He cried out and the effort and sound of his voice shot a stab of pain through his injured head.

Crying out again, he tried to stoop over to enter the low doorway but the pain and nausea overcame him and he fell to his hands and knees.

When he could steady himself and his vision, he looked around at the disarray and emptiness before him. All the things of value that were gone suddenly paled into oblivion, as he realized that Deh Neh Totsi and the children were gone also.

He screamed their names again and again as waves of pain swept over him and seemed to center and culminate in his head.

Slowly, his sanity returned and he realized that he must have a plan. How long had he been lying there in the snow? How long had they been gone? Were they injured?

The fire had not completely died and there was wood still there. He always kept several armloads inside to dry and he replenished it long before it was needed.

He took some of the smaller sticks and broke them to get the fire going again. Every snap seemed to reach up and slapped his head. As the fire grew, the cold and numbness of his extremities began to fade and the warmth brought hope and a degree of calm.

At last, he could begin to think.

He realized, even if he could overtake them, he was in no condition to fight even one warrior, let alone a whole band. The body coverings and foot coverings were fine for stepping outside for an arm load of wood, but not heavy enough to traipse off into a blizzard.

As his mind began to clear, he remembered the cave like structure that Chee and the boys had built last summer. In it was food and items that Chee called a coat and boots and other coverings for Deh Neh Totsi and the children. If the Raiders had not discovered it, there would be adequate coverings and some food.

He staggered his way to the Kiva like structure. The door, about ten feet up the wall, was intact. Stumbling several steps along the face of the cliff to where he had laid a ladder, he dug into the snow and exposed one end. Heaving it up out of the drift, sent waves of pain through his head and he closed his eyes and paused to regain his equilibrium.

Placing the top of the ladder against the cliff face next to the door, he slowly and painfully climbed up, found the end of the piece of rope that went down inside the door and lifted the bar to let the door swing inward.

The small two by four foot opening was the entrance to the cave which contained the food and supplies that Chee and his band of teens had left for them for the winter.

Even without a fire, the inside was a bit warmer and out of the wind. He began to put on some of the strange coverings they had left. He thought that they had called them socks and boots. There were also several packs that they had left. Ones that attached to the back and shoulder and rested on the hips. Greater weight could be carried with ease.

His rescue plan was simple yet perhaps impossible. He would find Sunflower and see if she could get Chee. She had called him up once before, so even if he was gone, she might get him back.

There were two problems: could he make it to their village, and could Sunflower get Chee? He could hardly walk even on familiar, level ground.

The even more improbable plan if Chee couldn't be found, was to form a small band of fighters that could overtake and ambush the raiding party, taking down the band of warriors so quickly that they wouldn't have time to kill their prisoners.

He knew he was not part of their tribe, but Sunflower, Azalia, Blossom and the young warriors, Lobo, Impala and Little Badger were his friends. The rest of the tribe he had met just once at the fall celebration and feast. Would anyone go to battle and risk their lives for him and his family? Sunflower and the little band of youthful friends might not prevail against a larger band of seasoned warriors, and the rest of the tribe might not even be willing to try.

But he could think of no other options. He must try.

He found a half box of energy bars on the shelf and He remembered how each night before bed the children would ask for "sweet stuff" and they would sit by the fire and break one bar into two pieces. Each of them would get one thumbnail size piece and make it last as long as possible; chewing it slowly and savoring every second. Then they all went to bed with the penetrating heat of the fire warming their coverings and the pleasant sweetness lingering on their tongues. Bedtime never brought an argument, but was a very pleasant close to the day. That's why there was a half box left, each bar lasted two days. With a half smile, he took four and decided to eat one now.

Even with these memories swarming into his mind, the waves of pain and loss still came as he made preparations for his journey.

Climbing back down the ladder, he hid it back in the snow drift along the cliffs and continued making final preparations for the long walk to find Sunflower. He ate as large a meal as he could and still walk the long distance. He carried enough food to last a few days. He had water bottles that were left by Chee and his friends that carried more easily than the home made, leaky water bags made of skins.

The warmth of the shelter, the food, water and a little time to rest had lessened the pounding in his head but it still throbbed and he still saw two of everything.

But the physical pain didn't compare to the fear and dread of the likelihood that he would never see his beloved family again.

With a throbbing head, the devastating pain in his heart and eyes filled with tears, Noh Tay Dah staggered down the trail towards the distant village.

More than a couple of miles down the valley, Deh Neh Totsi and the children were trudging through the snow, fighting the fear and anguish in their own hearts. She forced her mind away from the image of the still form of her husband lying in the snow and focused on the plight of her children. They were keeping up with the pace of the band only because the raiders were burdened with all of her family's possessions. All of the things that their friends had given them over the past year had brought much joy and made life so much easier. It was ironic that all those possessions were making her life easier even now as carrying them slowed down the pace at which the raiding party could walk.

In another hour or so they would emerge from this narrow valley into the wide desert valley. There the blizzard would hit them full force. Her best hope was that they would stop and camp and let the blizzard blow itself out. That would also give them an opportunity to see what all they had looted. Many of the items would be totally unknown to them. Even so, she imagined they would talk and argue for hours about what they were and how they might be used. She wasn't inclined to be helpful in that regard but on the other hand, interaction and talk might make her less of a nameless captive and more of a part of the group.

Their slower pace caused them to arrive at the big valley more than an hour later than expected, so, as Deh Neh Totsi had hoped, the warriors decided to make camp and wait out the storm where there was wood and some shelter.

The south side of the valley extended out into the desert for another half mile. There were some cut banks from times when the water had been high. There were spots where water had undercut rocks, making cave like alcoves to crawl under and get out of the wind and snow.

There was one large shelf of rock that tapered back at least ten feet and was eight or nine feet high at the front and at least twenty feet long from side to side. This was big enough for the entire group and the sandy floor would make a dry place to sleep. The snow had not blown in even halfway to the back.

Twenty steps farther on, another, smaller rock had been undercut, forming a small cave about eight feet long. The sandy bottom was dry and very little snow had blown in from the front. It was shaped like a half dome and a fire at the front would reflect the heat back towards the center from the ceiling and every side. They deposited their packs and straightened up to stand at the entrance.

One of the more surly looking captors had followed them. "You think you can sneak out when we aren't looking," he snarled.

Fortunately, the more mild-mannered leader had come over also and looked at their little alcove.

She turned to face him squarely, ignoring the first captor, and replied calmly. "I give you my word, we will be here in the morning."

The leader grunted and the ghost of a smile touched the corners of his mouth. They both recognized that there could be no escape under the circumstances. Fleeing through the snow with two small children would be slow and leave a trail a blind rabbit could follow.

He nodded and turned back to the group. The other growled, "we watch." And turned back also.

She ignored them both and began to gather wood. Under the snow the wood was still dry because the snow wasn't melting. Most of the trees had low branches that were dead and broke off easily because they were dry also. The children each carried a couple of small armloads and stacked the branches just under the shelter of the rock and at either end of the little alcove.

The warriors banter coming from the other cave caught her attention. One of the captors was brandishing the bow saw like a weapon, swinging it around or holding both ends and pushing it forward. Others argued that it was light and a hatchet or war club would break it in pieces, a spear would go right past it.

Seeing an opportunity, she moved over to their site. She noticed that they had not been gathering wood and wondered how they expected to stay warm at night. They would probably begin scrambling after some just before dark and not finding enough, they would come after what she and the children had gathered.

She stepped forward into their circle, held out her hand and said, "let me show you."

The warrior, who was swinging the saw around, wasn't too pleased, but again the leader tilted his head a little to the side as he stared at her, then at the warrior and said, "give it to her."

She took it firmly, turned and walked directly away from their group. "Come, I show you."

Without looking back, she passed a couple of piles of driftwood and brush to a large collection of wood of varying sizes. Choosing a three inch thick piece of wood, she pulled it part way out of the pile, shook off the snow and in seconds had cut off a three foot piece of firewood. Pulling it out further she cut another and then another until she was down to the end that could be broken by hand.

Grabbing another piece, she repeated the process and in less than five minutes she had cut an armload of good, longer burning pieces of firewood faster than any of them had gathered in the last half hour.

She handed the saw to the nearest warrior, picked up three of the longer pieces and headed nonchalantly back to her own cave and to her children.

They stared after her in amazement. Gathering wood was a pain. Small pieces that could be broken by hand were so small that they burned quickly. Longer pieces had to be laid over the fire sticking out from the fire at whatever length the piece happened to be and was in the way. It then had to be shoved forward every time the end burned off. At night you had to get completely out of bed to pick up a log and move it forward. These short sticks could be handled with only your arm getting cold for half a minute.

As these realities began to sink in, they looked at one another a bit sheepishly. One or two began to uncover larger pieces of wood and some of the others took turns learning to use the saw. Others began carrying the firewood back to the fire site. The searching for pieces to break was over. The need to try to stomp on a limb to break larger ones with your foot, was over. Moccasins were not made to break firewood so it was hard on the foot.

The fact that they had more firewood in less than half the time that it usually took, was not lost upon them.

Deh Neh Totsi again took the saw when the warriors were done, and cut enough to last for the night even though she would need almost as much wood as the larger group to keep a fire going all night. She and the children got all their wood by themselves.

After returning the saw, she returned to her cave. She dug into her pack and got an energy bar. Unwrapping it quickly she broke it in three parts and collected the paper. She cleared an area for the fire just under the middle of the opening to their cave, where the smoke would go up and out but the fire would be just enough inside to utilize most of the heat it produced. She also built a short reflecting wall on the outer side of the fire with some chunks of rock with flat sides. The first layer would be for a can to set up a little higher and heat faster. The second layer would set back three inches behind the can to capture more heat and reflect more heat into the cave. She also turned it a little so no one could see what or how she was cooking.

When the fireplace was ready, she took out the paper from the energy bar and crushed it into a ball and placed it in the center of the fire pit. She then built a little teepee of twigs, small and dry, directly over it. Then she built another teepee of bigger, longer sticks about a foot high over the little teepee, making sure to leave an open space to get a hand and a match into the paper.

When all was in place, she opened the little bottle of matches and took out one, then closed the little water proof bottle to keep the rest dry. Finding a dry flat surface on a rock, she struck the match and laid it against the paper. It flared up immediately and caught the dry teepee of twigs, which in turn burned up into the larger teepee and in seconds flames were flickering up two feet into the air.

Heat rises and flames go up. Teepees are the best way to start a fire.

The sudden light and leaping flame, immediately caught the attention of the group of warriors. Again, they stared in amazement. They were just now getting the wood stick that was swirling in the base, to heat enough to smoke. It was still far from a spark with which to try to start some dry Moss that everyone carried. Swirling a stick back and forth between the hands into a larger piece of wood was the primary and usually effective way to start a fire. But it took time and patience using very dry wood, very dry moss or the stringy inside of some bark, blowing on the embers until a tiny flame formed and then adding sliver by sliver to nurse those embers into a fire.

She and her children were the last to use the saw to get wood and they had a large, cheery fire going first.

The thought began to creep into their minds that her poise, no nonsense behavior, her unearthly scream for "Chee," and this skill of starting fires, might mean that she was a witch or a medicine woman. Whatever she was, it might be wise to not push her or her children too far or too disrespectfully.

Noh Tay Dah was not making great time. Even going downhill, he couldn't keep his eyes open for long or the swirling world made him nauseous and weak. He began a routine of opening his eyes long enough to see a tree or bush, then closing his eyes and walking the few steps to that object and repeating this procedure over and over.

It was slow going but the progress was steady. Every once in a while, he stopped and steadied himself and looked ahead. He needed to be sure he was on the trail to the village.

The snow was falling more gently with less swirling and less windchill. He could see a little farther and found where the trail to the village left the trail that the band of warriors and his family was taking.

It also meant that the trail was totally covered with more than a foot of snow and no one had broken a trail through it.

With a pang of regret and despair, he realized he was closer to his family right now than he was to the village. The urge was strong to follow the downhill, broken trail instead of making the long slog up and down the hills, forging his own trail to the village. Common sense prevailed and he continued on towards the settlement where he hoped to find help.

Again, it was step-by-step; finding a tree along the trail and making his way to it; pausing to take a couple of breaths; then slogging on.

He arrived at the "Spring of the Grizzly Bear" as they had all come to know it, but the sun was now far past straight overhead. As he remembered it with a degree of discouragement, this was about the halfway mark from his home to the village. At this time of year, darkness came quickly. Dismayed, he realized it would be dark before he arrived.

If wolves, mountain lions or grizzly bears sensed his weakness, they might decide to take him down in spite of their natural fear of man.

The throbbing in his head had not subsided and the dizzying nausea still began to sweep over him if he kept his eyes open for more than a few seconds.

As the afternoon crept on, the temperature was dropping, his energy was giving out and he was going slower and getting colder.

It soon became a mind-numbing mantra of "must keep going, must keep going," and placing one foot in front of the other by sheer force of will.

Suddenly, his head jerked up as a whiff of smoke sent a message through the fog in his brain. He must be near the village.

Nobody would be out in this cold snowy weather. They would be wrapped in layers of coverings against the chill. Some of the fires had been built up for a last-minute warming of the coverings before settling in to a family bundle for the night.

Fortunately, the hut of Sunflower and Azalia was at the near end of the village.

He staggered and stumbled the remaining steps. Falling to his knees, he slapped his hand against the hide that served as a door. He slapped urgently a couple of times and the flap was thrust aside.

He collapsed into the hut, almost falling into the lap of Sunflower, who was still on her knees as she pulled back the flap.

He gasped out in a voice somewhere between a wail and a whisper. "They take Deh Neh Totsi; they take Lay Leh Tso and Yah Doh Nay, they take everything!" And then he passed out.

Chapter 2

Azalia and Blossom were startled into consciousness. Sitting up quickly, Blossom grabbed Noh Tay Dah's hand with concern. "He is icy cold!" She exclaimed. "What did he say?"

"He say men take Deh Neh Totsi and children but not who 'they' are or where they take them," Sunflower answered while pulling the collapsed body of Noh Tay Dah into the hut.

"The fire is still going. I will warm a covering." Azalia said and picked up a deer hide to take out to the fire. She returned in a few minutes. Sunflower had positioned Noh Tay Dah on their mat and pulled some of the still warm pieces of fur they had been using around him. Azalia laid the warm hide over him and Blossom turned on the light that Chee had given them months ago. They seldom used it since they had to remember to put it out in the sun or it would cease to give light.

That's when they noticed his head. There was blood down the side of his face and in his hair. Closer examination revealed a large lump on the side of his head.

"That is bad!" Azalia said urgently. "When Whiteface knock me down, Chee say I must rest three days or the bleeding inside my head might kill me!"

"I remember." Sunflower replied. "The journey to here would be long and hard. He must rest. What about Deh Neh Totsi and Lay Leh Tso and Yah Doh Nay?"

"We must go! We must find them!" Blossom asserted. She was always ready for action even if she didn't know what action was called for.

"We don't know who took them. We don't know where they go," Sunflower lamented.

"Let's go back to Noh Tay Dah's home. We can track them in the snow." She said with agitation. "We must do something!"

Noh Tay Dah moaned and began to stir. His eyes fluttered open and he cried out hoarsely, "Deh Neh Totsi!"

He struggled to sit up but all three girls urged him to stay calm and keep laying down.

"Stay down, we are here to help." Sunflower said soothingly

"No! We must go! They take Deh Neh Totsi, Lay Leh Tso, Yah Doh Nay!" He cried out again continuing to struggle.

"You must rest! We must plan." Sunflower responded sternly.

"Blossom, can you find the boys?" Sunflower inquired.

"Yes! I know where they are." She said and muttered softly, "I know where everyone is."

Sunflower looked at her with a sudden surge of sympathy. Blossom's years as an outcast and in constant danger continued to surface in unexpected ways.

"Just tell them that Noh Tay Dah is hurt, Deh Neh Totsi and the children have been taken captive. Tell them to dress in their warmest winter coats and boots and bring their bows and arrows. We must plan," Sunflower said more softly.

"Azalia, go to Chee's hut and see if there are six packs there. Hopefully there are different sizes and especially a small one for Blossom. I know she will insist on going and her senses in the woods are every bit as good as Lobo's, but she can't carry a large pack.

"Set up each pack, then see if there are six blankets, food items; anything that we need to camp out in winter but still travel fast." She went on thoughtfully.

"I don't like to rummage in Chee's things, He might come back and not like it."

"Chee has not returned for two moons. Maybe never come back," she said in a strained voice. "But I know he would give whatever was needed to help Noh Tay Dah and his family."

At the mention of Chee, Noh Tay Dah aroused from his groggy semi consciousness and cried out hoarsely, "we must find Chee!" And then he sagged back.

"Yes, I hope we can find Chee." Sunflower said dejectedly.

Azalia went to the next hut to find what she could in Chee's things. "I hope he doesn't get angry," she muttered to herself.

Blossom returned and reported that the boys were gathering their things but would be coming quickly.

"Do you think Yul D'Vey would look after Noh Tay Dah?" Sunflower inquired of Blossom. "He needs someone to check on him and see that he is warm and has food."

"He is a good man." She replied, "he will help."

"Would you go and see if he will come now to see the situation and take care of things?" Sunflower instructed and Blossom trotted off again.

Yul D'Vey and the boys arrived at about the same time.

Yul D'Vey was a warrior but when the overwhelming attack by the Whiteface tribe had taken place, he was outside the village with no weapon better than a stick. Being outnumbered four to one, he could only watch from a distance as his wife and child were captured.

Sunflower had suddenly charged forward screaming for Chee and prevented the murder of Grandmother.

To everyone's utter amazement, Chee, a mythical warrior of stories and tall tales, had come. In only four strikes of his thunder stick, the attack was halted and his wife and baby and all the other captives were freed and returned. The white-faced warriors had retreated down the valley carrying their dead and wounded.

Chee had become a friend, not only to him but to all the tribe and especially to Lan Ah Kay (Sunflower) Coy Dee Wan (Azalia) and La Lin Eedah (Blossom). The boys, Lo Bay Ton (Lobo), Him Pal Say (Impala) and Roc San Lee (Little Badger). Yul D'vey would do about anything to help Chee and the young people.

Lobo was a full-grown warrior but not yet out of his teens. He had become an excellent bow hunter and was already respected as a leader in the tribe.

Impala was slighter of build but also an excellent hunter. He could glide through the woods like a mist, skip across a stream, yet seem to barely touch the slick rocks.

Little Badger was the youngest, the shortest but possibly the strongest, as he was heavily muscled.

Yul D'Vey assured them that he and his wife, Grandmother and probably others from the tribe would see that Noh Tay Dah had all he needed and get his rest.

With Noh Tay Dah safe in the care of others, the little band began their plans.

Noh Tay Dah did not know how many enemy warriors there were. There were "many." There had been enough to carry all of his possessions away. Since all of his possessions except his hides and skins had been carried there by their group in the first place, they figured there had to be at least ten or twelve.

As Noh Tay Dah remembered the path through the snow, he didn't think there could be more than fifteen or twenty.

Concluding that there were about fifteen seasoned warriors and only six in their group, caused some anxious glances at one another and a large dose of discouragement.

"What if we come upon them and kill several with our first arrows? Will they kill the prisoners before they flee?" Lobo asked.

"What if after a few have fallen, they attack us? When we take down deer, we get close to where they stand or we let them come slowly because they do not know we are there. We do not try to strike down ones bounding away through the trees." Impala reminded them.

"If the captors spread out and attack slowly going from rock or tree to another rock or tree, we could seldom strike one. It takes time to draw, lock on and release. The arrow takes time to get there. If you guess when he will jump and are wrong, you waste an arrow. If you wait until he jumps, he can get three steps before an arrow can get there and he is already behind the next, closer rock." Impala explained

"Once they get close enough to throw a spear or war club. we cannot stand ready to shoot. If we spread out, they will focus on one or two of us at a time. If we bunch together, they can throw a spear to drop among us and hope to get someone." Little Badger added.

"We cannot fight a large group unless we have the high ground and they must come to us across open ground with no rocks or trees," Lobo concluded. "We learned that in our first battle."

There was a long silence as each gazed ahead at nothing, hoping that some solution would become evident.

Lobo broke the silence as he turned to Sunflower. "Can you find Chee?" He asked solemnly.

Without looking up she said quietly, "I don't know. Chee thought his purpose was to help the tribe and fix Blossom. Since he knew of no other purpose, he thought the door would be closed."

"Do you know the way to the door?" Lobo persisted.

"We know where it was. We don't know if it is still there and we promised we would never tell where it was." Sunflower said with some exasperation. "We would be breaking our word if we showed you the door."

Blossom broke in rather vehemently. "Do you not know Chee? I have been quiet because I am young, but you have no plan. Do you think Chee would say 'I don't care about Deh Neh Totsi or Noh Tay Dah, you broke your word'? Do you not know how much he loves Lay Leh Tso and Ya Doh Nay? Do you think he doesn't care to know about them?"

"I made no such promise! I will go to Chee," she declared. She got up angrily and began stuffing things in her pack.

Sunflower got up quickly and went to Blossom. "I'm sorry, I was more concerned about what Chee would think of me than the problem of Noh Tay Dah and his family. We will all go."

"No! I will get Chee!" Blossom said stubbornly.

"Wait, let's think this through." Sunflower said softly. "If you get Chee you will have to come all the way back to here to start our journey. We could start from the door and take a direct route to where we thought we would pick up the trail. What if you slipped in the deep snow, and it will be deeper up on the mountain, and hurt yourself? We would be here waiting, and you would be there waiting and maybe freeze to death. We will all go!"

Blossom was getting over her anger and the idea of climbing the mountain in ever deepening snow was appearing more daunting by the minute.

"Okay. It is good to stay together," she relented finally.

It took only a few minutes to finish throwing a few more things in the packs. Picking up their bows and quivers full of arrows, they were ready to head up the mountain in the darkness.

"Where is your bow and arrows?" Little Badger said quizzically.

They all paused to look, and it was Blossom's turn to confess her subterfuge.

"Chee give me small thunder stick when there was an emergency and danger. I am not allowed to speak of it. He said to give it back when we were past the danger, then he forgot to ask for it before he left, so I keep it."

She looked down and said somewhat quietly, "it is better than my bow. I have practiced."

They looked at one another and decided it was not the time or place to debate the issue or inquire further, so they headed out.

The snow had stopped for the time being and the moon was out and three quarters full. It made plenty of light for hiking, but there was no obvious trail. When Chee used to come, he had deliberately come down by various routes so there would be no trail. Even when they had brought all the presents down after Blossoms operation, Chee still used two or three variations of paths so that there wasn't one obvious one.

Sunflower had paid close attention to all the general routes and lay of the land, so she was sure that she could find the way. After all, all the paths had led to one single path along the bottom of the cliffs to the door.

As they stopped for breath near the start of the cliffs, Lobo suggested, "if we stopped a few hundred steps from the door you could still say, 'I did not show them the door'."

Sunflower smiled, "we will stay together. I will trust that Chee will forgive me."

The way along the base of the cliff was mostly level and they arrived at its end in a few minutes. When they were only a dozen steps from the end they froze in dismay and disappointment.

Several had brought a flashlight that Chee had given them last fall. They were charged by sunlight and were fully charged now. Aiming them at the spot where the door had stood all they saw was a snowdrift. It wasn't very big, only a few feet thick at the bottom, and the wind had plastered the snow eight or ten feet up the face of the cliff. There was no door to be seen.

Azalia dropped to the snow, put her hands over her face and started to cry. Sunflower just stared in disbelief.

Blossom approached the drift and thrust her hand into the drift. The snow went up past her elbows almost to her shoulder and she touched the solid wall of the cliff. She took a step back in utter discouragement. At least it explained why Chee hadn't come back.

As she gazed out over the huge valley, she remembered something. Chee had reached through the door which he called a portal and touched a solid door only inches behind the portal. The portal itself was like a haze or mist only thicker and more defined.

She turned quickly and began to claw at the drift. As she pulled the snow away, the snow above would fall into the void she had made and she would start over.

"What are you doing?" Little Badger asked as he came up beside her.

"I want to remove the snow. Maybe the portal is still there." She responded with hope in her voice.

Little Badger looked at the narrow drift in the wall of the cliff and carefully pushed his hand through the snow. It met a solid wall right where he estimated the cliff to be.

"No door there!" He said sympathetically.

"No, if the portal is still there you would reach through it and touch the door!" She said with gathering hope. "Help me remove the snow!"

To humor her in this time of disappointment, Little Badger began raking down large double handfuls of snow. Suddenly he said, "what is this?" There, right in front of their faces, was a snowy looking mist.

"This snow doesn't come down! I grab it but it is nothing," he said musingly.

"It's the portal!" Blossom cried, "help us dig!"

The others jumped in immediately, pulling large swaths of snow away from the bottom as others pulled the snow down from the top. Soon the shimmery form of the portal took shape.

Reaching through they found a thin layer of snow against a wooden door. Blossom began scraping it off and pulling it back through the portal. In a short time, the portal was visible.

"But there is nothing there!" Lobo insisted. He looked behind the portal and the cliff was visible. He even shined his flashlight and the cliff was clearly there to see.

Blossom blurted out with enthusiastic glee, "Chee is there!"

"How can we tell Chee that we are here?" Azalia asked.

Inside the house I was having a restless day. I couldn't explain it. Sometimes I would think of my wonderful experiences and friends back in the tribe and grow a little melancholy.

"If you think you have completed the purpose of the portal, you're going to have to live with it. You have a life here too." Dorothy had said.

I nodded in agreement. Even though the tearful abrupt ending hadn't seemed like the end. I had left Blossom when I had said I would take care of her. The tribe was growing together with confidence and hope and I knew it wouldn't help to make them dependent on handouts and modern things that they couldn't replace when they were used up.

Were they relearning the old ways of making pottery, storing food, tanning hides or all the other practices required to live in that time and place?

Cam and Heather, Ben and Sharon thought I might be experiencing withdrawal symptoms or even PTSD of some kind. I felt it was more like the stages of grief and loss.

Almost every day, I would go to the shed and turn on the computers that ran the cameras on the other side. I knew there had been a big snowstorm with lots of wind. The portal was completely drifted over. If I opened the door half of the drift would fall in on me and I'd have to push through some of it to get to the other side.

Not that I was planning to go through. I was seriously considering the possibilities of a vacation type visit, but somewhere in the back of my mind, I suspected the lack of purpose seemed to make the possibility of the portal's closing a serious risk.

On the other hand, my work pack was still full and sitting near the door. Both rifles were in cases but leaning nearby, ready to hook on to the pack.

But then a weird thing happened as I was working on my computer. All the other distractions seemed to dissipate when I'm absorbed in computer stuff. The emails, stock market, news items, all get my attention and the agitation is put behind me. Which is why what happened was so strikingly weird.

About ten o'clock that morning, I got this overpowering feeling of angst. It was a combination of dread, apprehension, fear that some unknown thing was about to descend on me.

I shook it off and got a cup of coffee and returned to my computer, but some residue of it remained all day. That's why at about 9:00 PM when I had just sat down to watch the news, before going to an early bed, the buzzing of the doorbell caused me to almost jump out of my chair.

Sunflower suddenly remembered something from the very first time they had ever gone through the portal. Blossom and Azalia had stepped through and as she had stepped through, Chee had touched her arm.

"If you ever need to notify me, press this button." He had said and pointed to a small, round button above the inner door.

Of course, it couldn't be seen from the outside of the portal but she reached through and felt along the top of the inner door frame. There was the button! She pressed it in, but did not hear or feel anything, so she pressed it again and then again. There was no response but she thought it might take a minute if the signal was in the house and Chee had to get a coat or something and come out to the shed.

"What did you do?" Azalia asked.

"I remembered that Chee showed me a button the first time we were here. He said it would signal him. Let's wait a few minutes and see what happens!" Sunflower said.

As they waited impatiently in the cold, Blossom looked up in the tree about eight feet in front of the portal.

"What is that?" She said inquiringly.

"What do you see?" Sunflower asked.

Pointing up, Blossom said, "there! That funny looking round thing like an eye or the end of binoc'lars."

They were all gazing directly at the camera when the computer came up and turned on the outside cameras. Much to my surprise there were six faces looking directly at me.

Quickly I pressed the intercom. "May I help you?" I said in mock formality.

"Chee, we need you." Blossom shouted but further explanation was drowned out by all of them talking at once.

The fact that the boys were with them against my direct orders made me certain that whatever it was, it would be serious.

"Wait a minute and I'll open the door." I said, and unlocked the series of locks that made the door like a fortress.

"Okay, you can come in," I said.

"Is it okay? The door won't close?" Sunflower asked with apprehension.

"I can come to you but it will take a while for me to get ready," I said.

Blossom piped up immediately. "The Great Spirit make the door open for a reason. We have big reason," and she stepped through immediately.

That action seemed to decide for the rest of them and they followed her through.

Blossom ran to me and gave me a long hug.

"I miss you Chee!" She whispered in my ear.

"I miss you too Sweetie." I whispered back.

The others crowded around to give me a hug and the boys moved in with big grins and a shoulder bump.

"Let me lock up the door. Your snow is blowing in on my floor," I joked.

"We must go quickly," Sunflower asserted. "Noh Tay Dah has been seriously hurt and Deh Neh Totsi and the children have been taken captive."

"Did that happen about 10 o'clock this morning?" I said.

Their mouths dropped open and they glanced at one another. "How you know this?" Azalia breathed.

"I don't know." I said cheerfully. "Why did I show up just when you came hopping out of your hut on one leg, fighting with your boyfriend?"

"Boyfriend!" She gritted out. "He go to kill me!"

"Well, given the big long gashes you put on his arm, maybe he thought he had a reason." I said smiling.

Everyone smiled, a few snickered and Azalia realized I was joking to bring the tension down. Calm minds make better plans.

After a quick review of all the events leading up to their trip through the portal, I asked. "Okay, do you have a plan?"

"Not really, they are more than we are." Lobo said.

"Do you know where they are?" I asked further.

"No, but they not go far with much loot and two children," Impala said thoughtfully.

"Are they in a place where we could ambush them?" I continued.

They merely looked at one another and shrugged.

"Do you think they would kill the prisoners if we attacked them?" I continued. Sometimes prisoners were immediately killed both to dissuade the rescuers, since there would be none to rescue, and to keep a prisoner from joining the fight from behind them.

"I will tell you what I think and you tell me where you think I might be wrong. Tonight, they sleep and look over all the loot they have taken.

"Once they are gone in the morning, we will find their campsite and follow to where they turn north or south. Either way it will take them three days to get out of the valley. If they go south to the Whiteface, we will have two days to plan and find a place for an ambush. I do not believe they are Whiteface.

"If they go north, it is three days through country we know and where we can choose our battle.

"That is how I would begin to plan." I finished.

"That is all true but shouldn't we go now?" Lobo asked.

"Do you want to fight them before we know how many there are and in a place we have not chosen?" I asked.

"No." He admitted.

"Okay then, let's go into my house, have some hot chocolate, maybe some dessert and make a plan. We will get a good night's sleep in a warm dry place, while they have a bad night in a cold, wet and windy place." I declared.

My phone had been ringing constantly and I figured Cam and Ben were wondering about the door buzzing. I made a group call explaining the situation and the fact that I and my little tribe would be heading out tomorrow to try to rescue Deh Neh Totsi and the children.

"I thought you said your mission had been accomplished." Ben said questioningly.

"Well, that part of the mission that was obvious to me. But the portal is still open and there is still a major problem that I had hoped was not part of my mission."

"What's that?" Cam asked.

"We will discuss it at length when I get back. Right now, I need to get ready for this mission, which I hope doesn't take all week. We'll talk about it when I get back."

We all traipsed through the sliding glass door to the living room. The girls ran to give Dorothy a hug and the boys were lost in a glazed stare at things they had never seen or imagined.

Finishing up the hugs, Dorothy asked. "It's good to see you again, but what brings you here?"

Deh Neh Totsi and the children are captured. We must get them." Sunflower responded.

"And that means you need Chee." She said with resignation. "But, come in and sit down and I'll make some hot chocolate."

"Is anyone hungry?" I asked.

Before anyone could even take a breath to answer, Blossom declared, "I hungry!"

We all laughed, but they all said they could eat. The boys were hungry because they could always eat and the girls were remembering the food from their previous visit.

"How does pizza sound?" I asked the girls.

"Oh, that be wunnerful," Sunflower enthused.

Dorothy laughed and remarked, "we did eat a lot of pizza when you were here." She got her phone and began to place an order.

"What is peeza?" Little Badger asked.

"You will love it but you will see when it gets here," Azalia said enthusiastically.

"Is there anything else we need to get?" I asked.

The girls exclaimed eagerly and in unison, "ice cream!"

"Is that what we eat at winter celebration?" Impala asked.

"Yes, that is ice-cream!" Blossom declared.

"That good!" Impala said almost reverently.

The girls were so excited to show the boys around the house that we couldn't keep them still or quiet. I let them roam and question and explain for about a half hour until the pizza finally came.

We sat around the dining room table so we could keep the mess in one area. It is good that pizza was designed to be eaten by hand. The boys weren't very adept at utensils.

"Maybe you boys will understand a little better when the girls talk about their time here. They had many strange experiences," I interjected into their conversation.

"Fun as it is to eat our ice cream, we need to remember why we are here and begin to make some plans," I said seriously.

Chäptër 3

"It would take seven suns to show you just the biggest things they did while they were here. So, since we don't have time to do that, we need to focus and plan on how we can get Deh Neh Totsi and the children back safely," I admonished.

They looked a little guilty that they had forgotten about Deh Neh Totsi and their purpose here.

They settled back in their chairs and got quiet immediately. It would not be an overstatement to say we were about to make some life or death decisions.

"We will assume that tonight they are camped close to where Noh Tay Dah's valley meets the big valley. There are protected places to camp and available firewood there," I began.

"Let's assume they will go north or south so how we plan will be the same either way.

"We will be about a half day behind them and we can go faster, although they will be on the level ground. By the end of the first day, we will go up a side valley to camp while they will camp close to the valley.

"There will be no water where we camp but we'll be able to melt snow. They will have to do that too. We will stay even with them until we find a wide space with a finger of land that extends out into the valley. They will either go around it out into the valley or find a low spot to go over it.

"If it is a narrow pass with sides, we can be on both sides and demand that they stop. If they don't, six of them will be struck down by your arrows immediately.

"I will focus on protecting Deh Neh Totsi and the children. Any warrior who takes a step in her direction will be stopped immediately.

"Remember, we are there to rescue them, not kill unknown enemies. We will adjust our plan, even at the last minute, to deal with whatever we face.

"Now let's get a good night's sleep and be ready in the morning," I concluded.

"Can we take shower?" Azalia asked plaintively.

"Showers!" I exclaimed, "it would take two hours for six people to shower and another hour to fix your hair."

"Is shower what you show us in days of hot sun?" Lobo asked.

"Yes! You said you liked it." Azalia responded.

"It good in hot sun. Not good now." Impala interjected.

"No need shower." Little Badger declared.

"Girls can shower." Blossom said eagerly.

Everyone turned to look at her. "I thought you said you didn't like water." I said in disbelief. The others nodded.

"This good water. It warm!" Blossom grinned.

"Oh, okay! Shower, Fix your hair. Do whatever, but we leave at first light," I said with resignation.

"Come on boys, I'll show you where you can sleep in a soft, warm, peaceful and quiet place," I said.

Dorothy got out the hair dryers for the girls and showed them how to use them.

I got the bacon, eggs and pancake mix ready for the morning. I guess I was designated as breakfast cook.

The morning arrived all too quickly, but the sizzle of bacon and the aroma of coffee, as usual, encourages people to get up.

"How did you sleep, boys?" I asked.

"I almost not want to sleep. I like soft warm place." Impala said, still in some awe of a "bed" that wasn't a skin on the ground.

"I hope remembering it helps keep you warm tonight," I grinned.

"Girls, help Dorothy clean up while the boys and I get whatever we think we might need for a three or four day trip."

With everyone working quickly, we were packed and ready shortly after dawn. We put in a couple boxes of energy bars and some MRE's I had found at an Army/Navy store.

Back through the portal, it was only a few hours to the Grizzly Spring where we rested and filled our water containers.

Everyone was traveling easily with good boots and only three quarter full packs. Blossom was certainly bigger and stronger than she was last summer.

It suddenly dawned on me that she wasn't carrying a bow, nor were any arrows visible.

"Blossom, where are your bow and arrows?" I asked curiously.

We had paused for a short rest and a drink of water and everyone turned to look at Blossom to see what she would say.

She looked around somewhat guiltily but faced up to the truth. "I have little thunder stick you give me." She said defensively.

"I thought I loaned it to you and you were supposed to give it back," I said, raising my eyebrows.

"You not ask for it." She said, not looking at me directly.

"Do you know how to use it?" I asked.

"Yes! You show me. I practice. I go far out in dry Creek and strike the wall. I take two steps back and strike two more. I take all apart and put in more little sticks that make thunder. I find best way to hold and point and after two trips, I go ten steps. I hit little box I draw in dirt on wall every time. You leave little box full of little sticks. I not use half of box."

She paused, waiting for my reaction to her lengthy explanation. The others seemed to be holding their breath, not sure what reaction to anticipate from me.

"How big a box did you draw?" I asked unexpectedly.

She held her hand apart about eighteen inches and then about two feet high.

"About the size of a man from neck to waist?" I asked.

She nodded, obviously relieved that I didn't seem angry.

"I hope you're right." I said, and settled back into my pack and started off.

The others looked at one another as though they thought some major crisis had been averted, but adjusted their packs and headed out with me.

The boys took turns breaking trail and it was only a little over an hour to the stream. The storm had not totally covered Noh Tay Dah's tracks, so we followed them until they curved north on our old trail. We angled slightly south and found the tracks of the invaders along the stream.

We didn't bother to try to sort out numbers. We would work on that at their campsite.

As we drew near to the end of the valley where it widened out and met the big valley, we slowed down. It was possible that they had not left yet, although I doubted they would stay there. But just in case, we went slowly and quietly.

As we approached the section with the cut bank and overhanging rocks, Lobo motioned us to stay while he went forward to see if there was anyone there.

In a few minutes Lobo whistled like a bird, giving the 'all clear and come' signal so we moved on to where Lobo was standing in front of a large rock overhang where the black circle of a fire had recently burned. Off to the left was another, much smaller rock overhang also with the charcoal residue of a fire pit.

I motioned to them to count the depressions in the snow to see how many warriors had slept there. Sunflower and I went over to where Deh Neh Totsi and the children had stayed. Some of their firewood was still neatly ranked in one end of the little alcove.

Sunflower was poking around in the snow and found an empty can with the paper peeled off. I smiled. Deh Neh Totsi was planning ahead with some fire starter.

We went back to the others to see what they had found. They had counted twelve beds and three places where they piled packs but some could have slept with the packs also.

So, we were facing twelve to fifteen warriors to our seven. Of course, they would underestimate the girls and especially Blossom when they saw us. That would actually be in our favor.

After a short rest and one more look around, we headed out on their trail. They were at least four or five hours ahead, assuming they didn't leave as early as we did.

It seemed that Deh Neh Totsi and the children had not been harmed and had survived the hike and the cold night.

We followed the same trail they were on. Letting them break the trail through the snow made it easier for us. If they were four hours ahead of us, it would take us eight hours to catch them even if we traveled twice as fast as they were going.

Measuring some of the strides they were taking, we figured they weren't pushing themselves or their captives, and given the times they stopped, milled about and set their packs down, we just might be able to go twice as fast.

Our packs were designed for hiking and rested on our hips more than our shoulders. They were carrying their loot like potato sacks and it was wearing out their arms and ultimately their backs. We found places where things had fallen out of their packs or perhaps a pack had fallen apart and spilled everything. These spots were obvious from the indentations in the snow and the tracks that showed that they gathered around to pick things up.

At these spots, Deh Neh Totsi and the children went off a few yards to sit on a rock and leave us a clear set of tracks that showed that they were okay and doing well.

At every hilltop, no matter how small, one of the boys would forge ahead and scan the next valley and ridgetop, checking to see that the trail continued and that no head was sticking up to watch their back trail.

The warriors we were following would have no concept of binoculars, so they would not watch with much thought of concealment. If they could hardly see a full body walking along their trail, surely someone following could not see a head and upper body standing still and looking back.

After about six hours, we became more cautious. We knew that about two hours ahead was a deeper Valley with some cut banks and brush very similar to the campsite they had used the night before. Since the days were short and the nights cold, they would want to stop early enough to make preparations for the night, cut wood and get a fire started before dark.

As we came near the top of the ridge before the dry wash, we stopped. I suggested that two of them go to check out this valley. Impala and Little Badger volunteered immediately.

"Go west at an angle instead of following the trail," I advised. "Use the binoculars to see if there's a trail leading over the next ridge to another valley. If you can't find one, go down the ridge just far enough to confirm that this is where they are making camp. You only need to get close enough to hear and be careful that those going out into the valley bottom to get wood, don't look back and see you. We just need to know if this is where they will spend the night?

"Signal us from the ridge instead of coming all the way back and we will join you. Be careful!" I concluded.

They left, angling off to the west and disappeared over the ridge.

We brushed the snow off of some rocks and from the space in front of them so we could sit, lean back and rest. I'm sure I was probably the most tired of all of them. Youth always wins out in these situations which call for endurance.

It wasn't twenty minutes before Impala and Little Badger reappeared on the top of the ridge. They waved and we got up, put on our packs and hurried to join them.

They motioned for us to be quiet. Sound travels a long way in the still, crisp air, so they reported in hushed tones

"They camp along bank of dry stream bed," Impala reported. "They across from big rocks on far side of valley."

We could see the rocks across the valley so their campsite was about a half mile down this ridge.

"Let's go to the next valley and find a place to camp." I said, "we can look for a good ambush site somewhere up ahead and make our plans."

The site we found was at least a mile and a half from our quarry, and since it was in the next valley, any smoke drifting down the valley would not go near them.

Our site was similar to the one our quarry had used the night before. It was an alcove under a rock ledge where water had washed out a spot about six feet in depth and twice that in length with a sloping ceiling starting at six feet in height at the middle and curving down on each side of the opening.

Being higher up the mountain, the valley was narrower with steeper and higher sides. There were a number of juniper trees growing in the bottom and up both sides which made our campsite invisible beyond fifty yards in any direction.

Firewood was plentiful and a couple of armloads from each person almost filled the front of the cave. We would have a warm fire all night long.

I dug the extra ponchos out of my pack which met with general approval. They work for both a moisture barrier from the ground and a wind barrier around part of the body.

After the fire got started, we put the coffee pot on and kept adding snow as it melted. We soon had enough water for four cups of hot chocolate and I suggested that the boys get the first cups, since they would need to get awake constantly to replenish the fire.

The girls each wanted the other to take the extra cup and when they couldn't decide they offered it to me.

"I couldn't possibly take the hot chocolate that belongs to one of you." I said dramatically. "I wouldn't be able to sleep tonight knowing I had stolen the hot chocolate."

They just laughed at me and decided the extra hot water would melt snow more quickly so they began piling in the snow and soon had more than four cups boiling.

I handed out an energy bar to each one and they began digging around in their packs for canned food. A couple cans of beef stew and a couple cans of fruit would make a good meal. As they finished their hot chocolate, they would scoop a few cups of clean snow back into the pot.

Since the frames of the packs were about three feet tall, and the sloping ceiling came down to three feet high towards the back of the cave, we set them in a semi-circle in the alcove to make a backrest. Now we could sit in the semi-circle inside the cave with the fire in front. This way we were out of the wind and the heat of the fire came directly toward us and also reflected down on us from the ceiling. By sitting on one end of a blanket and bringing the rest up behind us and over our shoulders, we captured most of the heat and made a warm place to interact and relax.

We all needed to re-hydrate, and sipping and talking made for a cozy interlude before we turned in.

It was a great opportunity to get a report on how things were going since I left.

"Blossom, do you feel that the tribe has accepted you? Are things like you expected?" I asked tentatively.

She paused thoughtfully for a while before answering. "Everybody is friendly but I don't go to other huts. Everybody greet me where I go. Nobody frown or say 'go away'." She replied.

"Well, it is winter so there's not a lot of outdoor social life," I opined.

"What do the rest of you think?" I continued.

Lobo spoke up immediately. "She is accepted. All were reminded that she warn us of the Whiteface and lives were saved."

Impala and Little Badger agreed. "Lip is fixed, there is no curse!" Impala said.

Little Badger added, "people say more about Yul D'Vey talk then Blossom lip."

Everyone laughed and Impala said almost in awe, "that surprise everybody!"

"Everything was like a surprise and so different that the fix of lip was just part." Azalia responded. "Everyone sit in awe of beautiful lights, strange, wunnerful food, strange music sounds."

Sunflower summed it up with thoughtfulness and insight as she often did. "It all work together so that there is so much to talk about that lip and curse not important anymore. It also seen by all that we are family and that is first."

"Blossom is sister," said Little Badger with such fondness and sincerity that several exchanged glances.

Blossom finally spoke softly. "I know I safe in tribe but I feel even more warm and safe here with family." Her eyes seemed to glisten a little more brightly in the firelight.

She was snuggled in beside me so she scooted forward, turning to look straight at me and said, with what I hoped was mock sincerity, "it be good if our father was here more with family."

Before I could object, the others pounced gleefully.

"Yes! Father should be with family." Lobo asserted solemnly.

This was Azalia's turf and she entered the fray with enthusiasm. "Fathers who really love their children give them 'sweet stuff' and ice cream and pizza. But did our father bring ice cream and pizza? No! He bring beef stew in can!"

Everyone laughed and before I could defend myself, Sunflower, who also loved to tease, jumped in. "When you come to see us, we let you stay many days. We feed you and listen to much talk, big stories; but we visit you and you chase us out early next morning."

Again, they all laughed and nodded in agreement, as that is what had just happened.

"Okay, okay!" I finally broke in, "but what kind of children would take their loving father on a long, long hike in the middle of winter, in the middle of a wild blizzard and make him gather the wood and make the fire and cook the meal and sleep on the cold hard ground?"

"No, no, no!" They were all saying good-naturedly at my exaggerations.

I pointed at Azalia and said, "you didn't even offer me a hot shower."

This turned the exaggeration back to them and they all laughed good naturedly.

After the laughter had died down, Sunflower commented. "You see, Chee, even after a long journey, little food and cold hard ground, we are happy and laughing and warm in our hearts because we are together. It is better when we are all together. Even with the danger that we may face tomorrow, our hearts are light, our spirits feel free, because we are together."

Azalia added somewhat wistfully, "we still need you Chee. Not just to get the garden right and how to get the white powder for the acorns, but many things we not remember all the details."

Lobo spoke up with a serious expression. "We have need of leaders. Some want to lead by demand and people do not like. Some don't want to earn respect. Some do not make decisions and do."

Impala spoke with a reverent tone, "I remember father of Lan Ah Kay and Coy Dee Wan." He had slipped into the given names of Sunflower and Azalia as they were known before my arrival. "Coy Dah Mahn was great leader."

They all murmured in agreement. There were several minutes of thoughtful silence as old memories resurfaced.

I spoke quietly, "it is good to keep long memories of great men and women and wonderful parents."

Again, there was a murmured response. We sat for a while finishing our cup of hot chocolate and remembering people and events that helped to put our lives in perspective.

Tomorrow we would face a fierce enemy and we must be rested and ready. The lay of the land and circumstances would choose our actions for us.

Deh Neh Totsi and the children were tired. She planned to get the fire going, get the three of them fed and get to sleep as quickly as possible.

The bully, who seemed bent on harassing her, moved towards her site, which was only fifteen steps from the rest of the band.

"You make our fire!" He commanded.

She had just started gathering the wood for her own fire and they had not yet started to get any for theirs.

She stopped and stared at him for an uncomfortably long time. He shifted his eyes and she walked on and dropped the armload next to where she would build her fire.

"You build fire!" He demanded more belligerently.

She looked past him and responded. "I don't see any wood to build a fire."

"You get wood!" He demanded again.

He was the largest of the group. Apparently used to throwing his weight around and making others back down.

All the others had paused to observe the confrontation.

"So, you are chief now?" She sneered at him.

Her plan was reckless and did not stop to consider what would happen to the children if she were killed or injured, but she had had enough.

Turning her back in a curt dismissal, she reached inside her coat and grabbed the hilt of the large hunting knife she wore at her belt. She watched his shadow and knew exactly when he would be right behind her. Her plan was to turn quickly and thrust when he was one step away. She would turn, throwing up her left hand which he would undoubtedly grab but it would also keep him from seeing the knife in her right hand.

Most people would try to pull away from him but he would not expect her to step toward him and bury the knife up to the hilt in his belly.

The chief saw her reach into her coat and guessed her purpose. He immediately gave a loud and forceful command to the bully, who was still three steps away.

He angrily wheeled around to object but the chief fiercely commanded him again and he sullenly complied. Adding insult to injury, the chief told him to get an armload of wood and cool off. To lessen the ignominious humiliation, the chief commanded everyone to get some wood and prepare for the night.

The chief paused to look at Deh Neh Totsi who was still somewhat shaken by what she had almost done. Tilting his head to the side, he gave the ghost of a smile and nodded three times. She knew immediately that he knew what she had been about to do and in stopping the confrontation he had saved her life as surely as he had saved the bully's life.

The rest of the band would not have let the killing of one of their own go unpunished.

She nodded in his direction, lowering her head in acknowledgment.

She also knew that she was not done with the bully. He had been shamed in front of everyone and could not grasp that his bullying did not bring respect. If he had paid attention, he would have noticed that everyone seemed to enjoy seeing him put in his place. As with most bullies, his tactics merely caused resentment and he would never command respect as a leader.

When her fire was going, Deh Neh Totsi went back towards the other site, collecting some small, dry wood together and shaping it into a small tepee, with some larger wood over that. She then went to her fire and found a piece of bark about the length of her lower arm and a hand in width.

Taking some was dry grass from under a nearby limb that the wind had uncovered as it blew around the tree. She put the grass and some small twigs on the bark and went back to her fire.

She wasn't about to let her little fire sticks and paper be seen by these men, so she took a stick from her fire and lit the tinder on the bark. It began to flare up immediately and she went to the other site and put the fire from the bark into the tepee. It began to catch and in only the time it took to take three breaths, the flames were leaping up and catching the bigger wood.

She straightened up and met the eyes of the chief who was watching her as she worked. She nodded at him and returned to her children.

She and the children opened a can, making sure they were not observed. After devouring it they chewed on some dry meat. Making water from snow would take a while. Each cup full of snow gave about a quarter inch of water which was about four swallows. They would spend most of their evening getting rehydrated.

As they waited for a cup of snow to melt, Lay Leh Tso asked timidly, "Mother, will Chee come?"

It caught Deh Neh Totsi by surprise. She had given up hope in that direction. If Noh Tay Dah was dead, who would go to find Chee? Did anyone know where Chee was and how did you find him? Sunflower had apparently called out to him and he had come. Why would he hear the cry of Deh Neh Totsi? She was not of that tribe.

"I do not know my child, but if he comes, he will have a plan so we must pretend we do not know him, or these warriors might kill us and attack him immediately." She said with little hope in her voice.

"Maybe he come as a grizzly bear. They would not kill us because they saw a bear." Yah Doh Nay said hopefully.

"If he did come as a bear, we must not let them know it is Chee." She said, more to give hope and a narrative to the children.

"Maybe he sneak in and kill some and when they rise up and grab spears he run into the darkness. Then when they sleep again, he come and do that until they are all gone!" Yah Doh Nay said, building his own fantasy.

"We must wait and be ready." She said, "we don't know when he might come."

That hope might keep them going through their long journey.

The next morning was a repetition of the first. None of the warriors were anxious to get on the trail before the sun was up, adding a little warmth to the morning chill.

Deh Neh Totsi got up at sunrise because that is what she usually did. This morning there was the added incentive, because the bully might get up early and do something before the chief was able to stop him.

She melted some snow for water for the children. A can of fruit and some more of the dried meat made a small breakfast. Another couple of days and she would be out of food.

How could she find food for the children in this bitter cold, snow-covered waste land?

It was a little warmer this morning. The snow was settling and not as deep as yesterday. The first hill was a gentle slope and not too high. There were a scattering of juniper trees and lots of sagebrush. She couldn't help but enjoy the beautiful scenery and the snow-covered peaks far to the east.

She also noticed that the bully had decided to walk with those who came behind her and the children. He was undoubtedly looking for another opportunity to bully her. As they went over the crest of the hill, they saw another long slope down into a wide valley and then a long finger of land that went hundreds of steps out into the big desert on their right. There were cliffs straight ahead. They would either have to find a break in the cliffs or walk all the way out into the desert to go around the mesa that formed the end of the long hill.

They were relieved to find that there was a break in the hill and it would serve as a pass between the cliffs and make the long trip around the ends unnecessary.

They began their descent down the long slope on this side of the valley. Suddenly, Lay La Tso grabbed her hand and jerked it excitedly. Two figures, still little more than tiny dots, were walking along the face of the cliffs on a course to intercept them.

Deh Neh Totsi's heart jumped. Quickly she paused to whisper in her daughter's ear. "Do not let those behind us know what we see!" She said urgently.

Quickly she pulled Yah Doh Nay close to her and said, "do not let those behind know that we see someone coming."

"Is it Chee?" He asked excitedly.

"We do not know but do not look and do not speak. Just keep walking as you normally do. Pretend you see nothing," she urged

Chee and his little band broke camp at dawn. They were a valley ahead of the warriors who had Deh Neh Totsi and the children, but they wanted to be in place at the right place and time to execute their plan.

The boys with Sunflower and Azalia would go down the far side of the long finger of land to the narrow pass and come over to this side just after the cliff walls ended. They needed to get in position without being seen.

Blossom and I would follow the cliffs on this side to the path, walking in plain sight but adjusting our speed to intercept the warriors before they entered the pass.

We made no furtive movements but walked openly and nonchalantly in the morning sun.

"Now remember, when we get to them you repeat and translate everything they say to me. Don't say 'he said' or 'that one said'. I'll see who is talking and follow their conversation."

"Don't interact with Deh Neh Totsi or the children until we know the situation."

"I do it, Chee. But maybe they all talk at once," she said.

"Just say as much as you can of what you hear. I will try to figure out what they will do and what they are thinking," I said.

The warrior band was strung out along the trail with seven in the front, then Deh Neh Totsi and the children and then five more warriors behind them. They began to bunch together a little and then stopped in two groups with a gap where Deh Neh Totsi had been. Blossom and I approached and headed towards that gap.

Den Neh Totsi had wisely taken the children ten steps back from the trail, brushed off some rocks and sat down to rest out of the way of whatever was to happen.

"Do you have your little thunder stick ready?" I asked.

"It ready, Chee," she answered.

"When we stop, you stay three steps to the side and slightly behind so I can swing my rifle in either direction and you won't be in danger. And you take the ready position and get set!" I cautioned.

"Okay, let's engage!" I said and walked to the side of their path right towards the gap where Deh Neh Totsi had been.

Chapter 4

We positioned ourselves right at the front of the second group and ten steps back from their path. Deh Neh Totsi and the children were directly across from us, so any shooting would be to the right or left and not endanger them.

I had seen the trail made by Lobo and the group coming over the hill and taking positions behind rocks and trees. They had stayed behind a cluster of trees so their trail was not visible from the way that these warriors were going.

My group was in place and all was ready, so I decided to meet the situation head-on hoping to keep these captors confused and uncertain.

"We have come for Deh Neh Totsi and the children," I announced loudly.

Blossom translated and they looked at one another in a mix of disbelief and amusement. Here was some strange looking man and a little girl challenging a large group of armed warriors.

Grinning, I tilted my head to the side, raised my left hand and wiggled my fingers in a greeting towards the children.

When they looked at their mother for guidance, she smiled and waved back, so the children did too.

A warrior at the back of the group on the right, snarled out and Blossom translated, "I kill him and take his things!"

"You made a mistake in taking Deh Neh Totsi and her children. You will return them to me and all that you have taken and I will let you go!" I said again loudly so that all could hear.

Again, Blossom repeated my commands.

The incongruity of the situation was leaving them speechless, but also irritated. The little girl voice was issuing commands and ultimatums.

It probably sounded like watching a tense cops and robbers show and dubbing in Mickey Mouse, Huey, Dewey and Louie voices.

The brutish looking one who had spoken first, jumped in again. He was bigger but shorter than the others and obviously was trying to assert himself.

It was also obvious that he was not the leader and didn't command the respect of the others.

Blossom translated, "I go get little…, and she do as I say."

"Chee! He call me bad name!" Blossom said indignantly and then continued with her translation. "He say, 'I beat her so she do what I want'!"

I glanced at Blossom. She was more mad than scared. I said to her in a low voice, "if he takes a threatening step in this direction, you take him down."

"I do that Chee! I ready!" She replied and I heard the click of the hammer being drawn back into full cock.

The audacity of our demands and our apparent vulnerability was keeping them paralyzed with indecision. They perceived no threat and knew they could proceed whenever they chose.

Suddenly, the bully growled something and started towards us. Before he took his third step there was a loud crack of thunder from the little .22 Magnum derringer. It was not only loud but reverberated off the cliffs in front of us for a doubling of its effect.

The big warrior jerked to a halt like he had run into a tree and his left hand grabbed his upper chest on his right side. The shock of the bullet exiting through his shoulder blade turned his legs to rubber and he fell to his knees.

The rest of them stood there in shock. How could a little girl with no obvious weapon produce such a sound and get such results.

The warrior beside him helped the wounded bully pull the covering down over his shoulder revealing a small hole that was oozing blood. Then, as the covering garment was pulled down the back, the warrior looked behind him at the exit hole and his face told the story. The exit hole of a hollow point bullet is considerably larger than the entry hole.

I looked down at Blossom and said, "it went a little high and to the left."

"You say wounded enemy better than dead enemy," She gritted out. "I strike where I aim!"

The wounded warrior raised his head and cried out some kind of command.

Blossom translated urgently, "he say, 'kill the boy!' Chee, he say, kill Ya Doh Nay!"

"Okay, I've got it," I said.

The warrior who was standing a little towards the back of this group dropped the bag of loot and raised his spear. He walked directly towards Deh Neh Totsi and the children.

Deh Neh Totsi leapt to her feet, pulling the children around behind her.

By the time the warrior with the spear separated out from behind the group, he was only a few steps from Deh Neh Totsi.

It was enough space, and I pulled the SKS up and shot him through the leg.

His leg jerked out from under him and spun him sideways. His spear flew off into the sagebrush and he fell face first into the snow. He rolled over and screamed in pain.

Blossom cut in, "he not fix weapon. He cannot strike again! We get him now!"

As they gathered themselves to charge, I put two quick shots into a bush right in front of them. The bullets, striking the bush, flung the snow all over them and stopped this attack. Another would follow shortly.

"I can strike each of you two times and still not need to fix my weapon." I shouted and Blossom shouted the translation.

This gave them something to think about and I turned my head and shouted, "Sunflower, Azalia, come!"

Two figures emerged from behind some trees fifty yards up the trail. The captors had all turned to look when I turned my head and shouted that direction, and the two approaching figures held their attention.

"Fifteen steps back and ready!" I shouted.

Before they were in position just opposite the group of seven warriors at the front, they recognized that they were women.

As Blossom translated, one growled to the others, "he come to us with women and children."

Before they could use that as an excuse to attack, I again turned my head in that direction and shouted, "Lobo, Impala, Little Badger come!"

Three more figures stepped out from behind rocks that were about ten steps from where the girls had been hiding and came down the trail made by the girls. Before they got into position, I looked up the hill opposite the side where my group had stationed themselves and gestured to my imaginary army to stay in place.

It had the intended effect as they became even more confused trying to estimate how many enemies might be arrayed against them.

The boys took their places on each side of the girls. They all stood with one foot in front of the other with their arrow nocked and ready to draw and shoot. Their bows were obviously superior weapons to the spears of these warriors and it was obvious that these young people knew how to use them.

With all of us in position, I pointed my rifle at one of the two remaining warriors on my side and nodding to Blossom I said, "go to your friend and stop the bleeding or he dies." She relayed the message and he went.

"You were right," I said to Blossom. "Two enemies wounded, four warriors out of the fight."

I pointed my weapon at the lone remaining warrior on my side and commanded, "step back!"

When Blossom issued the command, he obeyed immediately.

"Sunflower, get Deh Neh Totsi and the children and bring them over here." I nodded to Blossom to begin translating. "If anyone takes a step towards them, take him down."

The ones up the trail got the message also.

When Sunflower reached Deh Neh Totsi, everyone fell into a group hug. Sunflower and Deh Neh Totsi each took the hand of one of the children and walked quickly to our side. As soon as they were clearly past the warriors, both children dropped the hands they were holding, and rushed to Blossom and me.

"I know you come, Chee!" Yah Doh Nay cried as he rushed in for a hug. Lay Leh Tso headed for Blossom to get her hug.

"Watch your weapon!" I warned Blossom.

"It not set to strike!" She replied but disengaged from Lay Leh Tso.

Up the trail, one warrior raised his hand and said to Lobo, "I talk to Chee?"

Lobo assessed the situation. There was no posture or evidence to indicate a threat, so he took charge and said, "you may go, the others will stand where they are."

This was the leader, finally revealing himself, and he approached with dignity but no sign of aggression."

I turned to Blossom, "you did a great job. Would you like to help with the children?"

Nodding her head, she returned the .22 magnum to the pouch where she kept it and quickly joined them as they moved back jabbering and talking over one another telling all that they had gone through.

As the chief approached, I motioned to Sunflower to translate and Deh Neh Totsi joined us as well.

"You are Chee?" He said, it was more of a statement than a question.

"Here is my spear. We are your prisoners." He said solemnly.

"We did not come to take prisoners. We came for our friend and all that belongs to Noh Tay Dah," I informed him.

I turned to Sunflower, "did you tell her?"

Deh Neh Totsi looked at us questioningly.

"Noh Tay Dah is alive. He came to get us. He wanted to come but we made him stay and rest," Sunflower said earnestly.

"Aaa-iii-eee!" Deh Neh Totsi screamed jubilantly. "Children, father is alive." She sang out and the children squealed excitedly and ran from one to another of us giving us hugs.

"She is medicine woman." The chief said seriously with a slight nod of his head towards Deh Neh Totsi.

"Why do you say that?" I asked curiously.

"Husband lies dead in the snow, she does not look at him. She knows he will rise and go to ones he know. When we leave, she turned face to sky and scream your name louder than any war cry, and you come. When one push boy and he fall into snow, she turn on man and say 'when Chee come, he strike you down.' When man raise spear against her, you strike him down. She do other strange things. She is medicine woman." He assured me matter-of-factly.

"Tell your warriors to bring all that belongs to Noh Tay Dah, Deh Neh Totsi and the children, and put it here before her," I told him.

I signaled the rest of the group to let them come. They came one by one and dropped hides made into baskets, filled with the family's possessions until there was a large pile of hides, skins, clothing, utensils, pots, pans, knives and even the hatchet and saw.

She had stood and faced each warrior as he approached, looking him in the eye and seeing him drop his eyes and then lay her things at her feet.

"Is anything missing?" I asked Deh Neh Totsi.

"Are any of your men trying to steal anything by keeping it hidden?" I asked the chief.

He turned and looked at each one to see if they had been honest. He turned back to me and said, "I believe they have returned all."

I looked at the pile with some skepticism. It looked like more than we could carry back.

Deh Neh Totsi turned to me and said, "it is more than we can carry. May I give some away?"

"It is yours to do with as you wish," I said.

"Even though they did us much harm, the chief was kind to me and gave protection more than once. They have a long journey with wounded ones. They need some things," she responded.

She and Sunflower began to go through the pile, tossing things to one side that she thought she could do without.

I said softly to Sunflower, "are their gifts from the celebration two moons past still in my hut?"

"They are there, Chee," she affirmed.

I turned to Deh Neh Totsi, "we can replace almost everything that is here. You only need to take back things that we couldn't replace."

"May I give gifts?" She said.

"That might be a good way to end this whole unfortunate situation," I said hopefully.

She turned to the chief and pointed to one of the warriors. "Tell that one to come," she said firmly.

The man in question, looked surprised, then worried. Why was he being singled out. He came hesitantly, watching carefully at where I was pointing my rifle.

Deh Neh Totsi stepped forward and handed him the bow saw. "You give this to me when I ask. I give it to you now."

He took the saw in bewilderment and backed slowly to his companions.

"The man who is struck down has paid for his actions; he will need warmth," and she handed a blanket to the chief to give to the wounded man.

She next pulled out the long kitchen knife. She handed it to the chief, "I almost give it to you when you come in my home." He actually smiled and nodded at the memory.

She left some more blankets, a couple of pots, some of Noh Tay Dah's shirts and a coat.

She and Sunflower decided how much food we might need to get home and set almost half aside to leave with the warriors. All the larger hides she kept and most of the children's clothing.

When they were done sorting, we would be taking only about half of the things that were stolen. Even then it was as much as we wanted to carry by the seven of us, not counting the three children. They would each have a pack of their own, to carry a few of their own things.

The iron hatchet was Noh Tay Dah's most prized possession. Indeed, any hatchet was highly prized in the tribe. It cut wood, broke and shaped stone and as a weapon it would split open a head clear down to the neck.

She picked it up and took the several steps to stand directly in front of the chief. A concerned and uncertain look clouded his face. If he attempted to defend himself, he knew I would strike him down with the thunder stick.

She looked him in the eye for a long moment. She truly was regal as she stood straight and tall, totally in command of the situation.

"Maybe she is a medicine woman," I thought.

"You strike down my husband from behind before he even see you!" She said in a ringing voice and her gaze went to each one who was standing behind the chief.

Sunflower was translating for me.

"Two of you have been struck down in return, is it enough?" She asked in a voice and look that took them all in.

"It is enough." The chief replied.

"Then there is peace?" She asked.

"There is peace." He said seriously.

"Then I give you this to confirm that there is peace." And she handed him the hatchet, handle first. He looked genuinely surprised.

"It is a great gift." He said with appreciation.

"As a sign of peace, I give you this." And he pulled a necklace from inside his shirt and over his head.

It was indeed an impressive gift not only for its beauty but apparently for its significance. His men murmured and glanced at one another recognizing it as his insignia of leadership.

It was on a rawhide string but the medallion was silver with markings of some kind. On each side going up the string were several beautiful sea shells. Between the seashells were odd shaped pieces of bright red coral. It was truly a beautiful piece of art.

"Since we are at peace, I give you this food, blankets, coverings and all that you see on this pile," she said, pointing to the pile she was leaving behind. "These are things you may need on your journey.

They all seemed impressed and somewhat confused by the strange turn of events.

They didn't even cast their eyes on the other pile to see what was in it. In a place where even the women were warriors and had great medicine and a child could strike you down and not even have a thunder stick, it is best to do what is to be done and leave.

While they were preparing to leave, I beckoned to the chief to come with me for a chat. Azalia came along to interpret.

We brushed the snow off of some rocks, clustered about fifteen steps north, and sat down.

"What is your tribe?" I asked.

"We are called As Te Kah," he replied.

I wondered if the word "Aztec" had come from this.

"One of your men said I needed to fix my weapon. Have you seen other men who had thunder sticks?" I asked.

"Yes, many," he replied. "They have coverings that are hard and shiny; head coverings also. Spears and arrows do not go through. Our people cannot fight them. They are cruel and kill many. Women and children are struck down. They make slaves and beat, torture and burn. The women they take for their own use."

He paused, looking into the past with pain and horror.

"We look for a place, but we could not live here." He gestured at the surroundings of cold, waterless wasteland.

"Our people are scattered in small groups, finding water and shelter where they can. We try to find a place and go back to get ones who are left." He explained.

"There is more cold and snow as you go north and I do not know how many tribes are there," I said. "I do know this, where these mountains and those mountains come together there is a place to go over to another river. There are tribes there but I do not know how many or where they have villages. Perhaps there is a stream where you would find plants and shelter. One tribe I know, and if you tell them, you are friends of Chee, they may help you and show you a place where you could live in peace." I concluded.

He thanked me and we stood and clasped forearms.

His men had bundled together the things that Deh Neh Totsi had given them, and we parted in peace.

It was already afternoon. The days were short. We were all tired. We decided to follow the trail back to the previous camp where Deh Neh Totsi and the warriors had camped the night before.

It was a weary but joyful group that set down the packs and surveyed their surroundings.

"I wonder if anyone will help a tired old father get firewood?" I said in a somewhat whiny voice as I untied a small bow saw from the back of my pack.

Deh Neh Totsi's head jerked up in concern, but Azalia replied with a laugh. "Maybe someone help," and she took my arm and pointed to a small pile of brush out in the gully.

The boys and Sunflower looked up grinning and Deh Neh Totsi relaxed, realizing it was good natured banter. She looked off into the distance with misty eyes. She and Noh Tay Dah often joked in this manner, and it reminded her that she sorely missed her husband, and missed belonging to a tribe. These people were the closest thing she had to a tribal family and she missed them when seasons passed without seeing them. She couldn't help but wonder if there was some way they could stay together.

Each of the boys was bringing in an arm load of wood even before Azalia and I had our nicely cut pile. At least ours were bigger pieces that would last longer at night.

Yah Doh Nay and Lay Leh Tso brought the wood that was left over from their stay from the day before, since we would all stay under the one large rock overhang. It didn't take a half-hour to get things laid out, a good fire pit built and a fire started.

"Why don't we used about ten cans of food and have a feast tonight? It will be less weight to carry tomorrow?" I suggested.

"That sound good!" Blossom called out from the far corner of the cave where she was playing and chattering with the children.

Everyone laughed. "If she hears 'eat or food' she is suddenly there, with cup or just hands out," Little Badger grinned.

Sunflower was studying the situation very seriously. "Each can make four parts. Each person get four things all be different but all get four."

"The girls can't have baked beans!" I said severely. "They make fun of my beans in front of my friends and say that is all I know how to cook."

"But we also say, you cook beans good," Azalia replied with a grin.

"Okay, boys get beans," Lobo declared.

A chuckle ran around the circle. Sunflower made sure Deh Neh Totsi understood the banter so she could enjoy the humor.

Fortunately, there were enough beans to go around. Mixed vegetables weren't as popular but the beef stew was a hit. Since there were ten helpings in two and a half cans, some people would miss something or get two of something. By the end of the meal everyone was trying to trade helpings.

I traded my peaches to Blossom for her vegetables. Lobo saw an opportunity when the two little ones were getting full and traded his pears for them to divide and they each gave him a full portion. Of course, we all objected but he just grinned and dug in.

Deh Neh Totsi just shook her head and waved her hand dismissing all the bartering and confusion that had just taken place over a simple meal.

Often the back and forth slipped into their own language and was too fast with too many talking at once, so I was totally left out. I didn't mind. Deh Neh Totsi and the children were being folded into the group and anything that took their minds off their recent trauma was healing to them.

As twilight turned to darkness, we gathered in closer around the fire with ponchos and blankets.

During a lull in the conversation, Deh Neh Totsi asked plaintively, "will Noh Tay Dah be well?"

Sunflower translated and I replied, "head wounds are serious but if he has rested for three days, he should recover. We will look carefully when we get there and if he will do what is necessary to heal, it should be well."

"Because we can't see the wound inside the head, we look for other signs. Pain in head, dizziness, slow thinking, eyes don't work right and this could include many other things. We will look at many signs and there will be a slow increase in activity. Do nothing for three to five days, take short walks another three to five days. Then increase the time and distance but always checking for the problems. Find problems, slow down. No problems, keep doing more. Bluebell (Val Dah Vey) had a concussion and seems to be completely well. But she was not struck as hard."

"Getting Noh Tay Dah well will be our first, most important job," I concluded.

She nodded soberly.

The children were sitting next to us taking in our conversation with unusual quietness, when Blossom said seriously, "we pray Great Spirit and Great Spirit Son make him well."

"That is always the place to start, because we know He hears us," I said.

"One more thing," Deh Neh Totsi said. "Could we walk all the way to our home tomorrow?"

"Boys," I called over to them on the other end of our half circle. "Can we make it all the way to Deh Neh Totsi's home tomorrow?"

They discussed it briefly among themselves. They seemed pleased to be consulted and I was pleased that they were willing to take leadership responsibilities.

Lobo answered for all of them, "we start after sun come up, we get there before sun go down."

"Well then, let's get a good night's sleep and get up at first light," I concluded.

Blossom wanted to sleep with the children so we tucked them in between us, throwing an extra blanket over the three of them. They were out before I could get settled into my sleeping bag.

It was bitter cold at dawn but there was a heaviness to the air, and as the sun began to strike our campsite, it gave promise of a warm day.

The boys built up the fire. Everyone added snow to the coffee pot and the cans from the night before were set out around the fire and kept full of snow until we had enough water for everyone to have a drink. We then added to the water bottles for the trip. We would be somewhat dehydrated by the time we got to Deh Neh Totsi's home.

I dug out ten MRE's and we had a quick breakfast. It also made the packs lighter and allowed us to redistribute everything more appropriately.

The hike to Deh Neh Totsi's home was without incident. We found a spot where the creek wasn't totally frozen over and got all the fresh water we needed. We passed the trail where Noh Tay Dah had turned off to go over to our village. In another hour we arrived at their home.

We all paused to take in the sights that told the story. There was the indentation in the snow and scattered wood where Noh Tay Dah had lain. There was blood in the snow.

The half teepee front to the entrance of their stone enclosure, was demolished and the poles tossed aside. The tracks leading towards the kiva-like storage cave indicated that only a single person had gone there and that was most likely Noh Tay Dah getting supplies and clothing for his journey.

Suddenly there was a muffled cry from inside the cave. We all rushed in. Sunflower was standing over Deh Neh Totsi who was kneeling and clutching something to her breast.

"Her marriage vessel is not destroyed!" Sunflower exclaimed. "It is a good sign that all will be well!"

Deh Neh Totsi knelt there in silence for several moments, gathering her composure and collecting her thoughts. The marriage vessel is like a wide vase with a spout on each side. It is the symbol that the two will eat and drink from the same vessels as they go through life together.

She rose, still clutching the vessel to her and with her eyes shining she declared, and Sunflower relayed to me, "it is well!"

"You can all sleep in here tonight," she declared.

I wasn't sure how we all might fit but we would deal with that later.

"Let's see if we can put the teepee back as it was," Lobo suggested.

The boys and I began assembling the poles together. Noh Tay Dah had put mud and clay between the poles to make a tight, waterproof room where the fire would be just outside the cave far enough for the smoke to go up and out the top of the teepee, but keep most of the heat directed inside into the cave. We wrapped the teepee with ponchos to make it relatively airtight and waterproof at least on a temporary basis.

Blossom and the children worked diligently bringing in small armloads of wood from Noh Tay Dah's wood pile. The girls organized the supplies and set the food aside so we could plan our last two meals before we left.

"Do you have enough food for when we get back to your village?" I asked.

Sunflower looked somewhat concerned. "We are very careful to make small meals to get three of us through until spring."

"Is there food in my place?" I asked.

"We not use your food but Blossom bring some sometimes." She answered with a somewhat guilty expression.

"Blossom! Is there any food left in my place?" I called over to her.

"There is some but not much," she answered.

"Each week Little Badger or someone bring food from cave for everyone but it only lasts four, five days." Azalia added.

"We will take food from our cave," Deh Neh Totsi declared. "We will share all we have. How long Noh Tay Dah not come home?"

"Let's plan for the next week or two and I will go for more food," I said. "Boys, what are the chances that we could get a deer on the way home?"

"Remember first hunt?" Impala said thoughtfully, "you say, no hunt near village in summer. Wait for winter. Get deer close to village! There two valleys where maybe deer. We hunt on way home!"

"Go to cave. Bring what is there," Deh Neh Totsi instructed.

The boys headed over to the cave, found the ladder and climbed in. There wasn't a lot but it would amount to a couple of days of food for all ten of us.

Blossom announced, "we hide trail."

There was a rather distinct trail from the home cave to the kiva cave on the cliff. The children ran back and forth from the wall then out into the wooded flat area between the home cave and the spring. Soon the signs of children playing some game had totally obliterated the trail from the home cave to the kiva.

Inside the teepee structure, Little Badger had arranged the wood against the side of the teepee opposite the entrance to the cave.

"We sleep in teepee. Keep fire going." He declared.

He then put several packs on the ground inside the base of the teepee on the left and right sides as a windbreak. Two of them could sleep between the fire and the packs and reach the wood with one arm, lay it on the fire and not even get out of bed.

As the evening settled in and a sharp chill returned to the air, we sat in a tight little circle in the main room of the little home, drinking hot chocolate and enjoying one another's company.

As the conversation lagged just a little, I turned to Deh Neh Totsi and asked a question about what she had overheard from her captors. Perhaps I could learn more about the conquistadors than the warriors' chief had related to me.

Chapter 5

Leaning closer to Deh Neh Totsi, I asked, "Did you hear your captors talk about a large group of strange warriors with unusual coverings and weapons?"

Sunflower interpreted for us and everyone got quiet to hear about the strange things.

"Yes!" She began, "they talk much about many battles. They have great fear of them. Arrows, even spears cannot strike through the coverings. Their weapons are like long sharp knives. They have spears, longer than our spears but with long points harder than stone. Some ride on great beasts that run like the wind and catch any who run away.

"They strike down and kill all that oppose them. They destroy all old ones and all little ones and make slaves of all who can work and carry large packs.

"They say they could not fight them and not many could escape. Many tribes and villages are destroyed. Strange warriors with coverings have no honor, no pity, they respect no one. They have no mercy. Some they torture and kill for no reason. They just like to destroy, burn, torture and kill because it makes them feel that they are better than all others."

"How much is truth, I don't know," she concluded.

"Do you know how far this way these warriors have come?" I asked.

"No. Captors say they come in bands followed by great numbers, more than can count. Nothing can stand against them," she answered.

Shaken by Deh Neh Totsi's answers, Sunflower turned her head toward me and asked, "Do you think they will come here?"

"I believe that someday they will come but they look for the soft yellow stone. If they do not find any they leave," I answered.

"But will they kill and destroy those who are here?" Lobo asked.

"They would, but not if you are not here or they can't find you," I suggested.

"Where we go? Where we hide? Impala asked.

"We will talk about those things and make a plan," I said.

"Which is greater, a grizzly bear or a rattlesnake?" I asked

"A grizzly bear," Little Badger answered immediately.

"Have you ever seen a grizzly bear hunt a rattlesnake?" I continued, "if you hear a noise at night and sit up and there is a porcupine or a skunk in your hut, who will leave your hut first, you or the skunk?"

They all laughed, "I leave quick!" Impala chuckled.

"And who would just grab the porcupine and throw him out?" I asked.

Again, they all nodded and laughed at the picture. Lobo caught the implications. "Easy to kill skunk or porcupine but only when you plan and have right place."

"That is right!" I replied, "there are ways for a small group to fight a large group, but it must be done carefully and with an understanding of how they think, and what they fear. Find a weakness, avoid their strength. If you can't strike them with weapons, strike them with fear."

They all sat quietly pondering possibilities and the seriousness of potential warfare.

Does war and death always lurk in the background of human existence? Are peace and serenity only to be enjoyed as interludes and thus should be valued and remembered for their rarity?

Rather than go to bed in such a somber mood, I suggested, "let's focus for a moment on the fact that we are full of hot chocolate, dry and warm, and gathered together with ones we love, trust and care for."

"We have had many adventures together. Some dangerous, some scary, some funny but we have shared them together, and we are connected by them. We will have many more adventures. What is important is that we are together."

They all murmured in agreement, bringing a more relaxed and cheerful atmosphere as we turned in for the night.

We awakened with the first rays of the rising sun striking the teepee and sending little slivers of light into the entrance of the cave.

As tightly packed together as we were, when one got up, everyone had to get up to keep from being stepped on.

Sunflower, Azalia and Deh Neh Totsi did a quick assessment of what might be needed for their fire group, and most of the deer hides, utensils and clothing were taken back to the kiva. If Noh Tay Dah returned, the things should be here, or if they needed something, they could come and get it.

Sunflower and Azalia also knew what was in the bags of Christmas presents and when Deh Neh Totsi would indicate that she was sure she needed something or other, the girls would say, "trust us, you don't need to take that. You will be in our fire group."

Shortly after a quick breakfast everything was packed and ready to go.

The three older boys went on ahead while we finished the last inspection, giving Deh Neh Totsi and the children some time to look around and say goodbye to their home. None of us could know how long, or even if, they would ever live here again.

We were a somber and quiet group as we took up the trail that the boys made leading us back to the village.

In less than an hour we came upon a place where the tracks and fresh indentations in the snow indicated that the boys had dropped their packs to look for deer over the next hill. Apparently, there were none there and they had returned for their packs and moved on.

Twice more we found similar spots.

Sunflower lamented, "I hope we have fresh deer meat. Few deer taken this winter."

"Frankly, I'm glad they didn't get one right away. Think of how far we would have to drag it."

Blossom said matter-of-factly, "Great Spirit give us deer when we need it."

"You are becoming quite the expert on how the Great Spirit works," I said dismissively. "How would you know how the Great Spirit works?"

"Great Spirit always work," she said seriously, "most time we don't see it."

"Wow!" I thought to myself. "She knows more than half the theologians in the twenty first century."

"Well then," I said. "We will just have to leave it to the Great Spirit to give us what we need."

In another hour we were at the Spring of the Grizzly, or Grizzly Spring, or whatever they were calling it. The boys had stopped for water here also. There were only a couple of likely valleys between here and the village where deer might hang out. At the pace we were moving, it might take three hours to get there.

We were not far behind the boys since they had made several stops to check out likely valleys. Suddenly, we heard some whooping and hollering from only a half mile or so ahead. It didn't sound like a war cry or shout of distress or danger.

The terrain was a long slope down from the mountain and a long straight path around the side of the hill. While it was covered in various evergreen trees of all sizes, there was no valley or cover from which to stalk deer.

We came upon them shortly in a mostly open area, and they were field dressing two deer and chattering excitedly among themselves.

"Great job!" I called out, as we got close enough for them to hear.

As we got closer, we could see that both deer appeared to be well fed and in great shape.

"How you stalk deer out here?" Sunflower asked incredulously, as we all took off our packs.

"We not stalk deer, they come to us!" Little Badger said grinning.

The boys were still full of adrenaline and talking over one another.

"Slow down, start at the beginning and tell the story," I said.

Lobo began, "we not see deer all day."

Impala jumped in, "we not even see tracks."

Lobo continued, "suddenly, we see movement uphill. Then we see deer."

"We count six," Little Badger interjected.

"They come this way," Lobo added.

"We stand right over there, in open place. We can't move or they see us," Impala said.

"We can't take off pack!" Little Badger put in.

"We don't move, deer go behind tree, we put bows in position and nock arrow and stand ready," Lobo continued.

Little Badger, "we remember you say no kill doe, maybe have baby."

Impala, "how we know? No deer have horns, what you call them?"

"Antlers," I replied.

"No deer have antlers now," he continued.

Impala, "four deer come out behind those trees. No antlers."

Little Badger, "Lobo whisper,' do we take one?' Then two come out behind."

Impala, "see, little horns start! And Lobo whisper again, 'I take last one,' and Little Badger, me take first one."

Little Badger concluded, "Lobo whisper, 'ready, go' and we all shoot together and two fall here."

They all paused to take a breath and we all murmured our approval.

I glanced at Blossom who was grinning from ear to ear. She raised her eyebrows at me, glanced up and nodded her head. I guess the Great Spirit knew exactly when, where and how we needed a deer and He gave us two.

Carrying full packs and dragging two deer made for slow going, but with eight people it was doable. We made four teams with one guy and one girl and took turns. The boys took some of the weight from the packs Blossom and I were carrying so that we could keep up with everyone and take our turn dragging a deer.

There were still a few hours of daylight left as we came around and over the last hill. We came in at an angle along the side of the hill, so that we would have a slightly downhill path to the tree just up from the girls' hut where they skinned out many of the deer that they brought in.

In fact, this was where Sunflower and I had skinned the deer and divided the meat of the first deer we had taken just after my arrival last spring.

With just a little more than a hundred yards to go, we saw Noh Tay Dah emerge from my lean-to that was attached to the big tree beside the girls' hut.

Lay Leh Tso screamed, "father!" And dropped her pack and ran. Ya Doh Nay struggled to get out of his pack but finally dropped it, racing after her.

Little Badger and Deh Neh Totsi were dragging a deer and I gestured to her to drop her pack and go. She almost flew down the slope and arrived only seconds behind the children.

We all stood there grinning and enjoying the excited, joyful scene of their reunion. I was concerned they would knock him over and give him another concussion.

Impala stepped in to help Little Badger, while I picked up Deh Neh Totsi's pack; Azalia got one of the children's packs and Blossom picked up the other.

Everyone took the packs to the girls' hut to sort, while Lobo and I began to hang up the deer. We didn't need to rush the skinning and processing since the weather would keep the deer well refrigerated.

As things began to get organized, and slow down, we paused to assess our situation.

The lean-to that we had built for Noh Tay Dah and his family was still there. The Christmas presents for them and all the extras from Blossom's presentation to the tribe at Christmas were there also.

Most of the stuff in my lean-to was mine and included some dried and powdered food and a couple dozen cans of assorted fruits, vegetables, beans and stew.

The lean-to for Noh Tay Dah's family had been built as a temporary structure and the tarp was partially caved in from the heavy snow. Some of the wood structure had broken or fallen out of place. It not only was in need of repair but needed to be strengthened and made airtight to better hold the heat.

We turned to look at Noh Tay Dah and his family but they were oblivious to us. The boys had built up the fire and the little family was seated on the log next to it wrapped together in a blanket with a child snuggled onto each lap.

We all glanced at one another and smiled. This had been an arduous and dangerous journey but that little scene made it all worthwhile.

Turning back to our immediate problems, I suggested, "why don't one of you boys cut some steaks, a couple of you can get some wood, the girls can make supper and I'll stay out of the "kitchen."

They laughed and I added, "I'll see if I can fix their lean-to enough to provide a sleeping space for the family and rearrange my lean-to for a small space for me."

"Do you boys have a place for the night?"

They nodded and I concluded, "let's get to work."

I decided to let Noh Tay Dah and his family have my lean-to as it was a little bigger and in better shape. Rearranging stuff all around the sides for the night would help keep out wind and cold and some quick repairs on the strings holding the front in place would be enough for now. We could take all of my stuff to what had been their lean-to tomorrow and put all of their stuff with it.

That lean-to would take some work.

Getting the snow off the collapsed part, putting the unbroken poles towards the center and letting the sides slope down and over the bags and boxes would serve for the moment. It gave me an aisle down the middle where I could sleep and we would remake the whole thing later.

Among the bags and boxes that I began to stack to each side and the back of the lean to, was the tent that I had planned to take back, along with the camp stove, heater, extra-large kettles and utensils from the Christmas dinner celebration of Blossom's acceptance back into the tribe.

After the celebration, I had left rather abruptly because of the danger of the portal's closing and hadn't taken any of that equipment with me. The fact that the portal remained open meant that my purpose was not completed. That brought me a certain amount of joy because I loved and missed these people in this place. It also brought a great amount of dread and trepidation because I was gaining more certainty as to what that purpose was.

I pushed it from my mind, certain I would need to wait for more guidance, hoping the development of circumstances would be clear enough that I couldn't miss it or avoid it.

Then there would need to be a considerable amount of consultation with my team to decide what to do and how to do it.

For now, getting ready for the night and checking on Noh Tay Dah's recovery from his injuries were the most important issues.

The tribe had heard about his injuries and the capture of his family and the successful rescue mission of their own young people. Now, upon their return, everyone wanted to hear the story. The little fire circle was getting filled to over-flowing with well-wishers, curious and hoping to find a little excitement during the boring days of winter.

I approached the girls with a proposal, "we can't very well eat in front of half-starved people who are coming to celebrate our return, so we may as well feed them as well."

All three of them looked at me like I had lost my mind. The boys had returned, each with a load of firewood, so I said to them, "we haven't distributed the fresh meat so we could use it. Put away the loin steaks and slice off the round steak. We have the large kettles that I brought for the last celebration and we can make a large batch of barbecued beans."

"I'm good at cooking beans so I'm told!" I said, and raised my eyebrows at Sunflower and Azalia.

Even Deh Neh Totsi, who didn't speak English had recognize the word "beans", and observing our interactions, was laughing.

She made a motion of pushing me away and said, "kitchen."

Everyone laughed and Sunflower said in both languages, "he will cook beans, so he can be in kitchen."

The boys quickly sliced the steaks. Blossom and Violet went to invite the other fire groups and to bring Grandmother and her skillet and her chair… and a blanket… and the two children.

Bluebell and Yul D'Vey, who had checked on Noh Tay Dah a couple of times every day while he was recuperating, came to help also.

Four skillets with four steaks each would feed a third of the tribe, so we could prepare the entire meal in an hour.

"So, who is going to tell the story of your adventure?" I inquired.

"We all tell it!" Lobo answered.

Apparently, that is what they were used to doing, as one would talk others would jump in with clarifications or details or something. Sunflower and Lobo, as the oldest of the group and Deh Neh Totsi as the principal character did the most talking.

Since I didn't speak or understand the language, I busied myself reorganizing the kitchen for the last round of meals, which would be to feed ourselves.

They must have done a good job as storytellers judging by the rapt attention and responses of the audience. The only part I think I understood was when I heard "La Lin Eedah" followed by several of them throwing their arms out and shouting "boom" in their loudest voice.

I had forgotten to tell them not to mention anything about Blossom having a "thunder stick". I guess that ship has sailed, the horse is out of the barn, the cat's out of the bag or however you want to say it.

Violet had stepped in to help me, and when I said, "don't you want to hear the story?" She had replied, "I hear story tomorrow."

She had started her presence with us as a little pest, always showing up for food. But in incident after incident in little things and big, she had displayed a genuine spirit of helpfulness and loyalty that was truly impressive in a child so young.

I reached out and gave her cheek a gentle squeeze and signed as I said, "I love you. Thank you!"

She smiled happily and stepped over to give me a hug and said, "I love you!"

I remarked, "how do you know English?"

She answered, "Blossom teach. I learn."

I said slowly, "I will teach you too."

She smiled, "that good." She paused hesitantly, "that be good."

I grinned at her, "that is good."

She repeated, "that is good!"

She got real serious and began fishing for words. "Blossom say… You… Hut… Big, big beautiful… You… Me see? She was doing gestures with each word as well and she was definitely communicating.

"I can show you pictures," I said gesturing also.

"Yes!" She nodded and smiled brightly.

The storytelling was over and the tribe was drifting back to their huts.

Violet began putting the smaller steaks into the skillet and putting more wood on the fire. Azalia came over to give her a hug and a few words. Azalia looked at me and nodded approval. She also had a special place in her heart for Violet, because she had stayed with her in a time of danger.

"Everybody sit down and get comfortable. Violet and I will run the kitchen." I said, waving a large spoon and a meat fork like a weapon.

"Kitchen can't run!" Blossom said disdainfully.

"It run when it see him come!" Sunflower said gleefully, catching the play on words.

Everybody laughed… At my expense… Again! I just grinned, delighted at the progress with the language I had taught them.

Blossom, who recovered her energy faster than anyone I knew, jumped up and said, "I help."

"Great, there's the can opener. Open six cans of fruit, whatever you find, and dump them together into that deep pan." I instructed. "The meat will be done in a few minutes and there's enough of the beans left over for everyone except Sunflower and Azalia."

"What!" Sunflower declared, "we always say 'we like your beans'."

"Many, many beans," Azalia whispered.

"Big beans, little beans." Sunflower pretended seriousness.

"Red beans, brown beans, black beans." Azalia nodded in agreement.

"All right," I said, and with my voice getting lower and darker, I ground out threateningly, "from now on you get broccoli."

Everyone was laughing and Azalia asked, "what is broc'ly?"

In my best villain voice I growled, "you will see!"

By this time, the food was ready and Blossom and Violet took the plates to everyone.

When we were finished, I carried the kettle of fruit around while Blossom and Violet spooned out a cup full to each one.

Noh Tay Dah seemed to be doing well, but it was still too soon to declare him healed. With Sunflower to interpret, I emphasized he needed three more days of rest.

It was late; there were plenty of blankets to go around, so we headed to our huts for a night's sleep. The girls invited Violet to stay with them.

The next morning, we got up after the sun had begun to warm the air.

"We have eaten all of the food that was meant to last you until spring," I observed. "I must go and get some beans," and I glanced sideways at Sunflower and Azalia.

The boys had just arrived and overheard our conversation.

"It is two moons until the trees bud and the plants begin to grow," Lobo said seriously. "We go far for deer and sometimes no find. We no more find some near village. Like you tell us, when first snows come, we find deer, but after two moons they all go away."

"We have dried meat and plants in cave but it almost gone," Little Badger said grimly.

"What everyone eat last night same as what they eat for half-moon." Impala said sadly, "children hungry! Everyone hungry!"

"Some meat taste bad," Sunflower acknowledged.

"Two times Blossom find animal with sharp pins. We give two back legs to Grandmother, Sweet Pea and Chip. It help, but not much," Azalia added.

I hadn't realized they were this low on food. At least they now had an idea of how much they needed to get through the winter. I wasn't going to let them starve, but they needed to realize the value of a garden and the diligence needed to prepare enough food.

"If we add only a little to each one in the tribe for one moon, it would weigh as much as I weigh, or as much as Blossom, Violet, Sweet Pea and Chip altogether," I said.

They all looked at me skeptically. "Well, maybe not quite that much, but close," I asserted. "You are all starving, remember?"

They didn't quite see the humor in that so I dropped the subject.

"I need to go back through the portal to meet with my advisors and get ideas for what would be the best supplies to get."

"We go too?" Azalia asked excitedly.

"Yes! We go too!" Sunflower and Blossom jumped in immediately.

"You say you show me hut. You take me too?" Violet piped up. Of course, she didn't have time to formulate the sentence in English, so she had Blossom ask for her.

This all naturally opened the door for the boys, who chimed in, "we go too?"

"I should meet with my advisors and Dorothy first and see what they say. I'm pretty sure they will say 'no, it is not a good idea'," I said.

"They not say that, Chee; they nice!" Blossom said confidently.

The upshot of it was, since they had all, except Violet, been there already and it was only one night, and I may be a hopeless pushover, we decided to go.

In a few hours we were up the hill and through the portal.

"Hi, I brought guests!" I said to Dorothy as we entered the house. She rolled her eyes but any forthcoming lecture wouldn't be delivered in front of the guests.

"The girls made me do it!" I said defensively and she had to laugh as she said, "right!" And turned her attention to our little entourage.

"Take off your coats and boots and I'll make some hot chocolate." She said, then added, "are Deh Neh Totsi and the children safe?"

My phone had started ringing the moment the door bell on the portal had been activated. All the rest of my advisor group had been left hanging when I had taken off suddenly to go after Deh Neh Totsi and the children and what sounded like a potentially big battle.

"I need to return these calls to my advisors. By the way, this is Violet and this is Dorothy," I said.

"Dorothy would love to hear about the rescue. Why don't you all sit in the big room and tell her about the adventure?" I suggested.

"Can I show big hut to Violet?" Blossom inquired.

Forgetting to wait for an answer, they skipped away to see everything and get Blossom's version of what they were seeing.

Since Sunflower and Azalia spoke English better than the others, they began filling Dorothy in on the details while they prepared the hot chocolate.

I got on the phone with Cam and Heather and Ben and Sharon. After hearing about the food shortage and finding out about the additional guests, they decided an in person meeting was in order.

"See!" I said, "you're just as excited and curious about these kids as I am."

Heather replied, "We know you, you are planning to get the whole tribe here, aren't you?"

Ben chimed in, "why don't we go to the deli and get fried chicken with side dishes and bring dinner back to your place for us all.

"We sold another bar of gold since the price went up another couple hundred dollars an ounce, so we have plenty of money in the account for food."

"Don't forget cake and ice cream," I advised. "That seems to be a big deal for them."

Returning to the living room, I announced, "guess what! Cam and Heather and Ben and Sharon are bringing supper to us and they are going to eat and visit with us.

They all cheered excitedly. Dorothy wiped her brow in mock relief

Blossom and Violet had returned or at least were passing through, when Blossom asked, "we see Wiley?"

Wiley Coyote and the Roadrunner had been a staple of the girls viewing on the TV when they had come to get Blossom's lip fixed.

The boys and Violet had seen my computer but nothing the size of the TV nor the action and excitement of the Roadrunner. They were mesmerized immediately.

With everyone temporarily occupied, I began searching online for beans in bulk quantities. By giving each person just a quarter pound per day it would take almost four hundred and fifty pounds to feed the tribe for a month. Of course, beans would soak overnight and double in volume, so we might get by with about two hundred and fifty pounds. When added to their stew, it would be a second source of protein and might be enough to fill their stomachs.

In no time the afternoon was gone and the "advisory committee" arrived with the evening meal. The girls rushed to greet them and exchange hugs.

"This is Violet," I said, putting my hand on her shoulder as Violet hung back, not sure what to do.

"It's wonderful to meet you. We've heard a lot about you!" Heather exclaimed.

"Pleased to meet you!" Violet responded.

"You speak English too!" Sharon exclaimed.

"Blossom teach," She replied.

"This is Lobo, and Impala and Little Badger!" I said, introducing the boys.

Cam and Ben did the forearm clasp, shoulder bump that I had described a number of times. I wasn't sure about the protocol for greeting women, but Sharon and Heather handled it nicely by giving them a short hug and smile. The boys took it all in stride.

The meal was delicious, and just right for everyone and for the occasion. The conversations were noisy and animated as there was a continual mixing of pairs, small groups or occasionally the whole group interacting on some topic or another.

Sharon noticed that Violet was not able to follow the rapid conversations so she began a private conversation with her using slow simple words.

"What is it like where you live?" She asked slowly.

Violet answered, searching for words, "cold… dangerous… Whiteface come." She was gesturing with each word to be sure it was understood. "Take… Me…" She continued and her face showed the fear and trauma she had endured when she was captured. While it was now more than a year and a half since that raid she was still dealing with some PTSD from time to time.

"Take…" And she used both hands in a grabbing motion. "Throw down… tree…" And she smacked her hand against her head to indicate her head striking the tree. "Chee… strike. Man fall… All go." And she waved her hand indicate that they left.

I had noticed the conversation dwindling as different ones became aware of her relating her story. While everyone knew it, they had not heard her tell it.

"Chee… fix head… give covering… shirt. I no give back." She smiled impishly and Sharon laughed.

"Chee… me… dance. It… make… good". She took a deep breath. "Now… I… good" and she smiled cheerfully.

She was suddenly aware the room had grown quiet and looked around a bit startled.

"It is good!" Azalia declared and moved to her quickly and gave her a hug. We are happy she is our friend."

Everyone smiled fondly and murmured their approval.

Chapter 6

Dabbing the corner of his eye and looking around the group, Ben said, "okay, let's get back to making a plan."

Lobo and Sunflower apparently took his glance to mean they were "in' and excitedly joined our advisory group, both to give their perspective but also to hear the concerns that we had about creating dependency.

Reassurance came first, "Money, what we use to trade for things, is not a problem," Cam said. "Since you gave us the yellow stone, we have enough to get what you need."

"What we want to be careful about, is causing your people to depend on us and lose the ability to take care of yourselves when the portal goes away," Sharon explained.

"As long as we can help, we will help. One way we can help is to guide the tribe in figuring out how much food is needed to get through a winter," Ben added.

"Let me make a few points," I broke in. "The tribe has been killed and looted. They had almost nothing of value left. Not hides for blankets or clothing, no store of food left, no leaders with the energy or understanding to lead.

"These two and these friends that are with them took on the whole responsibility of survival without resources or experience and have brought the tribe to these last few months of winter. The tribe has responded pretty well. They fell a bit short on the food gathering, but they have no resources to preserve food except drying which is all done over an open fire.

I think they have done a remarkable job, and I am proud of them," I concluded.

Sharon responded, "one of our concerns is that every time Chee leaves, we worry that he might not come back even if the portal is open, he might be killed in some battle or by other dangers. If that were to happen, we wouldn't know his fate, and you might not either. There would be no way that we could continue helping you," Sharon concluded.

Sunflower responded, "we work hard but we are not chiefs. We think we have much but quickly it is gone. Every time Chee leave, we think maybe he not come back. We have no one to say 'we must gather more'."

"We thank you for all you do for us. It is why we live now. We all be dead if you not give coverings, foot coverings, blankets, food.

"We sorry we not do enough," and she hung her head in discouragement.

Sharon responded sympathetically. "Don't be discouraged. We know you have worked hard under danger and difficulties. We just want to emphasize that we don't know when the portal will close and we don't want you to depend on Chee being there and everything stops working because you were expecting help from him."

Lobo spoke up, "because we young, some not listen. What need done, we do. We can not do for everyone."

"We understand," Sharon said gently. "That's why we are all here tonight. We aren't criticizing and we all want what is best for all of you. But if we could not help now, would the tribe survive?"

"Yes!" Lobo declared, "we hunt harder. We find food. We survive!"

"That's the spirit," Ben exclaimed. "And for right now, we can still get what you need for the next few months."

"I think it is important that I bring this up now, although not for discussion." I began seriously. "The portal is still open therefore there is most likely still a purpose. From what I know and from what I foresee as probable, we will have some very serious discussions and decisions to make, and things are going to get much worse and more dangerous before my purpose is completed."

There were a few moments of silence as we all weighed the possibilities of such a somber outlook.

Finally, Heather spoke softly, "you are speaking of the conquistadors, aren't you?"

"Yes, but now isn't the time to discuss it," I said. "It will require very deliberate, thoughtful responses and actions, with an eye towards history and the survival of many tribes. I think we will need to ask the Great Spirit for help, too," as I glanced quickly towards Blossom."

"It will certainly take things out of the realm of the abstract and theoretical," Cam said thoughtfully. "And right into our laps."

"On that note, let's get our supplies and containers and get food to the tribe," I said cheerfully.

"Right! Okay, what do you need?" Ben responded.

"We have some food." Sunflower said, "we make stew with dried plants and roots and dried meat every day."

I mused out loud, "beans, rice, lentils, what makes the most sense for this situation?"

"Beans will double in size when soaked," Heather suggested.

"And we could get a couple different kinds," Dorothy added.

"I figured a little less than a quarter pound per person, per day would suffice as a supplement especially if they swell up when soaked," Cam opined. "That's about two hundred and fifty pounds per month."

"Perhaps you should get enough flour to make fry bread a couple of times per week. Of course, include some baking powder, and salt and a gallon of oil." Sharon added.

"How about a big can of fruit twice a week for each fire group?" Dorothy suggested, it would provide vitamin C and be a special treat."

Each one volunteered to look for one thing or another and have it ready by midday tomorrow. And with that the meeting ended with goodbye hugs all around.

The next morning, Dorothy and I got some heavy-duty plastic tubs with snap on lids, some measuring scoops and a couple of small containers for each fire group to have a week's supply of beans and flour.

Everything was gathered and put through the portal by noon.

"Realizing it was meal time, Sunflower asked excitedly, "can we eat at hamburger place? Boys and Violet not ever see such a place."

"We have come this far so we might as well try that too," I replied resignedly.

We piled into two cars and went to the nearby family restaurant, where the girls had been before, and introduced the boys to burgers, fries and ice cream sundaes.

The boys and Violet were so full of questions and exclamations that they didn't even try to speak English and they all reverted to their language. Of course, I had no idea what kind of information they were receiving.

Returning home, we all said our goodbyes with big hugs for Dorothy, and I made sure to give my "advisory council" members a quick call to double check that nothing had been forgotten.

After going through the portal, our first job was to get what was needed for food distribution down to the village. We would bring the rest of the food later.

The girls selected two or three people from each fire group to learn how to soak the beans and how much to use. They already knew how to make fry bread so it could be made immediately for the evening meal.

"So that none of you need to take on another job, why don't you put someone in charge of weekly distribution?" I suggested. "Someone who understands the distribution is per person, per seven suns so they can make everyone understand that it must last the whole week."

Lobo spoke up immediately, "Grandmother would do a good job."

"Yes, but it be more work than you think. Lifting bags, lifting tubs, seeing who get what is right. Much to remember." Sunflower observed.

"What about Bluebell?" Impala asked.

"She would be good!" Azalia agreed.

Blossom interjected slowly and thoughtfully, "Mor Dak Sah need help. He not able to hunt. He always sad. He not talk. Maybe no friends. Maybe it make him feel needed. Maybe he want to do something."

We all pondered that idea for a moment.

Lobo was staring at Blossom with a strange look on his face. He glanced at me and said, "someday I be chief. Chief must know and lead people. Blossom more chief than me."

"Blossom is right. Sometimes we should look for one who needs to be needed as much as the job that needs to be done," I said.

"Did you ever miss a deer when you are hunting?" I asked.

He grinned, "yes! More than one." Then he added, "worse than this is wound. I strike high and back. We track deer all day. Sleep under tree at night. Next day, find deer in high grass. I feel bad all day. I not like wound deer. Leave to die." He said with some emotion.

"And what did you learn?" I asked.

"I learn take time. Do not think you better. Do not quit until find wounded one." He grunted, "maybe I learn more things."

"Being a great chief is not that you know everything and never make a mistake." I said, putting my hand on his shoulder. "It is admitting a mistake and learning from it. You will make a great chief!"

He smiled and nodded.

All three girls decided to talk to Mor Dak Sah. They explained the situation and what was expected and how to do the job.

His first reaction was negative, but they explained in more detail and emphasized how important it was that the food needed to be distributed evenly and regularly.

"We know you do it good," Blossom said encouragingly.

"You help me?" Mor Dak Sah asked.

The girls all said "yes" but they noticed that he was looking carefully at Blossom when he said it.

The food distribution was in place, Noh Tay Dah and his family were safe and sound, and everyone noticed an improvement in Mor Dak Sah's well being.

With these things in place, I decided to head back home.

While the farewells were heartfelt, there were no pleas of "don't go," or "we want to go!"

I hoped that meant they were accepting that they must take the responsibility for their survival.

I was to find that it was far more complicated than that.

By late winter, it seemed advisable to return to the village to see how the food distribution plan had worked and if we had sent enough food through. We put several sacks of beans and flour through the portal which I stored in the barrels at the stash site. We had put a fresh apple in my pack for each person and filled all the little empty spaces and my many pockets with energy bars.

My head had barely peeked over the hill when a shrill voice cried out, "Chee is coming!"

That was followed by the murmur and shouts of voices passing on the information.

The girls and Violet raced towards me, Noh Tay Dah and his family were all standing in front of their hut, and Grandmother, Chip and Sweet Pea had joined us. The hugs and greetings were heartfelt, and the boys showed up soon thereafter.

"How has the food held out?" I asked.

"It is enough," Sunflower answered.

"Mor Dak Sah do good job to give out food," Azalia said.

"He have friends. He talk. He laugh!" Blossom said happily with that beautiful smile of hers.

Sweet Pea walked up and stood in front of me. She cocked her head to the side, looked up at me with those big, beautiful eyes and charming smile and said, "Sweet stuff?"

Everyone was grinning at me and I suggested, "why don't you send her out to get deer? They would follow her home and you wouldn't have to hunt or drag them in."

They all laughed but nodded in agreement.

I pulled out three bars and pointed to Grandmother. Sweet Pea skipped over to her and handed her all three bars. Grandmother broke one in three pieces and put the other two in her pocket for later.

"Here is an energy bar and an apple for everyone," I said, taking three apples to Grandmother.

When I gave these to Deh Neh Totsi, she put three of each in her pockets and proceeded to give each of her family a quarter of an apple and a quarter of an energy bar.

"Who would like to go with me to take an apple and energy bar to everyone?" I asked.

All four girls and the three boys volunteered and we were a happy noisy group making our way through the camp. It was like going house to house caroling, except they had never heard of caroling.

Blossom took my hand to lead us around, lest anyone might think my hand could belong to anyone else. It was a great opportunity to see and greet everyone. They all looked warm, happy and healthy.

Back at the girls' fire, we sat and talked and ate a sweet honey crisp apple.

"It looks like the food helped get everyone through the winter," I remarked.

"Yes!" Azalia responded. "With other food from summer that Little Badger bring from cave each week and boys get two more deer."

"We go far for deer," Impala added, "we take pack, camp out. Sometimes two, three days."

"Carry pack, drag deer all day, hard work," Lobo agreed.

After a few more bits of news, we ended our time together and headed for bed. My lean-to had been used by Mor Dak Sah to store and distribute the beans and flour. A quick perusal of what was left indicated that he had done a careful, diligent job.

With all the tubs and supplies, as well as containers that they would consider my personal stuff, there was barely enough room to set my pack and roll out a bedroll. At least very little cold air would flow through my sleeping space.

Actually, I used two sleeping bags as a mattress, a goose down bag to sleep in plus a couple of blankets on top. It was soft, warm and dry.

The next morning after a leisurely breakfast and a warm cup of coffee, which I had stored away several visits previous, I was ready to face the day.

Winter days weren't fast and frantic like summer days but the time was filled with more than the usual firewood gathering. It was also more difficult to do while trudging through the snow.

We made a couple of trips to bring the rest of the food down to the village. The weather began to get warmer and the snow was melting off of all the ridges and the east and south facing slopes.

Several groups made trips to the river and even though it was running high and muddy, they caught fish in the pools and eddies near the shore.

The trees were budding, the flowers and other plants were coming up, the cattails were putting up shoots, and more food was becoming available every week.

It was time to go back home to report and assess the situation.

As I was getting my pack ready, I heard a loud commotion on the western upper part of the village. Loud voices, obviously raised in anger and more than just two parties in disagreement.

"What is that about?" I asked with some concern.

"I don't know but it sounds serious," Sunflower responded. "We better go see." She added.

Azalia and the boys went along and Blossom and Violet joined us as we were making our way up the valley.

Arriving at the scene, Sunflower asked what was going on and Azalia translated so I could get the gist of it.

"He steal my pot of stew," one woman was shouting.

"I no steal!" The boy answered back.

"He not lie. We not have pot of stew," his mother asserted.

This continued back and forth with Sunflower hardly able to get a word in and Azalia not being able to interpret fast enough for me to understand, except that one woman accused a boy from another fire group of stealing her pot of stew and the boy and his mother denying it. Soon, the rest of both fire groups started shouting their opinions and denials which quickly turned into threats.

I put down the urge to blast a stew pot off of the fire with my .357 and splatter them all with hot stew. Instead, I held up both hands and shouted "enough!" And Azalia didn't even have to translate, as they got the message.

As they quieted, I asked the woman, through Azalia, "why do you think he stole the stew?"

"He come to fire. Stew gone," she answered indignantly.

"I come get Lo Dah Tay. We get wood together," he answered quickly.

"He lie. He steal!" Her voice started to rise.

I think I refrained from rolling my eyes, as others on both sides began voicing their opinions again.

Again, I held up my hand, "did you see him take it?" I asked.

"No!" She admitted, "sneaky thief, take at night," and she glared at the boy.

"I no thief!" He shot back.

"Whoa, whoa, slow down, I said. "She didn't say you were the sneaky thief that time. We are making a little progress here."

Turning to the boy, I said, "come here!"

He came and stood in front of me, frightened but determined, Azalia translated.

"What is your name?" I asked.

"Loc Nos Pahn," he replied. "When Whiteface come, I taken. You come, they let me go, I no lie to you, Chee."

I put on my most intense scowl and asked, "did you steal the pot of stew?"

He looked me straight in the eye and answered, "I no steal, I no lie!"

I stared at him intently for a few seconds and he stared back.

My back was towards the two fire groups and I was facing my group and had stooped over to be at his eye level. I gave a quick smile and winked, and he exhaled in relief and returned to his mother.

My face was all serious when I straightened up and turned towards the fire groups.

"Let's see if there is evidence. Can Azalia and Sunflower look in both huts?" I asked.

I didn't know if that broke norms and protocols but if they objected and especially if just one side objected, it might tell me something. Both sides agreed and the girls began their inspection.

Turning to Blossom and Violet, I instructed, "you girls go and get a pot out of my hut. If we don't have a good replacement, we will get one. Also get three days of beans and flour. Have Mor Dak Sah measure it out for you since he is in charge of that. Bring two cans of beef stew."

I took Blossom's hand and printed "beef stew" on her palm. She knew her letters but this would be easier to match than a verbal description.

"Boys, go up the valley and look for tracks. Then look at the side of that hill and especially along the top of the ridge. A shoe print, moccasin print or even a barefoot print would tell us something or give us something to match.

In a few minutes the girls returned. "We not find any stew pot except what belong to our fire group. We bring it"

Both sides were beginning to look a bit embarrassed at their behavior, but I decided to let it settle for a while.

We waited for Blossom and Violet to arrive accompanied by Mor Dak Sah. His change in attitude from the angry, sad, morose, recluse that he had been, to the cheerful, helpful, dispenser of the supplies, had raised his status among the people considerably.

Sunflower explained the situation to him.

The new pot and the extra food mollified the woman who had made the accusations.

In a short while the boys returned with information.

Lobo said succinctly, "we find tracks."

Given the short report, devoid of any explanation, indicated that he thought it ought to be discussed in private.

"Let's go and make up our packs and then investigate what you found," I said.

"That good!" Lobo said, and he and the boys went to get their packs and bows.

Again, I raise my hand and Azalia interpreted. "We must all work together, seek truth, trust one another." Pointing to the two young boys I beckoned them to me. I put a hand on a shoulder of each one. "These are good boys. They are friends. Value your friends and be at peace with them. If you are wrong, say you are sorry. If any are sorry forgive them."

That was enough preaching for today, so I beckoned to the girls and we headed back.

I did notice that the two mothers had moved in for a hug and then everyone drifted back to their respective huts.

The boys came over with their packs and equipment and related what they found.

"We see tracks of only one. We think it a man. He come down side of ridge then no tracks into village. Then tracks over ridge. Join tracks come down. Same tracks go up. One person. Maybe join others up mountain." Lobo explained.

Impala added, "tracks go up, short steps, like he carry something."

"Well, we don't know if there is a war party or a family or a tribe. They are probably without food so be careful. Even if they are not an enemy, people will do whatever they can to get food for a starving family," I warned.

"We want to move quietly and see them first!" I suggested.

"Who is the best tracker?" I asked.

"I am." Lobo and Impala answered in unison.

We all grinned at that, so I asked. "Do you have a protocol for tracking as to who tracks and who watches ahead?"

Impala answered with a grin. "We let Lobo track. We stay to side and watch sides and ahead."

"The rest of us will stay behind but able to see you. My thunder stick can strike far ahead," I said.

The boys headed out; the girls and I fell in fifty to a hundred yards behind. We would move in closer as they crested a hill because an ambush would be out of our sight when they went over a hill.

More than an hour into our hike, we headed up a longer, steeper hill that turned out to be the top of a cliff overlooking a valley and a meadow with a nice stream.

We crawled to spots behind rocks and trees near the edge of the cliff to survey the situation.

The cliff wasn't high. It went from thirty to forty feet of sheer cliff along the side of the valley and another fifty to eighty feet of sloping hillside from the cliff to the valley below.

Right beside us, there was a collapsed part that formed a steep access to the top of the cliff. It was here that the thief had come out and gone back into the valley.

Set back under some trees, where the forest met the valley, they had established a campsite. Their campfire was burning and there were people lounging about.

We had three sets of binoculars to surveil the site and count the people. We were only about four hundred yards away. Our three little groups moved closer together so we could comment and share what we were seeing.

Blossom, Violet and I shared my big binoculars and Blossom was detailing her findings.

"I see stew pot beside fire," she said.

Impala grunted an affirmation.

Lobo said, "without binoc'lars I see warrior and wife maybe. Young man and woman with baby. Four between Azalia and Sunflower size; three, more small than Blossom and Violet. One lies under tree. Maybe sick. Woman take food. Pull him up, put in food, lay him down. Maybe some in hut. Maybe some in woods.

One by one, Sunflower and Azalia then Impala and Little Badger confirmed the number as from twelve to maybe fifteen people, unless there were others gone from the site.

We studied them for over a half hour. Lobo noticed no weapons although any number could be leaning against the back side of a tree. There were no other visible pots, jars or food containers of any kind.

Sunflower, Azalia, Blossom and Violet confirmed that they looked weary, gaunt and thin.

"They not move like warriors," Impala observed.

Violet, who was new to the binocular's, was continuing to look while we turned to trying to assess what to do. Suddenly she remarked, "man bring pot."

We all turned to look.

"You think he see us?" Little Badger asked.

"No," Sunflower surmised. "I think he take pot to village to return or maybe fill up again or change for other pot."

"Boys, remember that open area at the bottom of the ravine about ten of the one hundred step distances?" I asked.

They all recalled coming through it and some noticed the large rocks along the hill and some big trees.

"Let's set up an ambush there. Far enough that he can't warn his group and secure enough that he can't escape," I proposed. "Maybe he will tell us his story and who his people are. I think we should help them if we can."

"They need help, Chee," Blossom agreed.

We arrived at the little clearing and set the ambush.

Azalia, Blossom, Violet and I would step out to greet him. In quick succession, Sunflower on his right, then Little Badger on his left would step out. If he turned back, Impala and Lobo were coming behind him.

We could see from his walk, even going downhill, that he was exhausted and mal-nourished. I hoped he would stop and listen.

When he arrived at the center of the little clearing, Azalia and I stepped out about ten yards in front of him with Blossom and Violet a step behind and off to each side.

I raised my hand in the universal sign of peace. He stopped with a startled look on his face. He immediately glanced left and right and Sunflower and Little Badger stepped forward. As he wheeled to run, Lobo and Impala were behind him.

He looked like someone had struck him with a big club. He almost collapsed then staggered a few steps to an old log that was lying half buried beside the trail and dropped his head into his hands. The pot dropped harmlessly to the ground at his feet.

Since he was coming from the south, I took a guess as to his origins and said, "Yaht'eh Hosteen," his head jerked up and a little bit of life seem to return to his eyes.

I pointed at him and said, "din'eh?" And he shook his head affirmatively and spoke a few words.

"Okay girls, here is where you try to remember common words of a trade language or words that Deh Neh Totsi taught you."

Again, he looked at us curiously and a little more hopefully and responded with some words ending with "Deh Neh Totsi."

Realizing that these few words didn't mean we spoke his language he spoke slowly, "Deh Neh Totsi din'eh."

We nodded and I gestured to all of us, then to my eyes to "see" and said, "Deh Neh Totsi."

He smiled and visibly relaxed as a wave of relief and hope swept over him.

"Okay girls," I said. "He's all yours. See if you can communicate."

They were much more skilled at sign language and there was some overlap in the languages as Deh Neh Totsi and they had discussed numerous times. In a few minutes they were relaying to me in bits and pieces what they were saying.

They were almost all from the Din'eh and Deh Neh Totsi was a relative who had been captured on a raid about seven summers past.

An evil tribe with hard, pointed head coverings and hard shells covering their bodies had come with terrible weapons that thundered, smoked and killed at a distance. They could not stand against them and they killed many. The rest fled and scattered. They come north but did not know plants to eat. Did not have warm coverings. They were cold and had no food.

Tears filed his eyes as he related that they were starving and the children were close to dying. One in particular was unable to walk. It was his son.

I pulled out an energy bar and handed it to Sunflower. "Take a little piece so he knows it is food and give the rest to him."

His response at the first bite was like all the others that had come before him. His eyes got big then closed in pleasure at the sweet taste filling his mouth. He immediately folded the paper over the open end and put it in his little bag at his waist.

He was obviously planning to take it back to his family.

I pulled out three more, gave them to Sunflower and said, "give these to him and tell him to eat one now for strength.

"Did he give you his name?" I asked.

"Yes, his name Cedo Bah Gay," Sunflower answered.

"Tell him we have food. Can we go to his camp and feed his family?" I asked.

Again, he fought back tears as hope and despair seem to fight for expression on his face.

"We have nothing to trade," he lamented.

"Tell him he has a treasure worth trading for," I suggested. "There are few things of greater value than a true friend."

It seemed to strike a chord in our little group as they all murmured and nodded in agreement. Blossom and Violet were standing on each side of me and they both stepped over to me and hugged an arm.

He looked a little bewildered but hope was in his eyes as he stood, took my forearm and leaned in for a shoulder bump.

He said something in a voice strained with emotion which Sunflower interpreted as, "you will have no better friend."

The boys, without hesitation stepped in for a forearm grasp, shoulder bump.

"We need to plan," I began. "Azalia, you interpret so he knows what we are talking about.

"We have enough food for about two or three meals."

"Have you ever hunted this far?" I asked the boys.

"One time," Lobo answered. "Many deer. We take one. It take half day to get up break in cliff. Much work. Could not drag, only carry. Lift, hold in place, lift hold in place again, again, again. Much work."

He looked like the very memory was tiring him out.

"Well, this time the deer will stay in the valley," I said. "Can you boys get a deer this afternoon?"

"Where do we get more food for so many?" Little Badger asked. "There is little left in cave."

I responded, "as we said when you came to my home and met with my people, we are able to get whatever you need. But if we give everything this winter and you don't learn how to prepare for next winter will you starve then? If the door closes, will you live?

"I have food but it is up at the door. We will have enough."

Lobo spoke up, "I hunt, I get deer, Impala and Little Badger get food. You and girls take all this food and feed people. We eat when we come with food."

"Very good," I exclaimed. "Planned and spoken like a true chief!" And I slapped him on the shoulder. Turning to Impala and Little Badger, I said, "tell Mor Dak Sah to take out enough for one week for each fire group and we will get more when we return."

"Also," I added, "there is a box of energy bars and after you put beans and flour in your packs, put cans of food in until your pack is full."

"Everything you now have in your packs, we will put in our pack."

There was more than we could fit in, so we used Impala's pack.

"Get a pack out of my hut and use it too," I said.

The two boys went back to get the food and Lobo stayed with us until we got down to the valley. He then headed out to get a deer.

"Okay, let's go meet our new friends!" I exclaimed cheerfully.

Chapter 7

It didn't take long to get back up the hill and work our way down the cut in the cliff to the valley floor. Lobo left us there immediately to get a deer.

It was a beautiful little valley with a good-sized stream running down the middle. The meadow on each side was covered with tall, brown grass, interspersed with new shoots of green and lightly sprinkled with the earliest of spring flowers.

"Identify plants that we can get to make stew. They probably don't know our plants."

As we made our way across the valley, all of their people picked up sharpened sticks to defend themselves.

"Spread out a little. You never know what desperate people will do." I warned.

We stopped a little less than a hundred yards away and Sunflower interpreted my instructions to Cedo Bah Gay.

I told him, "You go ahead and tell your people who we are and why we are here and when they put down their spears, we will come in."

Their campsite was back along the very edge of the forest where they had some big trees under which they built their small shelters. They simply used a limb for a ridge pole and lay poles and sticks and chunks of dead trees against the ridge pole to make a tent. The tree kept most of the rain and snow off of them and the crude tent stopped most of the wind.

The campfire was simply built on a flat spot between two large trees where they could gather for warmth. Since they had no pots or pans, there were no stones or any kind of fire pit.

The fact that we had two women and two children, made our party less threatening. The younger adult male was the only one who needed some persuasion from Cedo Bah Gay and I noticed that he put his spear a little apart from where the others stacked theirs, so he could get to it quickly if he needed it. A little caution is to be commended.

We were still a dozen steps from their campfire as Cedo Bah Gay came back to us and said, "you are welcome at our fire."

"Tell him to give everyone a half of an energy bar," I said to Sunflower.

He knew what that was now and he nodded approval.

Sunflower and Azalia took some from their packs and with the three that he already had, there was enough to go around. They didn't need to know that we had more, with more coming.

The reaction of each one from the first bite was the same as it was everywhere we used them; a dreamy smile, a wide-eyed amazement, an assumption that something so good couldn't come from really bad people. Even the skeptic with one eye on his spear seemed to be won over. Energy bars were better than a whole cadre of diplomats.

There was a more ideal campsite - at least for us - about twenty steps to the side of theirs and he immediately gave us permission to camp there. Two huge trees, a jumble of rocks, some logs nearby would be all that we needed.

Upon finding a good spot to set out our packs, we left them and returned to meet our new friends.

It was immediately clear that they were close to the point of starvation. The baby in particular was in danger and the little son of Cedo Bah Gay and his wife may be beyond our help. He didn't have enough strength left to sit up, and the unknown plants they were trying to survive on were beyond his ability to chew and digest.

"Blossom and Violet, bring my pack." The two rifles still clipped on it would make it too heavy for either of them by herself.

"Azalia, would you find a pan, a can of chicken soup, a can of peaches and the can opener. We must get some nourishment in him now before we do anything else."

The girls arrived with my pack and Blossom remembered that she had the can opener and went to get it.

In my pack was a bottle of pink ant-acid that I always carried with me and some plastic spoons.

"Sunflower, ask his mother sit him up."

We put one spoonful to his mouth and he took it and swallowed.

Sunflower was in full nurse mode now and handed me a bottle of water before I asked. He took several spoon's full of water which wet his mouth and washed the medicine down his throat as well.

By this time, Azalia had returned with the cans of soup and peaches and Blossom had the can opener.

"Open the peaches just enough to pour out some juice. Azalia, put one can of chicken soup and one can of water in the pan and set it on the edge of their fire. We don't have time to set up our fire pit.

"Blossom and Violet, get firewood for this fire first, then some for our site," I instructed.

The other children were stirred up at all the activity of their visitors, and went with Blossom and Violet to see what they were doing and they all returned with an arm load of firewood.

Azalia had the pot ready and put wood on the fire to heat, at least to a comfortable warmth.

Sunflower had the peaches can open and handed it to me.

"Give his mother a spoonful of juice so she knows what he is getting," I instructed, as I put a few drops on the spoon she was holding

She cautiously sipped at the sweet juice, turned and said something to Cedo Bah Gay. Apparently, they had a similar fruit where they had come from.

Sunflower took the spoon and gave their little boy a few drops. He seemed to recognize the taste as well, as he swallowed the spoonful immediately.

"Open the can a little more and give him a couple of spoon's full with a little bit of the peach with it and we'll see if he keeps it down."

He swallowed it immediately and we kept him in the semi upright position for a little while and fed him a half of a peach. His mother stroked his hair, speaking to him in a low, calm voice and finally laid him back on his sleeping pad.

"Sunflower, ask her to watch to see if he keeps the food down and we can give him some chicken soup a little later," I said.

Sunflower relayed the message and she nodded.

As we stood up, we noticed that their whole group, except for the children who were with Blossom and Violet, had been clustered together watching intently and with some apparent amazement.

Cedo Bah Gay looked at his tribe, looked at us and spoke. His voice was filled with emotion as Sunflower interpreted, "your people work together and save my son, make much happen, fast. Each know what to do."

"Yes," I said proudly. "We have done many things together. We almost think and do as one!"

With the newly acquired brood following Blossom and Violet, the girls and I went back to our site to get organized.

We built the fire pit using a couple of stones with a point protruding out so pots or skillets could set over the fire instead of just beside it.

Sunflower left with the bow saw and the younger children to bring in bigger pieces of wood for the evening and night fire.

We suddenly realized the whole tribal group had moved our way and was watching in amazement again. We seemed to keep forgetting that both saws and pots and pans were strange and new.

Sunflower had cut several more, larger, three foot long, pieces and told the children to take some back for their own fire. Seeing Sunflower and Azalia working motivated the teens, who looked to be about Azalia's age, to begin to help. When Sunflower and Azalia tried to move some logs into position around our fire, everyone jumped in to help and made a fire circle big enough for both groups to be together for the evening.

Sunflower and Azalia knew without asking that I would want both groups together for the evening meal and time to visit.

Azalia called out that the chicken soup should be warm by now and we went back to see how Cedo Bah Gay's son was doing.

Not only had he kept the food down but was alert and smiled at us.

Sunflower fed him some broth, then included some bits of noodles with the broth.

"How much has he eaten?" I asked.

"About a cup," she responded.

"That should be enough for now," I said. "We will give him some more this evening and some more before bed if he'll eat it."

"Blossom," I called. "Bring the small blanket out of my pack, please."

She found it and brought it quickly. It was similar to flannel but a little heavier material.

"Would you do the honors?" I asked.

She rolled it out, then spread the blanket over him. As the warmth spread over him and he felt the soft texture surrounding him, his eyes popped open just as Blossom was tucking it around his neck and shoulders. He reached out weakly and touched her face, then drew his hand back and closed his eyes.

"I think you have a boyfriend," I said teasingly.

She looked at me, then smiled and said impishly, "maybe!" And got up and went back to our campsite.

The mother was enthralled with the blanket as well as the improvement in her son. Word circulated quickly about the strange covering and everyone came by to gently touch it and step away quietly so as not to awaken the boy.

It was getting along towards evening when Violet called out, "Lobo come, drag deer."

"Let's go help him," I said, and Violet and Blossom ran ahead to help drag it. It was a large, well fed, mule deer buck. Lobo was looking pretty tired from his efforts.

The girls had grabbed the rope and were pulling it along by the time I arrived. I tossed him an energy bar, grabbed onto the rope and we all completed our walk to the campfire together.

"Azalia, introduce Lobo to everyone. Sunflower, you and I will give a demonstration on how to skin and cut up a deer." I said, as I dragged it a few more steps past our campsite and under a sturdy limb about eight feet off the ground.

We threw two ropes, about five feet apart, over the limb, tied them to the two hind legs, pulled the deer up about five feet and tied off the ropes to each side.

"Okay," I said, grinning at Sunflower. "The winner gets two points but we lose two points if we nick the hide and three points off if we go through the hide."

"Good," she said. "What do I win?"

"Ooooh, pretty confident," I replied. "What do you want?"

"I want you to cook for me and bring me my food for three days," she said.

Azalia had begun to interpret our banter since everyone had gathered around to watch what we were doing. I began to realize that this was a lesson, win or lose, that men and women can and do work together and this group needed to learn it.

There were a number of exclamations and murmurs around the group as they realized this was a charged and daring challenge.

Our group just grinned. We had been working together for a long time.

"And what do you want?" She asked.

"You will stand before all of us and declare loudly, 'our leader is smarter, prettier and nicer than me'!"

Lobo and the girls laughed and cheered. Their teens were catching on to our banter and some cheered and some hissed - which was their version of a boo.

We were both ready with skinning knife in hand, so as a last gesture I raised both hands and cried, "who is for me?"

There was a lot of laughter and a few cheers.

Lobo stepped forward, raised both hands and shouted, "who is for Sunflower?" And everyone cheered and then all burst out laughing as I slumped my shoulders and fell to my knees.

I got up, grinned at Sunflower, and said, "let's go!"

Our cuts were almost identical. Out the inside of the leg, around the leg just below the foot and then pull the skin down the leg, using the skinning knives quickly, wherever the hide stuck to the carcass too tightly.

Since I was stronger, I was slightly ahead pulling the hide down the leg, but from that point on down the main part of the carcass, it was obvious that she was more deft with a knife and more experienced.

"Ready to pull up?" I asked, as I saw her waiting for me to catch up."

We both laid down our knives, untied the ropes and pulled together until only the nose was touching the ground. It was obvious, as we worked together, that there was no competition except for the skinning, as I tied my side first and waited for her to get the knot tight.

We attacked the second half at exactly the same time and she immediately pulled ahead. She stopped as I cut the hide from the breast bone to the chin as only one person could make that cut.

Then we jumped back in to finish the front legs and down the neck, which she won handily. She had probably skinned more deer in the past year than I had skinned in my whole life.

She stepped back with a smirky grin as I finished my side of the neck. While I was down with my knife in hand, I removed the head, leaving the hide attached. Lobo stepped in and laid out the hide and rolled it up with the head into a neat package.

Sunflower began to cut out the loin for steaks tonight. I ceremoniously took her knife and an arm and marched her to a seat on a log by the fire, given that she was clearly the winner.

Everyone laughed at our antics, but I saw the members of their group look at one another, trying to take in the strange but joyful and productive ways our group interacted.

Azalia already had the liver thin sliced and salted, the firewood was neatly stacked, the campsite was comfortable and functional. Of course, we had equipment and utensils that they had never seen before.

Suddenly, Blossom and Violet paused in their activity, as some movement across the valley caught their eyes. "Look, Impala and Little Badger come."

We all turned to look. The boys had gone above and beyond in their collection of food and equipment. It was much more than I had expected and they were tired and staggering under the weight.

"You brought a lot of stuff," I remarked with some awe.

It had been a long hike with a lot of weight. They collapsed onto the ground against the log but tried not to appear too tired in front of our new friends.

"Give them an energy bar to hold them until supper," I urged.

After two bites, they became self-conscious of eating in front of others who had been literally starving and they put the energy bars in their pockets.

I was amazed at Impala and Little Badger's thoroughness. They had tossed in a package of paper cups, some paper plates and even some spoons. I didn't think we would teach anything about spoons on the first meal.

As I was about to ask how we were going to prepare supper, it was obvious that they were ahead of me again.

Violet and Blossom were busy mixing a powdered fruit drink in the big pot. There were five cans of beans sitting beside the smaller pot, apparently waiting for me. Lobo was returning with six or eight willow sticks to cook steaks and liver, and Azalia was mixing up a batch of fry bread.

Sunflower stood up. I grinned at her. She and I both knew that sitting there doing nothing was more like a punishment than a prize.

"I ask younger ones to go to other fire and cook liver and steaks." She grinned at me and added, "you cook my steak!"

"It's a deal," I said with a smile.

Impala and Little Badger stood up too and added, "we go too! Help make sure things go good."

Lobo quickly followed. Since Cedo Bah Gay's group hadn't built a fire pit, they had to hold the sticks over the fire. Little Badger went to find some short sticks with a "Y" and used his big hatchet to drive them into the ground around the fire to rest the cooking sticks on.

"Blossom and Violet, why don't you give everybody a cup of fruit drink to get started," I said, as I began opening beans and dumping them into a pot. Adding a jar of Bar-B-Q sauce to the mix, I stirred it in and left it to simmer.

"Tell them to keep their cups," I added.

Everyone was delightfully impressed with the new experience of this sweet flavored drink.

The girl from the younger couple came over to Azalia and said something. It seemed to be an offer to help, as Azalia got out another frying pan and showed her the process.

Since the baby and the sick boy wouldn't be eating the regular food, there were thirteen of their group to feed. Cedo Bah Gay's wife went to feed their sick son and Sunflower went along to help.

The six sticks with two pieces of liver on each one was just right for cooking the first round.

The little butterfly steaks would fit three to a stick, so Lobo asked Violet to help the boys cook the steaks so the teens from their group could eat. Azalia paused the cooking of the fry bread as they were getting ahead and the young woman who was helping her, needed to eat.

Blossom, Azalia and I began serving. Everyone gathered together and they all sat down on the logs around our fire pit.

The meal was enthusiastically received and appreciated. It's hard to beat Bar-B-Q beans, well seasoned liver, and some fry bread.

Sunflower and Cedo Bah Gay,s wife returned, talking animatedly.

"He is much better!" Sunflower said happily, "he keep food in stomach. He sit up and eat more. She help him walk to hut to sleep. He not walk many days, she say. He sleep now."

"That's wonderful," I said. "I think they will all be doing better now with some food in their stomachs."

Little Badger spoke up suddenly, "I forget! I have food for baby. Bluebell say Sunflower fix!"

He dug out the bottle and formula and gave it to Sunflower who went to the young couple to explain what it was and what was involved in preparing it. When their supper was over. We cooked for ourselves. We made sure it was the same meal that we had prepared for them. I even made Sunflower's plate with an extra piece of steak, and delivered it to her with much ceremony and when our group laughed and cheered, they joined in.

As the evening wore on most of us put on something a little warmer. Some had leggings, some had a fur to throw around their neck. It was still early in the year and the nights got cold.

Blossom came to me and said, "girl not have good covering. She get cold."

I glanced over at the four young teens and saw what Blossom was talking about. One had a decidedly inadequate covering. It was a deer hide with a hole for the head to go through. It had been trimmed like it was made for someone much smaller. It was a tunic design, going down front and back with a few laces to hold the sides together. It was too small to pull completely together, so there was a two to three inch gap down each side from under the arm. It was also too short. Whereas most coverings come below the knee, hers was a few inches above the knee.

I had somewhat noticed during all the activity and mingling, but having been around teens who all too often wear shorts and short sleeve shirts in the winter, I didn't think anything of it.

Beckoning to Azalia to come and translate, we went to Cedo Bah Gay to inquire.

Thinking back and trying to remember various incidents and interactions, it dawned on me that this girl always seemed somewhat alone. Even now with the cold moving in, families and couples were moving together. The other three teens were sitting tight together and this girl had space on both sides of her. Another impression that thrust itself on my consciousness was that I had seen her smile only once. When I delivered the plate to Sunflower, they had joined our laughter and I noticed that she smiled for a moment.

As Azalia translated, I inquired, "who is the young girl sitting by herself? She seems to not belong to anyone here."

"It is true. She is not of our tribe. We find her as we flee. She starving, like us. She help find plants and roots. We share," Cedo Bah Gay answered.

Blossom chimed in, "Chee, we give her shirt? She cold!"

I turned to Cedo Bah Gay, "if we give her a covering will others feel bad that they do not get something?"

"No," he replied. "We have some coverings but there is none to share. They be happy for her."

"I get shirt?" Blossom inquired excitedly. "I give her my shirt?"

"She probably is a size or two bigger than you," I replied. "I always lose a shirt every time I come through the door. Why should this time be different? Besides one of my large shirts will work as a blanket at night."

Blossom hurried off to dig out my shirt and returned quickly. I turned to Cedo Bah Gay. "Do you know her tribe?"

"No, she come from east. Other side of big valley and river. We come from south and west," he explained. "Maybe escape from Whiteface tribe. She not speak our words. Maybe she speak some of your words"

"The Whiteface again," I mused. "Thank you and we will see if we can help her, if that meets with your approval?"

"It is good," he replied.

Blossom held up the flannel shirt she had chosen from my pack.

"You give to her?" She asked.

"No," I replied. "You and Azalia give the shirt and see if she will talk. Maybe her language or what she learned from the Whiteface will enable her to communicate with us."

The girls loved to give, whether food, clothing or supplies. They had experienced enough hardship and deprivation to know how significant help and friendship were.

Back at their camp they had just run out of food themselves, yet here they were, cooking, giving, serving and finding joy and fulfillment in the process.

They approached the girl as she sat forlornly on the cold log, hoping to catch at least some warmth from the fire.

It became apparent that they had many words in common. They unrolled the shirt and unbuttoned the buttons and helped her get her arms in the sleeve. She responded like others, by bringing the soft material up to caress her cheeks.

As they were explaining the shirt, I heard the word, "Chee." Her head came up as though she had been struck. The girls pointed to me and their conversation grew excited and animated.

Azalia beckoned me over and began to translate.

"She say girl in Whiteface camp tell about 'Chee'." Azalia said, "it must be Roh Dah Bey."

The girl stood up and asked, "you are Chee?"

"That's what they call me," I replied. "Where did you hear that name?"

"Girl in Whiteface camp tell me. She have white in hair like these girls. She adopted. I slave, so we not talk much. She in hut up river. I am downriver. Sometimes we talk and she tell of her family. Her tribe and many others believe Chee is great warrior long ago. Sometimes he come and help. Her father say Chee not real, only story. Her sisters say he is real and will come and help.

"One day Whiteface attack. They kill her father and mother and take her and others captive. Chee did not come. But she say 'sometimes I believe he real and will come, when Great Spirit send him.   Maybe he someplace else when Whiteface attack'."

"She not sure he is real or not real - only story.

"Then, one day, Whiteface go back to attack and take food and captives, but Chee come and make them give back everything and kill some and wound some and Whiteface come back say 'Chee stop them'.

"Then she believe he is real, and will come for her someday. Will you come for her too?"

My heart sank. I was in no position to go to the aid of someone with a hundred warriors ready to fight and avenge their comrades.

"Is she safe and does she have food?" I asked.

"She is safe," the girl answered.

"I am not the one who decides when and where I go. If I am to help her, it will be at the right time and right place," I said.

"Tell us, how did you get here?" I asked.

Others from our group joined us to hear her story. Azalia interpreted for me as we sat around in a small group, and she sat on the log and began.

"Sometimes captives try to escape. The Whiteface send fast running warriors to catch and bring them back. They call them 'catchers.' They beat them almost to death. Some do die. But it is lesson to not try to escape.

"After time, some think they know a way and so they try again.

"This time the plan look good. Go at night. If many go, they cannot catch all. Soon they set day and time. I not think good to go but after days of much trouble, I say 'I go too'."

"We run for long time to get far away. We get to mountain. We climb and climb. We think we free. We come to valley. We tired. Stop for drink. We go up little hill and looked back. They are coming. They fast and strong. We run fast as we can but they are faster.

"I cannot keep up. I see big pile of rocks and spires. I turn and run there. The others go on, then the catchers run past. I crawl far back and into small space and hide.

"Soon I hear screams and cries from far down Valley. Then there is silence. After long time, I hear them come. There is crying and sometimes a thud and a cry, as one is struck again. I lay there long, long time. Not move. Almost not breathe.

"After sun almost down, I crawl out with no sound. I hear nothing. They all gone. I go down Valley. I come to place where they catch them. Each one they catch they bring to big flat place. There is much blood and two bodies. The ones they think plan the escape are dead. I not stop. I go far around and keep going.

"Soon I come to big creek, night come. I cold and hungry. I try sleep. Morning come. I go, come to larger creek. I go down to find a warmer place, then I hear voices. I too tired to run. They will kill me because I go no more.

"Then I hear children and I know it is not the catchers. I look out from hiding place and see these people. They are tired and go slow. I come to them. They give me some food and I follow.

"We come to river and I warn. River go to Whiteface. Whiteface kill and capture. They decide to go across river. Come up this creek to this place.

"We not know plants or roots, cannot get deer. Sometimes rabbit but give to children. We hungry.

"Great spirit send you to us. Maybe we live."

With that she hung her head and looked so forlorn that the girls all crowded around to give her a hug.

"What is her name?" I asked.

The girls inquired and replied, "she say her name is Lark Soh Kim."

I looked at her intently and repeated her name with a smile.

So it was that we seemed to have inherited another girl.

"She sleep with us tonight?" Blossom asked, "she sleep between Violet and me. Our sleeping bags help keep her warm and we put big blanket over all three of us."

"The big blanket you are putting over you three wouldn't happen to be my big blanket, would it?" I asked sarcastically.

"You not need blanket, Chee. You have good warm sleeping bag," she said with that impish grin.

I was still getting used to the new Blossom. The transformation from wild forest waif with a cleft lip, that had made her "the curse of the tribe," to the confident, healthy little imp who wormed her way into the heart of everyone who knew her, was like a miracle.

Sunflower went over to check on the baby and Cedo Bah Gay's son. The young mother of the baby was profuse with thankfulness for the improvement of her son. He was sleeping peacefully, which also meant that the parents might get some peaceful sleep as well.

Cedo Bah Gay's son was also continuing to improve. He was sitting up in their tiny hut, wrapped in the warm blanket and chattering away.

Sunflower warmed up the last of the chicken noodle soup which he ate hungrily.

"He's still hungry, Chee," Sunflower said.

"Were there any beans or fry bread left?" I asked.

"Should he eat that food?" She asked.

"Try about a quarter of a piece and see if he keeps it down. If he does, we can try more of it and some different food tomorrow," I said.

Slowly, but surely, everyone wandered off to bed and I found a soft spot on the backside of the tree just a few steps from the campsite.

I think we all felt a little guilty in our warm sleeping bags or bedrolls with them just huddled together against the cold.

Chapter 8

I woke up with a start. Blossom was kneeling beside me and shaking me. I started to sit up and ask what was wrong, when she put a hand over my mouth.

"sh-shah," she whispered. "Men come. Some have shiny head coverings and black hair on face. Others from tribes like us."

"How far?" I whispered.

"About half hour. Maybe quicker. They stop, build fire, but not sleep. They wait for sun come up," she whispered back.

"How did you discover this?" I asked quietly.

"I hear deer run up valley. I feel danger in my spirit. I go see, back up in woods so valley in moonlight and I in dark. See man from tribe come slow, look over camp and go back. I follow. See their fire and see men."

"How many?" I whispered.

"Maybe four with hard, pointy, head coverings. Maybe six tribe men." She answered.

"Okay, get Sunflower and Azalia. I will get the boys up. Then Violet and Lark Soh Kim," I whispered as I rolled out and laced up my boots. "Tell them to take coats and weapons and leave everything else."

Our group was up in minutes and ready to go. They knew to wait silently as they got ready. They would get the information they needed to know when they needed to know it.

"Sunflower and Azalia get the couple with the baby, I will get Cedo Bah Gay and the young couple. You girls get the teens. Be emphatic! No noise! Leave everything but coverings," I whispered intensely.

Unfortunately, rousing them out of there huts and nests into the morning cold in absolute silence was impossible, but I didn't think any noise would go far enough down the valley for the enemy to hear.

I beckoned everyone in close and said tersely in a loud whisper, "we will be attacked at dawn. We must go in silence."

There were several gasps and a few murmurs.

"Blossom, remember the tree near the stream, with the pile of rocks on the little hill, just to the right of the tree? Lead the group right between the tree and the mound and go to the cut in the cliff, but do not go up. After the attackers see that we are gone and it starts to get light, they will see the trail and come to attack. Watch! Then have the teens start climbing the cut," I said. "The attackers will focus their attention on those climbing out."

I turned to Cedo Bah Gay, "follow Blossom! She has the plan and we need to know you are following it."

"Blossom, do you have your little thunder stick?" I asked.

"Yes," she said.

"When your group is in place, come a few steps back down the hill between the attackers and these people. If one of the attackers gets through, let him get about ten steps from you and fire center mass. Go with the Great Spirit!"

Giving her a little hug, I smiled and said, "lead your people!"

I beckoned to the boys and Sunflower and Azalia, "we will follow and make a plan as we go."

We trailed behind until we approached the tree and the little hill.

"We will set an ambush here," I said, gesturing towards the mound to our right.

The top of the mound was a jumble of rocks that reminded me of the comb on a rooster's head. It was parallel to the stream and facing back towards the trail we had been following.

"Let's set our battle plan and Lobo will direct it.

"Little Badger and Sunflower will be on the end closest to the trail, and will strike first. The rest of us take positions along the top. I will be on the end. Lobo, take the highest position and see how they attack and direct us from there.

"Let no one see you until Lobo directs us.

"Here is what I think will happen. They will discover that we have left. We left so suddenly that we didn't take our things. They will see our trail and with the sun just coming up, they will see all those up by the cliff.

"They will each be so eager to be the first to kill or capture, that they will run as fast as they can to catch us. Probably, one or two will be faster and get here first.

"Lobo will signal Sunflower and Little Badger to rise and strike. Signal when the attackers are about twenty steps before the tree so that they will know where their target is before they even rise.

"Have a second arrow ready in case you only wound or miss. Not that either of you would miss," I said with a wry smile.

The touch of humor helped to ease the tension and prepare them mentally for the battle that was to come.

"Lobo will have to instruct us about the rest. If they are bunched together, you all may need to rise and strike. If there is still one coming ahead of the others, have Sunflower and Little Badger strike him too. That way they don't know how many are here.

"The conquistadors have thunder sticks. If they stop and aim, tell everyone to 'get down' quickly.

"They won't be able to keep up with the native attackers so they should be far behind.

"Lobo will tell us if the native attackers keep coming and if they are coming all together. He will signal who is to rise and strike.

"I will take the Conquistadors.

"Any questions?" I asked.

They all nodded their heads and got ready to move into position.

"One more thing," I said grimly. "We have always fought to win, but this is a different kind of fight. The conquistadors will never stop killing, torturing and raping. They deserve no mercy and none can leave here alive. If even one escapes, they will be back with more and more fighters until these people and then all of your people are dead or captured. They will not stop. They must be destroyed!"

They were taken aback by the vehemence and intensity of my speech. In the past we had even made friends with foes in some other battles. This was indeed a different attitude.

We settled into position as the first light began to brighten the sky.

Shortly thereafter we heard the shrill war cries followed by the thunder of several guns.

I had hung a shirt on a branch just outside the fire circle in a way that would let it move in the slightest breeze. I hope they were shooting at that and not filling my good, goose down sleeping bag full of holes.

It was also an immediate confirmation that they were bent on killing first and only taking captives if anyone was left.

The war cries stopped as suddenly as they had begun.

It was getting light enough to try the binoculars. The sun was just hitting the peaks to the west of us and full daylight would arrive in minutes.

The binoculars revealed that the war party had found our trail leading across the valley and was preparing to follow. It was about a quarter-mile from the campsite to the base of the cliff and there was now sufficient light to detect details.

Suddenly, there were yells as the attackers spotted our group at the base of the cliff.

Immediately, Blossom sent the teens up the cut in the cliff.

The attackers responded as I had hoped. Thinking that their quarry was about to get away, they broke into a run. A half dozen defenders throwing rocks down the steep cut in the cliff could hold them off for hours.

The conquistadors, with their metal armor, heavy helmets bouncing on their heads and large cumbersome hand cannons, wouldn't even attempt to keep up with the fleet warriors.

Lobo was in position to watch with only the top of his head visible among the rocks and the rest of us stayed hidden.

Suddenly, he took a step down the hill and further out of sight and held up one finger. Sunflower and Little Badger moved into a crouch behind the rocks with their bows ready and arrows nocked.

"Now!" Lobo whispered loud enough for them to hear.

Both rose together with their bows aimed at the spot where the warrior should be, locked on and let fly. Both arrows struck the warrior in the upper torso and he threw up his hands and fell.

Since they were both still hidden from those coming down the trail, Lobo held up one finger again and motioned to strike.

The warrior in the second position had seen the first runner fall, but probably thought he had tripped over something so his focus was on the man sprawled ahead of him on the trail. He didn't even see Sunflower and Little Badger as two arrows struck through him also.

The five warriors who were following sensed that something was wrong, when two of their group had stumbled and hadn't gotten up. When they slowed their pace out of caution, they also bunched up.

Lobo held up his right hand, open with all fingers spread out, which indicated five warriors, and waited.

They were still coming, but had slowed down to a walk.

Lobo got his bow ready with arrow nocked, and waited patiently. Just before they reached the spot where they would have seen Sunflower and Little Badger, Lobo moved his hand in a small circle beside his shoulder and motion forward. Sunflower and Little Badger needed only to step forward and they would see the trail and the group of warriors who were bunched together. Lobo, Azalia and Impala simply popped up with bows drawn. Four arrows found their mark immediately. Lobo had deliberately not released his arrow because the warriors, who were bunched together, shielded the ones behind.

Two arrows struck one, one arrow was dead center on another and one warrior was struck a little low and to the side. The two who were mortally wounded fell and the one wounded staggered back. That left the other two exposed. They had been shielded by the front three, and Lobo dropped one immediately. Before Lobo could nock his second arrow, the others had released their second arrow. Two arrows struck the last warrior who had remained untouched and two more struck the one who was wounded.

Since Lobo was busy directing his part of the battle, I kept an eye on the conquistadors. They paused and brought their weapons into position to fire. The firing process was cumbersome since they had to hold the heavy hand cannon while applying a glowing piece of rope to the hole in the top of the barrel.

"Everyone down!" I shouted and all five went flat and made sure they were behind a rock.

There was a thunderous, sputtering roar as the four hand cannons fired independently.

There was a splattering of pellets against the rocks and I surmised that they were using multiple pellets like buckshot.

The harquebus was the hand cannon of the conquistadors and was used by other armies in Europe in the fifteenth century. It was a smooth bore, hand-held weapon that was heavy and not very accurate beyond sixty or seventy yards. With no rifling in the barrel, a single ball would quickly veer off in one direction or another. That is why they often used multiple small pellets. This shot didn't go as far and did less damage but the chances of hitting something were increased.

(The harquebus was the forerunner of the blunderbuss which came a hundred years or so later.)

An early harquebus did not have a stock to rest against the shoulder so that one could sight down the barrel. Instead, there was a long continuation of the barrel that went back under the arm and behind the shooter. This extension was often sharpened on the end like a backwards bayonet.

Since it took an experienced shooter about a minute and a half to reload, the barrel, used as a club or the back end serving as a bayonet or spear, was often used more in battle than the firing of the weapon itself. A charging army didn't take a minute and a half to go a hundred yards.

Part of the difficulty was that the firing was done with a special rope that, once lit, only kept its glow for a short while. If you remembered to blow on it once in a while to keep it glowing or it wasn't raining, it might be ready to fire when needed.

It was also difficult to keep it pointed in the right direction while trying to get the hot coal on the end of the rope into the little hole at the back of the barrel.

The big advantage was that when fifteen or twenty went off almost as one, the tremendous roar and the rolling cloud of blue gray smoke struck terror into the hearts of people who had never seen such a thing.

In this case the four weapons didn't produce as much roar or roll enough smoke to frighten my little group, because they had already heard the 30.06 and the rapid fire of the SKS.

My interest was whether they had seen their warriors fall and would decide to retreat or keep coming. My guess was that they were arrogant enough and confident enough in the protection of their armor, the superiority of their weapons and the fact that bows and arrows didn't go very far and definitely wouldn't pierce their armor, that they would come anyway.

That was the main reason I hadn't fired my weapons. They didn't know I was there and they had never seen or heard of weapons like I had.

They were still two hundred yards away. Their first volley was designed to flush out the rabbits and they would hunt them down after they slaughtered the ones on the cliff.

We all waited patiently while they reloaded. Sunflower went down behind the hill a little and came up to where I was.

"Remember warriors who had Deh Neh Totsi? One say 'he not fix weapon, we take him now.' He think you must do what they do now?" She asked.

"Yes," I said. "They had seen the weapons of the conquistadors, and thought I would have to do many things to make my weapons strike again.

Lobo broke in, "what do you want us to do now?"

"We wait!" I said, "as they get closer, you may show yourselves and watch them. If they prepared to strike with their weapons, get behind the rocks.

"We want them to come close. If I have to take long, careful aim, it might give them time for one to get away. They think they can walk right up here and shoot us all and we can't do anything about it," I explained.

"Go ahead and show yourselves. They will think you are getting ready to run. If they look like they are going to strike with their weapons, get down immediately," I warned.

"You want we should strike with arrows?" Lobo asked.

"No, their shining armor protects them. That is why they are not afraid of your arrows. If they come close enough that you could strike them in the face you might take them down," I answered.

Only about half of my head was sticking out above the rock so they had no idea what I was. Not that they would have cared. I might be a child hiding there. It wouldn't matter to them.

At about fifty yards, they began to separate; two to one side and two to the other, to come around the mound where we were located.

I got up on one knee and leaned against the side of the rock. The SKS was just like a little stick if they were noticing it at all. Taking out the two on the right would be the best choice, as they would soon be out of sight on that side of the mound. The two coming around my side had nowhere to go.

The first shot would be easy; after that there would probably be moving targets.

Lining the sites on the target farthest to the right, I carefully squeezed the trigger. He jerked backwards, dropped his weapon and crumbled. He had not completely fallen, when my second shot hit his partner. He too jerked backward and fell immediately.

Perhaps the crack of my rifle was so different from the sound of the harquebus that they were used to; or perhaps, it was that the second sound came from somewhere that they couldn't locate. And, there was no thunderous roar, there was no huge cloud of smoke, so the two remaining simply stood there staring.

Since I needed to fire quickly, I used the double tap method with two shots a half second apart on each of the other two conquistadors.

The field was clear and our ambush had worked perfectly. Our little group stood, raised their bows above their heads and let out a loud, "aaii-eee."

Blossom and Violet responded immediately with an "aaii-eee" of their own. The rest of the group were still in a state of shock and awe. Five teens had stood firmly and calmly as seven large, full-grown, experienced warriors had attacked in full force. Four heavily armed conquistadors with weapons that had killed many and put their entire tribe to flight; who had armor that no weapon could pierce, had fallen like pine cones from the top of a pine tree as if a squirrel had casually bitten it off.

We climbed up to the base of the cliff where everyone was waiting.

Sunflower beckoned to the teens, who had climbed up the steep chute to distract the oncoming warriors, to come down.

The view from where they were waiting was only about a hundred yards across the stream and up the hill from where we had prepared our ambush so that it was like a seat in a big arena watching a re-enactment of a battle.

They all crowded around to congratulate and comment on what they had seen. As the hubbub subsided, Cedo Bah Gay stepped forward, his eyes still wide with amazement.

"This is more than I have ever seen in my life," he began breathlessly. "You did not direct the battle! Lobo pointed and waved and it was done. They all acted as one! The girls stood and were as brave as any warrior. They took down the enemy with more accuracy than any I have seen."

Azalia was having a little trouble translating, as his words came in a rush with even some stammering, but all had seen it with their own eyes.

Lobo was a little embarrassed with the high praise, as were Sunflower and Azalia.

He slowed down a little, but still with awe in his voice, "you say 'listen to Blossom' and I think 'what does little girl know?' But she give orders like old warrior, then…" And he paused with even more amazement, "she direct teens up the cliff, then she say 'stay here' and she walk down to stand between us and the warriors who come to kill us!"

It was Blossom's turn to be embarrassed. She came over and tucked herself between me and my arm. I grinned at her and whispered, "we won't tell him about your secret weapon."

"Blossom is the one who sensed the presence of danger and came to wake me up at night to plan and get us all to safety. You have seen the heavy packs that Impala and Little Badger went to get for you. You saw the care of Sunflower for the baby and your son. Lobo is a great hunter and leader as you have seen. You have seen Azalia prepare food for many and learn many words so she can translate for me. Violet is a faithful and true friend to us.

"We have all stood together as warriors against great danger and strong enemies and we have traveled and explored together.

"But more than all of these, we are family and friends. I would trust my life with any of them," I said as I looked at them proudly and fondly.

All in our group murmured assent and nodded seriously.

It was obvious, as their group glanced around, that they were traveling companions, thrown together and functioning together out of basic necessity and not much more.

As my eyes glanced over their group, I noticed Lark Soh Kim standing a little off to the side and not connected to anyone. The "too small" deerskin and the flannel shirt that we had given her was wrapped around her against the morning chill. It struck me that this was the sum total of her possessions in the world.

She was gripping the fingers of her left hand with her right hand in an expression of anxiety and indecision. I pause to look at her and our eyes met, so I smiled. She immediately, came forward and stood before me, obviously conflicted about something.

In a trembling, almost desperate voice, she asked tentatively, "you teach me be warrior like them?"

Azalia was there to translate and I said, "most of the things you need to know, I can't teach you."

The crushing disappointment that washed over her face was heart wrenching so I continued, "the things that make a great warrior are not just fighting skills. Things like a good heart, courage, taking responsibility, helpfulness, doing hard work with a cheerful attitude. These are all skills that come from your heart. These things will show on many occasions and in many circumstances so we will see it day after day and know if it is real. Trust and acceptance must be earned."

She looked a little less wounded and I glanced around my group searching for a little help.

Blossom jumped in immediately, "she have good heart, Chee."

Somewhat to my surprise, Sunflower, usually the cautious one, spoke up, "I see much of what you say is in her." She said seriously, and Azalia nodded in affirmation. They had had the most contact with her on a work level.

I glanced at the boys, not sure if they would venture into this territory or not. Again, to my surprise, it was Lobo who spoke thoughtfully, "she have hard life but keep going. She have little but have 'thank you' in her heart for food and shirt."

He grinned at her, and said, "maybe we have room for new little sister."

He said it in both languages so Azalia didn't need to translate.

I turned back to her and said, "I guess we will see how it works out." And I held out my hand for a handshake.

Too overcome for words, she brushed my hand aside and stepped close for a hug. Blossom joined in, then Violet and then one after another they all gave her a hug, even the boys.

Turning to face everyone, I said, "let's go back to our campsite. They didn't have time to do too much damage. We also need to bury those who have died. And one important thing. Do not go near the conquistadors. They carry disease and sickness that could kill you all. Do not touch any of their things unless it has been cleansed by me," I warned severely.

"Let's plan our day before we go back to the campsite to eat," I suggested.

"Would two of you go back to our village for a pick and the two shovels? We need to dig a big grave."

"Any food you find in my lean-to you may eat, except all the energy bars. You may have one there and one to eat on the way back." I said and grinned at them, "bring as much of the canned food as you can but not a heavy pack this time."

Impala and Little Badger headed up the chute and the rest of us headed over to the campsite, making a wide circle around the bodies lying along the trail.

For the moment we had lots of meat and a good variety of other food.

The site was relatively undisturbed. The shirt I had hung up to make them think someone was standing in the semi darkness, had a lot of holes in it and the sleeping bags where the three girls had been sleeping had some holes, but when the attackers realized we were gone, they didn't destroy anything. They were planning to go back and take it all after they had dispatched us.

After a good meal and a general cleanup, I advised, "let's take an hour and get back some of the sleep we lost and let the food settle. We have much work to do today."

After the early rising, general activity and excitement of the morning, everyone was looking tired. They, of course were only a step or two away from starving. I on the other hand, just felt like a nap.

It was still before noon and the boys wouldn't be back for a couple of hours, so we could kill some time. The sun was warm and there was hardly any breeze, so it was a good time to nap.

The hour went by all too quickly, but there was much to be done.

"Girls," I began. "Take all the women and girls who can go, and search up the valley for plants and roots that Grandmother taught you."

"Lobo," I said turning towards him, "you and I will make up some fishing poles and take the men and boys downstream. I assume this stream should have fish."

"It look good," Lobo responded.

Since we all carried fishing gear in our packs, we easily had enough to put together three poles.

We went to a flat spot with no bushes or tall grass and practiced swinging the sinker out to a designated spot.

We then put a hook on the line, and I took Cedo Bah Gay out to the stream.

It is exciting to watch someone fish for the first time. The anticipation, the tug on the line, the jerk to set the hook, the flopping fish coming out of the water, then, the sheer joy of success. He was as excited as a kid at Christmas. I thought I might have to pry the pole out of his hand to let someone else learn.

By this time, Lobo's group was done practicing so we put hooks on the end of the line about two feet past the sinker.

Approaching the pools from an angle that would not frighten the fish, everyone caught a fish on his first try. We pointed out the most likely places where fish might be lurking, reminding them that only two or three fish could usually be caught in one pool before the others grew wary and wouldn't bite.

We showed them how to clean a fish, although they knew the principles of field dressing animals. We made homemade stringers from a willow shoot and warned them not to take more than they could eat unless they were drying them for later use.

"Remember, you have a whole deer hanging there that you need to eat," I reminded them. "Let's take no more than two fish for each person today. The girls will show you how to cook them."

Lobo was not as skilled as the girls at translation but he knew enough of both languages to help us communicate.

Cedo Bah Gay said wistfully, "how we get such sticks, what you call line and hooks? If we have this we not starve."

"We will give you these and some extra hooks, line and sinkers, I said. "They will get lost over time but maybe you will find a way to make hooks from bone."

The women and girls got back about the same time with roots that cook up like an odd shaped, skinny potato and some wild onions and other plants.

The boys were excited to show their fish. The biggest fish was caught by the smallest boy and he was almost bursting with pride while soaking up the congratulations.

The campsite became a hive of activity, with cleaning, chopping, cooking with new utensils and metal pots and pans. The chatter, laughter and, camaraderie were things that had been missing for them over the last several months.

Lark Soh Kim came over with Azalia to interpret and explain, as she gestured towards the activity going on all around the campsite. "All this food, right here, and we starve. I must learn all this. This more important than be warrior!"

"It all goes together," I replied. "You will learn it all. You will be a good student."

She beamed as Azalia told her what I had said.

Impala and Little Badger were back before lunch was ready, so the boys and I went out to find a gravesite that looked like easy digging and was away from the activities of the group.

"We will all dig this afternoon. I'd like to get this chore over before evening," I said grimly.

With all the men and boys helping, we got an adequate grave dug in a few hours. As quickly as one got tired another jumped in to keep the dirt flying. Even Lark Soh Kim came out to take a turn shoveling. With Azalia to translate, she affirmed, "I must learn how to do this."

Her efforts evidenced more grit and determination than skill but she did it. My estimation of her continued to grow.

Dragging the bodies to the gravesite, took some time as I insisted that I was the only one who would touch a conquistador. Their armor would be great as an object lesson for everyone to see what they were up against.

I confiscated the harquebus from each one along with the firing rope, black powder and shot. I also took their swords that would make better machetes than weapons against bows and arrows or spears. Any kind of weapon would help these people feel a little safer.

I stacked the harquebuses and equipment and prepared to leave. Little Badger would oversee the filling of the grave.

"Where you go, Chee?" Lobo asked.

"I think I should go back and report," I said. "We need more food and supplies but my main reason for going is to wash off all my clothes and everything else to protect everyone from the disease and sickness that clings to the conquistadors. Do not touch anything that was theirs until I get back and clean it."

"Explain this to the others. I cannot even hug them goodbye after touching the soldiers and I don't want a long explanation or a scene," I explained.

He smiled at the remembrance of some of the previous scenes. "You leave hard work for me."

I pulled on my pack, which was mostly empty, and headed for the chute up the cliff.

Blossom and Violet saw me heading for the cliffs and cried, "Chee!" And ran out to follow.

Lobo intercepted them and explained why I was going.

Again, they called out and I turned and waved. They waved back but made no attempt to follow. It was encouraging that they obeyed an order delivered through Lobo.

I stayed high on the mountain, went around far above the village and came to the portal.

Dorothy didn't need to touch any clothing or anything connected to the conquistadors either, although she was probably inoculated against anything they might have had. She selected a complete set of clothes and tossed them down the stairs while I washed all of the things I was wearing and took a long hot shower. She also went to the garden store and got a dozen spray cans of the strongest disinfectant that she could find.

It took a while for me to finally feel clean. Dressed in a set of dirty work clothes, I set about spraying and wiping down every piece of equipment I had touched until I felt that it was clean also. Then I took another shower and put on clean, casual wear that was light and comfortable.

Now it was time to meet with my advisors. How were we to deal with more people, more problems and then the conquistadors?

Chapter 9

Back home a good meal with Dorothy and the "advisory council" at one of our favorite Mexican restaurants helped bring me back to the present. Along with the good banter, sharing of news about people and things, my mind had been cleared for some objective problem solving. "We've got dessert back at our house. The things I need your help with would probably best be discussed in a less public place," I said.

As I related all the activities and problems back in the tribal lands, a somber atmosphere overtook our gathering. The story of the escape and despair of Lark Soh Kim, coming to the point of starving, without possessions or even adequate clothing, brought tears to the eyes of some.

A small remnant of a tribe, starving, without hope and some sick to the point of death, was like piling on.

The fact that the Whiteface had hunted down and killed or unmercifully beaten the runaways was a timeless reminder of the depravity that can beset humanity.

The arrival of the searchers that included conquistadors, highlighted the danger. "These people were shooting before they even knew who was in a sleeping bag. They were primed to kill and destroy." I related.

None of us could have foreseen the tragic circumstances that would embroil us when the portal made its first appearance in the back yard.

And yet the growth in abilities and willingness to learn of my little group and even the whole tribe, was bringing hope and joy. Lobo was emerging as a true leader. Impala and Little Badger were showing themselves to be competent and energetic. The girls were knowledgeable, instinctively helpful, quick thinking, courageous and very adept.

Clearly, the new problem is, we now have a small, struggling tribe to rescue from despair and danger. Both tribes need provision, help and guidance for a little while longer if they are to survive.

The conquistadors were coming into the valley. And even if all the tribes banded together and outnumbered them ten to one, it is doubtful that they could defeat the conquistadors with their armor and hand cannons.

"So how do you think we should proceed?" I concluded.

"Well, number one where do you think this all ends?" Sharon asked.

"Yes, why is this your problem?" Heather added.

Without waiting for an answer, Ben chimed in, "you can't feed and protect everybody. In fact, if the conquistadors are destroying tribes to the south and they are fleeing north, this exodus of refugees may never end."

"What do you think you should do?" Cam asked.

"Well, as you point out, the problems aren't going away," I answered. "But here is where my struggle centers. The portal is still open. It stayed open when we backed off and looked at the situation as potentially finished. Blossom is healed and received back into the tribe. They almost made it through the winter so if those two things were the purpose, then we expected the portal to close.

"Who are we to say what the portal should do?" Heather remarked.

"If it's open, aren't we exactly where we were at the start?" Cam questioned.

"If the portal remains open, maybe we should conclude that its purpose has not been fulfilled, or could it be that *our* purpose hasn't been fulfilled?" Heather mused.

Ben interjected, "My question is, if there is no remaining purpose, then why was this coincidental, serendipitous, good fortune of having all this gold fall into our hands that enables us to get supplies and equipment? We still have so much."

I responded, "as the proverb says 'don't withhold your hand from doing good if it is in the power of your hand to do it,' We have the means to accomplish something good even if we can't foresee exactly what that might look like."

"So, what do you think we should do?" Sharon asked.

"I believe these people were thrust into our sphere of influence for a reason. I don't think our response should be any different than what we do every week. Those who have a need and come across our path, we help. We don't go out looking for the homeless and addicts, but when we see an immediate need, we help.

"I'm not looking for all the hungry people but I think we should help feed those we come upon, or that come to us.

"I'm not going to go out to destroy conquistadors or enemy tribes, but if they come after us, we should fight and defend those under our care."

"What about creating dependency?" Dorothy asked.

"I look at their situation like we look at an accident victim," I responded. "We provide care, shelter, food and whatever it takes to get them well. Don't get them hooked on drugs, but give them something to ease pain until they get well."

"In the same way, we should teach them to hunt, fish and gather fruits, nuts and plants. Until they reach self-sufficiency, we supplement their food resources."

"If they face an enemy, we give them help and/or we give them the means to fight and defend themselves."

"That's where I am right now in my thinking," I concluded.

Cam responded, "the portal is open; the need and opportunity exists; we have the resources to support your efforts; so, I propose that we continue on with our involvement. Whatever it takes. Whatever they need, whatever you need. Then we evaluate again. Keep us informed."

"You need to be careful," Sharon added. "These violent encounters seem to happen pretty often."

"Trust me," I said sincerely. "I don't seek trouble but it's a primitive, hard existence in that time and place. I will be careful."

The rest of the evening sped by as we switched to lighter banter with plenty of wit and humor. After these exchanges on more pleasant subjects, we said our goodbyes and they departed.

The next few days were spent in finding supplies: beans and flour along with the other incidental items for bread making and some flavoring for meat and beans.

We also found some cans of soup that are reconstituted by adding water, doubling or tripling the amount from the can.

We found cases of canned fruit for special occasions and searched for high calorie, fatty foods which are opposite of the modern diet.

Most of this would be stored at my stash and some put in my lean-to.

It took most of another day to get all the supplies through the portal and safely stashed with my other stuff.

Another night on a memory foam mattress in a warm house, sounded really good, so Dorothy and I went out for supper.

The next morning, I headed through the portal early, loaded down with about twenty pounds each of beans and flour for Mor Dak Sah to distribute, and proceeded to the village.

All of my crew had returned and were busy with their tasks. Little Badger was getting the next week's dried food from the cave.

"There only enough for one more week after this," he said seriously.

Lobo and Impala were out hunting for the next few week's meat supply.

The girls were sorting and arranging food and supplies in my lean-to and around their hut and fire pit.

Lark Soh Kim was helping but was somewhat at a loss about where she fit in, or what she should do. I was glad to see her with a coat, even though it was too big but it was warmer than my shirt and more functional than a blanket.

"Blossom, Violet, are there shoes and clothes in my lean-to?" I asked.

"Yes," Blossom replied. "We give coat to Lark Soh Kim but not know if okay to give other things."

"Will you and Violet go through the clothing and see if you can find a T-shirt, pants, socks and shoes. She should have an outfit like each of you have. If you can't find the right size, we will check the stash or I'll go and buy something," I instructed.

"Think of it as 'shopping'," I said with a grin.

"We get Azalia help," Blossom grinned back.

Noh Tay Dah and his family were working around their hut and fire site. They waved as I approached. The children rushed to me for their hug and I got down on one knee to receive them.

They chattered away about something but I didn't understand any of it. Sunflower was looking our way and I motioned for her to join us to translate.

Turning to Noh Tay Dah I asked, "is your head better?"

"Yes!" He replied and Deh Neh Totsi nodded also.

"Are you walking every day?" I continued.

He nodded again as Deh Neh Totsi answered, "we walk every day. Now he carry wood for fire. He fix hut with bark. Keep out rain. Make warm." She said proudly.

Turning to Sunflower, I asked. "Did you talk about the people we found?"

"No," she answered me directly. "Not have time. Not know what you want to say."

"Very good," I said. "We will need to plan a time to tell them their story and see what they think. Tell them we want to talk to them about our journey when there is time."

Deh Neh Totsi looked questioningly at us, but nodded and said, "we want to hear."

With the tasks that lay ahead of us, it was almost like starting over but that's what springtime is all about anyway.

The snow was melting off of the hillsides and was mostly confined to areas protected from the sun. The gullies were still filled, but access to the river valley was now available.

Sunflower and Azalia took most of the younger women and girls down to gather the early spring shoots and find open spots to dig roots. Several men went to keep watch for enemies and bears. Bears fresh out of hibernation were often ill tempered.

Blossom and I began designing a regimen of training for Lark Soh Kim and Violet.

Violet was a gentle spirit with a strong impulse to help and desire to learn but she was still young and had not been tempered by the harsh, rigorous life that Blossom had endured.

Lark Soh Kim was intense, driven and almost obsessed with trying to become like Sunflower and Azalia.

As we were getting the bows, practice arrows and targets out and placing them up the hill away from the village, I asked the girls, "do you always use a person's full name or is it ever okay to use a short form?"

"Could I call to Cedo Bah Gay and say 'hello Cedo' or do I need to always say his full name?"

Blossom translated my question and the girls discussed for a minute.

"When we just talk together, we use short names." Blossom asserted. "Sometimes I say 'Lan Ah' to Sunflower when we work. When you there, I say 'Sunflower'. When I tell someone in tribe, I say 'Lan Ah Kay'."

"So, it's like formal and informal?" I asked.

Blossom looked at me with head tilted forward and eyes rolled up like a schoolteacher looking over glasses and said, "no know these words!"

I laughed, "okay, ask Lark Soh Kim, should I always say her full name or can I call her Lark, or does she want a new name like all of you have?

"In my language, a lark is a bird that sings a beautiful song in the evening just as it is getting dark. It is so beautiful that when someone sings a beautiful song, we say 'she sings like a lark'."

Blossom relayed the message and Lark Soh Kim responded with a wistful, faraway look and a trembling lip

"My mother sing beautiful song when I little. Maybe someday I sing beautiful song too. I like you call me Lark!"

Blossom's translation was also in a softer, more serious tone. She had wondered for years if there would ever be a song in her heart too!

"Okay! Lark it is," I said cheerfully. "Violet has had some lessons with the bow, so Blossom, show Lark the safety protocols and how to shoot."

She looked at me with a slight frown then figured out what 'protocol' must mean and proceeded.

Blossom's demonstration shot was very close to the bull's-eye and while she tried to appear nonchalant, I could see that she was pleased with her effort. They were eager students and she was a good teacher and soon they were putting most of their arrows into the target.

I pulled out a slightly stronger bow for Lark and moved the target back another ten feet. She adjusted quickly, but Violet wasn't as skilled as she was younger and smaller.

After about a half hour, we stopped to rest.

"Let's take a break and practice English. When we are on a journey or in a battle all of my instructions are in English," I said.

As Blossom translated, we began where we had started with the others a year ago, except now, with Blossom to translate, we didn't have to rely on signs and gestures alone.

I also wanted to make good use of our time and give Violet the opportunity to shine. Not only did she have a head start on vocabulary and word usage but this was in her wheelhouse.

Lark was a warrior spirit, intense and more physically skilled. Violet was a scholar spirit, thoughtful, introspective and social.

After another session of practice with the bows and arrows, we headed back to the lean-to to put them away.

While Blossom was still with us to translate, I asked Lark, "are your coverings comfortable and do the foot coverings fit?"

"They feel strange," she replied. "But they are warm and fit good. I like!"

I noticed, as we went our ways, that Lark went immediately to get firewood for the evening meal, Violet began setting things out at the fire pit and Blossom put the bows and arrows away in my lean-to and instinctively straightened my sleeping bag and smoothed out the blanket.

She came over to me and sat down, leaning her head against my shoulder. Her thirst for love, attention and reassurance was almost unquenchable. We could sit for long moments and communicate all we needed to say without a word being spoken.

We finally broke the silence at the same time and with the same word, "Lark…"

We looked at each other and laughed.

"She will be a great warrior," I said.

"She have good heart, Chee," Blossom added.

"I hope she realizes that she is not in competition with all of you and that she can find happiness and acceptance by being herself. We need to be her friends as well as her teachers," I said.

Sunflower and Azalia arrived back from the plant and root search with the women and girls.

"Shoots starting to come up. Ground where sun shines is soft enough to dig. We find roots, we have enough food for two, three days. More is growing quickly," Azalia said enthusiastically.

"That sounds great," I responded. "Would you have time now to talk to Deh Neh Totsi and Noh Tay Dah about the people in the other valley?"

It turned out that all of our group wanted to share in the telling of our adventure, so we invited them for our evening meal. We began with the mystery of the missing food at the fire site that had led us to begin tracking the thief. We went on to describe finding them and discovering that they were starving and didn't know the plants of this country.

As I feared, their penchant for storytelling meant that almost every incident required comment from someone. Even Lark was eager to share her story.

It was when I spoke of our introductions to those people and mentioned Cedo Bah Gay that Deh Neh Totsi broke into our narrative.

"I know people in my tribe who name Bah Gay," she said with interest.

"I thought that they might be from one of your villages which is why I wanted you to hear their story," I said.

"Yes! Tell me more!" She exclaimed.

Of course, that meant that the next two hours were filled with 'the rest of the story' and I must admit that they were all pretty good storytellers.

"Would you like to go and meet them and see if there are ways we might help them?" I asked.

"Yes!" She said excitedly, "when can we go?"

"Well, the boys brought back a deer so we have meat. The girls got a three day's supply of plants and roots," I mused. "So tomorrow the boys and I will go to get packs full of supplies. The next day we will go back to the people in the other valley and see how they are doing."

"Get all of your gear together. Get a pack and sleeping bag for Lark. Get whatever Noh Tay Dah's family needs and we will be ready for the trip," I concluded.

"Are the children going with us?" I asked.

"No!" Deh Neh Totsi answered, and Sunflower interpreted. "They will stay with Grandmother and Chip and Sweet Pea. It will be fun for all of them and there is possible danger on this journey."

The next morning the boys and I went for food while the girls collected the gear and cooking equipment. We wouldn't need too much since we had left our first batch with the small group of refugees.

It was still morning when we got back and the girls turned their attention to filling everyone's pack with enough food for both groups for a couple days and some left over to leave with the refugees.

A little past noon I heard Blossom calling frantically, "Chee! Chee! Come quick I find wolf, she hurt, she have little ones, they going to die. We need help!"

"Hurry!" She urged as she grabbed my arm and started pulling me up the hill.

I hurried after her, trudging up the hill past the patches of snow.

"Wow! She is one big wolf," I exclaimed.

"See Chee! She hurt!" Blossom exclaimed.

"She's not hurt so much that she couldn't take your arm or leg off if she got her teeth into you," I said seriously.

"See, her back legs don't work and she have two little pups," Blossom added urgently.

The she wolf was standing on her front legs with bared teeth, slathering jowls and growling in a menacing manner. The two pups were tucked in close beside her.

"We help her Chee. She can not hunt, she die, little ones die" Blossom urged.

"That is true," I admitted. "The kindest thing to do is put her out of her misery."

"No Chee!" Blossom cried. "Pups need milk! Pups need mother! We help!"

"So, you are going to walk over and scratch her behind the ears and say 'don't worry mama, we are here to help'," I said somewhat sarcastically.

She narrowed her eyes and looked at me with a frown. "No, but we could bring food," she said adamantly.

"Blossom, you are kind and tenderhearted but that she wolf can't hunt, and even if we feed her, she is too severely wounded. She won't live very long." I said gently. "Feeding her would just prolong her pain and suffering."

"But the little ones could live. If momma wolf live, the pups get milk until they big and eat meat. We help them, Chee!" She said pleadingly.

"She is severely injured. She might not live long enough for the pups to be weaned," I explained.

"How you think she get hurt, Chee?" She asked, changing the subject.

"Well, I would guess that the big long gashes along her flank, her back leg and side, were made by a grizzly. She would not attack a grizzly without a good reason, so I'm guessing the pups came out of the den, probably for the first time given their size, about the time a grizzly was nearby. He decided they would make a small meal so he went after them. She tried to distract him by charging in and jumping back and got to close. He wheeled and took one swipe that caught her along the side and threw her into a tree or rock with such force that it broke her back.

"Perhaps the pups had retreated into the den or if there were other wolves, they might have harassed the bear into leaving, then they left and she couldn't follow. The little ones came out when they got hungry. So, she started crawling on her front legs to find water."

"She is either taking a rest or too tired and injured to go on," I concluded.

The wolf had left the defensive position and was lying with her head on her front legs but with her eyes still watching our every move.

"This ravine only has water when the snow melts but the nearest stream is two small hills over, to the stream that comes down to your village," I concluded.

"Then we bring food and water," Blossom declared.

We argued for the next ten minutes.

"If she gets strong enough to leave, she will hole up somewhere and die there," I argued.

"If we bring food to her here every day, she will stay!" Blossom asserted.

"What if she gets strong enough to move and comes down and waits behind a tree and jumps out and grabs you as you walk by?" I said.

She just looked at me, like, "if that's your best argument, this argument is over."

"What about the pups? They are wild animals who will grow to be as big as their mother. They could kill somebody if they got mad or tried to steal food at a campsite," I argued.

"I make them listen, Chee!" She declared.

"Okay here are some rules. You never come here by yourself to bring food or for any reason. You must have someone with you. If you break the rules, I will put all three of them down. Do you understand?" I said firmly. Without giving her time to answer, I continued.

"Also, after the mother dies and you are working with the pups, if they injure or attack or threaten without reason, anyone in our village, I will take them down. Do you understand and agree?" I said adamantly.

She reluctantly agreed.

"Blossom, these are wild, dangerous animals and you must prepare yourself that this may not work. I will not wait until someone is injured or killed to take them down. How would you feel if Chip or Sweet Pea were injured or killed because these wolves no longer feared people and didn't obey either?"

That made her think, but she still wanted to try so we began to plan.

We went back to the village and got several strips of meat and a few bones that hadn't been boiled yet.

Water was the greater need but we didn't have anything other than a skillet that was flat and stable enough to make a water dish. I would have to go back to get a dog dish.

We took the meat up the hill to the wolf. A half mile hike, two or three times a day, ought to get me in shape.

Again, we were met with a ferocious warning but it didn't last as long and she immediately attacked the meat that we tossed to her.

For about a half hour we stayed twenty feet away so that we would be "with" her, but well out of reach. When she had downed all the meat, which took about three gulps, she settled down and the pups came to get milk.

We left quietly. We had talked to her most of the time we were there, so she would get used to our voices.

I went back through the portal to get a bag of dog food and a wide bottom, water dish.

Getting it in front of the wolf was the first big problem. We used a twelve foot pole with a "Y" on the end and made it like a tennis racket to set the dish on and extended it to within three feet of the wolf. She was not happy with the intrusion into her space. Once it was in place, we taped the bottom half of a gallon jug to the end of our stick, poured a little water in it and got most of it poured into the water dish.

For all her fuss about intruding into her space, she immediately lapped up the water. The second try was met with some growls, but she didn't try to back away and actually moved in to start drinking before we were done pouring.

Because of the length of the pole and the awkward delivery method, we were able to give only a few cups at a time, and our third attempt hardly seemed to bother her.

The next step was to see if she liked dog food. We delivered it in front of her with the same method and poured some on the ground. She sniffed it a few times, then tasted it and quickly ate it up. She then laid back down and rested her head on her paws, watching us with what seemed to be a little less hostility.

The pups moved in to nurse and we moved to the uphill side. If she decided to attack, she would have a lot harder time getting to us.

Her eyes never left us but she seemed to accept that we were not a threat.

Chapter 10

With the final items for our packs and equipment put together the night before, we set out just after dawn the next day. We anticipated a slow hike given the size of our group and the weight we were carrying so it was about midmorning when we came to the cliffs and the steep, rocky gash where we could climb down.

The close encounter the struggling tribe had with the invaders a few days before had made them more alert and they spotted us across the valley before the first one of us made it to the bottom.

The view from the top of the cliff was beautiful. The tall brown grass was like a carpet from that height and the new shoots coming up was making the valley much greener than it was before. There were significantly more wildflowers sprinkled into the mix adding a delightful display of color as far as the eye could see in both directions.

Blossom, Violet and Lark had stopped at the top with me, and Blossom interpreted as Lark remarked, "much danger in beautiful place. You think they welcome me?"

I replied thoughtfully, "your new coverings make you look older and bigger but you are still you. They are still the same. Even if you didn't feel accepted by them, they took you in and shared their food with you. Now you have new friends and great opportunity but you are still you. Be confident, be friendly, let them know that you still respect and appreciate them, they will welcome you."

The others had slowed down and waited for the four of us at the bottom of the chute so we could all go together.

They in turn, had stopped their activities and came together to wait for us.

Cedo Bah Gay and I greeted each other warmly, then turned to the others to greet them too. They all looked healthier, more vibrant and were friendlier than before.

I beckoned Noh Tay Dah and Deh Neh Totsi forward to meet Cedo Bah Gay.

Sunflower took charge and within a few minutes of the formal introductions, Cedo Bah Gay and Deh Neh Totsi were engaged in animated and lively conversation. As soon the others heard the conversation in their own language, they crowded around.

The rest of us just stood there observing their excitement, but I noticed those in our group were all smiles and not feeling neglected.

I stepped over to Lark and stood between her and Blossom and said, "I think we will all be welcome when the excitement wears off."

It was only a few minutes for the three teens from their group to break away and approach us hesitantly. They said something to Lark and she responded. Blossom turned to interpret, but I shook my head.

"Unless you hear something that is concerning to you, let them talk together with privacy," I told her.

After their short greeting, Lark took the initiative and stepped in to give the smaller teen a hug. The other two crowded in and Lark hugged the girl then the boy and then there was a group hug.

She looked at me and raised her eyebrows and smiled. I nodded and smiled back. She had gone from barely included to hero status.

Since Sunflower was no longer needed for translation, she joined us and remarked with a smile, "they all know her family and when she was taken captive, and we may have to stand here all day if we wait for them to finish."

Since each of us had been carrying a heavy pack for the last several hours, we were happy to just stand there and rest for a while anyway.

Suddenly a very thin young boy made his way toward us. We recognized him immediately. It was Cedo's son who had been on the verge of starvation when we first met him.

Out of respect for a leader and to follow protocol, he gave me a quick perfunctory hug as I dropped to one knee to receive him. He then turned to Sunflower who also dropped to one knee for a little longer, more heartfelt hug. But I noticed that he was looking at Blossom the whole time he was hugging us.

Letting go of Sunflower and turning towards Blossom, he suddenly became hesitant and unsure. She was standing between Violet and Lark and he didn't seem inclined to hug everybody, but he was obviously in great emotional turmoil over Blossom. He took a hesitant step then stopped with indecision. The effervescent Blossom took matters into her own hands and stepped forward to give him a hug.

I was surprised that Blossom was a whole head taller and his extreme thinness made Blossom look downright robust.

His hug was more of a clinging to, and in thirty seconds he looked like he had grown two inches and had advanced three days closer to health and vitality.

He stepped back and was awkwardly embarrassed until Blossom put him at ease with some kind of verbal greeting.

The rest of our party was grinning broadly but fortunately had the good sense to keep their mouths shut.

Sunflower may have been the nurse that tended to his needs in what looked like his final hours, but it was Blossom who put the warm blanket over him and with the warmth a surge of hope. It was Blossom's face he saw as his eyes flickered open and brought him back from the very brink of the abyss.

He might die of old age and still have that vision bringing him hope each night as he drifted off to sleep.

We made the assumption that it would be permissible to use our old campsite although it was quickly observed that they had been using it for cooking at least.

It was a while before the conversation with Deh Neh Totsi began to subside.

Lark also, was chatting pleasantly with the teens. They were obviously impressed that this shy, lonely, skinny, poorly dressed, half starved urchin was now a confident, superbly dressed, and as far as they knew, Lark was now a member of our exceptional band of disciplined, competent fighters.

Her self image had taken a few steps forward. If these teens saw her as already a part of our group, maybe she could begin to see herself that way also.

Blossom was standing with me with her arm around my arm watching Lark's interaction with the teens and her newfound poise and confidence. After a few moments, Lark came over to us and Blossom translated, "they welcome me, Chee." She said almost in awe.

I smiled at her and responded, "the girls assured me that you had a good heart and you showed it to me there. They saw you suddenly as above them but you made them feel equal and accepted. They will always remember that and now I see a good heart also.

"Remember when I said there were things I couldn't teach you? You just showed me that you have right things in your heart and you will bring them out when needed."

"Thank you, Chee," she responded modestly. "I will try."

Blossom was still holding onto my arm so I turned and hooked my left arm in Lark's arm and we walked casually over to the fire pit.

The boys were putting the sleeping bags and mostly empty packs at the same places each of us had slept before. Sunflower and Azalia were sorting the items for the evening meal, breakfast in the morning and the rest of the food on a pile to leave with Cedo Bah Gay's group. Violet was organizing the fire pit, putting out pots and pans and bringing the items for the evening meal to the fire. She had also gotten the fire going.

"Sunflower! Remember when we were getting things for each fire group and you didn't count yours because there were only two of you? I'd say your fire group had grown a little," I said smiling at her.

"Yes, it has," she agreed, looking up with a smile.

I turned to Violet and said, "I'm proud of you. You are a good worker!"

Blossom had taken the job of interpreting all the English for Lark. Her face softened and she almost whispered as she responded, "Chee make everyone feel special."

Violet stood up and said cheerfully, "I like make food."

"Wonderful," I responded. "I like to eat food."

I heard laughter behind me and realize that Blossom was interpreting everything for Lark.

"What do you like?" I asked Lark.

She responded with a grin, "I like eat food!"

I smiled at Blossom and nodded approval. Her faithfulness in helping Lark fit in was improving the fluency of her English as well.

The evening meal was a happy occasion. Our girls did all the cooking except for the venison, which was done on sticks over the other fire. We did have to eat in shifts, often with only one or two items together, depending on what pans or kettles became available to cook the next batch. No one seemed to mind if the meal started with beans or vegetables or ended with fish and meat or vice versa or in any other order.

Everyone sat around talking and as they got up for other helpings, they always seemed to return to a different group so the mix was changing constantly.

I even got to hold the baby while the parents went to fill their plates. He now looked healthy and contented and it felt good to know that we had discovered this group in time to actually save lives.

Cedo Bah Gay came over with Sunflower and sat down to talk.

"We thank you and all of your group for food and other items to help us cook and catch fish," he began. "But we have no one skilled with an atlatl to hunt deer. We have no weapons or fighters to protect ourselves from war parties or men with silver suits. Do you know of a place that is safe?"

"We will have a meeting with the tribe when we return, and talk about what can be done. There are places and possibilities that we have discussed. The tribe may suggest a better place and may even find some way to help.

I do not know when I will leave here, so it must be decided by the tribe."

"You will leave," he asked.

"I do not belong here. I believe I was sent for a purpose but when that purpose is done, I will return to my place, and stay there" I explained.

"But you will come back to help if we need help? We can send someone to find you? Sunflower knows how to find you?" He said all of this with a hint of concern creeping into his voice.

"Sunflower knows that I will come if I can but the time will come when I cannot return," I said.

He looked puzzled and concerned but didn't press the issue and we prepared to retire for the night. I noticed that everyone was already in bed which was a little strange because I was almost never the last one in bed.

The valley was beautiful in the surprisingly bright moonlight. The distant cliffs were clearly visible in the silvery glow and I didn't even need a flashlight to find my sleeping bag.

As I pulled the top back to crawl in a lump towards the bottom suddenly moved. I jumped up and folded the top back further to find a snake slithering out and across the top of the bag.

"Aaiieee!" I cried out and jumped back tripping over a limb lying off to the side while the snake slithered away. Suddenly the camp was filled with a great commotion as everyone jumped out of their sleeping bags and nine faces were peering at me from ten feet away to see what was wrong.

Make that ten faces, as Cedo Bah Gay came rushing back fearing that some kind of attack was in progress.

As I found my breath and my heart rate began to come down, I noticed that no one was rushing to help or inquiring about what had caused me to cry out so loudly.

A closer look showed that only Cedo was showing genuine alarm. The others appeared to be suppressing their emotions with great effort and the emotion being suppressed was mirth.

Apparently, the snake in the bedroll was no accident. They all knew it was there and had been waiting for my reaction.

I'd been had!

Sunflower moved over to Cedo to interpret what was going on while Blossom was whispering to Lark.

"Okay, you've had your fun and somebody is going to be in big trouble," I began firmly. The grins only got a little wider except for Cedo, who only grew more concerned that a serious rift in the unity of our group was about to erupt.

Lark was still a bit apprehensive but she didn't know how any of us would react to this provocation.

"I will find out who did it and when I do, they will be in big trouble," I warned.

The grins remained, except for Cedo, who seem to think the amusement at my plight was as bad as the prank itself.

"I know the boys didn't do it because they are afraid of snakes," I stated matter-of-factly.

There was an immediate objection from the boys.

"See, if you had done it, you would have agreed so that I would no longer suspect you. The fact that you would sooner be suspected than admit you are afraid of snakes, indicates it wasn't you," I continued.

"Azalia didn't do it. I can't even picture her carrying a snake.

"Sunflower didn't do it. She is too serious.

"Violet didn't do it. She doesn't think like that.

"Blossom didn't do it. Although she would have if she had thought about it.

"That leaves Lark," I concluded.

The seriousness of my demeanor was finally wiping the grins off of their faces.

"Lark, did you put the snake in my bed?" I said severely.

She hung her head and looked around and said in a strangled voice, "yes, they say it be funny, be okay."

"Lark, come here!" I said sternly.

Several of the others responded with alarm, "Chee, we say…"

"Silence!" I commanded forcefully.

Lark was trembling and a tear started down her cheek. She thought she had destroyed all she had gained.

"Lark!" I said and reached out and took her into a big bear hug. "That was the biggest prank anyone has played on me in years."

She burst into tears and hugged me back in relief. "I sorry Chee!"

"Don't be sorry. Just be careful. I owe you one now!" I warned grinning at her.

"Chee, you scare us!" Violet said and there was a tear on her cheek but relief in her voice.

"Good," I said. "But you scared me first!"

Azalia added, "we think it funny and we glad you're not mad."

Impala said musingly, "we scare you but you turn it around and scare us."

Cedo Bah Gay had taken it all in and the relief from the high tension as well as the picture of me jumping out of my bed and screaming, overcame his emotion and he started laughing almost hysterically.

This set off our group and they began to laugh also. I took a step back from Lark, put my hands over my head and did a deep bow, "to the princess of pranks," I said sincerely.

They laughed and moved in to give us both a hug.

Cedo Bah Gay remarked to Sunflower, "your people are strange and different from any group I have seen." And he walked back to his bed shaking his head and still chuckling.

Blossom was still translating for Lark as I remarked to the group gathered around, "you know how much I love you and I know that you love me and each other. I also think that Lark is making a place in each of our hearts as well."

They all smiled and nodded in agreement.

When I went to my bed, I picked up my sleeping bag and shook it out. Just in case...!

The next morning, we said our goodbyes with a promise to search for a place that could be a safer home for this group.

Our trip home was without incident and everyone went to catch up on the things that needed done after our absence.

Blossom and I headed up the hill to check on our wolf rescue project.

We found the wolves in good condition. The extra food we had taken to them was gone, but they didn't seem particularly hungry. We would continue taking food and water several times a day for the next couple of weeks. Taking extra when we would be gone but feeding three times a day so we could sit and talk and get them used to our presence and our voices.

After a feeding, as we sat and talked on the hillside, Blossom mused, "how old are pups, Chee?"

"Good question," I answered. "They come out of the den to play at about three weeks. Assuming that is when the injury to mother wolf happened, and we have been bringing food for a couple weeks, they are about five or six weeks old."

"When can they live without mother wolf?" She continued.

"Another good question," I answered. "With us to feed them, probably in another week or two."

As though they understood that they were being talked about, the two little ones approached to within three or four feet and stared at us. We continued talking to them but made no move towards them. Apparently, they satisfied their curiosity as they turned and waddled back to their mother.

"I will get some doggy treats and we will bring some very small pieces of meat," I said. "I think it is time to interact with the pups and become the alpha male and alpha female of their pack."

"See how the pups lick at the face and mouth of the mother? They do that so she will regurgitate food for them. Not real appetizing from our perspective but the pups seem to like it," I said.

"They still drink milk," Blossom observed.

"Yes! It is a process. For a few weeks it will become less milk and more meat. At six to eight weeks their teeth will become strong enough that they can begin to learn to eat fresh meat."

I'm not sure what is in doggy treats but it's better than dog food and wolves like it too.

In the days that followed, we got some treats in hand and some very small pieces of meat, sat down and began to coax the pups to us.

Blossom was the first to touch one of the pups. The bigger one, which turned out to be a male, was bolder and more adventurous than the other. After tossing them a few treats when they came close, she held one between her fingers and waited for him to come and get it. He eyed it carefully, moving from one side to the other and then approached cautiously. Finally, he stepped in took it from her fingers and backed away a few feet.

She tried again and he took it immediately and ate it without moving away. This seemed to motivate the smaller one, who turned out to be female, and she crowded in to get her share.

Blossom was sitting cross legged on the ground and reaching out to give them the treats. The next time she didn't reach out as far and they had to come closer. As they ate the treat she reached past their heads and stroked the shoulder. They soon came to accept this without reaction. When we got up to leave, they scampered back to their mother.

Blossom was almost giddy with this success.

"See Chee, they not afraid," she said.

"Just remember, you can tame a wolf but it will always be a wild animal. Be prepared that some day, they may just take off, find a pack and not return to you," I warned.

The next few days we increased our visits and quickly they came to accept our presence and come to meet us. When we sat down, they would crowd around us and let us pet them and finally even jump into our lap to lick our face.

"We need to give them names," I suggested.

We had lots of fun with that. Everyone in our group had a bunch of suggestions until there were dozens and dozens of names. Apparently, most of them had meanings in their language.

Finally, I said, "Blossom, you need to just pick a few names and make the decision. You are the one who will work with the pups so you should decide."

After much deliberation she decided on Kih Ta for the male and Sah Sha for the female.

Now that everyone knew that we were trying to tame wolves, the pressure was on for a meet and greet.

However, the wolves weren't ready. Blossom and I weren't ready and we still had to solve the problem of a group of fifteen people needing to be absorbed into the tribe or relocated to an adequate, safer place.

"We need to make some time to discuss our problem of what to do with the new tribe," I told Sunflower and Azalia as we began to relax after supper.

"We do tonight?" Sunflower suggested.

"Let's send Blossom, Violet and Lark to round up the boys and one of you get Deh Neh Totsi and Noh Tay Dah since I don't speak the language." Then I added, "it will be good for Lark to be seen around so everyone gets used to her and knows that she is part of our group."

I made some hot chocolate while they were gathering our group together.

"We need to evaluate our options regarding the little tribe in the other valley," I began.

Nobody responded and Blossom frowned and said, "what is ob shun?"

I sighed, every time I spoke while thinking about a problem, I drifted off into vocabulary that nobody understood.

"We must think of choices about where we can put the other tribe so they will be safe and be able to take care of themselves."

"I will give a few possibilities and I want all of you to think of how it could work or why it wouldn't work," I suggested.

Trying to get the discussion started, I said, "Idea one, we bring them here to live together with the tribe."

"Tribe must vote first," Lobo stated.

"Many people to feed," Impala spoke up.

"It be nice to have more people," Azalia said wistfully.

"Lark, tell us what you think. You lived with them. Would they be a help or a problem," I asked. I thought she should be brought into the discussion and might have some insight.

Blossom had taken it upon herself to be the interpreter for Lark. Lark paused thoughtfully, "Cedo Bah Gay work hard but we still starve. Others give up, just wait to die.

"But they do need help," she added quietly, not wanting to be too negative about her friends who had taken her in. "I want to help them."

Sunflower broke in seriously, "we were discouraged and ready to die when you come, Chee. Now everyone work and help. Maybe our tribe help that tribe."

"Noh Tay Dah, you are welcome here but do you plan to stay or return to your other home," I asked.

He responded, "I want to go back but children still have fear and I cannot do all I did before."

"I understand," I said and nodded in agreement.

"Deh Neh Totsi, you know the tribe and the ways of these people. What do you think?" I asked.

"When people hungry and live in fear, they different," she said sadly.

Several murmured agreement and Lark spoke softly, "that true!"

"What about finding them a safer place where they could hunt and find plants and roots? I asked.

"There are deer where they are but they could not take one," Lobo observed.

"We show them plants that they can eat, but next moon those plants be hard and old and they must learn new ones like we did," Sunflower added. "You bring book and Grandmother remembers and shows us."

"What place more good than what they in?" Impala asked.

"But that place not safe," Little Badger chimed in. "They cannot stand against warriors and not possible to stand against conquistadors."

"Well, what do you recommend?" I asked.

"Maybe tribe let them come until they learn and then find place," Azalia said hopefully.

"Maybe we meet with tribe and tell all these things and ask what they say," Lobo asserted.

The others rallied around that idea and again I was impressed with Lobo's leadership. He listened to everyone, proposed a possible, and what would probably be, the best solution and the others seemed willing to follow his leadership.

"Remember, you must persuade the tribe and be willing to accept their decision. I will help but I never know when my time is done, so you all will be the leaders and the ones who will make the decision work. Plan who will speak and what points you want to make so everyone doesn't say the same thing. Then call the tribe together.

"Maybe some of you talk to individuals first. If Grandmother, Yul D'Vey, Mor dak sah and a few others are already on your side, you are more likely to persuade others," I advised.

"I talk to Yul D'Vey," Lobo said.

"I talk to Mor Dak Sah," Blossom declared.

Everyone turned to look at her with skepticism. Mor Dak Sah was still considered a hard liner but everyone had also observed that he seemed to be a changed man. They also remembered that Blossom was the one who recommended that he be in charge of food distribution and that had proved to be a good decision.

Lobo looked at her quizzically for a long moment, digesting the facts as he knew them and then nodded, "Blossom speak to Mor Dak Sah."

"Azalia and I will talk to Grandmother and some of the other women," Sunflower volunteered.

"Great!" I exclaimed. "Plan what you will say, tell them the good points; tell them some of the difficulties and how those could be managed and then, we will have a whole tribe meeting a few days from now."

Lobo's plan, along with my explanation, met with everyone's approval so we separated to plan our approach to certain individuals, and get everything in place for the meeting in just a few days.

Chapter 11

As soon as we had returned from our trip to Cedo Bah Gay's group, Blossom and I continued the care and feeding of the wolves and discussed what our next steps with them would be.

We decided it was time to begin a strict regimen of training. We used a verbal command, a motion and a physical positioning. We put them in a sitting position, said "sit" and then gave a treat. We then added the motion to the verbal command and in a few days at either the motion or the verbal command, they would sit.

After a few weeks we had added "stay, lie down and come" and were working on distant commands like "stop" which meant "freeze, don't move or hide" for when we would be hunting.

We talked to them regularly so they would know our voices and we used their names every time we addressed them.

It was also becoming evident that the mother wolf was failing. She had come to tolerate our presence and had stopped growling or making any threatening sounds or postures when we gave her food and water. It seemed she understood that the pups were being cared for and that we were the pack for them.

"Just remember, Blossom," I warned. "No matter how tame and docile she appears, she might be luring you into the range of her teeth like you lured the pups onto your lap."

I would bet that with her last breath she could still bite and jerk an arm hard enough to break a bone.

Every time we left and the pups attempted to follow, we would command them to "stay" and they would return to their mother and watch us go.

But they were getting to the age where it would be natural for them to go with their mother or the pack on short hunting trips, so we decided to try it the next time we visited them.

When we got up and started to go, we said "come" instead of "stay" and they seemed a little bit confused. It took only one more "come" and they bounded happily to us and jumped around our feet. It was only a quarter-mile to an area of sagebrush near the edge of the forest.

As we approached the sagebrush flat, Blossom and I separated a few yards and slowed down.

Very shortly, Blossom spotted a rabbit and raised her fist for the motion to stop. We both froze and the pups looked at us quizzically and stopped. She then pointed forward and we both moved slowly and cautiously forward.

The rabbit was still thirty yards ahead taking a few hops from one bush to another to get out of our way without being seen.

I looked over at Blossom, grinned and raised my eyebrows in a question. We didn't have a command or motion to "go" or "hunt" or "attack."

Blossom took things into her own hands and said in a loud whisper, "Kih Ta, Sah Sha, go!" And she started moving towards the bush where the rabbit was last seen. The pups trotted along with her and she quickened her pace. The pups kept up and suddenly the rabbit broke from its cover and took off.

Blossom shouted, "go," and ran after the rabbit. The pups saw the rabbit and the instinct to chase took over and they darted past her after the rabbit.

The rabbit had not reached adulthood by being slow and stupid, so outsmarting some gangly pups on their first outing wasn't a big deal and with a few zigs and zags it disappeared into a jumble of rocks leaving the pups sniffing and investigating every bush in the vicinity.

Catching up with Blossom, I joined her and we watched the pups explore the area.

"I guess point and 'go' is a good start on the hunting commands," I said laughing.

She said cheerily, "they do better next time."

"Kih Ta, Sah Sha come," she called and they trotted towards us.

As we went back into the woods returning to the mother wolf, they forged ahead and to the side, sniffing behind every tree or bush. Chasing had been great fun for them, catching and eating would soon become more necessary.

We returned to the village, where Lobo and the girls were discussing what each of them had learned from the conversations they held with the important ones in the tribe. I was invited to sit in, and found somewhat surprisingly, the responses were mostly positive.

Most of the objections centered around where they would stay and how there could be enough food to feed them. Most seemed to agree that just as they had been helped, it would be good to help others.

"Blossom, what did you say to Mor Dak Sah and what did he say to you?" I asked.

"He say it be good to help," Blossom responded. "I say Chee will help little tribe if they are here or if they be in another valley. If they in another valley Chee be there more than here. If Chee bring food, we all get more food if all are here."

I laughed, "Blossom, you made it all about food. You will have more and Mor Dak Sah will have more to give out. Benefits and job security! Very smart."

The others had to laugh. They had agonized over approaches and wording, appealing, explaining and answering questions. All that work and planning and all they needed to say was, "we all eat better!"

In spite of the simplicity and humor in Blossom's report, they all realized that there would need to be much preparation, planning and goodwill for the idea to be acceptable to the whole tribe.

If the solution of having them come to our village was unsustainable, they would have to move on, but perhaps they would have learned enough to better provide for themselves.

Lobo and our group needed to carry the load on this project. The people might agree to something if I pushed it, but would they stay on course if I were gone?

A meeting of the tribe was called for two days from today, which would give everyone time to think and discuss. There needed to be some discussion of the needs and problems that would be encountered, so we could begin to make a list of things to get.

In the meantime, life went on.

Blossom continued working with Lark on skills with the bow and arrows. Running up the hill and then shooting while still somewhat out of breath; setting the target at different distances and then turning to shoot and having only a second to judge the distance correctly. Blossom was a pretty thorough teacher and Lark was an eager and fast learner.

Violet also worked with Lark on English. She had begged to learn how to use the computer, so I showed her how to bring up a few programs. One was on vocabulary and the other on hearing and repeating conversation. This was a place where Violet could shine. She had a knack for language and loved to mess with the computer.

Lark saw these sessions as a necessary step in learning, a tool to be used, whereas with Violet it was a passion.

Lark wanted to communicate with all of us to be a part of the team. Blossom wanted to communicate and talk with me, and Violet just loved to learn.

Fortunately, Violet's passion to learn resulted in steady progress in language learning for all of them.

"Blossom, let's take Lark and Violet along to meet Kih Ta and Sah Sha. The wolves need to begin to meet the rest of the pack," I said.

Blossom ran to get the girls and they returned obviously excited to meet the wolves.

"We meet wolves?" Lark asked.

"Hey! You are speaking English. That is very good." I said slowly.

"Thank you. I try. Violet teach good," she went on.

"Very, very good!" I exclaimed, "both teacher and student."

They both beamed knowing that I could see that their work was showing progress.

Mother wolf expressed some displeasure that two strangers had come, so I told them to sit quietly about twenty feet up the hill while we gave her food and water. It was obvious that she was losing strength and the back legs were lying there and shriveling. Even though the infection of her wounds was ravishing her body, she ate and drank eagerly.

The pups pranced around our feet as we fed the mother.

When we went up to sit with Lark and Violet, the pups got shy.

Blossom and I sat on the outside with Lark and Violet between us. Kih Ta came to me for a treat and I talked to him and scratched his ears. Then I gave the treats to Lark.

We were sitting cross legged in a line and Kih Ta came around close to my knee and stuck his head around to look at Lark.

"Talk to him," I said. "He doesn't understand your words but he reads your voice."

She talked soothingly and held out a treat. It was too much to resist and he stretched forward to take it out of her hand but he backed around in front of me to eat.

It only took about a half dozen treats for him to just stand in front of her waiting for the next offering.

Violet and Sah Sha were having the same pattern play out on their side.

"If we do this a couple of times each day, they will see you as part of the pack," I advised them.

"The next day we added Sunflower and Azalia with good results, but decided to wait until after a decision had been made about the new tribe coming over before Lobo, Impala and Little Badger would have time to be included.

Tomorrow was the meeting with the tribe. Regardless of the outcome, we would be super busy for the next few weeks.

We decided that having a feast would set a more conducive mood for the meeting, so I went back up to the stash to bring back all the ingredients for a barbecue.

The boys had just come in with a deer and we got a front quarter to slice and dice to make the barbecue

"The deer return to streams where there is new grass," Impala stated.

"We see many deer. It will be good hunting now," Little Badger assured us.

Lobo and Sunflower were assigned the task of running the meeting. They would describe the situation of the new group and explain their need, then invite questions until a decision could be made.

Sunflower was nervous, "Chee, they will do like you say. You tell them what to do," she said.

"No, it must be the tribe's decision with no input from me unless they ask. If problems come up later, they will be more willing to work on things if it is their decision," I answered.

"You be the leader, I'll be the cook," I advised with a smile.

"I more like to cook," she muttered.

"You'll do a good job," I assured her. "Let everyone talk and listen to what they want to say. Then take a vote. Lobo will be there and keep order. They all respect both of you."

Feasts are always appreciated and well received and the mood was relaxed and jovial.

Bok Pon Day and May Bitah, Blossom's parents, came over to me as the cooking part was ending and beckoned to Azalia to come and interpret.

"You fix La Lin Eedah, we thank you," May Bitah said nervously.

"She is a very special girl," I said smiling. "We are all proud of her."

"We not know what to do. We put her out. She almost die. She suffer much!" May Bitah said, her voice wavering and her eyes filled with tears.

Bak Pon Day nodded, he was obviously struggling also.

"Remember these things," I said earnestly. "You did what you thought you had to do because of the decree of the tribe. You raised La Lin Eedah for a few years to be brave, determined and a fighter. When the Great Spirit makes a really special person, he often gives them hardship and danger; even loneliness and rejection. They learn to stand and endure until they become a great leader. La Lin Eedah will be a great leader."

Bok Pon Day finally found his voice, "you fix La Lin Eedah. She well, she happy, she have family. We not have curse again. Nobody! Never!" And he pounded his fist into the palm of his hand for emphasis.

"I nodded appreciatively at his determination, "she is still your child. You are still her parents. She loves each of you in her own special way."

"You help La Lin Eedah. You help all of us. It is good. These people who need a home. Maybe be good for all of us," he said.

"That is possible," I said. "It is for the tribe to decide."

Lobo and Sunflower did a great job of describing and explaining who the little tribe was and why they were stuck where they were. There were a number of questions which they handled well and then they called for a decision.

Bak Pon Day spoke immediately, "we wrong to send away La Lin Eedah and it be wrong to send away these people who need help."

There were many who followed his lead and responded affirmatively.

Mor Dak Sah chimed in, "I wrong to make La Lin Eedah a curse. She not a curse. She is wonderful person. Chee help her; Chee help us. Chee help these who need home."

After that there were only a few others who spoke up and they were all in favor. A few simply said, "we should help."

When Lobo called for a vote, it was unanimous.

I was pleasantly surprised at the outcome but it was understandable. La Lin Eedah was the illustration, all of my little group were the primary workers at this point and the few adults who might object were in favor.

It was probable that the easy assimilation of Noh Tay Dah and Deh Neh Totsi had been an influence also.

It was decided that the new people would have space just past where the girls' hut, my lean-to and Noh Tay Dah's family were located and in the beginning, they would make up their own fire groups.

The boys and I got busy building a good fire pit with protruding stones that let pots or pans set out over the fire.

The girls gathered long willow shoots that could be bent into the typical rounded top hut. They would probably make do with three huts to start unless they needed four smaller ones.

Deh Neh Totsi agreed to be the liaison between the two groups with all five of the girls agreeing that they would help get them settled.

The boys brought in a few arm loads of firewood to get them started.

I realized firewood was going to be a problem. The bow saws had made many more dead trees usable for firewood but there were dozens of dead trees that were too big for the bow saw. They needed a splitting maul instead of an ax to work them into usable firewood.

I added these to my list for my next trip. I know my advisors would look askance at the mission creep of setting up a welfare system for the whole valley.

Unfortunately, the threat of the conquistadors was an inescapable problem. It would have to be dealt with sooner or later or all the tribes for miles around would be wiped out or enslaved.

Tomorrow we would head out to bring the other group here.

In the meantime, we decided to take the boys to meet the wolves. It was somewhat amusing, as the boys seemed more apprehensive than the girls had been.

We used the same approach as we had with the girls. Blossom and I fed the mother, who was obviously failing in health, then we sat in a row and gave treats to the pups.

The pups were starting to lose the roly-poly look of their first stage, and were now bouncing around on longer legs on a bigger, more wolflike frame.

People giving treats wasn't novel anymore for the pups, so they quickly began taking the food from the boys' hands. As long as there were treats, who cared who was behind the hand.

The boys relaxed and enjoyed the encounter and the pups accepted that these additions were just another part of the pack.

Each of us had brought an empty backpack so we could go on around the hill to the stash and bring back as much food as we could carry. There were a number of food needs right now. The group we were going to get would need a meal for the journey and they would also need enough for a few days meals until they became acclimated in the new setting.

Our tribe also needed some supplemental food for a few more weeks. Mor Dak Sah was going to be happy to have a few weeks of food to organize and give out. After the boys and I returned to the village with our loaded packs, I decided to run an idea past Sunflower.

"What would you think of the idea of having some of the women prepare food at the new fire pit for the new people when they arrive?" I asked.

"That be wunnerful!" Sunflower enthused. "We ask Grandmother, May Bitah, Blue Bell. We ask Deh Neh Totsi too."

"Great!" I responded, "send someone to talk to the women and some of you set out enough food for... How many are we going to feed? Are we eating with them plus the cooks?

Doing the math, I said, "that will be more than twenty-five people."

"Lobo and boys be tired and hungry too," Sunflower added.

"Deh Neh Totsi!" Sunflower called out as she saw her coming out of her hut. "Tell us what you think."

After a brief explanation, she agreed that it was a great idea but she added, "maybe I need go, help talk to ones coming." Then she added with a grin, "Noh Tay Dah cook good as me."

Sunflower laughed and interpreted what she said.

"You are probably right, on both subjects," I laughed.

"Sunflower, why don't you and the girls get all the food and equipment out and ready so all they need to do is cook," I suggested.

"Tell the boys to lay out four tarps for temporary shelter and several blankets. I'll take Blossom, Lark and Violet to feed the wolves and then we'll be all ready for the trip tomorrow."

It was a crisp, cool morning with a promise of a sunny, warm day as we left the village.

Our packs were mostly empty since we needed food for only one meal and room to bring back all of the stuff we had left with the little tribe as well as any possessions that they had. We planned to be back well before dark.

"Let's make this a training trip for Lark!" I suggested. "Anything that is important for her and a reminder to all of us. Point out plants that are, or will be, good for food, berry bushes, signs of animals."

"There is where deer and wapiti rub skin off antlers," Little Badger pointed out.

Pointing to a nearby tree, Lobo exclaimed, "see scratches high on tree? Grizzly bear show how big he is by how high he reach. That big bear!".

Impala made the sign to "freeze" and we all stopped to see where he was pointing. There was a fox sitting on his haunches, watching us as we approached.

The girls were identifying plants, and on occasion, patches of blackberry bushes and current bushes that were now filled with blossoms.

"Each blossom make berry," Azalia explained.

Blossom, who was wandering off to the side of the little valley, found a large patch of strawberry plants that not only had lots of blossoms but a few tiny green berries.

"They start be ready before next moon," she assured us. "We come back get plenty!"

Not only were the lessons valuable but the time passed quickly and we soon found ourselves at the top of the cliff overlooking the valley and their camp.

We went down the chute three or four at a time so we wouldn't hurt anyone if we loosened a rock and sent it careening down the narrow cut in the cliff.

They saw us coming before half of us were safely down.

While waiting my turn, I gazed over the beautiful valley. It was greener than when we were here the last time, and the flowers were more profuse and varied. The breeze coming across the meadow and swirling up the cliff brought a pleasant fragrance. I was grateful for the beautiful scene.

We all made it down the chute without incident and were warmly received by the little tribe.

The baby was doing well, waving his arms and making noises at all the new people. Cedo Bah Gay's son was up and walking around. He was still extremely thin but none of them were robust.

After the greetings, we pulled the various cans and food items out of our packs to prepare the noon meal. It needed to be more than a lunch, to give them energy for the journey back to our camp.

But first we needed to propose to them the solution that the tribe had agreed to.

Again, I called on Lobo and Sunflower to explain the proposal, and give the official invitation from the tribe to join them, then more explanation of and how we thought it could work.

Cedo Bah Gay, obviously speaking for all of them was amazed that the whole tribe was willing to take them in and help them get settled.

"How can this be? They do not know us. We are strangers to them. Why do they think of us?" Cedo Bah Gay said in amazement.

The others in his tribe were equally questioning.

Sunflower began the explanation, "we starving too and close to death when Chee get us to try; he teach us what we should have known; he give us hope. All agree that they should help others who are like we were before."

Lobo chimed in, "he teach us to hunt with bow and soon we have enough food."

Azalia added, "hope make work easy and people are willing, Grandmother remember how to find plants to eat and everyone gather food."

Sunflower summed it up, "as Chee helped us when we had need, the whole tribe want to help you. Even now everyone is making ready for you to come. Will you join us?"

Cedo Bah Gay looked around. Suddenly, there was a look of hope, of direction, of purpose on each face. Even though they had been brought back from the brink of starvation, they were still defenseless and exposed to danger. This was not only an offer of shared food but an element of safety and companionship, of stability and a future.

"As I say to Chee, some days ago," Cedo Bah Gay stood and said before all of them, "you will have no better friend. I think we all say that to all of you now!"

His little tribe murmured assent but didn't know how to respond to the generosity and opportunity.

The father of the baby stepped forward and extended his hand to Lobo. They grasped forearms and leaned in for a shoulder bump. This broke the ice and the others stepped forward and included Impala and Little Badger in the heartfelt expressions of gratitude.

The women almost rushed Sunflower and Azalia to give hugs and what I assumed were expressions of thanks. They quickly engulfed Blossom and Violet also.

I had deliberately stayed in the background. This was a tribe to tribe decision. Lark came back to join me. She wasn't really in either tribe and didn't know exactly where she fit in.

After a few minutes, Sunflower raised her hand calling for their attention.

"Lark spoke to us for all of you. As she has become loved and accepted by all of us, we think we will love and accept all of you."

Lark almost gasped at the unexpected high praise. I reached around and gave her a quick side hug, and said with a grin, "see, your good heart is showing to everyone."

Their whole tribe turned to look at her with new eyes. The little, almost unnoticed, hanger-on was suddenly a person of stature.

Cedo Bah Gay came over and said simply, "we all thank you."

She responded with a mature appropriateness, "you take me in, save my life, I thank you."

Now that the invitation had been accepted, we prepared for lunch and departure.

The animated conversation, easy smiles and laughter was notable evidence of their new outlook on life. There was an eager anticipation of better days ahead.

The journey to the village was slow. Not only were they still struggling with the weakness of starvation, but the baby and Cedo Bah Gay's son slowed our progress even more.

Fortunately, after the arduous climb up the chute to the top of the cliff, the trail was downhill most of the way.

It took all of four hours to get to the village but the reception was overwhelming. Every person in the tribe came out to greet them, choosing someone to help by carrying their pack or whatever else they were carrying and walking with them through the village to their fire pit.

Yul D'Vey was carrying little Bob so Bluebell could carry the baby for the young couple. Of course, this was the perfect time to make introductions on a family to family level.

I was especially impressed that Mor Dak Sah and his wife connected with Cedo Bah Gay and his family.

The introductory conversations slowed the procession to a crawl so my group surged ahead to drop our packs and see if we could help with preparations.

The tribe had built a second fire pit to cook all the food. This would also be needed later to smoke and dry meat and fish. Some had brought in even more firewood so there was a huge pile near the site.

The tarps were arranged as tents, using limbs from the huge trees and would serve as immediate, temporary shelter while the new people worked on building their huts. The temporary tents were bigger, warmer and drier than what they had been living in for the past couple of months.

They dropped their packs in an area up the hill from the fire pits and tents. They would decide later who would be staying in which tent.

Noh Tah Day and the women, who were cooking for the new group, had outdone themselves in preparation. There was more food today than would be available for the next week, if I didn't get a crew to go up the hill and pack some more down.

I was especially impressed with the next part of their preparation. Some women from each fire group went back to their own fire and brought a kettle of stew, already hot and ready, along with everyone's cup in order to eat this meal, with the new people, all together as one tribe.

It was a great start on a new beginning.

Chapter 12

The shared meal as one tribe was a joyous occasion with lots of laughter as the vocabularies of common words were limited. Deh Neh Totsi was hailed from all sides as the universal translator. Lark was helpful also as she had picked up some of their language during the short time she had lived with them.

I simply went off to the side, observing with great appreciation the efforts everyone was making to be good hosts and guests and develop relationships. I didn't understand anybody and there were at least four languages being spoken not counting English.

Violet noticed, came over to take my hand and stand beside me, observing the scene before us.

"They all happy, Chee, "she said quietly. "It feel good to feel safe and welcome. It feel good to help."

"Do you understand any of what they say?" I asked with a grin.

"I like learn words. I learn many from Deh Neh Totsi. I understand many things they say. I will learn more," she said confidently.

"Yes, you will!" I said warmly, "you are learning English faster than anyone and soon you will pass everyone in that ability. I am proud of you."

She beamed, squeezed my hand and laid her head for a moment against my arm before joining the younger teens who were attempting to communicate.

It wasn't long before the meal was over and each fire group drifted back towards their huts.

Grandmother, Bluebell and May Bitah were cleaning, organizing and setting aside things they had borrowed to make the meal.

Deh Neh Totsi was pointing out the tents and supplies when one of the men pointed to the flat spot that was partially visible through the trees to where the garden had been.

"You grow food?" He asked her eagerly.

"Yes, Chee brought seeds to see what would grow." She responded and beckoned to Sunflower to come over and explain.

"We grow corn, beans, carrots, squash and other things," Sunflower explained.

"We know beans and squash but not other words. What are they like?" He mused.

"Wait, we have pictures," and she started for her hut to get a seed packet.

"What is picture?" He called after her.

She returned with the seed packets and he exclaimed with excitement, "that is maize! We grow maize, beans, squash too!"

Sunflower beckoned to me to come exclaiming, "they know how to make garden."

"Wonderful! Ask them if it is something they like to do and want to do," I told her.

Sunflower interpreted, "it is what we do for winter. It hard work, but you have water near and much ground that look good. Can you get seeds? Can we look for more space?" He asked eagerly.

"There aren't many flat places around here to make a garden," I replied.

He called to Cedo Bah Gay and the father of the baby and related what he had found.

We all walked down to the garden site and they began to look around. A short way down the valley, where the valleys came together and where the fire that the Whiteface boys had started was finally put out, there was a more gentle slope on the side of the valley. It had been covered in grass and bushes but the fire had burned most of the area before it was extinguished.

They walked down to the area pointing and exclaiming and finally, with both Deh Neh Totsi and Sunflower interpreting for me, they thought that corn, beans and squash would grow here.

They would have to carry water every few days but it was good land.

Pointing to the seed packets and with both Sunflower and Deh Neh Totsi coming up with the words one or the other might know, we talked about root crops and faster growing things like lettuce. I was also thinking of the possibility that potatoes and other things might grow in the original garden space.

With growing excitement, we went to get Yul D'Vey, Mor Dak Sah, Bok Pon Day and a few others to discuss the possibilities. Our puny little garden had been deemed a success. Would they like to have a very big garden that these people knew how to make?

Would those who gathered and hunted share with the ones who grew the garden, who would then share in the fall and winter?

Having tasted the produce last fall and throughout much of the winter the village leaders thought it would be good. With the new group getting settled and a few plans in place, Blossom and I went up to feed the wolves.

The mother wolf seemed weaker and the pups were growing every day. They ate and drank ravenously, as would be expected of wolves.

Since there were still a few hours of daylight left, we decided to take the pups hunting again. They were eager to go and ranged out away from us, back-and-forth from one side to the other.

As we approached the sagebrush area, we slowed down and spread out.

Kih Ta saw movement first and looked back and forth to Blossom and me, emitting a short sound that was somewhere between a growl and a question. We immediately made the sign to freeze and we all stopped. Blossom motion to go slowly. Both wolves move forward with slow crouching steps and then Blossom made a motion to go or attack.

They bounded forward. Kih Ta headed straight for the spot where he had seen movement and Sah Sha kept pace a few yards to his side.

Suddenly, the rabbit bolted with the wolves in hot pursuit. Instinctively, they attacked from each side so that every time the rabbit zigged or zagged it was turning into the path of one wolf or the other.

Too late, it realized it should have run in a straight line to safety, as the wolves converged on it from each side. It couldn't escape the sharp teeth and strong jaws and the hunt came to a successful end.

Blossom and I stopped about ten steps short to see what they would do with the rabbit. Was it just a game or did they know it was food? Sah Sha picked up the rabbit and brought it to Blossom and laid it at her feet.

We field dressed the rabbit and they ate that part with enthusiasm. Taking the rest of the carcass with us so they would keep the lesson to share their kills, we carried it back to where the mother wolf was. We handed it back to the pups and pointed to the mother. They proudly took it to her and she made a variety of sounds and licked their faces and then began to chew on the rabbit. Rather than "wolfing" it down, it became a shared meal with all three eating together.

We watched for a while. It wouldn't be long before they could hunt for themselves.

It was dark when we got back to the village. The girls were making stew. Lark, Violet and the boys were there so once again they had one of the largest fire groups.

Noh Tay Dah and his family had established their own fire pit and tonight they were hosting Cedo Bah Gay and his family. This also made the other fire group a little smaller.

I walked around the fire and came up between Sunflower and Azalia. I put my arms across their shoulders and they straightened up from bending over the cook fire and looked at me questioningly.

"I just want you to know that all of your work is greatly appreciated. We probably would not survive without you," I stated fondly.

There were a number of grunts and murmurs of agreement around the fire. The girls smiled self-consciously and Sunflower graciously said, "everyone work, everyone help."

"I know they do, and I'm proud of all of them. I would like to propose another trip."

They all gave me their full attention. "Remember our first hunt where you and the boys took down your first deer?"

They nodded and smiled with a far-off look in their eyes.

"Let's do a hunt to show our newcomers how it is done. Boys, are the deer back in the little valley?" I asked.

They nodded affirmatively.

Still focused on the boys, I asked, "is Blossom's bow strong enough to take down a deer?"

They glanced at one another for a moment and Lobo answered, "I believe up to fifteen steps it would take down a deer."

"Blossom, can you hit a target this big," making an eight inch circle with my thumbs and fingers, "at fifteen steps?"

She thought for a moment and said, "most of the time, not always."

I turned to Lark, "can you hit a target that size at fifteen steps?"

Blossom relayed the message but also nodded affirmatively. Lark responded in English, "most time, not all," and glanced at Blossom for approval.

"Lobo, if one of you takes Blossom and one takes Lark, one pair comes up the valley and one pair waits at the top, like our first hunt, would that be good?" I asked.

He glanced at the other two boys and they both smiled and nodded.

"Okay, Lobo you decide which of you will hunt and who will go with you and where you will go and work with the girls on what you expect from them and plan the hunt," I instructed.

Lobo grinned, "I plan hunt. Impala and Little Badger do hunt. Tomorrow, we plan. Lark go with Little Badger, Blossom go with Impala." He paused, "when we take trip?"

"Let's plan for the day after tomorrow," I replied. "Girls, plan the meals, equipment and all that we will need and we will take a trip!"

That met with everyone's approval. Blossom and Lark looked at each other with a grin and excitement in their eyes. It would be their first big game hunt.

"Can I go to?" Violet inquired timidly.

"Absolutely!" I said, "you will write down the things we plan and do. Then when Lobo is as old as Grandmother, he can look at your notes and remember what he should do!"

Everyone laughed and Lobo grinned and nodded.

Which reminded me, I needed to get a whole box of notebooks for Violet. She had gotten into the habit of writing everything down, and even now she could correct minor arguments about when things happened, new words, details of instructions and many other incidentals that we might try to recall.

It was also helping her learn English at a faster pace and with more precision than the others.

I inquired of Lobo, "what time of the day will you stalk the deer?"

"They will be in the valley before sun go down. We hunt before dark," he replied.

The next day started with feeding the wolves enough to tide them over until we got back, then taking a trip to the stash to get some beans and flour for Mor Dak Sah to dispense, and rearranging my pack for the trip.

When I got back, Blossom and Lark were carrying their bows and arrows, as well as a target, up the hill for some practice, so I joined them.

"Would you like me to help you make it as real as it will be?" I inquired.

"That will help," Blossom responded and Lark nodded.

"There will be signals so you know which deer Impala and Little Badger are choosing. It will most likely be a young buck and standing with a side toward you. This will be done before you get close to shooting distance so he won't be waving his hands around when you are only fifteen steps away.

"If the deer are moving up the hill, he might hold up his fingers to show where the deer is in line. Two fingers mean the second deer.

"Then, you should shoot together in rhythm. Remember to hide a step or two back from a tree or bush so you don't bump it with your bow or arrow.

"He will mouth a word like 'go' or 'now' or might just nod his head, and you will step to position. This must be only one step to the clear path to the deer. Then you draw, lock, release together in rhythm.

"You can't follow what he is doing or you will be late and the deer will move and you will miss. You know the rhythm and you will be together.

"Now let's practice the motion. Don't ever draw and release a bow when you don't have an arrow to shoot. So just pretend to draw," I reminded them.

"We never do that, Chee," Blossom said emphatically.

"Good! Let's practice then. Go to each side and get behind a tree but be sure you can see me. No arrows yet, just the rhythm."

After they got into position, I nodded and silently counted to four.

"You both released before I got to four. Remember step, draw, lock, release." I reminded them.

"The one short step is to put you in position. Step directly toward your target so you're in the right position to strike. Don't rush the aim. 'Lock' means lock your sight on the target, then release."

After a few dry runs, I put the straw target out fifteen steps and set it in front of a dirt bank.

"Okay, hide!" I said and put two fingers to my eyes and pointed to the target. In about two seconds Lark released an arrow and struck the target. Blossom was looking at me with some confusion. Lark was looking at me with some confusion also.

"I haven't said go or nodded yet," I said smiling at her.

"Oh," she said with her brow furled as in thought.

"Oh!" She repeated more loudly and her eyebrows shot up and her mouth dropped open.

I grinned at her and she shook her head and took a deep breath.

"Let's try again. Ready, position."

I paused for a moment and said, "you may have to be in a ready position, sometimes an uncomfortable position, and be perfectly still until the deer moves to the right spot. So, be ready!"

I paused again, put two fingers to my eyes, raised one finger to indicate the first target, then after another brief pause, I nodded and counted silently. At the count of four, they released together and at five, two arrows hit the target with almost one sound and both were closer to the center than they were to the edge.

"Very good, very good!" I said enthusiastically, "that is about perfect. Well done!"

"Okay, let's see if you can do it three times without missing," I challenged them.

They could, and they did!

"Now, let's move the target to twenty steps."

At twenty steps two out of three were in the eight inch circle and the penetration from Blossoms bow was deep enough to bring down a deer.

They were ready!

We returned to the village and I motioned to Lobo. He came over and I related how well the girls had done.

"Blossom's bow is strong enough at twenty steps and both can strike the right spot."

"We will explain how we stalk and strike and show the signals we use," he replied.

He called the boys and Lark and Blossom together and they wandered off discussing the details of the hunt. I got my pack together, like I would want it for such a trip, and checked with the girls to see if they had everything they needed.

"Do you have the cans of baked beans packed?" I asked with a grin.

"Oh yes! Of course!" Azalia said seriously, "we never go without beans! You might get so weak you could not make the trip back!"

"Not a problem." I said, "if I fall down, you will carry me!"

She just laughed and went back to whatever chore she was working on.

I went to my lean-to to finish a lesson I was developing. As our group had grown, it was getting harder to keep the cohesion and function of the group together. Ultimately that would result in less understanding and trust of one another in different circumstances. We needed to strengthen our unity to prevent that from happening.

On our first hunt there were only five of us. Azalia had not become an active part until she translated for me when the tribe came to see the bear. Blossom had come in from the wild that time as well but she was as wild as the animals we hunted so she fit in immediately.

Violet had never been on a hunt or faced a war party, so she was on the periphery of our activities. Lark was new and an unknown in terms of her skills and ability to function in the unit.

I was hoping this trip would draw us all together.

We didn't need to leave early or be in a hurry. The day was warm and sunny, the smell of spring with fresh flowers and budding leaves filled the air. The light breeze was crisp and invigorating. We hiked with a spring in our step and a peaceful joy on each face.

It took about two hours to reach the Grizzly Spring, as we had taken to calling it, and there was plenty of cool, fresh water, lots of firewood and fire pits from previous trips.

"Let's drag a few logs around so we can sit around the campfire this evening," I suggested.

The excitement of the hunt had created a need to work off some energy, so trimming some of the fallen trees, cutting them into manageable lengths and dragging them to the campsite was great exercise.

We had a late, light lunch since we didn't want the hunters to be sluggish with overstuffed stomachs.

We drew our packs up into the trees to keep animals from getting to the supplies.

Lobo went over the procedures and signals one more time and we set out for the valley.

There was a small ridge with some clusters of rocks about a quarter mile from the hill overlooking the valley. We settled into a nest of rocks to wait for the right time to begin.

It was only a short wait before Lobo turned to the hunters and said, "let's go."

We all followed discreetly behind and stopped a hundred yards short of the crest of the hill.

The five hunters went ahead to look into the valley and locate the deer, going the last twenty yards on hands and knees. They backed away from the top of the hill and Little

Badger and Lark headed up the hill to cross the valley and come down the other side into a thick stand of small trees and bushes.

We had moved forward just enough to see where they would go. There was a clear deer trail showing where they usually left the valley. Little Badger and Lark would locate just up the side of the hill about twenty steps from the trail.

Impala and Blossom waited about five minutes and headed down the ridge where they wouldn't be seen then go over the hill and come up the valley along the little creek.

Stalking meant moving and movement meant the deer might have opportunity to see the threat before they got close enough to shoot.

There were many small evergreen trees, lots of bushes and tall grass to cover both sound and sight.

Blossom was as good as Impala at stalking, having had years of experience at moving and hiding in the woods after she was cast out of the tribe. She was also much smaller and lighter.

The rest of us waited a few more minutes until Lobo beckoned to us.

"Crawl on hands and knees until you see deer. If you see them, they can see you, so move very slowly. There is log at top and some little pine trees to see under. Find spot and don't move."

The deer were a hundred yards down the meadow and off to our right. The breeze was coming across the valley so it was possible that they might catch our scent. I was hoping they were off to the right enough that our scent would stay west of them.

Once we caught a glimpse of Impala moving stealthily from one tree to another but the undergrowth was too thick for us to follow where he went.

After a few minutes, he seemed to just appear behind an evergreen tree about twenty yards from a deer at the farthest part of the small herd.

Impala turned his head to the right and nodded. We knew Blossom must be right there but we still couldn't see her.

He stepped to the edge of the tree, drew, locked on and released. Another arrow came out of a clump of bushes to his right, but we still couldn't see Blossom.

The deer took a half dozen jumps, crossed the stream and started up the valley. After another couple of jumps and it fell over and lay still.

The rest of the herd, had their heads up looking for the danger but Impala and Blossom had melted into the tall grass and were completely still.

The herd milled around for a few seconds then started up the valley. Several stopped to look back but could find no threat.

They fell into a single file and went up the trail. Although we couldn't see Little Badger and Lark, we knew they had to be in some little lane among the trees about twenty yards up the hill where they would get a clear shot.

Suddenly, one of the deer jumped, wheeled sideways, then back around and bolted up the hill past the others. In less than a dozen jumps, he crumpled in a heap and didn't move.

The rest of the deer, still not seeing any threat but sensing that there was one, bolted up the trail and into the deeper forest.

We waited a few moments and Lobo stepped forward and yelled, "Yaaa-Eeee!"

Immediately, there were four responses, as the hunters stepped forward, raised their bows and shouted, "Yaaa-Eeee!"

It had been previously decided that they would drag the deer out of the valley so that the herd might return more quickly.

We all divided up to go both directions to bring the deer over the hill and field dress it on this side of the ridge.

Blossom and Lark were ecstatic and grinning from ear to ear. They were both carrying the arrow that had struck the deer, probably as a keepsake from their first successful deer hunt.

They were both talking excitedly one after the other and over each other, relating the details of the hunt. I had never seen Lark so excited. She said more words in five minutes than I'd heard her speak in a whole day; and in what I assumed was three languages.

Finally, they slowed down a little and began to take turns. Violet translated for me and Blossom began again in English so I could understand.

Lark started, "Little Badger, good teacher. He tell me strike low because we strike downhill. He say 'this much'," and she indicated the distance, "and it hit right there." She said pointing to a spot right under her arm.

Blossom broke in, "Impala point to bush and I crawl in grass to bush and start to get up and deer right there," and she pointed in front of her at an invisible deer only a few steps away. "I look at Impala, he nod. We step, draw, lock, strike. Both arrows strike right behind shoulders. My arrow got a little bit high because so close."

Impala broke in, "her arrow deep enough and close enough to heart to be kill strike."

As the adrenaline wore off, they calmed down a bit.

"It just like we practice, Chee! It just like Lobo say, it just like Little Badger show me," Lark exclaimed as Violet interpreted.

I think she got another shot of adrenaline just reliving the hunt again. Of course, as a slave, she did what she was ordered to do with little appreciation or praise. Here she was a major success as part of a team.

Blossom came over for a hug and Lark looked around like she didn't know what to do next. I extended an arm and she almost jumped in to participate in the hug. Her loneliness, fear and rejection may not have been as severe as Blossom's, but it was still painful and emotionally damaging.

Violet, as the ever present translator, had tucked herself in between Blossom and Lark. Sunflower and Azalia saw the group hug forming and came in behind Blossom and Lark.

I looked over the heads of the girls and saw the boys looking on and said, "group hug, come join us," and they of the unemotional, aloof, serious attitudes came immediately and joined in.

Blossom would probably hug any and all, right through the afternoon. Lark seemed to be so overcome with the feeling of love and acceptance and unity of such a group that she was about to squish my spleen. She probably had never experienced a group hug as sincere and genuine as this.

This spontaneous expression of caring and belonging was a welcome reaffirmation of our love and commitment and it felt good. We hadn't had a group hug since last winter when I left after what we all thought might be our last time together.

The group hug slowly dissolved, each one backing away and returning to their tasks. I noticed the high intensity and emotions of the hunt mixed with the warmth and sincerity of their commitment and love for one another left them somewhat pensive and sorting out their emotions.

The boys finished the field dressing and we wrapped the liver in a plastic bag. We would skin out enough of one deer to take out a couple long strips of loin for steaks.

Supper was a happy, boisterous time. Even though the boys had taken a couple dozen deer for the tribe during the past year, they were still caught up in the excitement and thrill of the hunt that Lark and Blossom were experiencing.

By grilling two steaks or slices of liver on one stick, we could make a meal that we could all eat together and those who wanted more could keep on grilling.

I set up paper plates for the occasion and announced, "the sweet baked beans are ready! There's enough for everyone but Sunflower and Azalia!"

"No! No! We love 'sweet' baked beans!" Sunflower objected.

"Yes! You make 'sweet' baked beans very good!" Azalia said with exaggerated mock sincerity.

The boys grinned and filled their plates. Lark looked back and forth to determine that this was all in good fun before smiling and helping herself. In a moment she responded with her mouth half full of beans, "they good!"

"Don't say that!" Azalia said in mock horror, "you will eat beans for the rest of your life!"

The boys were grinning and nodding to keep the argument going.

"Okay." I responded with finality, "you shall have no ice cream!"

"Noooo!" Azalia wailed and the others all joined in until it sounded like a pack of lost coyotes. Then we all burst out laughing.

Lark was looking at us in total confusion since she had never even heard of ice cream. Her dazed expression set us off in another peal of laughter.

The meal was delicious. Somehow jovial conversation seems to make everything taste better.

After the meal, I said, "let's clean up from supper and build up the evening campfire. I have a special lesson tonight I think you will enjoy. Lark had asked if I could teach her to be a warrior like all of you. So tonight, I want to talk with you about how the Great Spirit makes the heart of a great warrior."

Chapter 13

The brightly burning campfire put a warm glow of comradery all around us. We had never talked in any detail about what makes a great warrior but I knew they were curious. They had all expressed a real interest in what that might mean and wanted to see if they might become great warriors.

"Lark, you asked to be a warrior like these," I said. "What did I tell you?"

"You say it must be in heart, come out when needed, but I don't know what that mean."

Violet was helping her find the right words but Lark did say it in English.

" Your English is getting much better!" I nodded in approval of her effort.

Continuing on, I said, "I decided to ask myself that question and go to the book of the Great Spirit to see if he had answered it. And he did. In many examples and stories.

"His book says, 'the Great Spirit is love!' But what is love?"

Azalia spoke up, "it is how we feel about…" She paused, suddenly realizing that the subject was too big for one word.

"Sometimes saying what we feel about different things is very confusing. Sometimes it is like trying to catch the wind. We know it is there but we can never catch it."

They all nodded in understanding.

"Do you love your new coverings, shoes, coats, shirts?"

They all nodded again and touched the soft, light fabric that was so much more comfortable than deer hides.

"Do you love a favorite color?"

This brought barrage of answers. "I love the blue sky" "I love bright green when sunshine strike leaves." "I love bright red of flowers."

"Do you love Grandmother?"

There was a murmur of affirmation accompanied by smiles at the thought of her.

"Do you love Grandmother the same as your coverings and colors?" I asked.

This brought the first step of our lesson home. All these loves are so different that they hardly mean the same.

"We have many words for love. Most of them you haven't ever heard of, so the Great Spirit gave us words to help us describe love that we can see.

"I found it very interesting, that one of the first words the great spirit uses to describe love is 'joy'.

"We sometimes use happiness but happiness comes from what happens and joy can be in us even when bad things happen. So, joy might include humor, fun and even more broadly, things that make us smile or laugh. We even use the word "enjoy' which means 'what brings joy in'.

"This is one of the reasons why we joke, and tease and have fun. It draws us together and we enjoy each other. A great warrior's heart finds joy in many things.

"Another word is 'peacefulness'. Joy and peace go together in that joy often brings peace.

"Remember a few moons past when we set out to get Deh Neh Totsi and the children back from the As Teh Cah?

"As we camped in the cold winter weather, you began to tell me what a good father would do and I was telling you what good children would do and soon we were laughing and teasing back and forth.

"That night Sunflower made an observation. 'Tomorrow we go into battle against experienced warriors who outnumber us, but tonight our spirits are light and we are happy together.' Such joy and peace is what love is about.

"Another word is 'kindness', treating others as you want to be treated. Azalia, remember when we hiked over the mountain and your leg wasn't all healed and strong yet, the boys took turns carrying your pack. You were embarrassed but it showed their heart. They wanted you with us.

"And Blossom when you were put out and became 'the curse of the tribe' it was this group seated around this fire who opened their hearts and we became a family.

A warrior's heart has kindness!"

"Another word, 'faithfulness' means you keep going, you finish the job. Sunflower and Azalia worked in the hot sun helping prepare a garden when they didn't even know what a garden was.

"Self-control is a tough one. The Great Spirit warns that your tongue is the hardest thing to control, meaning, what you say. Then, there is anger, hate, greed, selfishness. If we don't control these things, they will control us and we will make bad decisions and hurt one another.

"Another very important word is 'humbleness'. You must know yourself and know others. Value their abilities, if they have a weakness help them grow and become stronger. Never try to make someone fail so you look better. That destroys trust. This is an important part of all the other pieces. You don't think you are the best at everything so when you see goodness and love in others you can say, 'I wish I was as joyful as that person. I wish I could be as faithful or kind."

"Remember when the large army from the north came to attack us?"

There were murmurs and nods of remembrance around the circle.

"They were only two or three minutes from over-running my position and killing me. At that last minute, I sensed more coming behind me and I thought I was dead. But it was all of you and you sent six arrows into the line of warriors coming up the hill.

"I'll never forget how I suddenly felt. I was about to die but you brought a strange joy and peace.

"I would die with the greatest warriors I had ever known in all my life, and that was okay.

"The chief saw that too, and called off the attack. You continue to show your hearts as you bandaged the wounded and gave them a deer for the evening meal.

"Remember how they stood and saluted you?

"They saw that you have the hearts of great warriors.

"Remember the snake in my bed incident?"

Smiles, nods and outright chuckles followed that question.

"Remember, you thought I was really angry but it was a test not only of Lark but of all of you.

"You thought I was wrong to be so angry, didn't you?"

They nodded seriously and Lark was almost teary-eyed just thinking about it.

"But what did I learn? That all of you would stand for what was right even against me.

"Lark, did you notice that they all stood with you in facing my anger? That told me that they saw a good heart worth standing for.

"And Lark, I think you were somewhat scared when I called you over to stand in front of me."

She nodded vigorously.

"Did you think that your chance of being taught to be a warrior and be part of our group was gone?"

Again, she nodded.

"But you stood, looked me in the eye and said you did it. You didn't blame anyone else or lie about it. From that truth, I saw the heart of a warrior. Truth builds trust and I am proud to be allowed to help you become a great warrior, like these others."

There was a unanimous agreement and murmurs of support around the circle. Sunflower, who was sitting beside Lark, reached across her shoulders and gave her a quick hug.

"There is one more word that the Great Spirit emphasizes. Love is 'long-suffering' and He puts it in the list with joy, peace and other things He is building into our hearts.

"Long-suffering means to suffer for a long time. If you fell and broke your leg and were stuck between some rocks, a few hours would be a long time. At other times something may go on for many moons.

"All of you have suffered by losing loved ones, by having little hope of survival, by having only a little food and even worse things."

Several were glancing at Blossom and Lark.

"Blossom, you have a loving heart that we all see and enjoy, we might even say 'you are the heart of our group'."

Again, there were nods and murmurs of affirmation.

"Lark, we don't know all that you have suffered, but you don't show hate and bitterness, instead we see a thankful, truthful heart that is eager to learn and grow."

Violet broke in timidly, "Chee, I no have great warrior heart. I not like fight, I do not like war! Do I need warrior heart?"

"You make a good point. We have emphasized a 'warrior' heart, but we need to emphasize a 'great' heart which is really the same thing and it will be needed by everyone.

"Why do you think you are here in our circle tonight?"

She shrugged, "you say I can come."

Azalia broke in, "when I could not keep up, when tribe go to see bear, you stay with me. I was scared and tired and didn't know what to do. I could not go on but you stayed with me. That was brave. You show love and faithfulness, not for war but for help. This is great heart too. Chee, is it so?"

"Absolutely!" I replied, "we need great hearts to make peace, settle disputes and especially, to teach. Violet may become a great teacher who remembers these lessons and hunts and battles.

"She can take Grandmother's knowledge and pass it on to the children. She has a great memory and knows as many words already, as most of you. She is learning Deh Neh Totsi's language and will help keep peace and understanding between the tribes.

"We began with the heart of a great warrior but when the Great Spirit and his Son makes a great heart, it is shaped for whatever needs to be done.

"Sometimes war is thrust upon us and it is intense and hard but usually it is also short.

"Peace takes time, understanding and all these things we have talked about. Sometimes peace is harder than war.

"Violet will be a voice for peace.

"Prepare for war, but seek peace," I concluded.

There was a long pause as they were all lost in thought.

Impala broke the silence with a question, his voice was barely above a whisper. "Can we have peace with the Whiteface?"

There was a long silence as each one mulled over that thought in the light of what we had just discussed.

I waited for an uncomfortably long time before saying, "if the Whiteface come looking for peace, what will you do?

"Don't answer that now. It is something that you must sort out in your mind and spirit and heart in the days ahead."

There was little conversation as we turned in for the night.

Sunflower was overheard to mutter to no one in particular, "peace is hard!"

The attitudes were a lot more cheerful in the morning light and the activity of breaking camp and packing gear kept us all busy. The boys had built two travois to carry the deer. With lighter packs and lots of help, we were making good time getting back to the village.

In about a half hour, we stopped for a break and a drink of water.

As we had walked, I'd been thinking about next steps. "Is there anything in my pack that you need back in the village?" I inquired.

"Are you carrying cans of food?" Azalia asked.

"Maybe a few. Let's put them in other packs and I will go back to report and get seeds for the garden and more food to supplement your supplies," I said.

"That be good," Sunflower said. "The roots and plants are not yet plentiful and many fear going down to the river where Whiteface or conquistadors might be."

"Okay, you all go on to the village and I will go back and get supplies and other things I need." I said and waited for the inevitable objections or clamor to go with me. I was amazed that there was nothing; no response.

They all stood and waited as Sunflower came over and said, "if Great Spirit send you to help us and protect us, then the door will remain until the Whiteface and conquistadors can no longer destroy us. We all talk and think this is so."

That was a new slant and I wasn't sure about that myself, but if it made them feel more secure and accepting of the situation, it was probably good.

We parted and I headed up the hill, back to home, to Dorothy and my friends who help and advise me.

The meetings with my advisors were always pleasant and informative. The biggest issue, other than being suddenly trapped in the sixteenth century, had been dependency.

Whether we liked it or not, we now had a bigger issue.

After the pleasantries, and catching up on friends and family over a delicious steak barbecue potluck, including ice cream and chocolate cake, I gave my report.

"The new tribe was not only well received but they are farmers. At least in the primitive sense, they grow food as well as gather food and hunt." I concluded my report on the addition of the new tribe.

"It certainly sounds like they needed help, and you with your group of warriors saved lives," Sharon exclaimed.

"That's true but how much extra food are you going to need to feed them all?" Heather asked.

"They will need supplemental food for at least another month until some of the plants and berries become available. The garden won't be available until late summer and fall." I replied.

"What about the logistics? You have to transport hundreds of pounds of food to the village and store it in a dry place every week." Ben observed.

There was a pause in the conversation and Cam finally broke the silence. "It seems like we have been skirting around the biggest issue driving all this. If all these people are fleeing north, how far behind are the conquistadors?"

"Frankly, that's the real reason I'm here, and yes I've been avoiding the issue," I admitted.

"One little part of the story I omitted was that the little starving tribe was being pursued by four conquistadors and seven indigenous warriors bent on killing them all," I began.

"Blossom discovered their presence and surmised, correctly it turned out, that they would attack at dawn. We got up and fled to the cliffs and watched. When they did attack, they shot and speared the sleeping bags and a shirt I had hung as a decoy, proving that they were bent on killing us all without warning or mercy."

I continued to relate the whole story through the ambush and taking down of the warriors and all four conquistadors.

"That was some omission," Cam remarked dryly.

"Yeah." I responded with a sigh, "I haven't sorted it out and have no plan. But I can tell you this, arrows, even with metal points, won't go through Conquistador armor. The hand cannons begin to become effective at a hundred yards with buckshot that can inflict significant wounds. At fifty yards, it's a suicide mission.

"So, if there are thirty or forty conquistadors with hand cannons, they might be defeated with about three hundred warriors if the first wave was a suicide mission against the harquebuses; if the second wave was a suicide mission, throwing themselves against pikes and swords; and the third wave, if it was three steps behind the second might be able to knock the swords out of a few hands and ring a few bells inside the helmets. If they knocked them down by sheer force of numbers and beat off their helmets so they could crush some heads with a war club, they might destroy thirty or forty conquistadors." I concluded somewhat bitterly.

"That sounds rather dire!" Sharon reacted.

"Yes! It's worse than dire!" I exclaimed, "in the south they are destroying or will destroy the great civilizations of the Aztecs, Mayas and Incas. They are after gold and will murder and enslave thousands, in reality tens of thousands, to get it. Even worse if you don't have any, they will destroy just to keep in practice. They kill everyone who gets in their way.

"Read your history books. These are all facts!" I concluded

"So, you think you can change history?" Sharon asked incredulously.

"No, actually I don't. What I believe is that you can participate in history so that we become a part of what happened. Maybe we are an essential part of what happened, but it happens in times and places where little or no records were kept.

"We know the history and live in the result of it but have no records of who, what or how those results came to be. I believe we are tasked with influencing the 'what and how' of these results that we now know were made to happen."

My explanation left us all a bit dazed and confused.

They were all somewhat science-fiction buffs so thinking outside the box was not impossible.

Ben responded thoughtfully, "so you are saying many things could have happened, but of course, only one did. The most likely thing didn't happen so you need to make sure the unlikely thing that did happen, actually happens."

"That's a fair summary," I responded. "The conquistadors did destroy civilizations; they did find a cave of gold on the east side of the Sangre De Christo range. They conquered almost every tribe from Florida to California. They even made forays up as far as Wisconsin if that history is correct. They destroyed some tribes, left death and sickness wherever they went but didn't colonize these areas.

"With all due respect to New Mexico and Arizona, they were not typical destination spots in the sixteenth century.

"They knew gold was usually found in the mountains. That's why they destroyed the Incas. Look at Machu Picchu and Inga Pirca to see what terrain they were looking for."

Cam broke in, "so you think they should have looked in the mountains of Colorado?"

"Actually, they did," I exclaimed. "They mined gold in the Animus River in Western Colorado.

"If they had made the relatively easy trip up the front range, they would have discovered gold at what later became Denver City. It wasn't discovered until 1858, more than three hundred years later. The Colorado gold rush found gold all over the mountains of central Colorado."

"So, you think you are supposed to stop the conquistadors?" Heather asked skeptically.

"Yes!" I chuckled, somewhat drained from my recitation, "I am going to put a stop sign at what will become the border with a sign saying 'conquistadors go home' and then I'll be done."

"I'm sure that ought to take care of it," Cam remarked with an eye roll and a smirk.

Heather spoke up, "seriously, you think that is your mission?"

"Actually… Yes." I said with great resignation.

There was a long pause as this revelation was weighed against their assessment of my sanity.

"I'm not sure I'm ready to accept that," Sharon said somberly.

Ben spoke up thoughtfully, "do you all know Douglas Marlin?"

"I think we all do," Cam responded. "From church and many other social gatherings, most people call him 'Doug.'"

"Many also call him 'Doc' from his medical training in special ops," Sharon added.

Ben continued, "he has the special ops military background but he also is a science fiction aficionado with an emphasis on science. He was on the government task force investigating UFOs and was part of several 'paranormal incidents' investigations.

"Maybe you could pick his brain on the paranormal as well as the military aspects. Probably without revealing the portal or the situation you are in specifically."

Cam remarked seriously, "since you have no knowledge or experience in guerrilla warfare, I'd say you need to pick somebody's brain."

"Okay go ahead and set up a meeting. Are you all planning to be present?" I asked.

"If we are finding stuff that you need and buying and transporting, we ought to know what's going on in order to make the best choices," Sharon declared.

"Then, see when he's available. Let's go with the scenario of science-fiction buffs who like to propose scenarios and discuss actions and solutions." I suggested, "I'll get the things I need and head back tomorrow. I'll report back in a few days and see what you have found."

"Let me call him now. Maybe we could set a date before you leave," Ben suggested.

He then moved off to a quiet spot to make his phone call, while we packed up the leftovers, cleaned off the tables and put the dishes in the dishwasher.

"Would you like to take the leftover chocolate cake with you?" Sharon asked.

"If there are nine pieces, or twelve if Grandmother and the children are there, or sixteen if Noh Tay Dah's family is also present," I grinned.

She laughed, "I'll tell you what, it's just a flat cake so I'll make another tonight and bring it to you tomorrow by midmorning and you'll have plenty to share with that group. Not the whole tribe mind you, just your extended group."

"That would be greatly appreciated by all, I'm sure," I responded.

Ben came back with the phone still in his hand. "Doc is available in five days, that's next Thursday and I suggested another potluck and Bar-B-Q. Does that sound okay with everyone?"

Everyone nodded or said 'okay', so he turned back to his phone and declared, "next Thursday. Dorothy says to come for dinner at five so we have some time in the evening to create fantasy. See you then."

The meeting came to an end and I headed to the garden store to get seeds of all kinds that might grow in that climate and altitude.

I also went to bed early and got a good night's sleep.

Sharon came by as promised with a cake in a one layer pan, all wrapped in a box for the journey. We fastened it at the very top of my pack so it would stay flat.

The pack full of seeds and food was fairly heavy but I would be going downhill to the village.

Sunflower, Azalia and Blossom were there as I put my pack in my lean-to. The cake was set aside and left in the box, the seeds were set on another pile and the food was organized and put in an appropriate place with what was left of my other food.

I asked someone to come with me to take the seeds to Cedo's group and all three decided to come along.

We added Deh Neh Totsi, since she spoke Cedo's language but knew only a little English.

There were probably some things lost in translation, as I spoke to the girls, who spoke to Deh Neh Totsi who spoke to Cedo's people. But with the pictures and gestures about planting depth, what the plant was like, spacing, etc., we got most of the information transferred and questions answered.

After the evening meal, I checked on the cakes. With the whole cake pan and half of another, we could get a lot of pieces. I sent Blossom and Violet to get Grandmother and the little ones. Sunflower and Azalia invited Noh Tay Dah and family and then Cedo with his wife and son.

When the girls returned, Sunflower suggested that we make hot chocolate, as she had seen a large can of cocoa mix in my lean-to.

"It will be good with the cake," Azalia asserted.

None of us would argue with that, so we prepared for what had become a rather large gathering.

Blossom and Violet brought Grandmother's chair which became another source of wonder to Cedo and his wife.

The cake was sweeter than anything that Cedo's family had ever tasted and they ate as slowly as they could to make it last as long as possible.

The conversations were interesting and jovial, as lives and memories were shared and friendships deepened. All too soon the evening chill reminded Grandmother that she should get the children home and to bed.

Lobo carried her chair and took her arm to help her traverse the uneven ground to her hut.

Chip and Sweet Pea made the rounds to give everyone a hug and chatter like little socialites.

The party quickly, but reluctantly broke up. Such pleasant social interactions had been few and far between for Noh Tay Dah, Cedo and their families.

Again, I had to rearrange my lean-to in order to make an aisle to sleep in. My place was now the go-to for a storage unit.

Somewhere around midnight, I was jerked out of a sound sleep when a cold nose touched my face. I grabbed a handgun that was always under my pillow when I slept, and sat bolt upright in my sleeping bag. Two medium-size forms were staring back at me from just above my sleeping bag.

"Kih Ta, Sah Sha come," and they crept forward to snuggle against me, whimpering and whining as though in great distress.

I gathered them in and they licked my face and rubbed against me.

Blossom, who was in the hut on the other side of the tree, heard them and came over. They moved out to meet her, rubbing against her legs, then turning around to rub back the other direction.

She sat down at the head of my sleeping bag and they crowded onto our laps, but continued to get up and turn around and lay back down. The restlessness and whimpering was probably their way of telling us that mama wolf was gone.

"I believe mama Wolf has died and we are what they have as a pack or family," I said to Blossom.

"They feel frightened and alone, huh, Chee," she said.

"I think so. Wolves are one of the few animals that grieve a loss like the death of a pack member," I said.

The commotion had awakened the other girls and they came over to see what was wrong.

With heads held low and tails drooping they went around the legs of the girls and back to us. Each one reached down to stroke them as they went by.

"What we do, Chee?" Blossom asked.

"Are you girls interested in a short, night journey?" I asked.

"Where you want to go? You take wolves back to mother?" Azalia asked.

"No, we will move away from the village and help the pups grieve," I said. "Get coats and shoes for a short hike."

It was a moon lit night so we didn't need flashlights to go to the other side of the ridge that went down behind the village, then over one more ridge to an outcropping of rock that gave us a clear view of the night sky and the valley stretching away in the distance.

The pups had walked so close to us that they almost tripped us one after another as we walked.

We all sat down cross-legged in a circle. The pups went from one to another but didn't stop moving for long.

"Okay, let's have a wolf grieving ceremony," and I tilted back my head and did my best wolf howl into the night sky.

The pups came over and licked my face, then sat back on their haunches and let loose a high pitched, mournful howl towards the moon overhead.

The girls caught on immediately and began to join the howls. We simply howled at intervals. Sometimes just one of us, sometimes several at once. The pups would listen intently then join or respond at their own pace.

It was an eerie experience but we could see the change in the pups' demeanor. The droopy tail, the hung down head, the agitated movement began to diminish.

As the pups reduced the frequency of their howls, so did we, so that there were stretches of silence before they would howl and we would respond.

Suddenly, during one of the silences, a lone wolf, far away and up on the big mountain to the west, responded with a howl that was almost like a faint echo.

The pups' heads came up. They got up from the sitting position with tails up, prancing with excitement and went to each one of us to lick our face and prance away.

Apparently, the message they got was that mama wolf was okay, they were with their pack and life would go on.

As we headed back to the village, Kih Ta and Sah Sha scouted ahead and off to each side, sniffing bushes, trees and rocks. Their grief and loss were under control and put behind them, and they were ready to move on.

Tomorrow I would get the boys, go up the hill and bury the momma wolf.

Chapter 14

Life moved along at its normal pace in the village over the next few days and I realized my meeting with Doc Marlin was coming up tomorrow evening. After the evening meal, I called my inner group together to try to prepare them for what was ahead. My little cadre had grown to nine. All except Lark had been through the portal and had some understanding that I came from a very different place.

They knew I had a team helping me and getting clothing, supplies and equipment that was strange but helpful to their lives.

They also had grown to expect something a little out of the ordinary each time we went to the little "v" shaped sitting area overlooking the valley. That history made for a somber mood with heightened expectations as we seated ourselves and gazed out over the far reaches of the moonlit valley.

"As you may have guessed, I've brought you here to talk about a very important problem.

"You have seen the conquistadors with their weapons and armor. They are coming and we must be ready."

There was a chorus of exclamations. "When they come?" "How many come?" "They have thunder sticks, what we do?"

After the hubbub diminished, I continued. "I don't know when. Probably scouting parties will come first to see what is here. They will be looking for the yellow stone. If they do not find any they will leave. The problem is, they will torture and kill anyone in their way and they will keep on torturing and killing until they are convinced that nobody knows about the yellow stone."

"Don't even talk about the yellow stone, not even to each other. If someone heard you even talk about it, and they were being whipped and cut and burned, they might report that they knew nothing themselves but they had heard you talk about it.

"They would then start in on the one named even though that person knew nothing and had never said more than to repeat that the conquistadors look for yellow stone.

"You cannot imagine how evil, vicious and murderous these people are and I hope you never have to find out for yourself," I concluded.

"What we do, Chee?" Blossom asked obviously shaken.

Lobo added urgently, "even our new bows, arrows do not go through armor."

Impala spoke up, "we have shiny coverings from four that attack us. Nothing that we have can go into it."

"If they come in great numbers, like the army of warriors who came from the north, even your thunder sticks could not stop them." Little Badger reminded us. "You say to us 'in two or three minutes they run over us and kill us if their chief did not stop battle'."

"All of what you say is true," I agreed. "I tell you about this so you will understand what the danger is. Now we can plan to do things that might work so that they can't catch and kill us. We must understand how they think, what do they fear? Can they fight in the mountains?

"Sometimes they have warriors who will fight with them to get the possessions of other tribes that they consider to be their enemies," I added.

"Like the seven warriors with the four conquistadors who attacked us," Sunflower remarked.

"Exactly" I said. "Their mistake was separating and becoming targets. The conquistadors didn't know about my weapons, so they walked right up to us.

"Tomorrow I'm going back to meet with a man who has fought many battles and studied many more. He may have ideas that could help us.

"In the meantime, think of problems and possibilities. Have Violet write them down in her notebook and we will discuss them when I get back."

We returned to the village as a quiet, thoughtful group. The future looked to be filled with uncertainty and danger.

The next morning, I headed back to talk with my advisors and Doc Marlin. We planned to tailor our conversation so that different people would ask predetermined questions so Doc wouldn't focus particularly on me.

We hoped to be able to get helpful information without directly revealing what we were doing.

After the delicious covered dish dinner, we sat around with our coffee cups chatting and getting acquainted.

Heather started the conversation by talking about science-fiction settings. "When we write science fiction stories, we want them to be realistic. We wanted your real-world advice so our fiction stays believable."

Cam presented a scenario, "if we were out hiking and ran across an alien shuttle and made contact with a small crew, what would be a realistic outcome, in your view?"

Ben added, "they have the little translation box to translate our conversation back and forth. They need some food and supplies and we are inclined to help them out."

I interjected, "you have a high security level would you be obligated to reveal the situation to some government agency? There could be national security implications although they don't appear to pose any direct or immediate threat."

Sharon added, "wouldn't a good positive interaction be a foundation for future contact rather than some agency coming in and taking control? They would probably consider the aliens a threat and seize their shuttle craft."

Doc responded, "I do have top secret security credentials and, yes, the government agencies would probably fight over who would be in charge of taking the aliens into custody. But without any indication of a threat, I wouldn't bring in any government agencies.

"You are right to assume that they would have all kinds of motivations that could create a confrontation with a superior civilization. This could lead to global danger not just national security.

"So, writing a science fiction story about aliens but keeping it under the radar, so to speak, on a local, regular people level would be realistic even if a local, special ops guy was involved."

"Great," Ben continued. "It makes writing realistic scenarios easier even if it is science-fiction. People might think the ex-military guy would have to reveal the situation and the story would have to go in a different direction."

"Here's another scenario we've explored that could lend itself to a science fiction twist," I said, breaking in and changing the subject. "We are friends with a primitive tribe in South America. Loggers are illegally cutting the jungle trees. The government looks the other way for financial reasons. The logging company brings in mercenaries to clear the jungle of everyone who might get in the way. The tribal people must leave or die. Blow guns at twenty yards are not equal to rifles at two hundred yards.

"Leaving is a temporary fix because the logging will catch up with them again and they can't live without water and food which doesn't exist everywhere."

Ben illustrated the point. "On Star Trek the prime directive was that they were not to interfere with other cultures. In one episode they found a culture about to be annihilated by another much superior group and Captain Kirk and the crew concluded that the only way they could be saved was to arm them sufficiently to defend themselves. So, the captain had the crew make black powder rifles and gave them the ability to make black powder for their self defense."

"Drawing on all your experience, would you arm the natives in South America so they could defend themselves?" I asked.

Doc's answer was a bit long and nuanced but the conclusion was, "if the survival of the tribe depends on self-defense, it isn't a bad thing to give them the means to defend themselves. The danger is that their newfound ability and weaponry might cause them to be a threat to other tribes or set them against the government that otherwise might leave them alone.

"But, yes, providing for their defense would be a legitimate action." Doc concluded.

"Maybe on a more practical level," Cam interjected. "What about tactics? If you have a large powerful army coming against a small ragtag group, how does the little group stop the big army?"

"Well, that's not really a sci-fi question, that is, as you said, a tactical problem." Doc began.

"This is more my area of expertise anyway. Food and water; you have to have it and you try to diminish theirs.

"Terrain! Stay on the high ground except in some unusual, preplanned situation and have an escape route.

"Many tiny victories; death by a thousand cuts. Sneak in, take out two or three and get away.

"Sci- ops! Install uncertainty. Make them feel unsafe and vulnerable, playing mind games, preying on superstitions and fears.

"One of the most important considerations; get your non-combatants to a safe place so you don't have to play defense. You want to be on offense most of the time."

He concluded, "this brings you full-circle. Get your people back to food and water and in a safe place so you are free to move and strike."

We explored a couple more scenarios, carefully avoiding time travel and then urged him to talk about his experiences studying UFOs and paranormal activity.

It was quite entertaining and we all enjoyed the stories, and of course, we had gathered the information that would help us decide on a course of action should the conquistadors decide to come north.

As we prepared to go our separate ways, we thanked Doc profusely for a very helpful and entertaining evening.

"Glad to do it!" He replied, "I enjoy the subject and if I can be of any further help, please let me know. I miss these kinds of down-home get-togethers with good food and good friends."

After he had gone, I said in summary, "I would like to get started secretly training my small group in firearms."

"Are you sure that's the wisest idea?" Sharon objected.

"If a hundred conquistadors invade, there is no possibility of stopping them. If we arm thirty or forty people who had never fired a gun, we still wouldn't win."

"I propose that we start small, just my group and we start simply. Let's take a .22 Magnum, which is accurate at a hundred yards and carries enough power to penetrate armor. We will also train on a .243 which is light, has little recoil and can be effective for the girls. It is accurate out to three hundred yards and will still carry enough force at five hundred yards to get through the body armor worn by the conquistadors."

"The last training will be with the guys going on to a .308. It's heavy and has quite a kick but it is fairly accurate at five hundred yards and still carries its velocity and momentum out to a thousand yards."

I concluded, "we aren't fighting at a thousand yards but when an army forms in ranks, the target from the legs of the front row to the heads in the back row is ten feet in height and twenty feet wide depending on how many rows and how many deep and the angle of march."

"Basically, you lob bullets in, aiming five feet over those in the rear and a bullet can drop five or ten feet and still strike a combatant."

"It sounds like you've already done some research," Cam observed.

"I have! There are ballistic charts for the bigger weapons and I will carry the necessary information with me."

"I know someone who has a .243 that they might loan or sell to us," Ben said.

"I'll get ammo for the .243 and .308. I have the .22 mag covered. Be sure there's a scope on the .243. Also be looking for a couple more of each if we decide we need to get some quickly."

"I'm still not sure this is a good idea," Sharon objected again. "Isn't this stuff too modern to be used in the sixteenth century?"

"In principle, I agree with you, but it is better to be prepared and not need something than to need something and not be prepared." I observed.

"As for a modern weapon showing up in some burial mound; it will be marked off as an anomaly. Someone planted it. It got put in with the wrong stuff in a chain of custody error. Since it couldn't possibly be there, as it appears to be, then it wasn't there. The site was contaminated, so note it and move on.

"Would you want to ruin your career fussing about some relic in a contaminated burial site?" I said grinning at her.

"Let's hope you get everything collected and brought back through when you're done," Heather exclaimed dryly.

The next morning Ben showed up with a nice .243 rifle with a scope and in a carrying case.

With the two I carried everywhere, and the extra three with ammunition, there was at least sixty pounds of weaponry on my pack. I decided to leave the .308 and ammo in the shed and pick it up later. We wouldn't be using it until after three or four practice sessions with the lighter rifles anyway.

That left enough room in my pack for a couple of boxes of energy bars and a can of beans for Sunflower.

Back at the village, Deh Neh Totsi was working at her fire pit preparing her family's evening meal.

The girls were doing the same on the right side of my lean-to.

I waved to Deh Neh Totsi's family, turned and waved to the girls and went into my lean-to to deposit my pack and bury the two rifles in a mound of clothes, tarps and "stuff".

Blossom was at the front of my lean-to when I emerged, waiting to give me a hug and chatter away about what she had been doing for the last few days.

It was only a few steps to the girls' fire, where I ceremoniously gave Sunflower the can of beans. Everyone "ooohed and aaahed" and made melodramatic remarks like this was the most extravagant gift they had ever seen.

Sunflower just rolled her eyes and everyone laughed.

Azalia, Lark and Violet all came to welcome me back. The evening meal was a relaxed and pleasant time and when we were done and sitting around the fire, I broached the subject that was at the back of everyone's mind.

"I believe it is time to make some decisions about the war that threatens to come upon us," I began.

The mood immediately turned serious and they stared into the embers of the dying fire as though this would bring about some new revelation.

"When I arrived here, Sunflower was the first person I met. She was charging an army with a rock!"

They glanced at one another than laughed. Apparently, we were going to keep the serious discourse light.

"Azalia was fighting three armed warriors with her fingernails while standing on one foot."

They looked at Azalia and grinned at the picture.

"Violet was the most daring of all! She stole my shirt and wouldn't give it back!" I exclaimed with awe in my voice.

They laughed loudest at this remembrance, nodding in agreement. Violet just grinned.

"I say these things for two reasons; so that we can look at life with a touch of humor and to point out that the courage of each of you is beyond question.

"We added the boys because Sunflower said they were the best and she was right. Then we added Blossom whose spirit beat the wilderness and whose love captured our hearts."

They all smiled fondly, and looked at Blossom. She looked down, a bit embarrassed at the praise.

"And now we've added Lark," I said. "All of you saw in her heart, goodness and determination and she has proved to be the fastest learner in our group."

"Probably," I added. "Because each of you have helped her and taught her."

She nodded vigorously as she looked around at each one.

"My purpose here is this; to remind all of you to keep on doing everything that is necessary to live and survive and to help others. We have come to trust each other without question. But now we may have to do different things so that all the tribe may survive. You have already begun to do these things and take leadership. The boys mostly hunt and bring in meat. What if the boys were needed at a battle? Could you be the hunter for the tribe?

"What if we were separated into smaller groups and I sent Violet to each group and told one group to pretend to attack then run. Even if you didn't know that as you were being chased, we were setting in ambush to roll rocks down on them, would you run from the battle or want to stand and fight?"

"I believe we trust each other enough to follow instructions even if we don't know why," I concluded.

"We would follow instructions, Chee," Sunflower said, "why do you make it a question?"

"Because the rest of the tribe and others who may join us, might not agree. We must be so fully trusting of one another that we follow instructions even when everyone else wants to do something different.

"Our plan is to attack. So, you explain and attack. If others say no, don't count on them. Attack by yourself. Once you attack you are to strike and run. Some say 'no, we must finish the attack'. You still strike and run and if they will not follow, they will die.

"We trust one another even if no one else listens!" I said emphatically.

"Chee, I agree with Sunflower. Do you think we would not follow your plan?" Azalia said questioningly.

"Okay," I sighed. "Let me get to where I was going. What if each of you had a thunder stick?"

This thought struck home with considerable force.

"If we had thunder sticks, we could drive them out!" Blossom piped up.

"Remember the army of warriors from the north. In two or three minutes they would have overrun our position, killed us and taken our weapons.

"If we were in a bad position, out in the open or in a place where there was a high spot where they could shoot down on us, or they could surround us and leave us without food or water, they could defeat us.

"If we are caught in any of these situations, they might kill us and take our weapons and then nobody could stop them."

"We would still need a plan and others might say that with those weapons we could just go over and strike them down. Could you say 'no, the weapons have limits. We must follow the plan?"

Sunflower responded thoughtfully, "you think we could be like the conquistadors who walked right over to us because they had mighty weapons?"

"Yes! You must consider the distance. Remember the conquistadors were far out of range of your arrows but with their thunder sticks they struck the rocks you were hiding behind.

"Anyone can make an arrow go more than a hundred steps but you would not strike a deer to bring it down at half that distance.

"In the same way, the thunder sticks have limits and takes skill and practice to strike where you want them to strike.

"Others might want you to use your thunder sticks. That would not be allowed unless they were trusted and trained. Some would want to use it to bring down a deer but it makes a loud thunder and would tell the conquistadors where you are if they were close enough to hear."

"Okay," I concluded. "Let's tell the boys tomorrow and you girls can begin to plan a day trip. One day we hike out, shoot in the afternoon, stay overnight, shoot in the morning and come home."

"We will decide tomorrow on which day to go."

The excitement of striking with the thunder stick was going to ruin some sleeping tonight, I was sure.

The sun was barely up when I was awakened out of a sound sleep by Blossom and Lark standing at the front of my lean-to calling my name.

I responded groggily, "what's the problem?"

"Not a problem," Blossom asserted. "We want to go with thunder sticks today."

"But we haven't talked to the boys yet," I objected.

"We talk to them last night. They be ready this morning," Blossom answered.

"We haven't planned meals and gathered food and equipment," I objected again.

"Food is planned. We be ready in one hour." She said somewhat impatiently.

"I haven't finished my night's sleep," I said, and rolled over on my side and closed my eyes. "Go away!"

"We bring cold water. Help you get up." Lark said suppressing a giggle.

My eyes popped open and I sat up, "you better not get my sleeping bag wet. You'll be in bigger trouble than hiding a snake in it." I said with feigned anger.

This time they both giggled and Blossom said, "okay, you get one hour."

I flopped back down and closed my eyes, "okay, go away."

The boys arrived in less than an hour and the boisterous chatter and clanging of pots and pans was loud enough to wake the whole camp but it was probably intended for me.

I sat up, put on my boots and lace them up. The morning had enough of a chill that I put on a long sleeve, flannel shirt.

The boys would take turns carrying the .243 and the girls would carry the .22 magnum. They needed to get used to the weight of the weapon in their hands over a period of time. The guns would also stay in their cases to avoid any damage from inexperienced handlers.

We had enough ammunition for several shots in several sessions. The first lesson would be on gun safety and operation. I also took one piece of conquistador armor to see if the .22 magnum could penetrate it and at what distance it would still be effective.

It was a noisy, excited group that stepped out sprightly at the beginning of the hike. It was a good thing we weren't hunting. All the deer for miles around could hear us coming.

Of necessity, we had to take the wolf pups with us. There was no one to keep them and they wouldn't stay anyway if Blossom and I were headed off on a hike.

Everyone soon settled into their quiet, ground covering walk as the nervous energy wore off a bit. In a short time, we came to Grizzly Spring. We stopped only long enough to replenish our water supply and headed on toward the stream that came down from Noh Tay Dah's place.

By the time we came to a place in the valley where we had a hundred yards from bank to bank, we were close to the place where Deh Neh Totsi and her captors had stayed and where we had camped on our way back from that encounter. We decided to make that our base of operations for the night.

Across the stream and a dozen steps out into the valley was a mound of jumbled rocks where we could sit. It was also surrounded by several trees that would offer shade. We decided that would make a good place to give instruction.

After everyone was seated and comfortable, I began. "This is a dangerous weapon. We will no longer refer to them as thunder sticks. This is a .22 magnum, which we will call a twenty-two. That is a .243, which we will call a two forty three. Later, if things go well, we will add other names."

I proceeded to identify all the parts that were pertinent to the level of need; how each part worked and what it did.

"Never! And I repeat, never! Point a gun at anyone you don't intend to take down. Never assume the gun is not loaded. You always check!

"If I see you pointing it at people, if I see you forgetting to remove the magazine and check for a cartridge in the chamber, I will come at you like a grizzly bear and if you are careless several times, you will not get to shoot the gun again.

"Is that clearly understood!" I declared firmly.

They saw that I was intensely serious and they responded with serious nods.

"Lobo, come here," I said and handed him the .22.

He took it, turned away from the group, removed the magazine, and worked the bolt to check the chamber.

"Do I put the magazine back in the gun?" He asked.

"Great question. What do all of you think?" I asked.

There was a variety of responses.

"You are all right," I answered. "If we are looking at the gun to see how it works and feels, do not put the magazine in. If we are hunting or fighting you do put it in and you would check to see that there is a bullet in the chamber instead of seeing that there is not a bullet in the chamber. Always put the safety on.

"Remember how you shoot an arrow. You don't walk around with an arrow nocked to your bowstring. That is the ready position; then you draw back, lock on, release.

"If there is no bullet in the rifle, nobody can get hurt. If you are hunting or an enemy might be near, you do want bullets in the gun."

We spent another hour on threat levels and levels of readiness; handing the gun around and going through the safety protocols.

When I was satisfied that they understood and were operating safely, we moved to the next step.

"Let's look through the scope, lock on a target and dry fire. That means you will squeeze the trigger until it clicks. That is when it will fire; it won't fire now but it will when there is a bullet in the chamber."

When each had gone through this procedure several times, we broke for lunch.

While we were eating, I passed around a spotting scope so we could see our targets after each shot. We also looked through a rangefinder to practice judging distances.

"See those three trees together down the valley? How many steps to that middle tree?" I asked.

It became a fun guessing game but got them used to judging distances.

"Remember, a step is my big step not some little step. After you make your guess, Violet will tell you who is right," I said.

"I not know who is right!" She said plaintively.

"Look through this, hold it steady on the tree, and press this button. What do you see?" I asked.

"I see a six and a five then 'y' and a 'd'." She answered slowly.

"Listen carefully everyone," I looked around at everyone. "The 'yd' is a yard and a yard is a big step! How many of you said 'sixty five steps'?" I asked.

Their guesses had ranged from fifty five to seventy five. The boys and Sunflower had done more hunting and were the closest.

"See the big boulder all the way across the valley next to the cliff? How far is it?"

Again, they guessed and with the tree already identified, their guesses were all closer together this time.

"Violet, what is the distance?"

"I see one, two, seven yards," she answered.

"That's a hundred twenty seven yards. You all were a little short but you're getting close," I said.

"Each of you use the rangefinder on a few trees or rocks while guessing what you think the distance is before checking it.

"Just as it is with a bow and arrow, knowing the distance is essential. The farther you shoot; the higher you must aim. We will give you drawings of how to shoot at different distances later," I concluded.

Each one had their own paper target with a number assigned. We put sticks in the ground about three feet apart at fifty yards from the rocks where we would shoot.

"Youngest first," I said. "Violet, are you ready?"

"I don't know if I do right." She said timidly.

"I believe that with your attention to detail, you might be the best shot here." I said matter-of-factly. She smiled at my confidence and I guided her a little in standing and holding the rifle.

"Blossom, take the wolves about fifteen steps back and sit with them so they won't be spooked by the loud sounds," I instructed.

"Now, Violet, step-by-step do what I told you and put the crosshairs on the little circle at the middle of your target."

She squeezed off a shot and at fifty yards we could see the little black dot about two inches above and an inch to the right of the bull's-eye.

"That is great!" I enthused. "Take one more shot and put the crosshairs two inches below the circle in the center.

The second shot was even with the center and an inch to the right.

"That is great shooting!" I repeated, "here's the lesson on distance. The rifle is centered on a hundred yards. At fifty it is two inches high, at a hundred it is at center, at a hundred fifty it would be two or three inches low."

Next, I went through each step with Blossom, leaving her to shoot and taking the pups back to sit with them. They barely flinched when the gun went off.

Blossom's two shots were closer in height but both were to the right. Lark, Azalia and Sunflower had similar results.

"Let me adjust the sight. Since everyone is shooting to the right, I'll make it come back left. You boys better sight carefully if you want to keep up with the girls."

All three put their shots within an inch of center. Most were within a half-inch and Lobo had one that actually touched the center.

"Now let each of the girls take one more shot." All five put their last shot within a half-inch of center.

"Put your targets at a hundred yards and we will try again," I said. "Put a little circle around the holes in your target so we know which holes are new."

This time, the spotting scope was helpful. At a hundred yards, skill levels began to be manifested. Each of them put at least one shot out of three within the six inch circle.

Again, we marked out the existing holes and went back to try freestanding shots. At this distance the hunters, who knew how to take a deep breath and freeze in position as they locked on, were still hitting the paper, while the less experienced ones were missing the whole target.

Overall, I was impressed and encouraged. They were shooting at a good skill level and the afternoon shooting session came to an end.

Chapter 15

The days were getting longer and warmer. A lack of rain was creating drought conditions and the streams were beginning to run low. Even when the streams were flowing fully in the spring, the water would sink into the porous, volcanic sand and rocks of the huge valley floor.

Only during the wettest years did the streams actually flow into the valley and down to the river.

The boys put together the fishing gear and headed upstream. The girls were gathering some plants along the stream to make stew. Blossom and Violet were scouting around with the wolf pups and I was left with my morose musings on an unknown history.

A tsunami of horror was about to sweep over this land. To the south whole tribes were being destroyed and slaughtered. The tribes were not united and for the most part didn't even know of one another's existence.

Even if they were united and determined, they had little chance of standing against the weapons of the conquistadors.

All I know from history was that the conquistadors were stopped. How they were stopped and at what cost was never recorded. The indigenous people had only oral histories and the conquistadors avoided any records of defeats and failures.

This evening could possibly be the last time our little band would be together in an innocent, carefree campout. I would try not to spoil it.

The boys returned with enough fish to feed us for both days we would be here at our practice site. The wolf pups had caught a rabbit and brought it to Blossom. She skinned and dressed it, giving all the extras to the pups. Bringing the rest of it to the campfire, they roasted it for a while then cut it into small pieces to add to the stew.

As I had hoped, the jovial and boisterous, repartee was fun and encouraging.

"Are the children taking care of their old father okay this time?" Azalia asked.

Lark's head came up quickly to see where this taunt was going, but she relaxed and joined the laughter that followed.

"Everyone just left me sitting here by myself," I lamented. "Even my dear pups deserted me."

"We are sorry," Sunflower said with feigned seriousness. "There was nothing for you to do. We didn't bring any beans for you to cook!"

"What!" Lobo exclaimed. "We not have campout without beans!"

Everyone laughed as we recalled various jokes and teases from the past that were directed towards one another.

Lark spoke up, shaking her head sadly, "I only know one joke and I could not find snake to put in sleeping bag."

They all laughed as they gave a thumbs up to Lark and pointed at me.

"That's because I found all the snakes and put them in a sack and I will deliver them later tonight!" I responded.

As darkness closed in and the stars blinked on in a cloudless sky, the mood grew more serious. There is something about staring into a campfire, watching the smoke swirling upward above the leaping flames and the sparks flying up and dancing into the night, that promotes introspection and serious thought.

After a long silence, Lobo broke in gently, "you say conquistadors will come. We cannot stand against their weapons and hard coverings. Will we flee to the North? Can we flee far enough that they will not follow? Will you bring more thunder sticks or rifles that we can fight them?"

Sunflower added, "can we flee far enough and fast enough to escape? Can grandmother and little ones, those with babies not fall behind and die?"

I paused and took a deep breath. "I do not know what will happen. I do know that we will prepare. We will think what could happen and what we could do. We will talk and plan together."

"So much has been thrown on you all that others can't seem to understand. You had to learn to use the bows and arrows to get food. Only a few others worked to become good at it. You had to make a garden and the others saw too much work. I'm hoping our new friends will take that job and work to complete it."

"When the conquistadors come, it will be too late to prepare. So, we are beginning now. We will learn to shoot a rifle. We will learn when to fight, where to fight and how to fight."

"Chee, am I big enough to fight?" Violet asked plaintively.

"Well, yes and no. If warriors are coming and they get close, the .22 will take them down. If they get too close you can't outrun them or fight them." I answered.

"Actually, I have a special job in mind for you that you can do better than anyone else."

"What is it, Chee?" Several asked in chorus.

"She will keep track of the battles and movements of people and armies and keep us all working together," I said.

"How can she do this? How will she know? How will she tell us?" There was a barrage of questions.

"Remember the first time you looked through the binoculars? You thought the deer had jumped right up close to you. Remember after you got used to them, we let Noh Tay Dah and Deh Neh Totsi look through them and they jumped and looked startled as the mountain goats seemed to jump towards them?"

Those who were there smiled at that remembrance.

"Sunflower and Azalia, you were at my house and Blossom was far away in a big building almost a day's walk away. Dorothy took a little box and you talked to Blossom and me. You told me, 'you are not here but your voice jump here'!" I reminded them.

They nodded and I continued, "I believe I can get some little boxes to send voices."

They looked at one another, questioning what that could mean or how it would work.

"Let's say five of you go down the valley and space yourselves every three hundred yards. The last one is up on a mound and he turns and shouts, 'army comes', the next person turns and shouts, 'army comes' right up to the last who shouts to us, 'army comes'.

We grab our stuff and get away. The army gets here and no one is here."

"With the little voice box one person far down the valley could say, 'an army is coming but there are only about fifteen warriors and conquistadors only one is on a horse beast," I proposed.

"Now we can make decisions. Do we flee or are there some good places to set an ambush? Do we all hide and let them walk into a trap? Do the girls flee and let the fleet warriors chase them to a bunch of rocks where they turn and begin to take them down? When the slower ones stop, they are right below the cliff where the boys are hiding and the slow half of this army tries to scurry through the bushes like rabbits with no place to hide?"

"Information wins the battles," I emphasized.

They were listening and picturing the battles as I described them and nodding in understanding.

"One more battle where Violet directs," I said smiling.

"Violet is up on the high mountain with a small group. Impala and Little Badger are far to the south watching for the army. Lobo is up the mountain to get a deer. Sunflower, Azalia and Lark are with the village to protect and guide them to a new site if needed. Blossom and I are far to the north looking for places to set ambushes or hide the tribe."

"Impala and Little Badger calls but only Sunflower is close enough to hear, 'a big army is coming! We don't know if they will follow the river and come to the village or leave the river and go north.' Sunflower can reach Violet with the message. Violet calls Lobo to tell him to return to the village immediately. And she calls me to give me the message."

"I tell her to let us all know when the army starts one way or the other."

"Impala calls, 'they are leaving the river and going north.' Sunflower tells Violet. Violet calls me and we decide to meet at the next stream beyond Noh Tay Dah's stream at the valley where we rescued Deh Neh Totsi and the children. Violet calls Lobo and Sunflower. Sunflower calls Impala and Little Badger to meet at the village, and we all head to the meeting place to set an ambush.

"That is how Violet can keep us connected."

"She could also be connected to the tribe and tell Deh Neh Totsi to bring plenty of food to our camp so we can keep track of the big army without leaving our place and traveling all the way back for food," I concluded.

Lobo was gazing off into the distance somewhat awe-struck at the possibilities. "This is possible?" He almost whispered.

"Yes, and that is why I have hope," I said seriously.

They all looked at little Violet with new eyes.

"You think I can do this, Chee? I don't know how to make voice go far away," she said hesitantly.

"I will teach you. I know you can. I know you have the kind of mind that sees the details and I will help you put it all together in the weeks to come," I assured her.

"But first, we must learn our new weapons. Tomorrow you older ones move on to the .243 and longer distances. Tonight, let's get a good night's sleep," I concluded.

The next morning after a leisurely breakfast, we went back to the shooting range.

"This is a .243. It is bigger and shoots further than the .22. The big benefit is that it is accurate at three hundred yards and would still go through the armor of a conquistador at five hundred yards and even further.

"The downside is that the bigger the gun is, the bigger the kick against your shoulder. You have to learn to not flinch or move because of the kick.

"Let's set up our targets at a hundred yards for the first shots and see how it feels."

I took the breastplate of the conquistador armor and set it on a rock as a target also. We needed to see if the .22 Magnum would go through at a hundred yards.

"We will start with the boys. Hold the rifle firmly but not tensely. Shoot with the same procedures as the .22."

"Blossom, take the pups back a little further. This rifle will make a much bigger noise."

Lobo was first and the bigger rifle looked more comfortable for his size than the .22.

After the first shot, he turned and grinned at me. "It jumped and kick but not hurt me!" He exclaimed.

"Take two more shots and see if you focus on the kick so much that it makes you miss the target. That's what we mean by 'flinching'."

Lobo placed the next two shots within the circle without flinching.

Following Lobo's lead, the other two boys held firmly and placed all three shots within the circle.

The girls were a bit reluctant but they also absorbed the kick and hit the target.

"Ignore the kick and stay focused on the target," I instructed.

"Blossom, see if a .22 bullet will go through the conquistador armor."

It went through with ease which meant we needed to check it at two hundred yards.

"Let's angle down the valley to where we can shoot at two hundred yards," I said.

It took a while to set up the targets and armor, but they were eager to try the more difficult shots.

The .22 Magnum still carried enough speed and momentum at two hundred yards to go through armor. This was great news. We could pick off their army bit by bit by striking and staying out of the range of the harquebuses.

At two hundred yards, the boys were able to put two out of three shots into the target. Sunflower also put two shots into the target while Azalia and Lark each had one.

"Your discipline with a bow is serving you well. This is really good shooting," I said.

After each one had shot several more rounds, we went to collect the targets. On the way back, Lobo asked quizzically, "you say this rifle shoots five hundred yards. We cannot even see target at five hundred yards."

"Good observation," I responded. "Allow me to show you."

We were passing a mound of dirt that was typical of the Little Valley. We stopped there so I could explain.

"Pretend you are an army. You are bunched together, maybe marching. Make two rows and face the mound. Shorter ones in front, taller ones to the back.

"Now the whole group is one target. From the head of ones in the back row to the knees of those in the front row is about five feet. Four people standing beside one another not packed together is about ten feet. It is a five foot by ten foot target."

"Remember when the army from the north attacked us and you - foolishly I might add - came to save me. Blossom had a new, stronger bow and was shooting downhill. Her shot went high but struck one who was farther down the hill. The target wasn't just one warrior but a whole bunch to shoot into."

They all nodded at the remembrance while picturing my description in the current, visual illustration.

"So, we get five hundred yards from the army we strike the army?" Impala asked.

"Basically yes!" I answered. We would almost never engage with a large, well-armed army and let them get close. We would fight at our distance."

"The only time we would let them get as close as two hundred yards is if we were up a steep hill or on a cliff and had a good, fast escape route," I concluded.

"Chee, I have some hope now," Sunflower said. With determination in her voice. "Maybe we can win this war!"

"We will surely try!" I said as we arrived back at our campsite and began to pack for the trip back to the village.

Things at the village were going well, but to me, it had the feel of a calm before the storm.

I collected the rifles, put them in their cases and put them in my lean to.

Grandmother, Sweet Pea and Chip came to visit. The children and the wolf pups hit it off immediately. Our hyperactive pups finally had some human pups who were as hyperactive as they were. The rope toy that I had brought, became the fetch toy. Sometimes their throw wasn't very far and the pups would jump and catch it in midair. When the children got tired and flopped down, the pups came and snuggled against them to get scratched and petted.

I turned to Blossom and remarked, "I think someone stole our wolf pups."

She smiled knowingly and replied, "they come back when they get hungry."

Cedo and the men of his group took us to see the garden. While nothing was up yet, they showed us where they had planted various things. They had enlarged the garden area that we had made last year and had another spot about four times as large for a big cornfield.

"We need more maize seed to fill all that space," Cedo said as Sunflower and Deh Neh Totsi interpreted. I added it to my list for my next trip.

"This will be a wonderful addition to our food supply," Sunflower enthused, and everyone complemented them on their good work.

Before I left, I pulled Lobo and Sunflower aside and showed them where I had put the rifles.

"We don't want any guns visible or even known by any-one outside our group at this time but I want you to know they are there if needed."

"Lobo, I will bring a bigger rifle. It shoots further but strikes harder too." I said and grinned at him.

"Actually, it is very similar to my rifle so you have seen and heard what it sounds like."

"Imagine a big army with many cook fires. Fifteen or twenty soldiers around each one, sitting and relaxing. We need to get only eight hundred yards away. That's almost a half mile. It is eight hundred big steps and you thought fivr hundred yards was far."

"From a higher position on a hill or cliff, we have a tar-get that is about ten feet high and twenty feet wide. Once you know how much higher you should aim, you can drop every bullet into that target. Not all will hit someone, but if they do, they will still go through their armor at that distance."

"Wah!" He exclaimed, "they not even know where we hide."

"At dusk we could stand up and wave and they still couldn't see us!" I said.

"Will the .243 shoot that far?" Sunflower asked.

"I will get that info when I go back for supplies," I said.

"Everything here seems to be going smoothly so I'll head back this evening. I have many things to get and many more to order," I concluded.

The opening of the portal door notified everyone that I was back. Dorothy quickly arranged with the others to have a covered dish dinner the next evening.

Early the next morning, I started my shopping trip. Maize seed was first on the list but there wasn't much avail-able. I found some field corn that boasted a high protein content that could be ground for meal, and they found a hand- turned grinder to make the job easier.

Ammunition needed to be bought at different places so as not to raise questions. We needed only a few boxes for most of the guns we had. The .308 and .243 were the ones that required thousand round boxes.

Ben and Sharon arrived a little early and let me know that Doc Marlin was planning to come also.

"Won't that make our discussions a bit difficult?" I inquired with a hint of exasperation.

"Well, when I let it slip that we were getting together, inviting him was easier than trying to explain why he couldn't come," Ben said quietly.

"We are at the point where I have to requisition the real stuff. We need rifles, ammo and communication equipment," I said.

"We will just have to stick to the South American jungle tribes narrative," Ben said.

The others arrived soon after and our conversation was warm and cheerful.

We caught up a bit on family happenings and people we knew. The evening was flowing by quickly.

"So, what is happening with the incursion of the loggers into the tribal lands?" Doc asked quizzically.

Everyone glanced sideways at one another and I took a long drink of coffee to give me time to formulate an answer.

"The incursion is still a threat but it hasn't been forced upon us yet," I answered

"So, the scenario of invading loggers was a real situation not just a 'what if'? He inquired.

"That's pretty much the case," I said. "Part of my purpose this trip is to get some rifles and ammo for my little group," I responded.

"How is your little group doing?" Heather broke in trying to turn the conversation. I appreciated her help.

"You mentioned that they were doing some gardening. How is that coming?" Sharon asked hopefully.

"Great!" I said with some relief, "they have made it five times as big as my little garden from last year. Some of them have really taken to gardening."

"You tried some different stuff like carrots, beans and corn, didn't you?" Ben asked, "how did that turn out?"

"They loved it and decided it was worth continuing so I'm taking back more seed corn," I said.

"Where did they find open ground in the jungle?" Doc asked quizzically.

This time the sideways glances were hard to not notice.

"Well, as I understand it, there was a fire that cleared some land and we were using that area for the garden," I answered realizing we were getting into deep water here.

"So, was this land in the jungle proper or on land that had been already logged by the loggers?" He asked suppressing a grin.

I realized the jungle doesn't burn that easily until after it is logged and the brush dries. Nor would the jungle dwellers come out to land that had been logged over because it would be near the logging operation.

"Well, the fire burned a brushy area where there were no big trees," I said apparently unconvincingly.

With a quick grin, Doc said, "you mentioned you needed some rifles. I can help with that. What are you looking for?"

"I'd like a couple .308's and a couple .243's all with scopes," I said, breathing an inward sigh of relief.

"Why not AK-47s or AR fifteens?" He asked, "they have a lot more firepower."

"We wanted to keep things at a longer range for safety reasons," I said.

"How are you going to get long-range shots in the jungle?" He asked. He was openly grinning now.

Everyone was looking uncomfortably concerned so I grinned back at him and said, "there are areas outside the jungle where we would flee to, when we decide to fight."

"So, this isn't in a jungle and it isn't in South America. You aren't part of a militia now, are you?" He asked seriously.

"I will tell you this much. There is no militia. We are not operating in the United States but we are working in support of the interests of the United States, not against them," I answered firmly.

"I would be willing to volunteer to go with you," he said. "I have combat experience and a lot of other skills and experience that could be helpful in the situation you are describing."

"I appreciate that, but the decision would need to be made in consultation with my advisors. Your expertise could be valuable for the cause. These guys here are my helpers who get stuff, but they have never been in the field and don't know the people and situation in detail," I said.

"Maybe we could discuss it further after I get advice and permission. In the meantime, we do appreciate your help and insight and if you are amenable, we would like to get advice in the days ahead."

"I'd love to be involved, just let me know," he responded.

After Doc had gone, I turned to the others and remarked, "we didn't fool him for long. He still won't be able to guess a time/space portal but he figured out the subterfuge pretty quickly."

"Are you going to bring him in?" Cam asked.

"I'd love to have him, but necessary secrecy and the danger of no return may give him pause," I said.

"What do you all think? If he were to have the details, would he keep the secret?" I asked.

"I think he would and I think we would all feel better if you had someone with you who knows and understands combat," Heather replied.

"If we are all in agreement on this, we can let him see the whole picture during the next visit or two. In the meantime, here are my current needs. In addition to the rifles and ammunition I need a solar generator, a base communication system, handheld radios with solar chargers. I put some suggestions together and will get a pair of handheld units to take back to introduce to our group and explain procedures.

"Actually, I've already introduced them to the concept. When the girls were here, they talked on the telephone with Blossom and me when we were at the hospital," I concluded.

The next day after getting all the supplies on my list of immediate needs, I headed back through the portal.

The .308 was in the shed, ready to go, so I took it along with a few boxes of ammunition. My pack was full and every pocket had something in it, even if only a few more energy bars. It was good to be going downhill most of the way.

My lean-to was getting stuffed again. I would either need to build a new one or disburse more stuff. Mor Dak Sah was giving out fewer provisions each week so that everyone would work to provide for themselves.

Cedo's group got the seed corn and immediately went out to put in a few more rows. They would put in a few rows each week for a few weeks so that the harvest would be spread out longer.

Lobo and the boys were eager to try out the .308 so we planned a day trip. Sunflower decided to go so she could see if she could handle the heavier gun and strong recoil.

I also wanted to get Violet started on the two-way radios. I explained the on/off button, the press to talk, release to listen switch and what the channel selection meant. Later on, she might have to handle multiple channels. She also learned to use the solar charger to recharge the radio battery.

"Don't be concerned if something goes wrong and you forget what to do, we will be back this evening and will go over things again," I said.

"We will call in about an hour to practice, then a few hours later when we get to where we will shoot.

"I will say 'calling Violet, come in Violet, over.'

"When I talk, I press the talk button and when I say 'over', I release it and it is your turn.

"You press the button and say, 'I hear you, Chee, over'.

"After each time you talk, say 'over' and release the button so you can hear me talk.

"When we are done, we say 'over and out' and the other says whatever you want to say, 'okay', 'be careful', 'see you later', but end with 'over and out'. That means we are done talking."

"I try to remember, Chee" she said hesitantly.

"You will do fine. Remember this is just practice for fun. The hardest thing to remember is press to talk, release to listen," and I demonstrated on the unit I was carrying.

We headed out and in less than two hours were at the Grizzly Spring where we replenished our water bottles and I called Violet.

"Calling Violet, this is Chee, calling Violet, over," I said.

"Chee, I hear you. It work good. Where you at?"

The signal went dead so I assume she was done.

"This is Chee, remember to say 'over' so I know it's my turn, over."

"Oh, I forgot. Where you at? Over," she said.

"Very good! We are at Grizzly Spring and will call back in a few hours, over."

"Okay, I done. Over and out," she finished.

"Excellent! You are getting it right. This is Chee, over and out."

We needed to go only far enough that the sound of the gunshots wouldn't get back to the village. Towards the east and out to the edge of the big valley, there were small hills and scattered buttes that would give opportunity for some long-range shooting.

We skipped the hundred yard range and moved the targets out to two hundred yards to zero in. The first shots were more for the purpose of adjusting to the recoil. Sunflower handled it well but acknowledged that her shoulder hurt.

"You will get a .243, but in an emergency, you can handle the .308 as well," I advised.

After only a few adjustments to the scope, they put almost every shot onto the target.

Let's try some five hundred yard shots," I suggested and went to a cliff where the rangefinder confirmed a five hundred yard distance.

We stood two twelve-foot poles against the cliff to mark a ten foot wide target and scratched a line on the cliff face twelve feet up at the top between the poles. We also scratched a line two feet up to make a ten by ten target.

"I believe we will be able to see where a bullet strikes the rock face of the cliff," I said and pulled out my ballistics chart.

"Believe it or not, the .243 has less drop than the .308 at five hundred yards. The advantage is that the .308 with a much bigger bullet will do more damage to what it hits. At five hundred yards the .243 drops about three and a half feet, but the .308 drops about four feet." I instructed

"So, put the crosshairs exactly between the two poles and one foot below the top line and you should hit near the center of the square. Lobo's three shots were three and four feet from center and all were to the right and high.

Impala's first shot was also high and right.

"Let me adjust the sight just a little and you aim about two feet below the top line. Some rounds are better than others at a distance so we will assume they aren't dropping quite as much," I advised.

This time, Lobo's next two shots were closer in height and nearer the center.

Little Badger had the best shots. All three were within two feet of center and one was right at the visual center.

"As you can see, you probably won't hit an individual target but when a group is walking or marching or sitting around a campfire, you can strike the enemy and especially strike fear and not be in danger," I pointed out.

"One more thing; when you sight this time, look down the row of dots and see which dot is at the center of the target." All three sighted and counted and came to the same conclusion.

"That is now your zero point for five hundred yards. Use that point to fix on the target instead of guessing two feet down," I said. "This will make you even more accurate.

This time all three shots from each of them were hitting within a circle about three feet in diameter.

"Great shooting," I exclaimed. "Let's clean up. Always pick up empty shells. Not in the middle of an actual moving battle, of course," I added.

Little Badger spoke up, "that rifle kick hard. My shoulder sore!"

The others agreed.

Sunflower added, "it kick hard. I maybe not use .308."

"But you didn't flinch and throw off your shot!" I said, "and in a battle, you won't even feel it.

"Let's check in with Violet," I changed the subject. "You need to learn to use the little box too."

"Chee to Violet. Come in Violet. Over," I called.

Violet responded immediately, "this Violet. You sound close, we hear good." There was a click a short pause, then another click, "over".

I showed the boys and Sunflower how to press to talk, release to hear and say, "over".

Lobo tried it. "This Lobo. We shoot five hundred yards. Over."

"This Violet. Can other girls use radio? Over."

Impala had the radio, "this Impala. Chee say yes. We say hello to everyone. Over."

Each of the girls took a turn and Little Badger had a turn as well.

"This Azalia, where you shoot? Over."

I handed the radio to Sunflower, "this Sunflower, down valley, valley before Noh Tay Dah place. Down where valley wide to five hundred yards, over."

"This Azalia, that long, long way. Voice go far. We talk all over hill and valley."

"This is Chee, Violet, keep the radio on in case we need to tell you something. Over and out."

"This is Violet, over and out." Came the reply.

Chapter 16

The trip back to the village was without incident. We were tired and hungry when we arrived, but the rest of the girls had a good supper prepared and we dug in immediately.

The boys and Sunflower talked excitedly about the big thunder stick that could strike into an army at five hundred yards and more.

Sunflower remarked, ".308 kick hard, I use .243, it shoot just as good."

"But .308 hit harder," Little Badger said.

They sounded like a bunch of hunters at a camp touting the virtues of their various rifles.

It was a pleasant evening around the fire, discussing the tribe, the food supply and the lack of rain that they had experienced for the last few weeks. Fortunately, while the stream was a little lower, there was still plenty of water for everyone and the garden.

The boys decided they would head out early in the morning and go west to the higher elevations where the deer seemed to have migrated.

"We need to bring two deer so there is food for all," Lobo declared.

"We still don't want the rest of the tribe to know about the thunder sticks yet, so you will need to use your bows," I said.

They nodded in understanding and we all headed for bed.

The next day, about mid-morning, two of the men came rushing into camp with potentially bad news. They were on lookout duty and had gone out on a finger of land that ended in a mesa at the edge of the valley.

While the mesa wasn't as high as hills near the village, it was out far enough and high enough to see far down the river.

"Army come up river," they exclaimed breathlessly and Sunflower interpreted so I could hear what all the excitement was about.

As the hubbub quieted down a little, I asked, "how far down river are they?"

"They go slow, maybe whole day to here," they answered.

"Girls, get Yul D'Vey and Cedo. We must plan quickly," I instructed. "Sunflower, set aside a pack for you girls and give extra packs to each fire group. The most important item will be food, then clothing and bedding. You have gone out on trips enough to know what is needed."

They immediately began setting out packs and putting in food and essentials.

By this time Yul D'Vey and Cedo had arrived. Turning to Yul D'Vey I asked, as Sunflower translated, "do you know how to go down to the cave and pack in supplies? Are there ones who can operate the ropes?"

"Yes, several go down to cave. Others here use ropes," he answered.

"Let everyone decide about their things. What things they take, things they put in cave, things they leave here. Some of the things that they leave, we can hide in the rocky places up the mountain.

"Go, tell everyone to divide their things and take things to the cave. As soon as you can get your things ready, get your group to the cave and haul up baskets of supplies to store there."

"Sunflower, may I have Violet, Blossom and Lark to help take everything that must not fall into the hands of the conquistadors up to the stash? We will take all extra knives, bows and arrows, ammunition and anything that would help them.

"I will leave the .308 and three boxes of ammunition for Lobo. You can put it with his pack in my lean to," I concluded.

Getting the three younger girls together, I explained the situation.

"Violet, the radio may be the best weapon we have. Guard it carefully and keep it charged. Here is a box that you set in the sun whenever you can. This is a cable. It plugs in here in the box and in this hole in the radio to keep the radio working."

She went over the procedure perfectly.

"Turn the radio off at night. The radio will keep working at night if you had the box in the sun long enough during the day. If the radio doesn't keep working, turn it off to save the battery and we will talk as the sun comes up and as the sun goes down. We will set times during the day when we can turn it on together."

"I do my best, Chee," she said hesitantly as the weight of responsibility fell on her shoulders.

"Your best is all we ever need and you will be good," I smiled at her.

Lark and Blossom were waiting as I finished. "Load everything that I mentioned into your packs," I said.

Unfortunately, all the ammunition, knives and modern stuff quickly filled the packs and left little room for personal or camping items.

"We will have to get what we need after we put the ammo and stuff through to the shed," I said.

"What is shed?" Lark asked.

"Oh yes!" I said, "you have never been to the stash, the shed or my home." I said amusingly. "It is where I take things and get things that you see and wonder about.

"We don't know where the army is going, so we don't know where or when we will go. We just want to be sure the conquistadors don't get these weapons."

The trip to the portal went normally and both girls were a bit awed by how big a pile of "stuff" was at the stash. Blossom had seen it covered in snow when she went past and hadn't really observed it.

We went through the portal and into the shed. Lark was moving slowly and looking at everything and understanding nothing and I didn't have time to explain.

"Set all the ammunition on a pile and we will take what we think we need," I instructed.

"We must prepare for two possibilities. If they come up the river, we will meet them at the butte that overlooks the river. We will rain down strikes until they figure out where we are and come after us. Then we will run back, around the next set of cliffs and get above them again, and take out more.

"We will lead them away from the tribe that is fleeing even if only half of them chase us.

"Every trail we come to, we will cross and they will have to decide which direction to go and try to pick up our trail again.

"We know the country now; every cliff and every high spot; where the water is; and at every turn we will strike down a few more. "They will not get us easily," I gritted out.

"So, for this plan we pack light?" Blossom asked.

"Yes! Three boxes of ammunition, two or three bottles of water and lots of energy bars; two or three dozen," I said.

"What is other plan?" Lark asked, still staring wide-eyed in all directions at computers and piles of food and clothing.

"If they stay in the valley because they want to go north faster, we will ambush them or just let them keep on going," I said more calmly.

"We will pack as heavy as we can carry comfortably. Use all that is on the first pile but add a coat for at night, some fishing gear, another couple boxes of ammunition, and an empty gallon jug which we will fill when we know there is no water ahead.

"Before we set our ambush, we will make a stash where we can replenish our supplies and travel with light packs to the ambush and do the same thing we would do in plan one," I concluded.

"Let's go back out to the stash and get our light packs ready. Actually, I think everything we need is right here," I said looking around.

"Can we say hello to Dorothy and show Lark your home?" Blossom asked.

"Not now, if the army leaves the river and goes north, we won't engage them until they get two or three days up the valley and away from our people. We will come back here and pack for that trip, perhaps we will have time to see Dorothy then," I said.

"Make sure your light pack is ready but leave it here. We will take the big binoculars to the top of the cliff here to watch which way they go."

I began to toss items on a pile for the long trip, since my short trip pack was ready. I would want the rangefinder for sure if we were going to shoot at four hundred or five hundred yards.

Blossom had the binoculars out and was searching down the river.

"I no see any army," she said in a puzzled tone.

"Maybe they are in a little valley and will come over a hill soon," I said.

Minutes went by with no sign of anyone, let alone an army.

Suddenly a patch of color not consistent with the rest of the desert brush and bushes caught my eye. It was too far, several miles in fact, and moving slowly but it did appear to be moving.

"Let me see the binoculars," I said.

Looking through the powerful glasses, brought the image close enough to see that it was a mass of people but it was still too far to make distinctions.

"They left where it first turned west. They should have followed it for several more miles. There is no water where they are or where they are headed," I said.

Blossom and Lark both used the binoculars for several minutes.

"They go slow, Chee," Blossom said.

Lark added, "It will take them hours to get straight across from us and I don't see any sign of water."

Scanning the valley to the north, there was no evidence of a water source. They would be making a dry camp tonight.

"Let's watch for another hour or so to be sure they don't realize their mistake and head back to the river," I advised.

The girls filled the next hour using the binoculars to view places up and down the river and across to the line of mountains in the east. The snow-covered peaks looked much closer than they were in reality.

From where the conquistadors were, the mountains behind us undoubtedly looked closer and more likely to have streams coming down the valleys.

My guess was that they would be angling over during the next few days.

What they probably didn't know was that the valley was filled for a thousand feet down with porous volcanic rock and sand and the streams sank out of sight before they even tried to flow over the valley.

After a little over an hour, it was clear that the army was committed to going north and we had time to plan our long trip.

Going back down to the portal, I thought I'd better let Sunflower know what was happening.

I put the solar charger on a rock to recharge the battery and pulled out the radio.

"Chee to Violet, come in Violet, over."

"This is Violet, over."

"Is Sunflower there? We need to report on the army and our plans, over."

There was a short silence and Sunflower came on.

"This Sunflower, where are you, Chee? What is happening?"

There was silence, then a click, then "over."

"The army is going north. We will trail along and see where they go. You can tell everyone that the danger is passed for today. Over."

Sunflower replied, "everybody get ready and fill cave and have packs but they be glad not to flee. Over."

"Being prepared is always good. Violet, charge the batteries and we will talk tomorrow. Chee over and out.

"We've got time. Now let's introduce Lark to Dorothy and let her visit my home."

Blossom ran to give Dorothy a hug and introduced Lark, while I called my advisors. They wanted to meet Lark and find out what was happening to require such a trip.

"We'll bring pizza!" Ben said.

"Don't forget ice cream! That would be unforgivable," I joked.

They showed up within the hour with pizza and ice cream and fortunately, we had lots of soft drink.

Lark was awed into a tongue-tied state but Blossom was keeping the conversation going.

Before the pizza was gone, Blossom had pretty much relayed all the happenings and plans that I was there to report.

"Since you now know everything that is going on, we may as well skip the ice cream and head back," I quipped.

Blossom frowned at me and said, "after we eat ice cream can I show Lark your house?"

"Sure! I imagine I'll still have a few things to talk about while you're gone," I said smiling at her as Blossom and Lark headed out for the tour.

"Lark seems nice," Sharon said.

"Not just nice but highly motivated and intelligent. She also has a weird sense of humor that you all would appreciate," and I related the snake in the bedroll story.

"Now that I would have loved to have seen!" Heather laughed.

"Besides letting you know why I won't be checking in for the foreseeable future and to let you know that the conquistadors are now in the valley, there's not much other news."

After some general conversation, we called to Lark and Blossom to come and say goodbye to our guests and they departed.

On the spur of the moment, I called Dr. Silver to see if he could give a tetanus, measles, smallpox and whatever else was in the concoction, shot in the morning.

He was genuinely interested in the girls and was happy to set an appointment before regular hours.

"Can we do showers?" Blossom asked.

"Okay, showers and bed. We have an early start tomorrow," I said resignedly.

The next morning, we met Dr. Silver at 7 AM for the inoculation.

"Is this the young lady with the lip that needed repaired? They did a beautiful job. It looks wonderful," Dr. Silver said enthusiastically.

Blossom beamed and said, "thank you!"

We had explained the "shot" to Lark and knowing that the other girls have been given one, she took hers stoically and was pleasantly surprised at how easy it was.

We didn't waste any time getting ready to head out to continue tracking the path of the conquistadors. If we could hardly see a whole army, I was confident they would never see three of us among the trees and bushes in the foothills.

It was soon evident that they were angling towards the foothills where we were traveling. They probably would need water soon even if they were carrying some.

We crossed the stream that came down from Noh Tay Dah's place, drank our fill and filled all of our small bottles.

The next small stream was five or six miles farther north and I hoped we could get some water there, because the next stream after that was fifteen miles away over some rugged terrain. That's fifteen miles as the crow flies and we weren't crows and we weren't flying.

We angled up into the mountains as we approached the first stream and it was almost dry two miles before it reached the valley. We found a spot where it surfaced and ran a small trickle for about a dozen feet before sinking into the sandy soil again.

We dug a hole where it was coming out of the streambed and let the dirt settle for a few minutes. It was deep enough to fill our small water bottles and we decided it would be prudent to put at least a quart into our gallon jugs.

After a short rest we trudged on. At two or three miles per hour, we were about eight hours from the next stream.

Several times we climbed to the top of a taller ridge to search for the army but couldn't find any sign of it. If my calculations were correct, they were at least a day and a half from the larger stream that I expected would flow out into the valley due to its size.

The stream we were aiming for and the bigger creek, flowed towards each other as they came out of the mountains putting them only three miles apart where they entered the valley.

We reached the stream valley by early evening. We needed to watch for scouts looking for water. At least I assumed they would send out scouts to find water under the circumstances.

The stream bed was dry but I expected to find water not far up into the mountains.

There was a long finger of land reaching out at least two miles into the valley. The side of the hill was a cliff that got higher and higher as the valley sloped down. We needed to see what the other side of this mesa looked like. This side was like a two mile long, unscalable castle wall.

For tonight, we needed to find a campsite. Tomorrow we would hike down the top of the mesa and see how it ended and what was on the other side.

About a half mile up the stream we could actually smell water. The air was heavier and cooler but a sharp incline of jumbled boulders and rocks showed where a beautiful succession of tumbling water and waterfalls would rush down to the valley below during the heavy spring runoff.

Eagerly we climbed the Rocky barrier and found a delightful and beautiful spot.

A stream was tumbling over rocks at the back of a large, mostly level space of more than an acre. Against the cliff wall on the right was a sandy beach with undercut rocks providing living quarters at the base of the cliff.

Several large, old cottonwood logs lay along its beach and several large cottonwood trees provided shade.

In the center of the acre was a pond, lined with cattails on the left side across from the beach. There was also some brush and willows along this side from the beach to the rocks where we entered.

This was the endpoint of the stream, most of the year. The stream flowing in was small but much more than a trickle. The whole area was big enough and sandy enough that it all sank into the soil and rocks and none flowed out above ground.

As we stood staring at the beautiful setting and breathing in the cool air, I dropped my pack, grinned at the girls and declared, "this is a campsite!"

"Look, Chee!" Blossom said excitedly, "I see fish come up!"

Sure enough, there was a circular ripple spreading out from near the cattails.

We carried our packs and looked around for the most suitable spot to build a fire and set up camp. The alcove under the cliff was a logical site, especially if it rained, but the beauty and fresh air at the log made it a great spot too. We finally decided to camp at the log and retreat to the cave if we needed better shelter.

The beach extended along the side of the cliff for a dozen feet past the spot where the top of the chute began its plunge to the valley below. The chute was at least thirty feet above the floor of the little valley which sloped gently downward along the side of the cliff getting wider and wider as it made its way to the big valley.

From this little sliver of sand, we could sit and watch not only the few miles down our valley but miles of rolling ground covered in sagebrush and bushes extending far out into the desert.

The only indication of water was the scattering of junipers and cedars both in the little valley and on out into the big valley.

Our site was high and set back enough that only a large fire that cast a glow up the cliff could be seen from any distance. The tops of the cottonwoods would look like shrubs along the cliff.

We didn't need a fire pit. We hadn't planned to do much cooking. There was one small kettle in which we could heat water for hot chocolate and in the morning, we could have oatmeal with some sugar and powdered milk. Powdered orange juice could be put into one of our water bottles for a lunch drink tomorrow.

"Let's see if there's any more fish in the pond," I decided.

Now I wished I had brought my fiberglass, take down, casting rod and reel with lures or salmon eggs, but I'd hadn't anticipated that I would have the opportunity to fish.

Worms were hard to find but once I got a willow rod and the hook and line installed, we managed to find some bugs in the rotten wood.

I made a bobber out of a piece of aluminum foil by making a bubble like a chocolate drop, twisting the top to seal the air in and twisting it around the line. If the bug didn't float the bobber would keep it near the top of the water.

Keeping a bush between me and the water, I swung the bait and bobber out into the pond.

The ripples had not even subsided, when a good-sized fish hit the bait. I had to be careful not to break the line or the pole so I played it a little and got it close enough to shore that I could reach down and grab it. It was about fourteen inches long. I had seen only two longer cutthroat trout in all my camping experiences. One was netted out of a high-altitude lake when I worked for the game department, and one was caught out of a remote beaver pond.

Since the law that made it illegal to use a part of a fish as bait wouldn't be written for another five hundred years, I decided to keep the innards in case I needed them. The bug had worked well so I stuck with them and caught two more about twelve inches long at other spots along the edge of the pond.

One fish that size was enough for a meal so I quit fishing for the day.

We roasted them over the fire with seasoning salt and they were delicious.

Before the sun went down, we went out to that little sliver of sand at the top of the chute to look down the valley.

"Each of you look through the binoculars and search the valley for the army. It would be nice to know where they were," I said.

"We will also discuss possibilities. If there is no reason to engage, we simply watch them go. If we do engage, here are charts showing how high to aim for long distance shooting," I said as I handed Lark a sheet.

"Blossom, there is no point in shooting five hundred yards and farther with the .22 magnum. If you are shooting at a bunched group, it might scare them but it won't go through armor," I warned.

"At a hundred yards you are right on; at two hundred yards, the drop is three to six inches and at three hundred yards it's a foot to a foot and a half.

"Lark, you are on at two hundred yards and there's only six to eight inches drop at three hundred yards.

"You can memorize the average for longer yards, but we don't plan to engage in those distances.

"While you look that over, I'll call Violet," I said.

"This is Chee calling Violet. Come in Violet, over."

"This Violet. You not real loud. You far away? Over."

"Yes! We are twenty miles or more away and around a hill so the fact that you hear me at all is good. Over."

"Sunflower want to talk. Here is Sunflower."

"Chee this is Sunflower. We are all okay here. We are ready to go if we need to. Do you see the army? Over."

"We don't see the army now. We are ahead of it. We will see where it goes in the next few days. Put Violet back on and we will talk tomorrow. Over."

"This Violet. We talk tomorrow? Over."

"We plan to start early tomorrow so let's not talk until tomorrow night, understand? Over."

"I understand. I keep radio working. I be ready. Over."

"I know you will. I'm counting on you. This is Chee, over and out."

Blossom spoke up as our conversation on the radio ended.

"I think there is glow from fire. Look left of trees at end of valley and far out in big valley."

She had handed me the binoculars as she identified the place she was describing. It was also starting to get dark, so the glow should get more pronounced. "I think you are right. Depending on how early they start, they should be going past the end of this Mesa around noon," I said.

"Look! Down our valley but off to the right. I thought I saw movement," I whispered.

"What did it look like?" Lark whispers back.

Keeping our voices just above a whisper, I responded, "it could have been a deer but deer should all be in the high country. Besides everyone here wears deerskin coverings so people look like deer," I continued

Our rifles were back at the camp site some fifty or sixty yards away. The hill on the other side of the pond went up sharply to a ridge and the ridge angled up and got steeper as it disappeared up the side of the mountain.

Again, I saw movement and both Lark and Blossom saw it also. A harquebus at less than a hundred yards and shooting buckshot could take us out rather quickly.

Once again, I saw movement in the gathering dusk and I heaved a sigh of relief, "it's an animal coming for water."

Suddenly, Blossom squealed, "it's Kih Ta and Sah Sha!"

Sure enough! Their sharp sense of smell had enabled them to track us for twenty miles.

The wolves stopped long enough to lap up some water and then bounded around the outer side of the pond and into our arms… And faces… And legs.

We all dropped to a knee and accepted their enthusiastic greetings back-and-forth from one to another. In a few minutes they calmed down enough for us to get up and make our way back to the campsite.

We sat down with our backs to the log and the wolves trotted down to the pond for a longer more leisurely drink. They came back, tongues lolling out and dripping water and settled in, one between Lark and Blossom and the other between Blossom and me.

We would all sleep better with the wolves on guard.

"Let's pack tonight so we can get an early start. All water jugs must be filled. We will leave our packs halfway down the top of the mesa. If they see us and decide to come after us, we can run for a mile without packs then pick up our packs and head towards the next stream.

"When they see water, they should go back and guide the army around the end of the mesa to the stream.

"We will head for the high country, find a point and watch them," I concluded.

After a good night's sleep, guarded by the wolves, we got up with the glowing promise of dawn and put the last minute things in our big packs.

The packs were designed to separate the big pack and leave a large Fanny pack for hiking. We had water bottles in our pockets and the small pack had a water bottle and energy bars.

We also took ammunition, rangefinder and binoculars.

The only way to the top of the mesa was up the steep stream bed, then angle across the side of the hill to get above the cliff, putting us on top of the mesa. The top of the mesa was mostly flat with some bushes and boulders. The north side was a long series of deep gashes and ravines aiming down towards a valley about three miles away, A distinct line of green indicated a likely water supply.

There were a few scrubby looking trees scattered along the top of the mesa and one of them stood near the edge, where a larger, deeper ravine sloped steeply down. There was a jumble of rocks just over the edge near the top, where we could stash our packs and with the tree as sentinel, find them quickly when we came back.

"Let's get to the end and see what we can see," I said cheerfully. It felt good to get most of the weight off of my back.

The end of the mesa made a beautiful lookout spot. There were some large boulders along the top where we could hide or steady a rifle to shoot over.

Lark went around the end to the north. We had observed the south side as we traveled to the pond and found that a sheer fifty to sixty foot wall was protecting us on the south and east side.

There was one chute that could be climbed, but it was narrow and steep. From the base of the cliff there was a steep slope going down another hundred feet to the floor of the valley on both the south and east side.

From the base of the slope, the finger of land continued on out into the big valley for another half mile. It ended in another small mesa that wasn't very high. The ground fell away from this original long gradual slope down into the valley.

There were numerous patches of brush and some junipers and cedars scattered about from the little valley far out into the big valley.

We spent the next hour admiring the view, looking through the binoculars and guessing the distance to various trees scattered in front of us and checking with the rangefinder.

"Let's take note of certain trees to establish our five hundred, down to two hundred yard distances in case we need to shoot. From up here, two hundred yards looks pretty close," I said.

Suddenly, Blossom remarked excitedly, "I see them coming!"

We took turns watching them. They were still a couple of miles away and coming slowly. It would be more than an hour until they got here.

Making observations and counting was giving us a pretty clear picture of what was coming.

An arrogant looking leader riding on a mostly white horse was at the front. He was followed by a half dozen warriors with war clubs. A conquistador leading a pack horse was next, then came the army of conquistadors, who had long ago quit making any attempt at formation or marching.

The two lines of slaves were next. They appeared to be tied together with four-foot long chains going from neck ring to neck ring.

The last figure was a conquistador riding a chestnut horse with black mane and tail. He was flicking out a whip at the last person in each line, who staggered forward after each lashing, stumbling under the fatigue, dehydration and the weight of their loads.

Chapter 17

Every time he swung the whip he swiveled around and his left hand jerked the reins, and the staggering horse would throw its head. I guessed it probably had a spade bit that was cutting its mouth, making it open its mouth so it was drying out worse than normal.

It wasn't just the horse. The line of slaves was also staggering at every step and the two at the back seemed about to drop.

Suddenly the figure on the left who appeared to be a girl about Lark's size, fell flat on her face under her load and didn't move. The fall snapped the chain to the next ring tight and that woman was jerked backward and twisted to the side to keep from falling. The whole line of slaves jerked to a stop, all standing bent over and motionless.

The rider rode up next to the girl and lashed down viciously with the whip, but there was no response.

Angrily, he got off his horse, took something from his pocket and jerked the neck ring around. Apparently, it was some kind of key or tool to take the neck ring off. He tossed the neck ring and chain on the pack of the woman who was next in line and peeled off the pack the motionless girl was carrying. Grabbing her by the hair and one arm he heaved her off to the side where she landed limply with a thud, a lifeless bounce and short skid coming to a stop under some bushes.

The woman who was next in line had a child with her. She was probably allowed to keep the child while others were slaughtered so she would be compliant and expend every effort to keep going, hoping to keep her child safe.

The conquistador tossed her the bag to put on the child. It was heavy and she tried to grab one side to take some of its weight off her child. It also put them last in line and before they had gone a hundred yards, the lash had landed on the bare legs of the child. Her scream was so loud we heard it a half-mile away.

I suddenly realized that I had such a rage boiling up in me that my hands were shaking. I was sweating more than the midday sun was requiring and I had a really bad taste in my mouth from the bile backing up in my throat.

I fought to get control. Rage is not good for your health, mentally or physically nor for making sound decisions. I took deep breaths and focused on the things at hand that needed attention, and began to calm down. A drink of water helped and moving around a little let my muscles begin to function normally. I also knew there was nothing we could do at the moment anyway.

"Are your weapons ready and is your ammunition where you can reach it and reload quickly," I asked.

"Can we fight whole army, Chee?" Blossom asked.

"As long as we are up here on the top of the cliff and they are down there, we can strike them all day long. If they try to circle around, we leave," I answered grimly.

It took another half hour for them to arrive at the open spot just this side of the ridge.

The lead conquistador sent two warriors to the top of the ridge to see if there was any sign of water. I doubted if they could see the line of trees marking the next stream from that position.

The warriors moved thirty yards farther east where there were two trees for shade. The army moved to the three trees that we had marked as our three hundred yard mark. The slaves simply dropped where they stopped, enduring the heat of the sun.

The horse and rider stopped behind the slaves for the moment. The horse stood spraddle legged with its head down. The rider took his bota and took a long drink.

A bota was an animal stomach used as a canteen. It was wrapped in leather to protect it and had carrying straps attached.

One of the conquistadors approached the slaves with a bota. They saw it and reached out and asked for water. He just stood there staring at them then extended the bota out towards them. Their cries and pleadings were clearly heard at our position. He drew back his hand, laughed at their sufferings and poured some water over his head.

They slumped back down in utter dejection.

I lined the crosshairs in the scope of the 30.06 on the horseman at the rear, allowing for a six-inch drop and gently squeezed the trigger. The middle of the breastplate took a good portion of the impact, slamming him backwards over the saddle. His hands, flying up and back, jerked the horse's head viciously and it reared up. The conquistador's feet came up; he turned upside down and slid over the horse's rump and crashed on his head right at the horse's back feet. If the bullet hadn't finished him, a broken neck would.

The crashing of the conquistador armor against its heels, spooked the horse and it bolted towards the mesa and up the valley to our right where it finally slowed down, circled a few times, looking back and entangling its reins in some brush. Working the bolt quickly, I lined up on the one who had so cruelly mocked the plight of the slaves. At the impact he also reeled back, throwing up his hands and flinging the bota into the bushes behind him.

Everyone was on their feet, looking for where the shots could have come from. Since no weapon could shoot more than a hundred yards, their search parameter was only a third of the distance to where we were. Of course, they couldn't see us behind our rocks even if they did look far enough this way. They were also looking for a puff of smoke. The fact that they couldn't find any, was perplexing to them also.

The pack horse had continued to wander ahead and was munching grass some fifty yards to the left.

Suddenly, a hoarse voice cried out, "Chee, Chee," the cry was taken up with other words that I couldn't understand. The conquistadors turned angrily on the slaves.

"Okay," I said to the girls, "let's engage. Remember your shooting charts. If they are bunched together shoot fast into the group. If they take shelter and spread out, slow down and aim carefully for the right distance."

I stood up beside a rock and waved my arms, shouting as loudly as I could, "buenos dias, hombres."

It would have been more dramatic if I had stood on top of the big rock at the edge of the cliff but that wasn't going to happen. As it was, I was a full step back from the edge and had a big rock in front of me.

"Blossom, don't go over the edge," I said.

"I okay Chee!" She said and grinned at me.

Lark looked at us like we were losing it, then shook her head. It still confused her that we often used a little humor to calm things down.

I waited a few seconds for all the conquistadors to try to locate my position.

Again, I waved my arms and shouted, "aqui, hombres."

They spotted me at the top of the cliff. I guessed they were wondering how I could shoot two of them and get up the cliff without being seen. Anything that would keep them confused and guessing was good.

"Blossom, remember when we rescued Deh Neh Totsi? I waved to my invisible Army on the other side of the pass? The captors believed there were more warriors, since three boys and three girls would not dare stand against a dozen trained warriors?" I reminded her.

"You always wave at invisible Army," she said grinning.

"Well, they aren't always talking and they don't eat much," I said grinning back at her.

"Sneak back using the big rock to stay hidden. When I call, you come, so they can see you, deliver the message and walk back to my 'army'. Then sneak back up here behind the big rock," I said.

"Okay!" She replied and took off.

I waved again and shouted, "hable Engles?"

They looked around and then the leader barked a command.

A man, obviously not a conquistador, came from behind them and out from under the trees.

I took him for a scholar, although everyone around here dressed weirdly, so I could only guess.

Turning back toward my army, I waved Blossom forward. She came openly and boldly and I gave her two messages to deliver in the native language.

"Chee says, people of the valley, be quiet and patient."

"Warriors. You may leave or you will die!" She shouted in her loudest voice.

The slaves quieted and settled back. The warriors looked at one another but made no move.

The "scholar" began his journey to the mesa and I went to the steep chute to greet him. Everyone else sat down to wait and see what would happen.

He was a tall thin man with a scholarly look and definitely not the murderous, ruffian thugs that called themselves conquistadors.

"How'd you ever get mixed up with the conquistadors?" I asked.

"Couldest thou repeat thine interrogatory. Thou hast a strange form of English," he responded.

I thought to myself, "I asked for English but I forgot I'd be getting sixteenth century English."

"Verily thou art a man of education. My English doth come from another country," I said.

"Yea, I am tasked with recording the places, events and exploits of the conquistadors," he explained.

"Of a truth thou doest well to expose the rape, torture, murder and destruction perpetrated on innocent people by the conquistadors," I said sarcastically.

"Verily I say unto thee, thou hast spoken truth, but they will accept or dispose of what ever I scribe for their own purposes."

"Thou shouldest remove thyself from their company when the battle dost start, lest thou be struck down in the midst of them," I said.

"Thou shalt deliver the message exactly as I giveth thee and then thou shalt move halfway to the pack horse. If thou dost go all the way to the pack horse, thou shalt surely die."

"Understandeth thou these things?" I said.

"Verily, I am but a messenger. I shall give truth as I am told," he replied.

"Good, listen carefully. Say to Generalissimo, 'thou hast trespassed upon my land and hast abused the people of my land, therefore thou must pay before thou leavest.

"The Chestnut horse is mine, the pack horse and all that pertaineth thereto is mine and all the slaves are mine. Thou shalt leave these things and thou shalt return to thy people far to the south, all the way out of the valley immediately.'"

The scholar made his way back to the leader and I returned to my position on the cliff. I assumed he would try to get his horses before he left.

I was wrong.

The scholar made his way back with a message and I went to meet him.

"He doth decline thy terms and saith instead, 'verily, thou hast killed two of my soldiers so for a thousand galleons of gold thou mayest have the horses and slaves and thou must pay another thousand galleons of gold for the lives of my men. Otherwise, verily, we will destroy you and all who are with you and take all that thou hast.

"Thou shalt be tortured until thou tellest where thy gold is taken from the hills, thy young men shall become slaves to mine it and thy women shall be taken as servants and concubines'." He concluded.

"Wow! He is full of himself, isn't he?" I said.

"What meanest this expression, 'full of himself'?" He asked.

"Never mind. Here is my answer and thou shouldest deliver it loud enough that all his men hear it too. I will be watching their reaction and I will know if thou dost deliver it for all to hear."

"Thou dost whine like a dog. You smell as doth a pig. You bray like a jackass and if thou dost refuse to comply with my terms and leave immediately, I will destroy your army and send you back in shame and disgrace.

"All the land from where the river passest the end of the mountains to the far reaches of the north, belong to England and France and conquistadors are never to set foot here again," I concluded firmly.

"Remember, thou must remove thyself from the danger that shall follow," I added.

"Thou mayest regret thy brashness," he said sincerely.

Returning to the girls, I said, "get ready. We'll see what they do. Watch the soldiers when my message is delivered. Tell me their reaction. I'll watch the leader's face through the binoculars."

The leader suddenly jerked erect in the saddle and glared at the top of the cliff.

"That must have been the dog, pig, Jackass part," I thought to myself.

"Soldiers look like they laugh then quickly turn away, look down," Blossom said.

"Good, he apparently gave it just like I said it," I said. "Watch closely now."

The leader jerked the horse's head up and screamed orders that I could hear clear up where I was standing, and gestured towards the mesa.

They were scrambling to re-attach armor that they had loosened earlier to get some air, grabbed their packs and har-quebuses and assembled in a loose formation.

"As soon as they form up, you put four shots right in the middle of the group as fast as you can work the bolt and re-establish your sight," I instructed.

"Blossom will start with one shot then Lark will join in. It will sound like a whole army is up here," I added.

I noticed that the warriors were still off to the side and behind the Army. I had expected them to lead the charge. Perhaps Blossom's warning was being considered.

"Blossom, fire!" I called out.

A second after the sharp crack of the first shot, Lark's deeper, louder booming shot followed. Because the next three shots from each of them didn't come at exactly the same time and had different sounds, it sounded like an army had commenced firing.

Before the echo of the shots had died away, I fired five fast rounds aiming at the back row going left to right. I swung back and fired the same pattern at the front row.

I swung the rifle again to the trees where the warriors had been gathered but there was no one there. Looking a little farther out I saw a figure running across an open space heading east. I didn't think they would be a problem again.

The carnage at the center of the army was devastating. Several soldiers were hit two or three times and there wasn't a single soldier standing at the center of their formation.

I should have told Blossom and Lark to shoot to one side or the other also, but in effect they had been too accurate. Every shot struck something in the middle of the army.

I had spread my shots a little more so there were some at the front and back who would be wounded.

At each corner of the loose formation there were two or three left standing. Half of the army had been neutralized in less than a minute.

"Reload now while they attempt to get over the shock. If the arrogant little Generalissimo tries to re-form and charge again, we will be ready," I said.

The "little Generalissimo" was in shock also. This is not how wars were fought. Armies were to line up and charge and the harquebuses would mow down the first ranks before there was any engagement. Even if the other army had some harquebuses also, the conquistador armor would stop the small shot balls and only a soldier unlucky enough to get hit in the face would be injured.

These weapons that had decimated his army went through armor and even more unsettling was that he had not yet seen a single soldier.

I stood up and aimed my rifle at the leader. The English speaker was standing nearby.

"Tell him to gather his wounded and leave now!" I shouted.

Whether at that moment he understood that he was making a life or death decision, I'll never know. He turned towards his men and shouted commands and those who had sought cover behind a bush or in a small depression in the ground, stood up and began attending to the wounded.

I kept my rifle at the ready. If anyone made a threatening move towards the captives, I would down him immediately.

Those that they decided were dead or beyond help, they left lying where they had fallen.

There were about eight that were carried or half supported or limped along with bandages wrapped around various parts of their bodies.

Once again, I shouted as loudly as I could, "go east there is water there," and I pointed to where a couple of lakes were located in the middle of the valley. The English fellow translated my message and they were gone in half an hour.

"Let's take water to the captives!" Blossom declared.

"Not yet," I said. "The conquistadors may be planning to let us come down while they sneak back to ambush us.

"Get the binoculars and see if they have kept going. Call out to the people that we will come and bring water but they must be patient," I said.

As things quieted down, the wolves rejoined us, sitting on their hunches and waiting to move on.

Blossom called down with the message and several waved back to acknowledge they understood. After all they had endured and the surge of hope they were now experiencing overcame the immediate need of water.

"Blossom, remember the bad guy in the store who got up after I passed him, and I thought he would be unconscious for a while? He would have killed me with his knife if you hadn't had my back."

"When we go down, do not go near the conquistadors. There may be a conquistador too wounded to travel but still able to take revenge if you turned your back to look at something. A quick up thrust with his sword and you would be dead."

I continued, "when we go down, I expect each of you to follow my orders very carefully. Do you understand?

"Even the captives could be dangerous if they are so affected by the sun, lack of water and the abuse they have experienced that they mistake us for an enemy," I added.

We could see the conquistadors as they crossed an open area and it looked like they were all accounted for.

Waiting a half hour, we made our way down the chute to the slope, then on down to the valley below.

The wolves had trouble navigating down the steep rocks, but they made it.

"How many water bottles do we have," I asked.

A quick inventory showed that we each had four full bottles plus a little left in the ones we had been using.

We dropped our light packs in a pile about thirty yards before we got to the captives and left half of the water bottles with the packs. Telling the wolves to stay with the packs, we approached the captives.

"Blossom, get the bota that was thrown into the bushes and see what is left in it," I instructed.

The bota was half-full, which was more water than one of our bottles.

"Give it to the girls on the left and tell them to share."

The first girl took a couple of swallows and passed it on. So did the next and the next. When the third girl handed it to the young man behind her, he turned and gave it to the little girl behind him.

That gave me some insight into the kind of people we were dealing with. They shared and they put others ahead of their own severe need.

I turned to the girls, "give one bottle to the first three in each line."

Stepping between the two lines of captives who were still chained together and seated along the path that the con- quistadors had made, I took a bottle to the young man who had passed his turn to the little girl.

As I turned back to the other line, it struck me that the man in front of me looked familiar. He was a little older and bigger than the others and had been beaten unmercifully. I guessed that he had tried to intervene or protect some of the younger ones and they had made an example of what would happen if one stepped out of line. One eye was swelled shut, there was blood in his hair and down the side of his face and most of his face was swollen and purplish.

The most cringe worthy sight was his feet. They had taken his moccasins or whatever foot coverings he might have had, and forced him walk all the way barefoot. His feet were a mass of cuts and bruises and sand had collected on the oozing blood so that it looked like he had just stepped into a puddle of black goo.

He looked at me with recognition but also some apprehension. Suddenly, I placed him. He was the leader of the Whiteface who had attacked the village on the day I had arrived through the portal. That day, he had acted with caution and wisdom and we had ended our confrontation with a salute, but from a distance.

I squatted in front of him and pointed to my eyes and then at him to indicate that I recognized him and held out my hand. We grasped forearms for a moment before I handed him a water bottle. He immediately turned and gave it to the young woman behind him.

She had endured the whip often as the last in line and she had a dispirited, blank look about her that indicated she had coped, by not being here and she was still mostly gone mentally. She took a few swallows and handed it back to him.

I pointed to the bottle then to him and he drank a few swallows. The two young women ahead of him had a bottle so everyone had some water for the moment.

Suddenly there was an anxious cry and I turned abruptly to see Lark falling to her knees and embracing one of the girls. I presumed it was a friend from her time with the Whiteface.

Turning back to the leader, I gestured to the two lines and pointing to the two trees about ten steps to the side, he understood that they should move into the shade.

He called to them. They all got up and still being tied together, moved in two groups to the shade and sat down.

He gestured towards the neck shackles and I nodded.

"Blossom, tell him I must go and see if the girl who was thrown into the bushes is still alive, and they must wait until I return.

After she had relayed the message, I beckoned to her and Lark to follow me.

We went back to the packs where the wolves were waiting impatiently.

I gave them strict instructions, "do not go near the conquistadors. Keep your rifle in hand until I get back. Blossom, go over and bring the pack horse here and tie her to that bush where there is grass. Lark, go to the top of the hill, to the base of the cliff and look for conquistadors. If you see one, even if he is way out in the valley but coming back this way, you shoot at him. It lets them know we are watching and it will let me know to get back here quickly. Do not go near anyone until I get back!" I said urgently.

They both nodded seriously.

Immediately, I headed for the chestnut horse.

Approaching slowly, I talked to him and untangled the reins. As I suspected the bridle had a spade bit that had damaged the inside of his mouth and there was blood on the froth around his mouth and quite a bit of foam in his nostrils.

Taking the bota from the saddle horn, I uncorked it and put the spout at the corner of his mouth, pushing his head up a little to let some water run down his throat. He swallowed eagerly and was totally cooperative on the second try and took several swallows.

He needed his nostrils cleaned so he could breathe properly. A piece of cloth saturated with water felt refreshing and he shook his head from the tickling sensation then thrust his head forward to do it again. After three tries his nostrils were clear and I gave him another drink.

The next step in sealing our friendship was a small chunk of an energy bar. I had stopped bringing the chocolate ones as the weather got warmer, so this one was heavy on oats and honey.

For an animal dying of thirst, he produced an inordinate amount of slobber. With his head bobbing and making grunting noises, he did everything but salute and swear allegiance. I gave him another piece of energy bar all the while talking to him and letting him get the sound of my voice in his head.

When I stepped up and gently settled into the saddle, he tensed as though waiting for the pain in his mouth. Instead, I merely lifted the reins off of his neck and flexed my knees and said, "let's go."

He started off at a brisk walk back to the trail.

When we got to the spot where I could see the body under the bush, I got off and tied the reins in a spot where he could get some grass. I took the bota and gave him some more water which he drank eagerly.

As I got close to the bush where the figure lay, my heart sank and I cried out, "oh no!" as I saw a distinct white streak of hair coming down the side of her head.

Quickly, I pulled her out from under the bush and sat down in the shade, pulling her across my leg. There was a faint pulse but she was hot and in danger of heatstroke and dehydration.

Working hastily, I got my handkerchief, wet it thoroughly from the bota and began to wipe her forehead, cheeks and neck. I opened the bottle of drinking water and pushed my fingers against her cheek to pucker her mouth into a pout and poured a cap full of water into her mouth.

It was only enough to wet her mouth and begin to wet her throat. She attempted to swallow but her throat was dry and her tongue was swelled and almost shut off her breathing. I poured in another cap full and this time she was able to swallow and the inside of her throat didn't stick together. After several caps full of water, her eyes fluttered open and she croaked out a sound and her body jerked. She probably hadn't ever seen anything as strange as me before, so it must have given her a shock.

As I started to give her another tiny sip of water, she mustered the strength to reach up and pull the water bottle to her mouth, taking several good swallows.

Again, her eyes fluttered open and she said, "Chee" and some other words I couldn't understand and the corners of her lips twitched in a feeble attempt at a smile.

Again she reached out for the water and guided it to her mouth for a few more swallows.

I could almost see the water begin to seep out into her body. Her breathing became more normal and I continued to cool her face with the wet handkerchief.

She was reviving steadily and each few sips of water seemed to add strength and life to her.

Finally, I said, "Roh Dah Bey."

Her eyes popped wide open in surprise and she said, "Chee" and a whole bunch of other words.

She took another couple of swallows and struggled to sit up. I helped her to a sitting position and she wavered a little like she might pass out. After a few minutes, I pointed up the trail and made the sign for "go".

She nodded gamely but if she couldn't get up, she surely couldn't walk to wherever we might be going.

Slowly I pulled her to her feet but she didn't have strength to stand. I picked her up, turned and when she saw the horse, she gasped. I stopped and smiled at her and began talking both for her and the horse since neither one understood a word.

Whether the horse would carry double, I didn't know, but Roh Dah Bey was more like a pack to be carried than a second rider.

I had tied the horse next to a small rock that I could use as a stepping stone. Placing her legs over the horse's neck in front of the saddle so that her knees hooked over the neck, and with her resting on my left arm and shoulder, I mounted.

The reins were draped over the neck and if the horse bucked or bolted, we might be in a peck of trouble.

I kept talking and the chestnut stood quietly until I was settled and Roh Dah Bey was sitting sideways across the saddle in front of me, while I held her in place with my left arm. Gingerly, I reached over her and found the reins, flexed my knees and said, "let's go."

He started off at a careful walk as though he knew he had a precious cargo.

It took a little longer to return because it was uphill and the horse was walking more slowly. I decided to call him "Ranger" and included "Ranger" in every sentence so it would become a familiar sound.

Roh Dah Bey was getting stronger as we rode up the gradual slope to join everyone. She finally pointed at the horse and said, "Ranger."

I smiled, nodded and repeated, "Ranger."

As we rode up to Blossom and the pack horse, Blossom squealed, "Roh Dah Bey" and ran to us.

Slowly, I shifted her weight to my left arm and shoulder and stepped down, then dragged her feet across the saddle to my side and stood her gently on the ground. She still didn't have strength to stand, so we lowered her to a sitting position and put a pack behind her so she could sit up.

The water, shade and the presence of Roh Dah Bey, whom they had left for dead, was lifting the spirits of the captives. They called out to her and waved enthusiastically.

Blossom was kneeling beside her alternately giving her a drink and a hug, when Sah Sha trotted up and immediately licked Roh Dah Bey's face.

She cried out in fear and we couldn't help but laugh.

"Sah Sha, sit and be good," Blossom ordered and Sah Sha sat but was leaning against Blossom and doing her best to refrain from another lick on her new friend.

Roh Dah Bey was trying to make sense of her situation. There were no conquistadors; the captives were still in chains but seated comfortably in the shade. She had been rescued by a pile of brush and leaves, put on one of the great beasts of the conquistadors and had a wolf walk up and lick her face.

I motioned to Lark to come and join us and she and Kih Ta came down the hill.

"Did you see any sign of the conquistadors?" I asked.

"No, I search carefully as far out as I could see with binoc'lars. Up and down Valley, no conquistadors," she replied.

"Good, but they will probably be back when they get replacements," I muttered. "Blossom, take care of Roh Dah Bey and watch the animals. Give her water a little at a time and an energy bar as soon as she feels she can eat something.

"Lark, give four bottles of water to our friends. See if we have enough energy bars to go around. I'll get the tool to get the neck shackles off. We have to get everyone up and away from here to a safe place today and I have no idea how we are going to do that," I muttered, mostly to myself.

Chapter 18

The conquistador that was driving the slaves, lay where he had fallen. I fished around in his pockets until I found the tool or key, however it might work, and returned to the captives.

I went to the young woman who had been just ahead of Roh Dah Bey, and beckoned Lark to translate.

All of them had necks rubbed raw and some were bleeding from the nasty collars. I didn't want to push or twist the collars trying to figure out how they worked. Lark explained that I was practicing on the extra collar.

Fortunately, it was a simple push and turn to unlock the place where it was held together and it spread apart and released from the neck.

It was a quick process to unlock all the collars and cast them aside. It might be worthwhile to rescue the chains that could be used for many things later, but right now they could only be seen as cruel implements of bondage.

Blossom came over excitedly, holding the hand of a young girl about Lark's age and pulling her along.

"Chee, this is Lu Day Sah. She come home too!"

"Wonderful!" I exclaimed, "your parents will be very happy that you are here."

With Blossom translating, she explained, "Roh Dah Bey always say you will come. I not think so. I not think you are real person. We thank you." She stepped in and gave me a hug.

Blossom grabbed my hand, "see, I say they come back!"

"Yes, you did," I said with resignation. "However, we aren't home yet. You and Lark help Roh Dah Bey come over and join the group."

After they arrived, I said quietly to Lark, "I want you to translate so they all see that you are a trusted warrior in my tribe. When you speak about plans and directions and make decisions, they will know that you speak for me and they will listen."

Her eyes began to get teary. "You say I am trusted warrior, Chee?" She asked emotionally.

"Absolutely!" I said, "you have proved yourself over and over to me in learning, in effort, in attitude and you have stood with me in battle. I trust you and I'm proud of you!"

"Now don't go all girlie on me," I said with a grin.

She reached out to slap my arm but stopped when she realized we were in front of a bunch of strangers. She placed her hand on my arm in a queenly gesture and since she had her back to the group, she took the moment to wipe her eyes.

She turned to our audience in full control and ready to go.

"People, we must get to a safe place and most of you can hardly walk. The conquistadors will be back. They have lost men, supplies, horses and captives. They will be back!

"I don't know what to call you. We are not a tribe. There are ones from many tribes. You are not captives. You are free. May I call you friends?"

They glanced at one another and nodded approvingly.

"The only way we can get things done is to work together. These are young warriors," and I pointed to Lark and Blossom. "When they speak for me, do not think you can ignore them because they are young or because they are girls. You saw them defeat an army of conquistadors and they have stood with me in other battles. They are braver than many who call themselves warriors. I trust them with my life!

"We have many decisions to make. We must get to water and a safer place. Many of you need something for your feet. Some of you have moccasins that are worn through. We must try to repair those quickly.

"The girls will get water and supplies and we will rest and get ready to move before the sun goes down."

The young man who had shared the water with the little girl, spoke up. "My foot coverings are still good. I can carry."

I motioned for him to come forward. He looked like he was gaining strength after the ordeal and his foot wear was intact.

Another young man from the group of three stood up and declared, "I will go!"

Turning to Blossom, I asked, "do you feel safe with these people?"

Grinning impishly, she said, "Kih Ta, Sah Sha come."

The two wolves trotted from guarding the packs where Roh Dah Bey had been sitting and stood on each side of Blossom.

"I feel safe," she said still grinning.

I suppressed my own grin. She was the safest one in the valley at that moment.

"Don't rush, take a drink when you get there and hand out an energy bar for the trip back. It's only about a mile over there. Make sure the boys get the packs on right so they travel easily."

"Okay, everyone!" I turned back to the group and Lark began translating again. Open the pack you were carrying for the conquistadors, take everything out. Let's see what we can use."

Everyone was able to stand up, so I knew they were gaining strength. Most of them walked the few steps to where they had dropped the packs and come back under the shade, when I noticed the leader trying to step as gingerly as possible on his severely bruised and lacerated feet. I motioned for him to wait, walked over to the pack and took it to him. "What is your name?"

The way it rolled off his tongue and after three tries, and a little help from Lark, I think I got it.

"Roah Sun Obi," I finally said and a small smile turned the corners of his mouth.

The packs were all filled with typical camping supplies and personal items. The best item of all was that each conquistador carried softer shoes so they could take off their heavy marching boots and use the softer ones around the campfire at night.

"Lark, ask if anyone's pack has a foot covering that would be big enough for Roah Sun Obi."

After looking at several, none of which were big enough, I decided that I would have to make one. Looking at the bodies of the conquistadors, I found a pair of boots that were a little bigger.

Roah Sun Obi's swollen, damaged feet would never fit in a boot but I could use the sole.

Cutting the boot off of the sole provided a foundation. Taking the sleeve off of a long sleeve shirt would provide the upper.

There was a small roll of duct tape in my bag and I knew there was a bigger roll in my big bag, so I got started.

We put his foot in the cut off shirt sleeve like it was a tube sock, up to his ankle and taped it there. Then we folded the rest of the sleeve under his foot and up around the heel to just above the ankle and taped it there. The duct tape reinforced the fabric and formed the sock to his foot.

Next, we put the sole from the boot and wrapped it from toe to heel in whatever direction seem to hold everything in place the best. When we were done, his feet were encased in duct tape but the fabric next to his skin was soft and he had a solid, firm sole to walk on.

We stood him up to see how it felt. A smile lit up his face as he took a couple steps with greatly reduced pain. He nodded and pointed up the valley. He would make it.

For those with the bottoms of their moccasins worn through, we tried a couple of things. We tried taping a couple layers of heavy pant legs to the bottom, but found what seemed to be a better way.

Cutting the boot tops off and cutting the toes out, let the boot sole fit any foot within two sizes of the original. They wore their moccasins inside the boot and we taped from side to side and across the arch and front to back without going under the boot sole. There was no tape on the bottom to wear through.

By the time Blossom, the boys and the wolves got back, we were almost ready to go. "Fill the small water bottles from the gallon jugs and share as you shared before. Bring all the botas we've collected and I'll water the horses. Don't drink anymore bota water until we clean them." I warned.

We used the last gallon to refill, at least partially, the little bottles and our packs were a gallon lighter.

"Everyone who can walk, follow me," I said.

We went only a couple hundred yards until we found a rocky, hardpan surface. We sent them one by one at different spots, up the hill to the steep slope and around in front of the cliffs to the south side before going down into the valley on the south side.

"Try not to leave any tracks. This may buy us some time if they come back before we are ready for them." I explained.

Those not as able, went up the already worn trail towards the chute and stepped off to the side and around the hill where they were least likely to leave tracks.

"Roh Dah Bey, would you like to ride?" I asked.

She grinned and nodded.

"Ask the girl on the end if she would like to ride," I told Blossom.

The girl was like a zombie. There was little expression and it seemed like little comprehension.

She really didn't answer yes or no but stood there in indecision.

I took her by the hand and led her to the horse. If she didn't want to ride, I expected she would indicate it now. The back of her calves were swollen and covered in welts. I picked her up carefully and set her in the saddle. Roh Dah Bey was considerably lighter and I set her in front of the zombie girl. The saddle was big enough to hold both of them.

Lark was directing all the individuals who came around the hill and those who were coming to the chute, to keep individual paths so as to not leave any clear trail.

Blossom led the pack horse and I led Ranger, after telling him how proud I was of him, and gave him a quarter of an energy bar. He bobbed his head and rolled the sweetness around in his mouth and made little grunting sounds like English was his true language and he understood every word I said. Horses are smart that way.

Blossom found a stretch of hard ground to go off the trail and I found another. We kept our distance from one another and from the group which was coming together.

About a half mile up the valley we began to angle over to join them.

We moved slowly and it took another hour to get to the steep, rocky stream bed that went up about fifty yards to the pond. From the bottom side it looked like just a short cliff that angled over to join the main cliff. The valley angled off to the left and went on for several miles with a gentle slope up to the mountains and the beautiful trout stream.

We would not go that way but we would leave a trail that looked like we did.

Those who were obviously too tired to go much further or whose footwear didn't need more stress and wear, were directed up the rocky waterfall from near the bottom.

The rest of us, which was about half of the group, and the horses went up the valley and found a game trail. In a few hundred yards, Lark had peeled off person after person at spots where little evidence of tracks would be seen until the only ones left were Blossom and me with the horses, and Lark.

Finding good spots to get off the trail and up the hill, Lark went back along the face of the cliff directing those on foot to the side of the waterfall and up to the pond.

Blossom and I took the horses on around the end of the little cliff and back along the side of the hill and came directly to the southwest side of the pond. As we topped the rise and looked down into the little hideout, with the pond in the middle, we could see that everyone was already gathering at the big, downed cottonwood on the northeast side where we had camped the night before. We made our way down to the pond and let the horses drink first at the east end farthest away from where the water came in.

We also cut their drinking short, since we would water them several times later this evening. A little at a time is much healthier.

We took the horses on around the pond and tied them to a cottonwood tree about thirty yards to the side of our campsite. I reached up to help the zombie girl and she held out her arms so I could catch her and help her down. It was the first sign of her coming out of her catatonic state. Roh Dah Bey was gaining strength and was expending it mostly on chatter. The fact that I couldn't understand anything she said, didn't mean she would refrain from saying it.

Blossom chimed in at intervals to translate a little. "I like ride big beast. It fun. Are we going to keep him? Can we all ride him? Maybe he will run with us."

Blossom couldn't keep up translating, so she quit, but that didn't stop Roh Dah Bey.

If she and Blossom got started, they were liable to keep us up all night.

Roh Dah Bey leaned off onto my arm and shoulder and relaxed as I pulled her off the saddle and set her feet on the ground. She stood for a moment, then took a step and walked unsteadily to the camp area.

Zombie girl was still standing where I'd set her, so I took her arm and walked her to a log and helped her sit down.

Blossom announced, "drinking water is up where the water comes in. Washing water is at the other end."

The two boys who had gone with Blossom and carried our packs, were filling water bottles for those too tired to move or suffering with sore feet.

Lark was exercising her generalship.

Blossom grinned as she translated some for me, "campsite is for sitting, talking, eating. Girls sleep over there. Boys sleep over there."

There was more but that was the gist of it.

Blossom called to the two boys and I called to Lark, to unpack the pack horse.

The conquistadors apparently didn't know how to throw on a diamond hitch but they had a lot of rope that went back and forth and across the large canvas that went over and around the packs.

It turned out that the pack saddle and panniers were about the same as we used 500 years later. The canvass was about ten by twelve feet and we laid it out on the sand to receive the items from the packs as they were unloaded.

There were pots, pans, skillets, kitchen sized spoons, forks, small containers of spices, two botas full of oil, one full of vinegar, bags similar to a five pound bag of salt, twenty pounds of beans, ten pounds of corn meal and twenty pounds of whole-wheat flour, some knives and a hatchet.

"Lark, would you take these two guys up the valley and get a deer. They should be coming out to eat and go to water this evening."

"Blossom, show the women who are up and able, how to make fried bread. Today it will have to be tortillas since we don't have anything to make the bread rise."

"I'll get some help to carry wood," now I was sounding like the general.

"I also need to call Violet before dark," I reminded myself.

The rope that held the packs was in two pieces, so we had a nice rope for each horse to tie them out tonight.

The bundles of long dry grass can be tied into knots, then tied together into a small handle to make a horse brush. I went to zombie girl and held out my hand. Taking my hand, she stood up and followed me to the horse. I stroked the grass brush down Ranger's neck and shoulder then down a leg. He bobbed his head in appreciation and I handed the brush to her.

Twenty minutes later she was still brushing and he was still enjoying it. I directed her to the pack horse (which I named "Sage") and she proceeded to brush her down as well.

I hoped maybe the activity, repetitive movement, horse relationship, something, might help her snap out of it.

Some of them had stirred around enough to get wood and dry grass to start a fire. One boy was trying to spin a crooked stick on a piece of cottonwood. It was not going well. I tapped him on the shoulder and he stopped to see what I wanted. I gestured for him to watch as I built a nice teepee structure to start the fire under and added a small teepee over some balled up grass with some dried stocks of cat-tails. It was much too much material to start a fire their way and he pointed and shook his head. I pointed to my eyes and then the pile of wood and took a match out of my waterproof container.

When I scratched it on a rock and it burst into flames, I heard several gasps. Quickly I put the match to the dry tinder. It caught immediately and the flames started up the teepee structure and a fire was going in minutes.

Blossom came over with the women who had been instructed on tortilla making. They had two skillets so they put some oil and flattened dough on them and quickly had some bread.

Everyone crowded around to try it and while it was more like an unsalted cracker than bread or biscuit, they declared it delicious. Of course, they were starving so a cricket would probably taste like a T-bone steak.

We heard a rifle shot that didn't sound very far away. Everyone froze and looked around fearfully.

Since there were no other shots or sounds of battle, I assumed Lark had shot a deer.

This proved to be the case, as she and the boys dragged in a nice young buck about a half hour later.

There were a couple of short pieces of clothes line rope in my pack and one tree had an eight foot high limb to tie up the deer. The boys grabbed the knives that came with the conquistador stuff and proceeded to skin the deer.

Roah Sun Obi insisted on helping cut up the deer, so I dug in my pack for a good hunting knife. He hefted it in his hand, shifted it back-and-forth from hand-to-hand, smiled and said several things.

Blossom was standing nearby and translated, "he say thank you, it good knife, better than conquistadors!"

"Tell him it is his to keep, my gift to him" I said, and she relayed the message. He smiled in appreciation.

Beckoning to Lark and Blossom, we went over to sit on a log laying off to the side to talk.

"We have too many people and too many things to do. That is going to drive me crazy. Horses, injured people, food, conquistadors coming and I have to have one of you with me or I can't talk to anybody. We have to plan!" I said in exasperation.

They agreed but added, "they take care of themselves, let them do it."

"Well, here are some chores. Take the horses to water and tie them out. But we have to check them regularly or they may get tangled in a rope and injure themselves.

"Great work getting the deer, Lark. That will be the main food."

"And great work, Blossom, teaching them to make tortillas." They grinned and nodded.

"I'm going to call Violet and fill in Sunflower and Lobo and whoever else is there. Do not tell them that Roh Dah Bey or Lu Day Sah are here. Sunflower would grab an eagle by the tail and be here in an hour!"

The girls laughed at the picture that conjured up.

"We also must let them know that half of our group is Whiteface. And by the way, Lark, you have conducted yourself very well from being a slave to being a leader over the slaveholders. I don't know if you know any of these people other than the girl I saw you greet and hug, but I understand how this could be difficult. You have been fair, confident, leading without giving orders. I'm really proud of you!

"Blossom, you get along with everybody. That little girl thinks you are a superhero. Actually, because of how you conduct yourselves, they all look at both of you in awe. They see you are great warriors even though almost all of them are older than you." I paused for a moment to let that compliment sink in.

"Let's call Violet." I said changing the subject.

Turning on the radio, we got started.

"Chee to Violet, this is Chee, come in Violet, over."

"This Violet, is everyone okay? Are you coming back? Over."

"We are all okay but we had a battle and now have a bunch of rescued slaves and warriors. Some of them are injured so we are in a camp letting them heal. Over."

"I give radio to Sunflower. She want to talk."

There was a click as she transferred the phone.

"This is Sunflower. What battle? Who did you fight? How many were there? Are you all safe?"

She forgot the "over" but the click indicated she was listening.

"This is Chee. There was a scouting group of conquistadors using slaves who were without water, making them carry the conquistador's packs and being whipped to keep going. We didn't like it because some of the slaves were about to die. We confronted them and took down about half of them and the rest fled.

"They will probably get reinforcements and come back.

"We are all safe for the moment but the captives need several days' rest before they can attempt the journey to the village. Over."

"This is Sunflower. Do you want us to come and help? Over."

"We can decide that tomorrow. The plan at the moment, is to rest and heal for another day at least. Lark got a deer and there was food in the conquistador's packs. If we can travel the day after tomorrow, we will start out for the stream between here and Noh Tay Dah's stream. The next day we could make it to Noh Tay Dah's stream and maybe you could meet us there. One thing you need to know and I need to know, about half of these captives are Whiteface. Can you deal with this like you accepted Noh Tay Dah and Deh Neh Totsi? Over."

There was a long pause and I began to wonder if she was really that undecided about helping the Whiteface.

The radio crackled when she turned it on.

"This is Sunflower. Azalia and the boys are here. We all agree that if you and Lark and Blossom can work in peace with these people, so will we. The conquistadors are the enemy. Whether we have peace or war with the Whiteface can be decided when the conquistadors are gone. Over."

"This is Chee. Very good. There are very few Whiteface left to have war with. Truly the conquistadors are the enemy. Over."

"This is Lobo. What you want us to do now? Over."

"I want two of you to go up on the cliffs above the door and look for conquistadors coming up the valley. I still don't want everyone knowing about the door, so counting Violet there are six of you. They may send a big army or just a scouting party to see where we went. Whatever they are doing, I want to know.

"You can do a half day at a time. Scan carefully at mid-morning, early afternoon and early evening or you can do all day. Once they are spotted, the next pair take the radio and we will plan from there. Put Violet on. Over."

"This Violet. What you want me do? Over."

"Make sure both batteries are fully charged and I will call in the morning. Chee over and out."

Turning to Lark I asked, "give me your opinion of Roah Sun Obi."

She looked at me with surprise, then turned thoughtful.

"He is warrior, chief of tribe with other chiefs. He is fair, he listen, he does not brag, is there more you want to know?"

"That is good. I want him and maybe another to join us to plan the next few days," I said.

"Let's talk to him now and then you both take the horses to water and tie them to a tree on the hill across the pond. He can have someone chosen by then," I said.

"And both of you, eat and keep drinking water!" I warned.

Both girls came along to talk to Roah Sun Obi.

After greeting him, I said, "we need to plan the next few days so we are thinking the same way," I was going to say, "on the same page," but that would have no meaning here.

"Is there another here that you would like to join us, whose wisdom and courage you respect?" I asked.

"Each one here has shown great courage," he said tiredly. "You can choose two from among them, I did not lead them to victory or freedom."

"Lark, you are right. If humility is part of a great heart, he is adding much to his learning," I said.

She smiled and nodded.

Turning to Roah Sun Obi, I responded. "You are still a chief and your knowledge and wisdom are needed."

He looked at me for a long moment, then shifted his eyes to the girls. Lark nodded her head seriously.

He looked back at me and said wistfully, "you make warriors out of little girls, maybe they make me into warrior again."

I shook my head, "They cannot make a warrior. Their brave hearts can call out what is already in the heart. We all see a warrior. We are calling for it to come out because we need it and these people need you."

He nodded thoughtfully, took a deep breath and set up a little straighter.

"There are several boys worthy to be chosen to lead, but your girls teach me to look deeper. I will ask Wen Nah Paw, mother of Suh Han Paw, if she will help."

We all nodded in agreement. We had seen her courage, her care of her daughter, the quiet shepherding of the girls and the respect shown to her by the boys.

Roah Sun Obi stood carefully on his bruised and lacerated feet swaying for a moment to get his balance as he prepared to walk.

"He is good chief, huh Chee?" Blossom remarked.

"You're just saying that because he complimented you," I retorted.

"You would have chosen a boy, huh Chee?" She said impishly.

"Well, the advantage of a boy is they don't talk so much," I said.

Lark was grinning and translating every word to Roah Sun Obi.

"It take four of us to keep you out of trouble. Only two of us here and look at trouble you in!" She said with her grin getting bigger.

Roah Sun Obi had looked on with alarm, then puzzlement, then he burst out laughing and joined in.

"I think she say truth," and he started limping towards the campfire.

Blossom took my arm and bumped the side of her head against it playfully.

I noticed wistfully that the top of her head was only a few inches below my shoulder. She was growing like a weed.

"Take care of the horses," I said. "Then we need to plan."

Suh Han Paw came over and joined the girls as they took the horses out to graze. She was recovering from her ordeal faster than anyone.

The girls returned and Roah Sun Obi and Wen Nah Paw joined us.

Lark and Blossom decided it would be easiest for Lark to speak their words to me in English and Blossom would speak my words to them in their language.

"We are still in great danger and must decide how to go from here. What are your thoughts?" I began, and gestured towards Wen Nah Paw to begin.

She paused thoughtfully, "where are the others who fought with you to destroy the conquistadors?" She asked and glanced at Roah Sun Obi as though they had already discussed this.

He nodded in affirmation.

I responded with a grin, "it was just us three. The girls really like to make a lot of noise."

They grinned as they translated this, knowing I liked to throw in humor to keep things light.

Roah Sun Obi looked back-and-forth seriously, "we hear many weapons, see many conquistadors fall. Where was warrior who strike down man on horse? You were on top of cliff?"

Turning serious, I replied, "we have weapons that are much better than those that the conquistadors have. Otherwise, we would not dare to confront so many."

"But we see you talk and direct others," he said with a puzzled expression.

Again, the girls were smiling as they translated.

"I pretend there are many so the conquistadors will not know that there are only three of us. It keeps them confused and guessing which is a great advantage for us."

"If they knew there were only three of us, they would have followed us and caught us in the open and at close range, then ten of them with their weapons could get us before we could get ten of them." I finished grimly.

They both nodded seriously and Roah Sun Obi said quietly, "then we cannot stay here."

"No, we must flee," I replied.

"But some are so tired they can hardly walk and others have injured feet," Wen Nah Paw said with great concern.

"How long will it take these conquistadors to report to their camp?" I asked.

They both paused thoughtfully and looked at one another. Roah spoke first, "they not go far today. They stop at water and help wounded. They cannot go fast. Maybe five days maybe six."

We all nodded as the analysis seemed good.

Lark raised her hand and I nodded to her to speak. She spoke to them and Blossom translated to me.

"How long will it take for them to form an army to come after us?"

We all nodded appreciatively at the question. It could mean an extra day for us.

Wen and Roah had both observed and participated in one such preparation only a few days ago. Again, they looked at one another and Roah nodded to her to talk.

"They must get ones who will carry the packs. Going into battle instead of just exploring, they will not bring women and children."

Roah nodded and added, "if they bring big army, it take two days for all to be ready. If they bring scout army to see where we go and how many there are to fight, they get ready in one day."

Blossom looked at me and gestured to speak.

"How long fast army take to get here?" She asked.

"They could do it in three long days to the place where their people lie," Roah responded.

"So where do we want to be in nine or ten days?" Blossom mused questioningly.

"That is the next question, isn't it" I said.

Lark responded with some alarm, "if we flee to village, we make trail to village and the conquistadors will go to village. We could not stop them there."

"Excellent analysis! That is very true!" I said.

"Blossom, you know this country better than anyone. What are your thoughts?" I asked.

"To flee or fight?" She asked.

Roah almost choked. This little girl was way ahead of him on the issues.

"We flee and when they catch up, we fight," I said.

She responded with impeccable logic.

"We flee to valley where Noh Tay Dah and Deh Neh Totsi lived."

At this, Roah's head jerked up, "you know Noh Tay Dah?"

"Yes, he and Deh Neh Totsi and the children are very good friends of ours. You know them?" I asked.

"He not like warrior way. Others mock and not let him live in peace. One day he leave. No one ever see them again," he answered.

"Go ahead Blossom," I said.

"We go to valley, get Sunflower, Azalia and boys, maybe more. Those fleeing go all way to top. Those fighting have several places to take down many and move to the next place. They not get up valley," she concluded.

I looked at Roah and Wen Nah. "Well, how does that sound to you?"

"You know these places, Chee?" He asked.

"Yes, and it should work about the way she laid it out," I answered simply.

Armed with a plan and some time, we all felt better as we got ready for the night.

Chapter 19

The next morning, I found the girls and we went looking for Wen and Roah for a quick assessment.

"Will everyone be healed enough to walk in five days?" I inquired, "does anyone have injuries worse than yours, Roah?"

"I be ready," he responded.

Wen Nah Paw added, "Roh Dah Bey get stronger fast. Everyone do better. We all be ready."

Turning to the girls, I said, "Let's take care of the horses and make plans."

Suh Han was glued to Blossom, so we let her tag along most of the time. She wouldn't understand anything we said anyway.

"I wanted your opinion on a couple of things," I began. "I feel bad that I haven't told Sunflower and Azalia about Roh Dah Bey."

"I agree," Lark responded. "I would want to know."

"What about Mor Dak Sah?" Blossom asked, "he would want to know about Lu Day."

"What if we asked Sunflower about who would lead the tribe if she came to help us?" I suggested.

"That is good!" Blossom asserted, "if she think tribe need help, we don't tell her about Roh Dah. If she wants to come and help us, you tell her that Roh Dah is here."

"Or, tell Sunflower and Azalia to come but let them find out when they get here." I said, "that plan lets them take care of things there, then plan for the trip here and back."

We spent some time with the horses, taking them to water, petting and talking, feeding them treats and getting acquainted and comfortable with them. Then we tied them out on some new grass to recover and strengthen for the trip ahead as well.

It was later than we had planned, when I pulled out the radio to report in.

"This is Chee and company reporting in, come in Violet, over."

"This Violet and rest of us, you late, Chee. We start to worry, over."

"We are well and have formed a little planning group to be sure we are ready for the journey and probably a fight too, over."

"We ready to go too, Chee. Sunflower want talk."

"This Sunflower. Where you need us, Chee? Over"

"Is everything ready with the village? Is someone prepared to lead and knows where to go? Over."

"Everything ready. We all want to come, over."

"Be sure they set a watch every day. Bring all the bullets left there for each rifle. Bring a pair of soft shoes size ten. One man was made to walk all this way on bare feet. His feet are bad.

"Bring a few big cans of fruit. Let's talk this evening for last-minute details and plan to start early tomorrow, over"

"This Violet. Do I come or stay with tribe? Over."

"We would love to have you with us, but we need a voice with the tribe. Would you be willing to stay and talk for us? Over."

"That be good, Chee. I stay with tribe. Over."

"Thank you! Turn your radio on every hour for ten minutes if we need to talk or you need to talk to us, we will talk. We might forget sometimes or be real busy but sometimes we will talk. Don't worry if we miss some hours. Start this tomorrow after our group leaves. Tell those who have a bow to bring all the arrows they can fit in their quiver. Over."

"This Violet, tell me what is hour again, Chee, over."

"See the little flat place on the radio? What numbers are there? Over."

"Many numbers on shiny, flat place. Big number is in middle, over."

"Tell me what big numbers you see. Over."

"I see eight then two dots, one over other, then two then three. Over."

"That is what I see on my radio. So, they are together. It means it is 8:23 in the morning. The hour is the first number before the two dots. Every hour that number changes. The next two numbers will be zero and a number one through nine that changes every minute. When they go past zero nine, we are past the first ten minutes, so turn your radio on during the first minutes up to zero nine. If we don't answer or call you then, turn off the radio and wait for the next hour. Over."

"I think I see what you say," she said hesitantly. "Over"

"let's practice tonight. Let the hour go to nineteen, turn on the radio and call before the minutes get to ten. Over."

"I do it, Chee, over."

"You'll do great. Love you all, over and out."

Violet apparently pressed the talk button and held up the radio as they all shouted, "love you all, over and out."

The next few days were anything but rest days for anyone.

We disinfected everything pertaining to the conquistadors. The women divided the cooking chores among themselves and several began cooking all the deer meat to delay spoilage.

We encouraged them to eat all they wanted and even then, we would be trimming spoilage off of the meat before we had it all consumed.

The wolves were feasting on bones and in the last few days, more partially spoiled meat than they could hold.

Each morning we made the rounds checking on injuries like cuts and bruises.

Roah's feet were healing nicely. Those with welts from the whip were especially impressed with the cooling feel of the antibacterial spray.

The women snagged the big tarp so they wouldn't have to sleep on the sand. Suh Han insisted on sleeping between Lark and Blossom, to which her mother agreed, and the girls didn't mind. One poncho on the sand held all three of them.

I went about thirty steps towards the end of the pond where the sounds of the night would be louder than the sounds of the camp, and laid out my poncho as a ground cloth.

At this altitude even late summer afternoons could get chilly. Getting my pack, I rummaged around for my blanket. It was missing but a quick glance at the sleeping girls located it.

Blossom had gotten to it first and of course, what was mine was hers. I smiled ruefully. I'll get it back when it is time to pack. Besides, this was just a midafternoon siesta time which was revered long before that word had arrived in this land.

I stretched out for a quick nap and continued planning for the next week.

When 19:00 hours rolled around, I checked the radio. I breathed a sigh of relief that they were set on military time and Violet wouldn't be confused when the numbers all started over again after noon.

As soon as I turned it on, I heard Violet calling.

"This is Violet, come in Chee, over" then a few seconds later, "this is Violet, come in Chee, over."

"This is Chee reporting in, you are right on time Violet. Very good, over."

"Here is Sunflower, she want to talk. Over."

"This is Sunflower, we are packed and ready. Over."

"Don't make your packs too heavy, but add some energy bars if space and weight permit. You'll want to travel fast. Over."

"This Lobo, we have some room. We have extra bottles for water, over."

"Sunflower, are you ready to make nice with the Whiteface? Actually, these are mostly young men, women and children and some are not Whiteface. But we must travel, camp and fight together against the conquistadors, over."

"This Sunflower, I be okay, Chee, over"

"Violet, you don't need to say, 'this is Violet' over and over. Just say it about once a minute and if I'm on, I'll say 'this is Chee' and you will hear and answer me then, over."

"Since you guys are coming here, have your lookout search from a lower spot. Not at the door! Then Violet will report anything they see. This is Chee, see you in two days, over and out."

They all shouted back, "see you in two days, over and out."

The routines of the day were pretty well set, but I decided to try something different for the next afternoon.

I had brought a swimsuit which could act as shorts if I wanted to totally unload and relax. I also had a bottle of shampoo. Going to a secluded spot, I changed into the swimsuit, went to the end of the pool, waded in, got wet and lathered up.

One by one and then in groups, their curiosity got to them and they came to see what I was doing.

The pond was more than three feet deep at the end, so it was easy to duck under and wash all the biodegradable lather off and come up clean and fresh.

Handing the soap to Blossom and Lark, I said, "get all the women and go behind that big bush and show them how good it feels and smells to get all refreshed and clean. Tell all the men to go to the campsite and wait their turn."

The whole proceeding was causing quite a stir and discussion, but the guys all headed back.

I called to Blossom and Lark and pointed to Lih Ah. "This might make her feel clean and whole again, so get her and help her wash her hair."

She was sitting on a log staring vacantly into space, but went along with the girls.

"Remember Sunflower saying, that even the air felt clean and fresh? Have them take two or three deep breaths when they come up out of the water," I said.

I returned to the fire and waited with the guys. Soon the sound of laughter, squeals as one splashed another, and lots of happy sounding conversation filled the air.

One by one the girls and women got dressed and came towards the fire site with smiles and conversations which I couldn't understand, but brought smiles and nods from the guys. Several had the men smell their hair which now had a fragrant lilac scent that began to permeate the air.

Most of them had returned, when suddenly there was an agonizing, guttural wail that had such pathos and emotion it brought every one of us to our feet.

"Wen Nah," I said and motioned for her to go see what was happening.

It took only a few minutes for the ones remaining to get dressed and emerge from the bushes.

Wen Nah and Lark were on each side of Lih Ah supporting her and guiding her towards a log. She was sobbing uncontrollably and could hardly walk.

Roah motioned everyone to stay and he and I went over to see what had happened.

Blossom met us. "Conquistadors treat her real bad. It break her spirit. Pain all come out."

Blossom would understand and recognize the importance of a giant, cathartic release.

Wen Nah, Lark, Blossom and Suh An all had their arms wrapped around her. Roah and I reached in, placing a comforting hand on her head or shoulder.

As her sobbing subsided, the circle of hugs loosened and Wen Nah and Blossom sat her down on the log. They continued to sit beside her with their arms around her. She continued weeping, but self-control was returning. The rest of us made our way back towards the fire.

Lark came over to me and put her arms around my arm, laid her head against my shoulder.

"When I come up out of water, the air is clean and fresh like you say. Suddenly, I hear my mother's song in my heart and I feel like singing. It feel good."

I patted her arm and said, "someday I will hear you sing. That will feel good too."

With the pool empty of the women, the boys took their turn and came back refreshed, smiling and enjoying the aroma of lilac. They spent as much time fixing their hair as the girls did. Of course, they all had as much hair as the girls and were just as particular.

Later that evening, Blossom and Lih Ah approached where I was sitting.

"She want to say 'thank you'." Blossom began.

As Blossom interpreted, Lih Ah explained. "Conquistadors no more have me. I here now. I free."

"We will do everything we can to keep it that way," I answered.

Her eyes were clear and she had a smile as she stepped in to give me a quick hug.

The next day was filled with checking in with Violet, who informed us that everything was going smoothly at the village. We checked injuries, took care of the horses, ate meals, kept the watch at all times and got a lot of rest.

I was looking forward to my group arriving this evening if not sooner.

We called Roh Dah Bey aside to inform her that Sunflower and Azalia, or Lan Ah Kay and Coy Dee Wan, as she knew them, could get here today. She could hardly contain her excitement.

"Would you, Lark and Blossom like to plan a special surprise meeting when they get here?" I asked.

That got all three of them even more excited and they made their plans.

When they were done scheming, they went to tell Wen and Roah what they were planning. They, in turn, relayed the fact that reinforcements were coming so the rest of them wouldn't be alarmed that a band of heavily armed strangers was suddenly upon them.

Blossom, Lark and I went to feed and water the horses about midafternoon.

We decided it would be good to exercise the horses and take them around the hill to some fresh grass and save the close-in grass for tomorrow. We found a spot where we could see up the valley, let the horses graze and sit and talk in the shade of some junipers. We didn't know where the little band would come into the valley. If it was farther west, they might come down the far side and miss us all together.

As I expected, we hadn't been there an hour until we saw some figures coming down the valley. Lark had the small binoculars and confirmed that it was our group.

We went over to a bare spot on the hill where we could be seen and as they got closer, we began to wave. They saw us immediately and altered their course to come to us.

After a few minutes of heartfelt greetings, we started around the hill. They were especially interested in the horses, since they had never seen one before.

"I'm really glad you are here. Blossom said it took all four of you girls to keep me out of trouble and we are facing a big chunk of trouble, so you better get busy and keep me out of it."

They all laughed at that and declared it true, but quickly grew more serious.

"How bad is it?" Lobo asked.

"It's definitely serious. We have fourteen people to get to safety. Most are worn out and injured to some degree. The only weapons they have are a few conquistador swords. And we don't know what is coming against us," I concluded.

"How you defeat first Army?" Lobo asked.

"First, they did exactly what we expected. They bunched up to march over us because they arrogantly thought they could march right over us. Second, I waved and gave directions to a large imaginary army like we did when we got Deh Neh Totsi.

"When the girls opened fire at the center of their army and then I added the SKS in a couple of sweeps across their ranks, it sounded like a big army. One of the men in the group of captives asked us where our army went."

Little Badger asked quizzically, "why they no shoot at you?"

"We were on a high cliff, three hundred yards away. We just dropped bullets into the big target they had nothing to shoot at," I responded.

"We will make plans later. Right now take a look at the place we found to rest and heal," I directed.

They all stopped to stare at the beautiful, secluded setting. The greenery around the pond, the sandy beach, the bright green cottonwood trees giving lots of shade made a picturesque, practical campsite.

"This is place to remember," Impala almost whispered.

"Let's stake out the horses here. We can bring them in close this evening. Now, let's go in and meet the folks," I said.

Since I wasn't sure what was planned, Lark and Blossom took over to do the introductions.

They directed our five guests to take off their packs and sit on the log and had all the others come around in front of them to be introduced.

It was a bit formal and my group looked a little uncomfortable with all those in front gesturing a quick hello, but all were grinning in a somewhat inappropriate way for the occasion.

Lou Day Sah was behind, so she wouldn't be recognized, but as soon as her name was given, my group all responded with exclamations of recognition and appreciation.

Before they could register any other response, Roh Dah Bey came up behind Sunflower and Azalia, put her arms around both of them, put her head right between them and said something in greeting.

The girls jumped at the surprise of being grabbed from behind but it quickly gave way to recognition and all three screamed with wild delight. Sunflower and Azalia jumped up then over the log and all three embraced in a screaming mass of swirling arms and legs and finally collapsed in a pile on the ground with wails and tears and all kinds of exclamations that I couldn't understand.

All the rest of us just stood there with misty eyes and broad grins. Blossom and Lark were weeping joyfully but Lou Day Sah's crying had a genuine note of sadness in it.

I beckoned to Lark and Blossom and we went to her to assure her that she would have her turn in a few days. She smiled through the tears and nodded bravely.

Lark and Blossom had laid out a poncho for a ground cloth about ten steps away from the rest of the women. They had pulled a small log around to create a barrier and privacy for the three sisters. They took their packs and set them against the cliff next to the poncho.

They probably wouldn't get much sleep tonight, so it was good that they weren't with the others.

"Blossom, where did you get the extra poncho?" I asked.

"It was in your pack," she answered matter-of-factly.

"You know more about what is in my pack than I do, don't you?" I responded with some sarcasm.

"Probably," she answered with that irresistible, impish grin, and trotted off to join the girls.

Lobo, Impala and Little Badger finally got to greet Roh Dah Bey and in a short while came over to where I was sitting.

"I like to get away from the camp sounds so I can hear the night sounds," I said.

"Trail here long and hard," Lobo asserted. "Can people make long, hard walk?"

"First camp back, no water." Little Badger explained, "hot, dry trail!"

"Not good place to run, hide," Impala added. "We must be two, three days ahead of conquistadors or they catch us in bad place."

"That reminds me, I haven't talked to Violet today. I should call her in a few minutes," I said.

The boys arranged their sleeping places and got what they needed out of their packs. They stacked all the ammunition they had brought and it certainly didn't look like enough to fight a war.

Those few minutes passed quickly and at the next hour, I turned on the radio.

"This is Chee, calling Violet, over."

"This is Violet. You not call all day. I worry! Over."

"Sorry Violet. We were busy. All of our people got here okay and we plan to head back the day after tomorrow. Over."

"That good. Everything here okay too. Over."

"Are the lookouts going out every day and have they seen any sign of conquistadors? over."

"They go three times each day. Take binoculars. Look for army. They see nothing. Over."

"You only need to turn your radio on each hour. You don't need to call unless there is something to report. I will do the same if I can. I really appreciate how well you are doing your job. Thank you! Over."

"I like job, Chee, it feel good when do something good, over."

"Keep up the good work. This is Chee, over and out."

Lobo was grinning broadly and shaking his head. "I see Violet, I see little girl. I hear Violet, I hear mother!"

I laughed, "I know what you mean. She will be the mother duck and we will all line up right behind her."

The evening chores had fallen into a predictable routine. The evening meal was the usual venison, cat tail shoots and tortillas. Sunflower and Azalia had brought some seasoning salt which was much appreciated by those who had never seen or tasted it before.

We also opened a big can of peaches and gave each person a half cup of peaches in sweet juice in a paper cup. We told them to keep the cup for more fruit tomorrow.

Sunflower had brought a sturdy pair of hiking sandals, so Lark, Blossom and I took them to Roah to try on. They fit well and using a shirtsleeve from a conquistador's shirt as tube socks, with a few cuts and some duct tape, the socks were fitting pretty well.

When he put on the sandals and stood up, he smiled like a schoolboy with an extra apple in his lunch.

"This feel good. I walk good tomorrow," he said and Lark translated.

After checking in with Violet, the boys and I sat and talked for about an hour after sundown and then turned in for the night.

The next morning most of the group was up by shortly after dawn. This would be a busy day. Everything must be packed and ready to go.

Even so, all the chores needed to be done. Blossom checked in with Violet, then we, including Suh Han, who always seemed to be with Blossom, watered the horses.

I couldn't bring myself to put the cruel, spade bit back in Ranger's mouth and I didn't have the tools to cut it off properly, so I set about making a halter out of thin nylon rope I always carried.

The pack horse already had a halter and Ranger would be led, so this seemed to be the simplest solution.

Just before noon, the three sisters still clinging to one another, came over to where I was working on the halter. They stopped in front of me and Roh Dah Bey said "Thang eu." And looked at the others to see if that was okay.

"Well, where did you learn English?" I asked, smiling. Azalia translated and Roh Dah Bey shrugged and pointed to her sisters.

"You—are—welcome," I said slowly, "keep up the good work."

The girls translated then they all smiled and nodded.

"Does she feel strong enough for the long walk tomorrow?" I asked.

Her response hardly needed translating.

"I ready!" And she bobbled her head just like Sunflower.

"Oh no!" I exclaimed and rolled my eyes, "not another one."

They all laughed and moved off to look around the little oasis.

That afternoon, I called a meeting of my group with Wen and Roah.

"We are traveling south. The conquistadors are coming north. Somewhere, tomorrow or on the next day, we will pass each other. We must be sure we are not seen," I began.

"They travel out in valley?" Lobo asked.

"Maybe. They could go to the water out in the valley because they know from those who went back, where to find it, or they might come close to the mountains looking for a stream. In that case, if they come very far in, they might see us or our trail and be only a few hours away. That would be bad!" I declared.

"Someone must always scout ahead of us and get on a high point and watch the valley. Maybe another could scout out our trail ahead so we don't come to a cliff and have to find a way around," I advised.

After some discussion, we had a plan in place and people ready to take responsibility.

That evening we brought the horses in close to graze, filled water bottles, set out the food for the morning and prepared to leave as early as possible. The wolves always returned from their hunting to sleep next to Blossom each night.

Even before dawn there was a flurry of activity. Blossom and Lark watered the horses and brought them in to be saddled.

We filled the panniers with everything but the breakfast pans and utensils and collected some packs from the smaller girls. We put the non-essentials from each of my seven people into seven of the packs being carried by the younger or smaller girls and women, until they looked like gunny sacks.

"Tell those without packs to help those who still have packs," I instructed the girls.

My group of seven carried water and weapons and a few personal items because they would be working with the horses and scouting. There would be two people to carry each pack that was left.

As soon as breakfast was over, we packed the pans and utensils, shared a can of fruit to lighten the load a little and threw on the packs. Actually, the panniers are lifted into place very carefully at the same time because they are heavy and need to balance each other on each side of the horse.

Two of the larger duffel bags were arranged longways with one on top of each pannier. Three were laid across the first two and across the saddle. Another was placed in front of the saddle and one behind the saddle.

The tarp was thrown over the whole set of packs and panniers and tucked in at front, back and all around.

The short cinch strap has a large ring on each end. The rope is tied to the ring on one side, goes over the whole pack down through the ring on the other side and back over the pack to the first ring.

"Pull down on the front rope and pull up on the back rope," I instructed Impala. "Little Badger, you pull up on the front rope and down on the back rope. Keep pulling until the ropes are tight.

I held the rope in place while they grabbed the two ropes right above the panniers. "Impala, put the back rope over the front rope and Little Badger put the front rope over the back rope and pull them apart making a little diamond. Hold them until I finish the tiedown."

Going under the pannier and around the back, up and through the backside of the diamond, around the back of the pack behind the saddle to the other side and the back of the diamond, all the way around the back, bottom and front of the pannier to the front of the diamond, around the pack at the front of the saddle to the other side, through the front side of the diamond, back around the front of the pannier then around to the bottom pull it all tight and tie the rope off from where I started.

We then tucked all the loose sides of the tarp under the rope, and that is how you throw a beautiful diamond hitch on a pack horse.

It holds everything in place; the tarp covers it all and keeps the load balanced while traveling and nothing will get wet in a rainstorm.

We left around the front of the pond traveling up on the hill where the horses had grazed. Everyone paused to gaze back on the little bit of paradise that had been ours for the past few days.

"Let's see if we can keep the conquistadors from finding our little pond. Go down the hill at different places and try not to leave tracks. Several of you go down the trail for a few hundred steps then come back up the trail. Everyone else stay on the trail so it is clearly going right past here and up the valley," I requested.

Lark and Blossom followed me with the horses over some rocks and hardpan until we came to the trail. At a couple of places, we wandered off the trail to the left for a few dozen yards before coming back to the trail.

If we kept the eyes of the trackers on the trail and our wandering off to the left, they might see no reason to explore up the hill. It was worth a shot.

After we had gone a couple of miles, I asked who wanted to ride the horse. Since only two of them had ever been on a horse for more than a few steps, they all raised their hands.

I had to laugh. If they each rode ten minutes and it took a couple of minutes getting each one on and off, it would take three hours and my group still wouldn't have had a chance to ride.

On the other hand, it gave them all something to look forward to on what could be a hard, dry journey.

The scouts were working overtime so we had to send them in pairs. Rest time meant walking with the group.

They would see a point to climb on one side of the trail or the other, where they could see out over the valley. They would hurry ahead, climb the rise or point, scan the valley for ten or fifteen minutes, come down and catch up. This would be done about every two hours today.

The scouts for the trail would travel ahead a mile or so and find a way around or over obstacles we might encounter.

On one occasion, the way up the break in the cliff was too steep and rocky for horses, so I rode Ranger and led the pack horse all the way around the end of the cliff and mesa to get into the next valley. It only took an hour or so of quiet solitude with beautiful scenery and I was back to the trail and angled right into the formation.

While it was hot, the fresh clean air with the smell of sage and cedar was invigorating.

Roh Dah Bey, with the rejuvenating power of youth, was walking easily.

If I had been beaten, starved, dehydrated, had heatstroke and left for dead, I'd still be in the hospital pushing my service button for a drink or asking for help to get out of bed!

We continued to give everyone a ride on Ranger, but I had a growing concern that if the conquistadors and warriors were making fast time on long days while we went slowly with short days, they could be upon us before we could get to a defensible position.

On the positive side, we were making better time than I had expected and as evening approached, the forward scouts, Impala and Sunflower, came back and announced that the little stream was only an hour ahead. That perked everyone up so much we made it in about forty-five minutes. My group went on ahead to go upstream a short distance and find a good campsite for the night.

We tied the pack horse to Ranger's saddle so Blossom could go with our group to set up camp. The rest of us then stopped at the stream for everyone to get a drink before heading upstream.

The site was adequate for the night and even had a good grassy area for the horses.

The planning group met briefly and I turned to Lobo and Impala, "all of you have worked extra hard all day but we need a lookout this evening," I began. "Lobo and Impala would you go back just far enough to find a high spot and look at the back trail?"

They both readily agreed.

"Thank you!" I responded, "keep in mind that they might send two or three or even more, ahead to see where we are also. Blossom, are you able to go with them and take the wolves? If anyone is near, the wolves will know."

She also agreed.

"Come back just as it gets dark if you don't see anything, take an extra energy bar to munch on while you're looking," I advised.

After they reported back and we knew we were secure for that night, we all headed for bed. Roah and his young men would set a watch a hundred yards or so on our back trail.

The next morning, we quickly ate breakfast, packed and got back on the trail in short order.

Lobo approached as we prepared to go.

"We not need to look out over valley today. Maybe we go back and watch back trail," he suggested.

"Good thinking," I replied. "Find a spot where you can see far back and have plenty of time to get on our trail and catch up."

"Maybe we go with you and find spot that be good," he suggested.

"If we were not so far ahead, you could get to us more quickly," I mused. "Let's see if we can find a good lookout point with an easy route for you to catch up."

"We close to valley where we get Deh Neh Totsi and children, we maybe stop on south side and watch trail come over North Hill," Lobo said.

"We are close to there now. Maybe the rest of us can get to the stream and up to where the stream splits in two. There are cliffs there. Maybe we can find a spot for an ambush," I said

It was almost dark when we got to our old campsite where the stream divided. Lobo and Impala hadn't shown up and I was getting worried.

I tried a call to Violet. "Come in Violet. This is Chee, over."

"This Violet, is everything okay? Over."

"The conquistadors are coming up Noh Tay Dah's Valley. They are following our trail but they will pass the trail leading to the village. It is possible that they might send someone to see where that trail goes. Set a watch to see if any come and be ready to flee. Understand? Over."

"I understand, Chee. We will set a watch, over."

"That's good, we will talk to you later, Chee over and out."

While we were debating whether to make camp or keep going, the boys arrived with the news we were all expecting and dreading.

Chapter 20

"They stop at old campsite where we camp coming back with Deh Neh Totsi," Lobo reported.

"How do you know that? That's four hours away!" I said.

Impala smiled, "we stand at campsite, look up valley. Up side of hill, far up valley is big rocks, stick out above trees. We see there, we go there see here."

Lobo added, "it take almost four hours to climb there. With binoculars we see campsite good. We see six conquistadors on horses and many warriors, how you say, both hands three times."

"Thirty?" Impala said questioningly.

"That would be thirty," I assured them.

"Maybe two, three more," Impala shrugged. "Hard to count."

"We only take one hour to get here. We not go down to valley. We come side of hill straight to here. No up, no downs," Lobo said grinning.

I smiled and nodded, "very good! Do you think they know we are close? Would they come up to attack us at night?"

Lobo and Impala looked at one another thoughtfully, "it hard to know. They could make camp. Come in middle of night, here at first light."

Impala brightened, "they unpack pack horse. Maybe mean they stay until morning."

"We will set out an armed watch tonight," I decided. "We will have all of us with weapons together at an ambush site and take turns sleeping at that site.

"If they wait until tomorrow, we will have a better ambush waiting. Tell everyone to sleep with everything ready to go at a moment's notice," I said.

Wen, Roah and my group got together to plan for the next day.

"Those of us with rifles will stand guard tonight," I began. "We all will leave early in the morning. Take only water, poncho, blanket and food. Put the rest with the pack horse stuff.

"Either we will all be dead or captured and won't need it, or they will be dead or fleeing and we can pick it up when we want to."

That sounded a bit harsh and fatalistic but it was what we were facing.

"Several miles upstream, it divides again. When we went with Noh Tay Dah and his family, we took the left stream.

"We will set our ambush just before the stream divides.

"Your trail will come out of the woods into the high meadow and we will be in the rocks and cliffs on the right.

"If enough of them get past us that they separate and come after you, you come back along the top of the cliff and roll rocks down on them. We will be coming up to the top to join you and make a stand as they come up," I said.

"Our group will try to stop them before they get past us.

"If they attack and we can't stop them, we will flee in two groups. One group flees and gets behind rocks and covers the second group, who will flee past and set up to cover the first group, over and over, moving up the hill.

"And Azalia," I said smiling at her. "Since their slowest one is faster than me, remember that if one actually runs after me, he is an easy target for the ones covering us."

She grinned and nodded, "that is good."

"I just hope that the ones covering are the best shots when it's my turn to run," I raised my eyebrows and grinned at her.

"Then I need rifle!" She said and bobbled her head like Sunflower would do.

Everyone burst out laughing. Lark translated for Wen and Roah and they just shook their heads. We were always goofing off at the weirdest times.

It did however, break the tension that was building over the coming battle.

"Wen and Roah, let everyone know how and when we will go tomorrow. But not the battle details," I added.

They went off to talk with the rest of their group. Beckoning my group in a little closer, I said, "that was plan two. That's what we will do if the first plan doesn't work.

"Let's try to think like they think. How many conquistadors are there?" I asked.

Lobo responded, "six on horses."

"What does that tell you?" I asked.

They looked at one another realizing they hadn't even thought to ask the question.

Impala responded with some sudden insight, "they not come to fight. They came to seek out how many we are and what our weapons do!"

Lark spoke up, "remember, Roah ask you where your army go?"

"Very good," I said. "When we got Deh Neh Totsi and children, I called out and you girls came. I called out again and the boys came, then I waved at others who weren't there but the warriors thought there were others waiting to come. And you girls thought they had surrendered to your beauty."

"That what we think too!" Lobo stated seriously, then all three boys broke out laughing.

The girls glared and then grinned, and Azalia, always with the wit and the last word said, looking as shocked and innocent as she could muster up for the occasion, "Yes, we always think that"

They were all laughing good-naturedly now, so I continued, "as Lark was pointing out, we waved and talked and gestured to my imaginary army several times. When we started firing it was proof that the army was there. It wouldn't enter their thoughts that two girls and an old man could have weapons to do what was done.

"Now they want to know what they are facing," I said.

"That is why they bring warriors. They don't care if they die," Sunflower said with disgust.

"Probably true," I responded. "But they are here to kill you so try not to be too sympathetic.

"So, what do you think they will do?" I asked. "Will the conquistadors charge their horses up the hill to ride over us?"

"I not think that." Little Badger said, "hill too steep and rocky."

"Do you think that they will ride in front, get off their horses and march up the hill with their harquebuses?" I continued.

"Not if they think there might be an army waiting." Lark replied.

"Right, so what would you do if you were the conquistadors," I asked.

Blossom spoke up, "I would send six or eight on death charge. Army have to shoot them, so you count shots. They think one shot from each weapon."

"So now you have six or eight dead warriors. Do you know how many are in the Army?" I asked.

"No." Blossom admitted, "maybe send half of warriors then all army must show themselves to defend."

"You are probably right," I said. "I think we will have to get all their attention and force them to do something with us.

"One other thing I would like to see. I hope those six conquistadors ride into rifle range." I said seriously.

On that note those of us with rifles went down to set a watch and the others went to get a few hour's sleep.

"Blossom, why don't you give your rifle to Little Badger and go back with Sunflower?" I suggested.

"No, Chee, I be with you. Wolves be with me. They warn us long before we know others are there," she said loyally.

"That is true, and I'm always happy when you're with me," I said softly.

Early the next morning, as the first glow of dawn was silhouetting the mountains far to the east, the campsite was alive with activity.

A quick, cold breakfast of leftovers, one can of fruit to top it off and everyone was ready to hide everything with the packs except the essentials we might need while fleeing.

With a good rest, a light pack and an army at our heels, we made the last few miles in record time.

We stopped to rest where the stream divided again. From here both streams were coming down a steep incline and the narrow valleys were bordered on both sides by cliffs that went up a couple hundred feet.

The first valley angled up almost straight north. The second Valley was longer and went west then curved northwest. A finger of land with cliffs on both sides jutted out between the two valleys.

We would defend the first valley from the eastern hill with an outcropping of rocks that was too broken and jumbled to be called a cliff. From the top of those rocks, the terrain was a steep slope to the top of the cliff on the east side of the valley.

"Roah, you take everyone up the northwest stream, get on top of the cliffs and prepare to throw rocks down on any who get past us. You will take out some and slow them all down until we join you at the top of which ever stream they take.

"Go! And be careful, especially on top of the cliffs," I urged.

Turning back to my group, we began to plan.

The rangefinder said the rocks were about a hundred yards from the trail. This is where the trail comes out of the forest to the tundra above timberline.

"This is where they will come when we begin the battle. Let's go up to those rocks and look down," I said and started up the hill.

"We will divide into two groups. Impala, Lark, Sunflower and Azalia are group one. Lobo, Little Badger, Blossom and I are group two. Impala will have my 30.06, Lark has earned the right to the .243," I said with a smile.

"We are one group unless we have to divide. We will divide if too many come up the hill at one time. Group one runs up to the next outcropping and covers us as group two follows."

"If they send one group at us and then the rest all wait until they see what happens, we let them come. Blossom you will shoot immediately at ones at the back of the charge. That will string them out a little.

"None of the rest of us will shoot. When they get thirty steps away those with bows will begin shooting. That will not be what they expect so the second group may charge or wait.

"Our big guns will wait. If the conquistadors ride within range, the big guns will get one or two shots to take them out.

"If the second group of warriors charge up the trail when the first warriors attack us, the big guns will be lined up on them and start shooting immediately, before they get spread out on the trail. If they wait, we wait.

"Impala, take the box of 30.06 bullets and my rifle when we divide into groups," I said and handed him a box of bullets.

"Right now, those with bows, see if you can drop an arrow on the trail at this distance."

Each one took a turn and all were within ten or fifteen feet of the trail.

"Remember, you are shooting downhill and they will be bunched together we hope, and on the defensive when whatever plan they had is disrupted.

"That is how we will start this party!" I exclaimed, with a grin. "Drink some water, have an energy bar and hurry up and wait."

The wait wasn't all that long. We could see them coming through the trees. There were some open spots and one meadow where we could use the binoculars to get a rough count. The original estimate was about right.

"Blossom, when the arrows start, you keep firing as long as you have a good target. Don't rush your shots. Lock on, squeeze the trigger, work the bolt." I said quietly.

"Everyone with a bow get ready. Rifles ready for a charge up the valley," I instructed.

Perhaps because they had conquistador backup with harquebuses, perhaps because they were chasing a bunch of women, children and once defeated, unarmed captives; maybe they didn't believe that there was an army around; maybe they were just arrogant. Whatever their thinking, they took no precautions as they walked out of the woods into the open tundra.

Coming to a stop, they looked in all directions and bunched up nicely.

"Bows ready!" I whispered loud enough for all our group to hear.

"Fire!" I said a little louder and four bowstrings twanged and the .22 magnum cracked loudly in the still air. Two of the four arrows struck flesh, one was overshot and one landed at the feet of the little knot of warriors.

"Fire again!" Four more arrows flew down the hill and all four struck flesh somewhere on a body.

Blossom had gotten off three shots and all three had hit someone.

Some wounds might not be serious but they were discouraging and debilitating in some way.

The attackers fled back under and behind the trees. Arrows and the little crack of some unknown weapon was certainly not an army with loud powerful rifles that they were expecting.

They located us immediately but couldn't tell how many of us there were. That produced more confusion and uncertainty into their plans.

"Remember, what I really want are the conquistadors," I said loud enough for all of my group to hear.

The conquistadors were coming closer in behind the band of warriors, screaming at them to attack.

There were at least six warriors wounded severely enough to be out of the fight. Not bad for the first round.

All they had seen so far were four figures with bows, and even at a distance they could tell that two of the four didn't look very big. Whoever fired the thunder stick with the sharp "crack" hadn't been seen but there were obviously three of them since the shots were too close together for one or two people to reload.

"Blossom, reload your magazine while they decide what they are going to do," I reminded her.

The conquistadors were inching closer, ordering and cajoling the reluctant warriors.

Suddenly more than a dozen warriors burst from the trees and headed up the steep slope, screaming out their war cries as they came. They were jumping to one side and then the other as they zigzagged up the hill trying to make themselves a more difficult target.

"What with all the screaming and running back and forth, they won't have enough breath to say "boo" when they finally get here," I chuckled.

Those who could hear my remarks laughed and Lark turned to look at me like I had forgotten that we were in a war, outnumbered three to one by big experienced warriors who were bent on killing us. I smiled and winked at her and she smiled slightly and shook her head.

The warriors were halfway up the slope and starting to slow down when I instructed loudly, "bows ready."

Four people with bows stepped forward and some of the attackers actually stopped to stare.

There was no army! There were only four kids and half of them were girls.

With a roar of rage at such arrogance and trickery, they rushed straight up the hill.

"Blossom and bows, at the thirty step mark, fire!" I shouted.

Four arrows found their target and at twenty steps four more went down. Blossom had struck a couple more and the few who were left hit the ground and got behind a rock or rolled into a low spot

"Bows, cease-fire. Stand in plain sight and watch.

"Blossom, if you can see part of an arm or leg sticking out from a hiding place, see if you can hit it."

Within a few seconds there was a "crack" of her small rifle followed by a yelp far down the hill.

"Got one!" She called out.

The conquistadors, who were still screaming at the warriors and not getting any results, must have decided to take things into their own hands. They were all the way up to the warriors hiding behind the trees next to the trail where it exited the woods into the open field.

At this point they were still too hidden behind the trees for us to get a clear shot, so we waited.

After a few minutes they rode out into the meadow.

They were obviously trying to make an impression. Whether it was for their warriors or us really didn't matter. To them, there was no army and arrows couldn't get through their armor so why not put on a show.

The spade bits made the horses pull their heads up and arch their necks and step a little higher.

They were riding two by two, and at a signal from their leader, they turned in formation and faced up the hill.

It was impressive and precise but I couldn't imagine them trying to charge with horses up a rocky hill that was so steep.

They appeared to see the folly of that as well, because they turned their horses in unison and rode about twenty yards into the meadow on the other side of the trail.

They even dismounted in unison in smart military style, took their harquebuses and with each holding them at a forty-five degree angle across their chest, advanced together back to and across the trail to start up the hill.

They would soon show everyone how real soldiers chased and destroyed a bunch of rabble off of a hill.

"Sunflower, watch them carefully. If they attempt to set off the hand cannons you call out 'everyone down'!" I instructed her loud enough for all of our group to hear. "Everyone have a good sized rock to jump behind if they do fire!

"Rifles ready!" I called out. "We will fire together."

Impala had dropped back and picked up my 30.06 and I gave him time to get set.

"Blossom, first one on the left; Lark second one on the left; Lobo, first one on the right; Impala, second one on the right; I'll take the middle."

Apparently, the three "children" with bows who were standing in plain sight, infuriated them. They were used to instilling fear. They were ten steps up the steep hill and no one was fleeing.

They paused, and Sunflower called out, "everyone down." We all jumped behind our chosen boulder.

There was a tremendous roar, blue/black smoke rolled forward and pellets splattered all over the rocks at the top of the hill.

"Stay down," I called out.

I wanted to be sure that one or two of them hadn't held their fire and were waiting for us to jump up. I peeked around the boulder and saw all six with the sharpened spear end of the hand cannons resting on the ground as they each began the reloading process. According to all I had read, that would be a minute and a half at best.

Since there was no evidence of an army, or any resistance whatsoever to their great military showmanship, they stood in plain sight, cleaning glowing embers out of their barrels in preparation for pouring in more powder.

"Rifles ready!" I called out and each one used the boulder they had jumped behind as a rest to steady their rifle on.

"Ready! Lock on! Fire! I shouted and five rifles cracked and thundered as one. My shots were strung out a little longer, since I was using the SKS and decided to double tap the two conquistadors in the middle.

Five of the six were blown backwards, landed on their backs and skidded on their shiny armor down to the trail. Even though the bullets easily went through the armor, the impact against the metal was tremendous.

The first one was staggering backwards and trying to get his feet under him, before he too, collapsed on the trail. The .22 magnum wasn't powerful enough to blow him backwards but it still went through the armor with devastating effect.

I doubted that the thunderous roar of our weapons was as impressive as the harquebuses of the conquistadors, nor did we roll out a cloud of smoke, but the effects were significantly more frightening.

All the warriors fled down the trail. Those wounded or hiding behind rocks on the hillside were in a quandary. Some couldn't run, some were afraid to get up to run so they all just laid there.

"Lobo, step forward and call to those who are left to tend to their wounded and prepare to leave," I said.

"Blossom, how much first aid stuff is in my pack?"

"Not much, Chee. We use most of it for captives." She responded.

"Get what we have and the roll of duct tape and let's see if we can help." I said grimly.

I wasn't in a particular mood to be of help to these who were trying to kill us, but they weren't quite so belligerent now.

Since the heavy rifles were not used on the warriors, most of their wounds were less severe. Only three had been struck mortally. The others had been able to see the arrows coming and attempted to avoid them.

One had thrown up an arm and took the arrow in his forearm. Others had tried to duck aside and were wounded with an arrow along the rib cage or in the fleshy part of their side, or in an upper arm or shoulder.

It was enough to take the fight out of them, but they could limp their way home, wherever that was.

"Little Badger and Azalia go up and bring the others down the valley to where they can see and be seen around the hill. Rest and drink water until these warriors leave.

"Lark, stand here at the top of the hill and be prepared to strike down any warrior who would try to attack us when our backs are turned.

"Impala, come down the hill part way and watch as Lark is watching while we help the wounded.

"Chief Lobo, come down with us as we help the wounded, and watch the horses. In front of the warriors you will give directions and instructions and strike down anyone who tries to go to the horses.

"Sunflower and Blossom, leave weapons here and let's tend to the wounded. You will give the orders and I will assist you by doing what you tell me to do," I concluded.

Lobo had looked at me and started to grin, but saw that I was serious and gave his attention to the task at hand. Sunflower and Blossom, who were used to bossing me around with good humor and at appropriate times, also saw that I was serious, as we headed down the hill.

Lobo took over, as I hoped he would, instructing the ones who could walk to come to the side and be tended to.

Blossom showed them how to take off the triple razor blade point, apply petroleum jelly and slide the arrow out. Sunflower applied the antibacterial salve, put a piece of towel over both the entrance and exit wound and fastened it with a pressure bandage of duct tape.

My job was cutting the towel in pieces and handing them to Sunflower as she called for them.

"Piece of towel," she called out and held out her hand and I placed the piece in her hand.

"Tape, this long," indicating the length and I unrolled the duct tape and tore off the designated amount and placed the end in her hand.

Blossom came with arrows and I placed them by the pack with the first-aid kit. She also, very carefully, handed me the arrow points which I placed in a side pocket.

One arrow had gone in between a warrior's hip bone and the bottom rib. Meeting little resistance, it almost went all the way through. It had stopped at the feathers and would require about twenty six inches of pull-through to pull it out.

"Can you cut it off at the feathers and pull it out the rest of the way through?" Blossom asked.

"Okay," I replied, and pulled out my multitool.

She held it steady as I used the wire cutters to cut off the end just below the feathers. We cleaned the end of any burs or points and pulled the last inch on through.

She waved me off and motioned to Sunflower, who ignored me and talked to Blossom and the patient. They were enjoying this bossing me around way too much!

I went to Lobo and suggested that he see if there was a leader who would be in charge of the trek back to where ever they were going.

"You give them two or three of the conquistadors botas so they can travel down the big valley to the river.

"Okay, you gesture and order me to go for the botas and I'll bring them back to you," I said.

He started to object, again saw that I was serious, so he pointed and told me to get the botas.

I brought them back and gave them to Lobo, who in turn gave them to the designated leader with clear instructions about leaving the valley and not coming back.

I also suggested to Lobo that he tell the leader to go to the conquistadors and take whatever they wanted to keep, or needed, to prove that they were dead.

We watched the warriors depart. The healthy ones carrying their dead; the wounded ones limping along favoring their injuries.

When they were out of sight we waved for Little Badger and Azalia to bring the group, while the rest of us rounded up the horses which hadn't strayed far.

"Do you understand why I had you give all the orders?" I asked.

Lobo answered, "you make them think we are the leaders and not someone not of the tribe."

"Exactly, if they thought I was in charge they wouldn't be afraid to come back again if I was gone," I answered. "What did they find out? They did not see an army. All their wounds were inflicted by young warriors and girls who were not a bit afraid of their whole band. When called upon, many warriors came from nowhere and took out the conquistadors and disappeared just as quickly. Then a group of warriors started to come against them from far up the valley. They didn't know who they were or how many. They left confused and uninformed and have suffered another defeat."

Soon, Roah and his group of former captives arrived.

"There are twenty-two of us, so we all could ride one third of the way back to the village with one person riding double with one group. All the horses will be led, since they have harsh bits in their mouths and we don't know if one might run off if not controlled properly."

I called Sunflower and Lobo aside, "we have seven horses. When we get to the hill just before the village, we want you seven to ride in to deliver Lu Day Sah to her parents. If everyone comes out making a lot of noise, get off the horses and lead them. We don't want anyone to get hurt by the horses getting spooked."

Everyone was excited to have a turn riding the horses. Even if they weren't controlling the reins, they enjoyed the full benefit of the feel and movement of the horse.

When we got to the turn off to the village, we stopped to rest, change riders and drink some water.

"Lobo perhaps you should send Impala and Little Badger on down the trail to be sure the warriors kept going. Tell them to be careful they don't get ambushed," I suggested.

He grinned and nodded, realizing I was giving more leadership responsibilities to him.

The rest of us went on to the Grizzly Bear Spring to rest and wait for Impala and Little Badger to catch up.

They arrived to report that the band was continuing slowly down the valley and were making no effort to watch their back trail.

There were still several among the former captives who were not fully recovered and were showing signs of fatigue. My group decided to skip our turn on the horses and let the others get a second ride.

Again, I was impressed that nearly all of them insisted that they could make it and to let others get their second ride.

I finally said to Lobo, "you need to select or appoint someone to select those who will ride and we will be on our way."

Sunflower and Azalia got their heads together and chose the riders in just a few minutes. The only adamant objection was from Roah, who thought that as leader of the group, he must set the example and walk.

When we reached the hill just before the village, we stopped and explained what we would be doing. Roh Dah Bey and Lu Day Sah were coming home after more than four years away. We would follow behind.

I asked Blossom to stay with me and translate. She readily agreed, but Lark objected, "she is member of the tribe. She must go with the tribe."

I called to Lobo, "there are nine people and seven horses how will you enter the village?"

Lark spoke up, "I must stay and translate for Chee."

"Then I will walk and lead; Blossom will follow me; Impala and Little Badger come next; then Sunflower and Roh Dah Bey, then Azalia and Lu Day Sah.

"We will go straight to the hut of Mor Dak Sah"

Lobo's procession went over the hill where they could angle into the center of the village and right up to the hut of Mor Dak Sah and his wife.

The rest of us followed on foot and stopped on the side of the hill where we could observe all that was transpiring.

The horses seemed to sense that this was a parade of some sort and brought their heads up, arched their necks and stepped higher than they did on the trail.

People rushed out of every hut to watch the spectacle. Most had never even seen a horse and here were their own people proudly riding right through their village.

They were so enamored with the picturesque high-stepping steeds that they failed to even notice the two new faces in the procession.

Lobo strode straight to the hut of Mor Dak Sah and his wife. The lineup of horses hid the last riders from their view.

Lu Day Sah tossed the reins to Azalia, jumped off the horse and ran to her parents. She was only halfway past the horses when they recognized her and all three screamed and fell to their knees in disbelief and hope and recognition all rolled into one at a volume that rivaled Sunflower at her best.

There were screams and cries and exclamations as the whole village converged on the emotional scene. Some of the women began the trilling sound of celebration.

Lobo called out, "dismount and lead the horses," and all the riders got off and began to turn the horses around to lead them away from the crowd.

Suddenly, there was another scream as Violet recognized the other newcomer.

"It's Roh Dah Bey, It's Roh Dah Bey," and everyone turned to look at the trio of sisters, each with a streak of light-yellow hair down the right side of her head. They were beaming broadly, but with eyes still filled with tears from the explosion of joy over Lu Day Sah and her reunion with her parents. They turned to wave, then turned back to lead their horses away from the crowd.

Lark and I watched the proceedings somewhat teary-eyed ourselves. She hooked her arm around my arm and laid her head against the side of my arm.

"I hope someday, I see my family," she said wistfully.

"I hope you can too," I responded quietly.

Noh Tay Dah and his family and Cedo and his group, were all standing in front of their huts watching the scene in the village unfold.

I called to Cedo and he came over and met Lim Begus, the boy from the Dineh.

Noh Tay Dah and Deh Neh Totsi came over to greet Roah and others they recognized. None of these were ones who had bullied them in the Whiteface camp.

It took a couple of hours for the excitement to die down, get the horses staked out and prepare our evening meal.

We simply unloaded the two pack horses into my lean-to and kept everything in a pile to deal with later.

After the evening meal our group went out to our log on the hillside.

We had grown in numbers. Violet was a vital part; Lark was the newest warrior and Roh Dah Bey was still an unknown. Her talents were yet to be discovered, but she was a fighter and a survivor.

"I am so very proud of all of you," I began. "You are tough, intelligent, capable warriors and I am proud to be part of this band.

"I love this place and the beautiful, peaceful view. I love each of you, individually and all together. As Blossom reminds us, 'we are family'."

There were murmurs and nods of agreement all around the semi-circle.

"But in the midst of all this beauty, peace and love for one another, we must now prepare for war." I said seriously.

"Why must there be war, Chee? The conquistadors have been defeated." Violet asked plaintively.

"Even the warriors who came with them have all fled," Azalia responded.

"Remember the bear?" I said, "Little Badger's arrow was like a big splinter and he didn't run away, he attacked!

"We have never gone after the conquistadors. They have always come after us. Each of our victories were just jabs with a sharp stick as far as the conquistador invaders are concerned. They will come to destroy us because it is their nature."

"What can we do? We cannot fight a big army!" Sunflower lamented.

"I believe that we will have no choice. Nobody with any understanding desires war. War is death, injury, captivity and destruction of whole tribes. The conquistadors will not stop. We cannot flee from them because they will keep coming until they find us.

"They are evil. They kill and steal and destroy. If they just wanted to control and rule over us, we could surrender. But that is not what they do. They kill all the old people who can no longer serve them; they kill the children because they are not here to build a future. They make slaves of the strong and healthy men and women, using them until they drop because they will move on and get more.

"They must be stopped!" I declared.

"But how can we stop them?" Lobo asked.

"I'm not sure, but I must go back and get rifles and equipment to fight and help from some who understand this kind of war," I said.

"You are sure you will come back?" Sunflower asked.

"Of all the times I have gone and come back, this time I feel most certain that I must come back to finish this war."

"If the battle must be fought, I cannot think of any group I would rather fight beside.

"Enjoy this time of peace; celebrate the return of Roh Dah Bey and Lu Day Sah; but prepare your hearts and prepare the tribe for war," I said with a sigh.

"War is not the path that we chose, but it is thrust upon us and we must be ready!" I concluded.

Hugging one another a little longer than usual, we whispered our goodbyes with voices heavy with emotion, glancing fondly to one another. With troubled hearts, and minds roiling with questions, We parted and I left them to climb the mountain in the dark, moonless night.

www.ingramcontent.com/pod-product-compliance
Lightning Source LLC
Chambersburg PA
CBHW051308300726
48976CB00002B/316